Praise for

"This ambitious, complex story spans the globe. Even when the intricacies of its plot are most challenging, we are fascinated and swept forward. Steinhauer has been likened to John le Carré and rightly so . . . Olen Steinhauer's Milo Weaver novels are must-reads for lovers of the genre." —*The Washington Post*

"Not since le Carré has a writer so vividly evoked the multilayered, multifaceted, deeply paranoid world of espionage, in which identities and allegiances are malleable and ever shifting, the mirrors of loyalty and betrayal reflecting one another to infinity. In this intensely clever, sometimes baffling book, it's never quite clear who is manipulating whom, and which side is up." —*The New York Times Book Review*

"Stunning . . . Readers are irresistibly drawn into Weaver's dogged struggle to unravel a complicated game of cat and mouse . . . Steinhauer is at the top of his game—but when isn't he?" —*USA Today*

"The plot unfolds with such ease, grace, and force that you simply don't want it to end. Which puts the work of . . . Steinhauer in the corner of John le Carré and Alan Furst, whose worlds of spies you want to linger in for as long as you can." —*Dallas Morning News*

"Excellent . . . Steinhauer is particularly good at articulating contemporary spy craft—the mechanics of surveillance and intelligence in the digital age and the depth of paranoia endemic to the trade. In addition, his ability to create characters with genuine emotions and conflicts, coupled with an insightful and often poetic writing style, set him apart in the world of espionage fiction." —*Publishers Weekly* (starred review)

"The best spy novelists have long shaded their stories with the gray of moral ambiguity, and Steinhauer works in that tradition while deconstructing James Bond even further . . . [In] this dizzying, dazzling array of hidden agendas and confused allegiances . . . all motivations are personal and the ultimate goal is survival . . . Another must-read from the best novelist working in the tradition of John le Carré." —*Booklist* (starred review)

"Thickets of tricky conspiracies, swamps full of secret agendas: Reader, you're in le Carré-land, guided there unerringly by one of the best of the newer crop."
—*Kirkus* (starred review)

"Superb . . . Steinhauer again propels spy Milo Weaver into an international whirl of lies, deceit and breathless action . . . Elevating [the] modern noir elements are Milo's moral complexity, and the rich, often ironic personal details of the lives of some very bad people indeed." —*Cleveland Plain Dealer*

The Nearest Exit

"Milo's back, and he's better than ever . . . *The Nearest Exit* should take its place among the best of the spy thrillers." —Associated Press

"Steinhauer's adept characterization of a morally conflicted spy makes this an emotionally powerful read."

—*Publishers Weekly*

"*The Tourist* was impressive, proving that Steinhauer had the ability to leap from the historical setting of his excellent Eastern European quintet to a vividly imagined contemporary landscape. But this is even better, a dazzling, dizzyingly complex world of clandestine warfare that is complicated further by the affairs of the heart."

—*Booklist* (starred review)

"Extraordinarily complex and compelling."

—*Library Journal*

The Tourist

"Here's the best spy novel I've ever read that wasn't written by John le Carré . . . It's a complex story of betrayal anchored by a protagonist who's as winning as he is wily."

—Stephen King, *Entertainment Weekly*

"Remember John le Carré . . . when he wrote about beaten-down, morally directionless spies? In other words, when he was good? That's how Olen Steinhauer writes in this tale of a world-weary spook who can't escape the old game."

—*Time*

"Smart . . . He excels when the focus is on Weaver, an intriguing, damaged man yearning to break free of his dark profession."

—*People*

"Olen Steinhauer evokes the work of spy novel greats like John le Carré with his new novel, *The Tourist* . . . As in the best of le Carré's work, the clandestine world of *The Tourist* is as much about bureaucrats as it is about black bag ops. Steinhauer has a solid grasp of the espionage world (either that or a fertile imagination) that enlivens his enjoyable story." —*Chicago Sun-Times*

"Justifiably praised for his novels set in Cold War-era Eastern Europe, [Steinhauer's] *The Tourist* is contemporary but equally intelligent, evocative, and nuanced."
—*Seattle Times*

"Elaborately engineered . . . He immerses his reader in the same kind of uncertainty that Milo faces at every turn . . . As for Mr. Steinhauer, the two-time Edgar Award nominee who can be legitimately mentioned alongside of John le Carré, he displays a high degree of what Mr. le Carré's characters like to call tradecraft. If he's as smart as *The Tourist* makes him sound, he'll bring back Milo Weaver for a curtain call."
—Janet Maslin, *The New York Times*

"This is Len Deighton country. *The Tourist* is a complex, contemporary espionage story told with wit and sagacity, and it offers up a dozen or more intricate characters who keep the action on target. While the international intrigue and cross-country chase are the stuff of traditional Hitchcockian entertainment, Steinhauer once again demonstrates how his economical prose can turn unrelenting paranoia into an exciting ride."
—*Boston Globe*

ALSO BY OLEN STEINHAUER

An
AMERICAN
SPY

OLEN STEINHAUER

St. Martin's Paperbacks

This is a work of fiction. All of the characters, organizations, and events portrayed in this novel are either products of the author's imagination or are used fictitiously.

AN AMERICAN SPY

Copyright © 2012 by Olen Steinhauer.
Excerpt from *The Cairo Affair* copyright © 2013 by Olen Steinhauer.

For information address St. Martin's Press, 175 Fifth Avenue, New York, NY 10010.

ISBN: 978-1-250-03697-1

Printed in the United States of America

Minotaur hardcover edition / March 2012
Griffin edition / October 2012
St. Martin's Paperbacks edition / October 2013

St. Martin's Paperbacks are published by St. Martin's Press, 175 Fifth Avenue, New York, NY 10010.

10 9 8 7 6 5 4 3 2 1

For Stephanie Cabot,
American agent

ORDER OF THING

TUESDAY, APRIL 22 TO
THURSDAY, APRIL 24, 2008

There had been signs, and it was more a measure of luck than intelligence savvy that Erika Schwartz was able to put them together in time. For instance, the military counterintelligence office, MAD, could easily have left her off the distribution list for their April 17 report on EU-related anomalies—a list they only added her to because they were preparing to ask for the use of an Iranian source in return. When the report came, it would have been easy to miss number 53, an item from Budapest. In fact, she did miss number 53, and her assistant, Oskar Leintz, had to draw her attention to it. He came into her new, large-windowed office on the second floor of the Pullach headquarters of the BND, the German Republic's foreign intelligence agency, slapping the report against his palm. "You saw the bit from Budapest?"

She'd been sitting, uncharacteristically, with a salad on her desk, staring out the window where, just over the trees, she could see distant storm clouds. Since her promotion two weeks earlier, she still hadn't gotten used to having a view; her previous office had been on the ground floor. She hadn't gotten used to having resources, nor to the look on people's faces when they walked into her office and shuddered, having forgotten that this obese, ill-humored woman now sat at Teddy Wartmüller's desk. As for poor Teddy, he was in prison. "Of course I saw the bit from Budapest," she said. "Which bit?"

"You haven't touched that salad."

"Which bit from Budapest, Oskar?"

"Henry Gray."

Of course, she'd seen number 53, but she hadn't connected the name because she'd only seen it once before, months ago, on another report from the same source, a journalist named Johann Thüringer. Now, with Oskar's prodding, it returned to her. She opened her copy of the MAD report.

53. JT in Budapest: On the night of 15 April, Henry Gray (American journalist—see ZNBw reports 8/2007 & 12/2007) disappeared. His romantic partner, Zsuzsa Papp (Hungarian), insists he was kidnapped. Her suspicion: either the USA or China. When pressed, though, she refuses to go into details.

"Gray is connected to Milo Weaver," Oskar helpfully reminded her, now stroking his thin mustache.

"Tangentially," she said, then noticed that she'd gotten some Caesar dressing on the report. She remembered Thüringer's observations from 8/2007 and 12/2007. In August, he reported that Mr. Gray had been thrown off the terrace of his Budapest apartment and was in a coma. The December report noted that Gray had woken in the hospital and eventually disappeared on his own. Soon afterward, an AP stringer named Milo Weaver had arrived asking questions about him. Gray had so far eluded the man . . . until now, at least.

She put in a call to a friend in the Hungarian National Security Office, the NBH, but there was no record of Gray leaving the country. There was, however, an old woman's bedroom-window eyewitness report of someone matching Gray's description being stuffed, dazed (perhaps drugged), by an Asian (Chinese?) into the back of a BMW on Sas utca, a five-minute walk from Gray's apartment. Though the witness didn't understand a word, she recognized English being spoken.

It was through another friend, Adrien Lambert in the French DGSE, that Erika learned that on the same night as the supposed abduction, at Budapest-Ferihegy's Terminal 1, someone in a Plexiglas-covered stretcher had been loaded into a private twin-engine plane. The aircraft was registered to a Romanian company called Transexpress SRL, a known CIA front. Passengers weren't listed, and while its destination was noted as Ruzyne-Prague Airport, there was no record of it ever landing there. Henry Gray had, in a bureaucratic sense, vanished from the face of the earth.

The little mystery gave her an itch, and she called Cologne and asked MAD for direct contact with Johann

Thüringer. Their immediate yes was a shock. Life on the ground floor, with requests taking weeks to be summarily refused, had steeled her for rejection. Acceptance simply wasn't part of her worldview.

So, giddy with power, she talked to Thüringer on a secure line to the Budapest embassy on Sunday, April 20. As per instructions from MAD, he had stayed most of the previous night with Zsuzsa Papp who, after enough drinks and terrified rants about how *no one* could be trusted, finally began to open up. She did not open up completely, he admitted, but along the line one name slipped out: Rick. *It's not a secret, I guess*, Papp had told him. *Not anymore. Henry worked with a Chinese spy named Rick. Spent an entire month with him. But in the end . . .*

"In the end, what?" Erika asked.

"Well, in the end she fell asleep. What I can piece together is that the CIA actually was after Henry because of this Chinese Rick. However, they left him alone for the past month, so why take him now? That's what Zsuzsa wondered. In the end, she believes the Chinese took him. I do, too."

Because of the Transexpress plane, Erika doubted that was true, but she didn't bother to correct him—partly because she didn't want to share with someone who would quickly report it back to another agency, and partly because of Andrei Stanescu.

Three weeks ago, Stanescu had flown to Brooklyn, New York, to shoot a man named Milo Weaver—payback for the death of his fifteen-year-old daughter, Adriana. Andrei had been helped in his endeavor by a

Chinese man named Rick—or, more properly, Xin Zhu.

When names connect so flagrantly, it pays to sit up and take notice.

If asked, Erika would hardly have been able to put her thoughts into words, but she did tell Oskar to keep an eye out for questionable American activity within the borders of Germany, particularly around the Berlin region, where Andrei Stanescu and his wife lived. By Monday morning she received an e-mail that pointed to two American passports—Gwendolyn Davis and Hector Garza entered the country through, respectively, Stuttgart and Frankfurt on Sunday, yet checked into the same Berlin hotel, the Radisson Blu. Neither name rang a bell with her or Oskar, but when the photos came through Oskar pointed at the black woman with large eyes. "Oh, shit," he said. "That's Leticia Jones."

Leticia Jones was one of two known Tourists, members of a peculiar CIA fraternity known as the Department of Tourism. It had for decades been a fable, a myth of a secret American department composed of otherworldly agents, who could enter and leave a city without a trace, but always littering destruction in their wake. It was the kind of tale you told spies before they went to sleep: the bogeyman. At the end of February, however, she had learned that it was more than just an intelligence-community legend, from a man named Milo Weaver, while he was tied up in her basement. Later, she'd sent a five-person team to America to keep distant surveillance. She wanted to know where this department resided, and who its members were.

The results had been interesting. Weaver met in a Washington, D.C., hotel with Minnesota senator Nathan Irwin, members of his staff, and Alan Drummond, the director of the Department of Tourism. Also in attendance were a man and a woman they later identified as Zachary Klein and Leticia Jones. A long night bled into the next day, taking these people to Reagan International Airport, then by car to 101 West Thirty-first Street, Manhattan. That building's twenty-second floor, they realized, housed the headquarters of the Department of Tourism.

However, this success was short-lived, for a week later secure moving vans appeared, and large men with shoulder holsters, watched over by plainclothes agents wearing more guns, gradually emptied at least three floors of that building so that by now only cockroaches remained on the twenty-second floor.

Leticia Jones was one of the famed Tourists, just as Weaver had once been. Now she was in Berlin with a man who could be another of them. Berlin, where there resided a Moldovan immigrant the CIA wanted for the shooting of one of their own. Add to that last week's renditioning of a man in Budapest who was, like Stanescu, connected to both Milo Weaver and Xin Zhu, and this was an arrangement of players that she could not ignore.

She rubbed her face hard, then looked up at Oskar, who was already grinning. He had an Easterner's joy of watching misery. "I suppose you're gassing up the car," she said.

"You're the big boss now," he told her, "which means

I'm more than just an underling. Someone else is gassing it up."

On the ride, she remembered her last conversation with Andrei Stanescu. Upon his return to Germany after shooting Weaver, she'd had Oskar and a couple of others pick him up at the airport and bring him to a waiting car. Oskar gave him a phone, through which she tried to make herself completely clear:

"I know what you did, Mr. Stanescu, and I do not approve, but if I let everything I disapprove of get to me I never would have made it to my twentieth birthday. We're receiving calls from the other side of the Atlantic asking for your arrest and your extradition to face American justice.

"I am not going to scold you. I won't even tell you that you are an idiot for shooting a man who, as I explained before, did not kill your daughter. All that is past. For the present, I will hold off the Americans for as long as I can, but I ask one thing of you, a single condition. You, Mr. Stanescu, will tell no one what you have done. You will not tell your wife, nor your brother. You will not tell your priest. It is the one act of your life that you will have to carry entirely alone.

"If it becomes too much, and you believe that you cannot hold your tongue any longer, then you will call me directly. Because I am the only person on the planet you can share this with.

"If you do *not* comply with this one request, the penalty will be immediate. You will disappear, and then reappear in America. Your life will be in the hands of strangers who know no empathy and care nothing about what you've been through. More importantly, your wife will lose a husband in addition to a daughter. We both know that she wouldn't be able to take that."

As far as she knew, he had followed her instructions perfectly, but still here they were.

She and Oskar took rooms in the Berlin Radisson Blu, and later that night, when one of her men in the lobby informed her that Davis and Garza were having a drink in the bar, she and Oskar went down to find them. She despised going out into the field, but the possibility of someone else getting this wrong was even more hateful. So she went personally to a table against the wall, settled down, and watched as Oskar, flanked by two Saxons who looked far less threatening than they really were, invited the two Americans for a drink. It was a sign of their coolness that they acted as if they'd expected this, which she doubted. Soon, Leticia Jones and the man known as Hector Garza were sitting across from her, the woman carrying a martini, the man holding something pink and fruity.

Erika introduced herself but didn't bother asking their real names. What was the point? She wasn't here on a fact-finding mission but to offer advice. They listened to her slow, measured English with feigned earnestness, and she pointed out that, given that they were on German soil, and given that their mission was now known, they could abandon it without shame. "Really, you can't expect a rebuke from your department head. Alan Drummond, right?" she asked and got confused stares in reply. "The point is," she said, "if you want to have a conversation with Mr. Stanescu, it can easily be done here—but in my house, you have to follow my rules. What you cannot do is shove him into some little plane, as you did with Henry Gray."

There was no reason to assume that either had been on hand for that abduction, but she noticed something tense in Hector Garza's features.

She could have shared more, in particular that she knew that these Americans had that morning parked a refrigerated truck painted with the insignia of the HIT grocery store in a private garage in Zehlendorf, but why bother? They would only come up with new plans, something Tourists were rumored to be adept at.

When they smiled and thanked her for the wonderful conversation—confessing, however, that they had no idea what she was talking about—she let them go without argument. Erika's people had placed two trackers on their truck, and there were now twelve men and women in Berlin whose sole task was to watch this pair.

The next morning—Tuesday, April 22—those twelve people watched as the pair parked their HIT truck outside Stanescu's Kreuzberg apartment building and followed his taxi as he headed in for his shift. However, along the way, the Tourists' pursuit was interrupted by two of Erika's men who smashed cars into the HIT truck at the corner of Gneisenaustrasse and Nostitz-strasse. Once that was accomplished, she called Stanescu directly and asked him to come to a restaurant along the Spree, the Altes Zollhaus, so that they could have a word. He arrived looking confused, having just witnessed a suspicious-looking three-car pileup on his way, but he was properly submissive. After offering wine and food and receiving disconsolate refusals in his broken German, she asked if he remembered a man named Rick.

Andrei stared at her. "I know one man what is named Rick."

"Well, the people in the truck that was following you know that you're acquainted with this man you call Rick, whom they call Xin Zhu. They are very interested in learning about him, and they believe you can help them."

"They are CIA?"

She nodded, her jowls trembling.

"But you attack it."

"They had a car accident, Mr. Stanescu." She placed a plump hand on the edge of the table. "That is not important to you. Before, I promised you that I would hold them off as long as I could, and I think I've reached the limits of my power. I don't think they're interested in prosecuting you for what you did to that man in Brooklyn. What they seem to want is information about the Chinese man, your Rick, who they believe sent you to shoot him."

Andrei leaned back, finally saying, "I can answer. Questions, I can answer."

"I'm sure you can, and I'm sure you will. However, we will do it my way, and not theirs."

"What is it, their way?"

She cleared her throat, and a waiter looked over before realizing she wasn't calling to him. She said, "They would have grabbed you and pushed you inside that truck, where there is a bed and a lot of drugs. You would have woken up in a plane heading somewhere. Perhaps to the United States, perhaps to Turkey—I don't know. For a minimum of a week, probably more, you would have been interrogated."

"And what is it, your way?"

She sighed. "I don't like it when German residents are dragged out of the country by other governments, particularly by friendly governments. You and I will go to a house outside of Berlin for, at most, three days. No drugs, just conversation. I will allow a single American on the premises to ask questions."

Two hours later, Oskar brought his phone. "It's the office. They've got a Gwendolyn Davis on the line."

In perfect German, Leticia Jones said, "So, does the offer still stand?"

The conversation lasted for one and a half days in a house off the E51 to Potsdam. Jones showed up early both mornings with a handheld audio recorder while Hector Garza stayed in his hotel room or strolled the shopping avenues, occasionally even buying shirts. Erika was surprised by this, having expected Garza to do the talking. After all, they had no idea how Andrei Stanescu felt about black people, nor how he would deal with a female interrogator. Leticia Jones wasn't just fluent in German, though; she had a remarkably welcoming presence that encouraged her subject to go deeper than simple answers.

The interrogation was also fascinating because Andrei Stanescu had only spent an hour or so in the company of the Chinese officer. What *could* he know about

Xin Zhu? Leticia Jones hadn't known this before their talk began. She only knew that Andrei had been handed a pistol in Brooklyn by a member of the Chinese embassy whom Andrei called Li. She knew that Li had been told by Xin Zhu to give Andrei the gun, and so it followed that Xin Zhu, or one of his representatives from China's foreign intelligence service, the Guoanbu, had been in personal contact with Andrei. Jones showed him a series of photographs until he identified Li as a man named Sam Kuo.

They'd finished dealing with the actual events leading to the attempted murder of Milo Weaver after just a few hours, and then Jones focused on the person of Xin Zhu. A physical description that began with that uncomfortable word "fat," then grew more detailed, his small eyes, his blunt nose, his full lips, the thin hair on the top of his head and the thicker black locks over his ears. His quiet way, as if by silence he could sap the air of indecision—"He is very convincing," Andrei said. "A thing in space. Hard . . . no, *solid*."

Their meeting had been preordained, Andrei believed. He had not been looking for it, nor even wishing it. He'd been a bitter man before Rick came into his life, full of hatred for all his fares and all the faces he saw on the street, and it was Rick who unexpectedly offered him a kind of salvation.

"He believes in order."

"Sorry, I don't understand."

"He said, *I believe in order of thing*."

"He believes in the order of things?"

"Yes. Exact."

"When did he say that?"

"When I ask if he is religious."

Knowing of Andrei Stanescu's Orthodox faith, part of Xin Zhu's argument had been to quote the Bible, lines of which—Erika knew from experience—could be pulled out to justify most anything. Zhu hadn't dug too deeply, though, sticking with the old standard. *"And if any mischief follow, then thou shalt give life for life, eye for eye, tooth for tooth, hand for hand, foot for foot, burning for burning, wound for wound, stripe for stripe."*

"Is he religious?"

"He did not say."

"What do you think?"

Andrei stared at Leticia Jones deeply, then touched the bottle of water in front of him but didn't drink. "Maybe," he said, but refused to commit himself further.

Leticia Jones did not bother to tell him that the man he had shot was not his daughter's murderer. It was beyond Leticia Jones's mandate—which was, as far as Erika could tell, to find out everything about the person of Xin Zhu from people who had met him personally, even briefly. What this told Erika was that the CIA knew embarrassingly little about the man, and it was desperate to learn anything.

Leticia Jones saved the most crucial question for the second day, and when she asked it, her tone was exactly as it had been the previous day: calm, welcoming, almost seductive.

"Why do you think he did it?" A pause. A gentle

smile. "Why do you think he helped you—a stranger—take revenge for the murder of your daughter?"

Andrei didn't need to think about that; he'd thought about it ever since March 28, when he'd picked up the big Chinese man from the airport and listened—at times exasperated, other times hypnotized—to his story. "Rick, his son was murdered. He know what it can do to a father. He know how going back to the murderer can make a father good when he is terrible. No, not good. Better."

"Better than good?"

"Better than terrible. He know this man that kill my Adriana. He sees injustice, he wants order. He believes in *order* of thing."

"So Rick is a man who makes order where there is no order."

"Exact."

"You like him."

"He give me gift. He don't know me, but he give me gift."

A gift, Erika thought, *that will ruin you once you've gotten past this wonderful high.*

Before calling the interview finished at 1:18 P.M. on Thursday the twenty-fourth, Leticia Jones rested her hands on the oak table that had separated them all this time, palms down so that each of her long, red-painted nails glimmered under the ceiling lamp, and said, "Herr Stanescu, after hearing all this, it strikes me that you really like Rick. Am I right?"

Andrei nodded. "He is very good man, for me."

"Which makes me wonder," she said, "why you would

be so open with us. Certainly you realize that we don't mean your Rick much good. We're not his friends. In fact, he's done some terrible things to us, and we don't forgive easily."

Andrei nodded.

"Don't you worry you're betraying him?"

Andrei smiled, then intoned, *"Give to Caesar what thing is for Caesar, and to God the things what is for God."*

You just take what you like from that book, thought Erika.

She walked Jones out to her car, and from beyond the trees they heard traffic humming down the highway. "So what did he do to you?" Erika asked in English. When Jones didn't reply, she clarified. "Xin Zhu, I mean. Kidnapping people off of foreign streets is no small thing."

Jones still didn't reply, only smiled, her feet crunching twigs.

"Tell Alan Drummond that if he wants to be a little less secretive, then I could have a look in our files. We might have something."

"Drummond?"

"Your boss."

"You haven't heard," Jones said, shaking her head. "Alan Drummond's out of a job."

"That's why they cleared out the offices of the Department of Tourism?"

To her credit, Jones didn't flinch. "All I know is he's in the unemployment line. Anything else is above my pay grade."

"Like what Xin Zhu did to you people?"

Jones shrugged; then Erika put a hand on her elbow, finally understanding. They looked at each other.

"He destroyed it, didn't he? The department. That would be . . ." Erika took a breath, wondering what this could mean, and how it might have been done. It was quite nearly awe-inspiring. A legendary department that had struck fear in the hearts of spies all over the planet for at least a half century, felled by a single angry man in China.

Leticia Jones wasn't going to affirm or deny a thing. She said, "You've been very kind, and the American people appreciate it."

"I doubt that."

Jones opened the door, then, as an afterthought, placed a hand on Erika's shoulder. "Well, I appreciate it."

"Not enough to tell me what Xin Zhu did to deserve this personality analysis?"

Jones got into her car and rolled down the window. "Xin Zhu did nothing, and everything, if you know what I mean."

"I don't."

A shrug, then Leticia Jones drove away.

By evening, both she and Hector Garza were on flights to New York. Erika asked a team to watch them, but somewhere on the road between New York and D.C., the two agents vanished into the cool American night.

Part One

IN THE HOUSE OF
SOCIALIST PHILOSOPHY

**FRIDAY, MAY 16 TO
TUESDAY, MAY 20, 2008**

1

The time Xin Zhu spent trying to be unheard could have added up to an entire life. Hours driving extra laps through a city, watching the rearview; accumulated minutes gazing into street-window reflections and standing in queues for bread or soup he didn't even want because his stomach was in knots. Sitting behind desks, thinking through cover stories and diversions and wondering how long ago his office was last scoured for bugs. Visits to cemeteries and bars and churches and empty warehouses and parking garages, only to find that his date wasn't going to show up. Meals lost sitting for hours in dark rooms, in airports and train stations and wet public squares, waiting.

Then today, driving the dull hour and a half from Beijing to Nankai along the G020, ditching his ten-year-old Audi and taking a taxi to the train station in tree-lined Xiqing. Waiting on the platform until the Qingdao train started to roll before heaving his large body and small gray overnight bag onto the last car. Hovering in the doorway as the station passed, watching for latecomers. All this, even though this same train began life in south Beijing, not so far from where his journey began. All this, just to meet someone who, like him, lived and worked in Beijing.

The story, which his assistant could be depended on to proliferate, was that Xin Zhu was on a weekend trip to Shanghai to gain 665 miles of perspective and consider his dwindling options. By the time the masters in Beijing realized—if they realized—that the big, silent man checking into Shanghai's Pudong Shangri-La was not Xin Zhu, it would be too late.

As the train headed southeast on its five-hour itinerary, he worked his way toward the front. He was a conspicuously fat man, and when he came upon others either he or they had to squeeze into a spare seat to allow space to pass. Newspapers, covered with photos of devastation—Sichuan province, annihilation by earthquake—were folded noisily to let him by. Occasionally, when coming upon young women with children, he offered a smile of sympathy as he raised his bag above his head, and they wedged themselves past each other. Finally, he found a pair of free seats in the front row of a clean, beige-paneled car. Zhu lifted the armrest between them and settled down gratefully before spotting more photos on more newspapers, rubble and weeping.

There was no other subject in the country, which almost made him feel guilty for this excursion. Four days ago, an earthquake had struck Wenchuan, in eastern Sichuan province, powerful enough to be felt more than a thousand miles away in the capital. The nation had mobilized. Nearly a hundred thousand soldiers were deployed, two thousand Health Ministry medical staff, a hundred and fifty aircraft. The confirmed dead totaled twenty thousand, but the published estimate was at least fifty thousand, which was probably low. In the face of that, what did the future of one fat spy matter?

It didn't.

As he waited for his breathing to ebb and the fine layer of sweat over his blunt features to evaporate, the ash-colored outskirts of Xiqing passed. The air was better here, and would only grow cleaner as they neared the coast. He, too, felt cleaner, being out of the capital. He always felt better in the field.

The conductor, a pleasant-looking woman in an immaculate blue uniform, darkened when he said that he wanted to buy a ticket from her. "You boarded with no ticket?"

"Last-minute change in plans. I had no choice."

"We always have a choice."

He could have ended the discussion by producing his Guoanbu ID, but instead he said, "My choice was to board the train or let my mother die."

"She'll die if she doesn't see your face?"

"The Qingdao hospital is out of blood. She'll die if I don't give her mine."

He could tell from her eyes that she didn't believe

him—at least, she didn't *want* to believe him. She finally said, "You think you can move into one seat?"

Zhu opened his hands to display his girth. "Plainly impossible."

"Then you'll have to pay for two seats."

She was modern in her hairstyle and speech, but Zhu recognized her lineage in the millions of petty dictators China had produced during the Cultural Revolution. Rules as badges, laws as weapons. He said, "Then I will pay for two seats," and reached for his wallet.

As the hours and the sinking landscape passed, he tried to put both Wenchuan and his personal troubles out of his head and watched the young couples that boarded and disembarked at each stop. They looked nothing like the peasant couples of his youth—they had clean teeth, fine clothes, modest jewelry, cell phones, and the sparkle of life about them, as if they could very clearly see what tomorrow looked like and were undeterred. He admired such optimism, even as the newspapers denied it with grisly photographs of collapsed buildings and helmeted workers digging through rubble to find corpses. The whole nation, perhaps the whole world, was watching as hope faded, and Xin Zhu was riding a train to the coast, rather than westward, to work alongside the volunteers. The first step toward helping others, he reflected with only a touch of self-consciousness, is to ensure your own survival.

As they left Jinan, one of his cell phones buzzed. "Shen An-ling," he said into it, his tone one of a man on vacation, "Shanghai is beautiful."

"So I've heard, Xin Zhu," came his assistant's thin voice. "I have also heard that, while you've checked into the hotel, you've barricaded yourself in the room. Might I suggest taking in the sights?"

Shen An-ling was pushing the cover a little too hard, which meant that he wasn't alone. "For the thinking I have to do, distractions will just get in the way."

"Nature, time, and patience are the three great physicians," Shen An-ling said, banally—and uncharacteristically—quoting proverb. "Don't think it can be rushed. You should get some air."

"I'll open the window. Is the office running smoothly?"

"We've been honored by a visit from Yang Qing-Nian."

Of course—Yang Qing-Nian, the right hand of Wu Liang. Who else would have asked why Xin Zhu was not leaving his hotel room? "Does he bring good news from the Supervision and Liaison Committee?"

"He brings good wishes . . . and a request for you to visit the committee at nine o'clock on Monday morning."

"I look forward to it," Zhu said with as much conviction as he could muster. "Make sure Yang Qing-Nian is comfortable. The best tea for Yang Qing-Nian."

His thoughts now utterly derailed, he hung up and took from his bag a small box of rice balls his young wife had prepared. He began to eat them, one by one, imagining Yang Qing-Nian in his Haidian District office, sniffing and touching everything, storing every detail away for his report to Wu Liang. *The place is a mess. They work like English clerks, noses to their screens. Stuffy, no open windows, and it stinks of cigarettes and peanut sauce. The place could do with a good cleaning.*

The irony was that Yang Qing-Nian and his master, Wu Liang, believed that they, in themselves, were enough to inspire fear. They believed that the appearance of Yang Qing-Nian, or anyone from the Ministry of Public Security, the domestic intelligence service, could throw him off his game, or leave him worrying all weekend in Shanghai about a Monday morning scolding. Were they his only worry, he actually would be in Shanghai, at a rooftop bar, enjoying a cognac and a Hamlet. Instead, all he could do now was ask a passing uniformed girl for one of her overpriced bottles of water.

It was nearly five when they pulled into Qingdao Station, which had been renovated for the Olympic boating competitions that would descend in the coming months. As he wandered the platform, bumping into hunched men lighting cigarettes, he gazed up at the freshly ubiquitous spiderweb ceiling of steel and glass. How much had it cost? With all the bribes and evictions that had riddled the great cities' expensive facelifts, no one knew for sure. Then, across the hall, he saw a long but orderly queue leading to a temporary Red Cross counter, handing over donations. Yesterday, the newspapers reported that donations for the earthquake victims had reached 1.3 billion yuan. Zhu walked toward the counter, paused, then approached a wet-faced old woman near the front of the line and gave her ten hundred-yuan notes, about 150 dollars, to add to her offering. She was speechless.

Outside, a bright late-afternoon sun was tempered by the Yellow Sea breeze. He set down his bag, took out a cigar tin, and lit a filtered Hamlet before joining a crowd of young people crossing Feixian Road. They passed two bright, packed restaurants—Kentucky Fried Chicken and McDonald's—on their way to Bathing Beach #6. The teenagers raised their voices and hurried down to the water, while he remained on the side walk, smoking and watching their lean, young bodies prance across the sand and dive into the sea.

Though his own people had been from the mountains, he had always felt sympathy for coastal people. They shared the pragmatic objectivity of their mountain brothers. He watched the out-of-towners flop in the water while the stoic locals looked on and sold them fried things from steaming carts.

The #501 bus was half empty, and he took a pair of seats in the back for the hour-long journey. An entire life could be filled doing these things.

The sun was low in the west when he got out in front of a high-rise on a broad avenue in Laoshan, at the foot of Laoshan Mountain. He was one of five passengers to disembark: two old women, a nervous pregnant woman, and a teenaged boy in a camouflage T-shirt. The old women left the bus stop together, the teenager was met by his mother, and the pregnant woman was met by no one. She sat on the bench, an empty polypropylene bag clutched to her large stomach, and lowered her eyes to the ground. She was, he suspected, crying.

Behind the high-rise he found the inconspicuous dirty-white Citroën Fukang in a small lot full of a variety of makes in a variety of conditions. Behind the wheel, a fifty-six-year-old man smoked with his eyes closed.

"Wake up, Zhang Guo," said Zhu.

Zhang Guo didn't jump; he was too full of himself for that. It was one of his most wonderful traits. Instead, he cracked his eyes and said, "You're late."

"Not by much."

"This whole thing is ridiculous, you know."

"So you're doing well, Zhang Guo?"

"The doctor says my prostate is preparing to explode."

Zhu tossed his overnight bag through the open rear window, then went around to the passenger's door. As he climbed in, the car groaning on its shocks, he said, "So things are about normal for you."

"I should be back in Beijing now, with Chi Shanshan; might as well fill my last days with her."

"I think she'll manage a day without your loving ways. Your wife will be the one suffering."

"How about Sung Hui? Is she as beautiful as last summer?"

"More so. She sleeps a lot."

"Good for her, but not for you."

"Perhaps it is good; my prostate is fine."

Zhang Guo flicked his cigarette out the window, then started the car. "It's remarkable how a man with less time than me can make jokes."

Zhu stared through a crack in the windshield at over-grown grass and more high-rises.

Zhang Guo said, "I'm not driving up the mountain."

"It's a good place to be alone."

"So is this car."

"Then let's drive around the mountain."

Zhang Guo sighed, put the car in reverse, and pulled out.

They began talking while they were still in town, stopping behind trucks and cars in worse shape than their Citroën, idling at lights as clouds of black exhaust billowed around them. Zhu brought up the earthquake, and they compared bleak estimates of fatalities, wondering aloud whom they knew in Sichuan, and which ones they'd heard from. It was a dismal topic, as well as unconstructive—the dead would not be raised by their concern—so Zhu asked some personal questions, giving Zhang Guo license to complain about life in his prestigious neighborhood of Beijing's Dongcheng District, his unbearable wife, his jealous mistress, and the atmosphere of paranoia that was enveloping the Supervision and Liaison Committee. "It's a place full of bad news," he said as they finally left town and started down the seaside highway that skirted the base of Laoshan Mountain and its famous spirits. To their right, the Yellow Sea opened.

"You heard about Wu Liang?" asked Zhang Guo.

"That he's preparing to destroy me?"

"The other thing."

"He's taking over Olympic security."

"And?"

"And it's a smart decision. Jiang Luoke wasn't organized enough."

"Jiang Luoke made the truce with al Qaeda."

"Which is only as good as the paper it's written on."

"It's not written on any paper."

Zhu clapped his hands twice.

Zhang Guo leaned into a turn as they entered the mountain's shadow. "Maybe we should have pushed your name," he said lightly, then shook his head. "Oh, that's right. You're the one who started a war with the CIA, then accused the esteemed Ministry of Public Security of harboring CIA vipers. I'd forgotten."

"You're being melodramatic."

"Xin Zhu, you killed three dozen CIA agents."

"Not quite. A few got away."

Zhang Guo showed him a pair of raised brows and flat yellow teeth, then returned to the road. "Of course, your mistake wasn't slaughtering the CIA. It was letting our masters learn of it."

"I didn't tell anyone."

Again, those eyes and teeth. "I'm guessing that your assistant, the one with the girl's name, boasted like a peacock after too many glasses of baijiu."

"An-ling is a unisex name. It's the kind of name you get when you're cursed with parents from the artist class."

"This is what happens when you hire from the artist class, Xin Zhu."

"Shen An-ling said nothing."

Zhang Guo took a dark, heavy hand off the wheel and patted at his shirt pockets until he'd found another cigarette. "The point," he said after slipping it between his lips, "is that Wu Liang has you cornered. He's got his ministry as well as the whole committee in a panic. Yang Qing-Nian is boasting that he'll get you dismissed."

"Yang Qing-Nian is a child, and he's terrified of the CIA."

"We're all terrified of the CIA. All except you, of course. People think you've gone *mad*. You realize that, don't you?"

Through squinted eyes, Zhu gazed at the long mountain shadow reaching across the water, smothering rocks and sailboats and white brushstrokes of wave. If he was mad, would he know? Or would it only take a coordinated effort by those he'd angered over the years to give him a proper diagnosis? Wu Liang and Yang Qing-Nian of the Ministry of Public Security, both ranking members of the Supervision and Liaison Committee, the Party organ that, among other things, oversaw discipline in their particular profession. Zhang Guo was also a member of that committee, from the Supreme People's Procuratorate, while Xin Zhu was merely a Guoanbu foot soldier. Could men such as these properly diagnose something he would never see in himself?

He said, "The committee also thinks the future of espionage lies in hacking California tech companies. They're afraid of their own shadows."

"That's possible," Zhang Guo said, "but now you've dragged me out to the edge of the country because you're afraid of *them*. What are we doing here?"

"The committee wants to talk to me on Monday morning."

"Does this surprise you?" When Zhu didn't answer, he said, "They want to know what all of us want to know, Xin Zhu. They want to know *why*. Why you set up a mole inside that secret Department of Tourism, and then, once the mole was uncovered, you killed thirty-three of their agents in all corners of the world. Without requesting permission. They think they know the reason—revenge. For the death of your son, Delun. But that wasn't the CIA's fault. It was the fault of some Sudanese farmers with machetes and sunstroke."

To their right, a peninsula reached out into the water, marking the halfway point of their journey around these mountains, pointing in the direction of South Korea. Zhu said something.

"What?"

Zhu turned back. "We've had this conversation before. Theirs is a causal responsibility. They killed an opposition figure in order to disrupt civil order in Sudan. Therefore, any deaths that result from that disorder are their fault."

"You can't treat a bureaucracy like an individual. Imagine if we were treated that way."

"I'd expect no less from the fathers of our victims," Zhu said, knowing as he said it that they would all be dead if that really came to pass. He waved at a parking area up ahead, a scenic outpost. "Pull over."

As they slowed and parked, two cars passed. One had Laoshan plates, the other Beijing. Zhang Guo nodded at them. "You don't think . . ."

"I have no idea," Zhu said, then gazed out the open window. Sea, horizon. He said, "It wasn't just revenge, you know. Everyone thinks that's what it was—the committee, you, probably even the Americans. Revenge factored into it, but it was also a practical decision. That's something I'll have to explain on Monday morning. By eradicating one of their secret departments, we have sent a serious message to the Americans, the same message we want to send with the Olympic Games. That we are the primary force in the world. We are a nation that has suffered long enough—that's the past. The present is this: We are a superpower of unfathomable riches, and we will not stand for interference, particularly from a country on the other side of the planet that still refers to itself as the world's *only* superpower."

Zhang Guo let that sit a moment before shaking his head. "Then they see fifty thousand die in Sichuan. Is this how a superpower takes care of its people?"

Zhu didn't answer, because he'd had this thought himself. Instead, he turned in his seat as best he could, reaching toward the bag he'd left in the back, but his hand only batted air inches from its handle. An involuntary grunt escaped his lips.

"Just sit back," Zhang Guo said, sighing.

Zhu did so, and, without looking, Zhang Guo reached his long right arm back and deftly snatched the bag. He tugged it up to the front and handed it to Zhu.

"Thanks."

Zhang Guo watched another car pass, then got out and walked around to where slanted trees framed the view of the sea. Inside the car, Zhu unlatched the strap and fingered at a thin file inside, finding a 4R-sized blowup of a passport photo. Here was the real reason for this meeting. He sat staring at it a moment, at the black woman, midthirties, before opening his door and placing his feet on dirt. The freshness of the salty breeze was a shock after the car's smoky interior. Down below, surf raged. "Come look at this."

Zhang Guo wandered back and took the photo. "Pretty," he said after a moment, "for one of them." He passed it back.

"You've seen her before?"

"Should I have?"

There was no sense being coy with Zhang Guo. "She's one of the ones who survived."

"One of the Tourists?"

"She went by the name Leticia Jones. We never did learn her real name."

"Why are you carrying around her photograph?"

Zhu sniffed. "A week ago she landed in Shanghai on another passport—Rosa Mumu, Sudanese."

A bang sounded as Zhang Guo hit the roof of the car with his fist, then walked away, feeling his chest for another cigarette. Once he had it lit, he turned back. "Where is she now?"

"She left Beijing last week, flying to Cairo. As for the week she spent here, we're just starting to piece it together."

"But why *would* she be here? An agent on her own

can't expect to do anything, particularly one that's blown."

"She did elude us for a week, all by herself. I only found out that she'd been here once she was gone. A border guard heard her speaking English to another Sudanese. The Sudanese tried to speak Arabic with her, but she didn't know it. It wasn't reason enough to hold her, but the guard noted her name for later examination. Someone from Sun Bingjun's department passed it on to me, as a query. I recognized her photo from my Tourism files."

Zhang Guo cursed loudly.

"It means little at this point," Zhu said, as much for himself as for Zhang Guo, "but she wouldn't be here without a reason; something operational, or just to scout opportunities."

"Opportunities for what? For an act of revenge against the great Xin Zhu?"

Zhu slipped the photo back into his bag. "I have no idea. I don't even know if she works for the CIA anymore."

"She had a forged Sudanese passport."

"The CIA doesn't have a monopoly on forged passports."

"Perhaps she's working for Wu Liang," Zhang Guo suggested.

"I've considered that."

"It was a joke, Xin Zhu."

Zhu gave a smile, but it wasn't a joke to him. None of this was. Wu Liang and the Supervision and Liaison Committee, the CIA, or any number of agencies he'd given trouble to over the last decades could be after him. After enough years, the idea of "the other" becomes faceless and broad, its tentacles ubiquitous enough to hide in every crevice.

"So what do you want from me, Xin Zhu?"

"I'd like to know what I'll be facing on Monday morning. Specifics. The precise examples they will use against me."

Zhang Guo nodded. "You'll have it by Sunday."

"As for the woman, I'll need to know if the Ministry of Public Security has anything on her."

This time Zhang Guo hesitated. He took a long drag and exhaled smoke that was instantly swept away by the wind. "Xin Zhu, two months ago you claimed that the Ministry of Public Security was harboring a Western mole, and then you cut it off from your intelligence product. When asked to show your evidence, you handed the committee notes detailing Chinese information owned by the Department of Tourism, information you said could only have been gathered by an inside source. The information could not be verified because the CIA had closed the Department of Tourism after your assault, but did that stop you? No. You demanded that the committee freeze the ministry's entire administrative section until someone had been arrested."

"I was ignored," Zhu pointed out.

"But not forgotten. You don't run the Guoanbu. You don't even preside over a core department. You've always been on the fringe, and you've always made enemies. My suspicion is that, on Monday morning, you'll be sent to preside over some township collective near

Mongolia while your office is closed down to make room for an elementary school. You're more trouble than you're worth."

"Does that mean you won't ask if they have anything on the woman?"

Zhang Guo stared at him, eyes large, then threw down his cigarette. He started to laugh. "Okay. I'll talk to the Ministry of Public Security. I've got someone who might help, just as long as he doesn't know that it's for you."

"Thanks."

"And you have no idea what this Jones did during her week here?"

"We have the hotel. We have one night at the hotel restaurant," Zhu said, which was not necessarily a lie, only a misleading omission. "What we need is help."

"What you need is to prepare a defense for Monday morning."

"What I need is a drink. Shall we?"

Zhang Guo approached and placed a hand on Zhu's thinning scalp. "You are one ugly, fat bastard. Sung Hui must be blind."

"Finally, we're in agreement."

2

Sung Hui was from Xinyang, a Young Pioneer and then a member of the Youth League whose enlightened proletarian worldview had earned her, at the age of twenty-three, a trip to Beijing for the Fifteenth National Representative Conference in 2003. Delun had met her first, him only twenty-one and full of fire for this beautiful provincial girl with the fierce Party line. Because his mother had been dead more than a decade, he showed off his girl to his father, and sometime during the next few years the lines blurred. Delun shipped off to Sudan to work for Sinopec. A riot of dark-skinned men hacked him up with machetes. That was April 2007. Three months later, Sung Hui moved in with Xin Zhu, and at first theirs was a home of shared mourning. Then, inexplicably, she asked him to marry her.

Since his first wife's death in 1989, a month before the June Fourth Incident in Tiananmen Square, Zhu had lost track of the nuances of living with a woman. With Sung Hui he found himself hesitating in a way he hadn't done since he was a teenager, musing over his replies to her simple questions and standing for too long in shops, puzzling over which brand of wristwatch she would prefer. More than this, though, was the protectiveness he felt. Sung Hui was twenty-eight, thirty years his junior, and he inevitably viewed her as a potential victim. Partly, it was the victimization he had seen and taken part in during his fifty-eight years; partly, it was the memory of his son being hacked apart in Africa. So he kept her separated from as many aspects of his work as possible, and to protect her he even lied to Zhang Guo, his oldest friend, about Leticia Jones's mission.

On Wednesday, two days before he met with Zhang Guo and five days after Leticia Jones, or Rosa Mumu, left China, Sung Hui's seamstress arrived at their apartment in a state of distress. Sung Hui made her tea and sat her in the kitchen, and after a series of questions learned that the seamstress's niece had been questioned at length by an acquaintance at the Blim-Blam, a rock-and-roll venue in the university area of Haidian, not so far from Zhu's office. The questions concerned Sung Hui and her life with her husband, her daily rituals and regular appointments. Sung Hui called Zhu at work, and he immediately returned home, then drove with the seamstress to meet the niece, who gave a description of the young man—Dongfan Beisan, early twenties, "very sexy," a musician. He played regularly at the Blim-Blam. His home was a mystery, as he had not registered his address with the authorities.

Instead of sharing this with the Ministry of Public Security and requesting a file on Dongfan Beisan, that night he brought Shen An-ling with him to the club, a dirty basement-level cellar on a narrow, grimy hutong choked with parked bicycles. The Blim-Blam was full of children drinking beer from plastic cups and wearing soiled T-shirts and jeans, disheveled hair, and expressions of complete boredom. The Ramones played from fuzzy speakers. The teens' boredom flickered briefly at the sight of two men in suits entering their lair, one an enormous, balding older man doing his best to touch nothing, the other a nearsighted, soft-skinned man who squinted at everything in surprise. The rock-and-rollers had no idea what this could mean.

On a hand-drawn sign inside the door, they had learned that the two acts of the night were the Pink Undergarments and Dongfan Beisan's band, Just Teenage Rebels, and they would be playing in memory of the Sichuan dead. Zhu and Shen An-ling approached the bar; a long zinc affair salvaged from the demolition of the Yugong Yishan Bar—another casualty of Olympic grandeur—and asked the bartender for the bands' dressing room. That provoked a laugh. "Right over there," he said, waving at the far side of the club, where teenagers were drifting in and out of a ragged opening in the brick wall.

Beyond was a dim corridor that stank of piss and led to a unisex bathroom with girls checking eyeliner in cracked mirrors and boys smoking and kicking each other at the urinals. Shen An-ling looked like he might be sick.

Through an open stall Zhu spotted three skinny young men with long hair, one in tight leather pants, another with drumsticks shoved into his jeans pocket, sharing a joint. By that point, however, the intruders had been spotted, and the girls were packing up their pencils and scooting past them to leave. The boys by the urinals left still zipping up. It was the drummer who first saw Zhu and Shen An-ling, and he nudged the one in leather. The third, in a T-shirt and knee-length shorts, looked over and panicked, dropping the joint into the toilet.

"Just Teenage Rebels?" Zhu asked.

The one in shorts whispered something, and all he caught was the word "producer."

"Yeah," said the one in leather. He, like the girls, was wearing eyeliner. "We're Just Teenage Rebels."

Shen An-ling clapped his hands together, clearly over his shock. "And you, I'll bet, are the great Dongfan Beisan."

A slow-witted, stoned smile. "That's right, comrade." He came out of the stall finally, shoving his fingers into his pockets, playing nonchalance. "You guys from Modern Sky?"

Modern Sky was a large, independent record label. "How did you know?" asked Shen An-ling.

"I *knew* it!" said the one in shorts.

Quietly, the drummer said, "No, they're not."

For a couple of seconds, no one filled the silence. Then Zhu said, "Dongfan Beisan, can we have a word in private?"

"Any deal we make is for all of us."

From behind, Zhu heard a laughing girl approach, see their backs, grow quiet, then turn and leave. Shen An-ling said to Zhu, "They're not serious enough. I told you this was a bad idea."

"You're right," Zhu answered, then raised a plump finger to point at Dongfan Beisan. "You looked serious, but I'm often wrong."

The one in shorts nudged Dongfan Beisan. "Go on, it's cool."

The drummer said nothing. His face was bleak.

Dongfan Beisan licked his dry lips, then glanced back at his friends. "Tonight, one for all. Trust me," he said, then high-fived them and approached Zhu and Shen An-ling, fingers back in his pockets. "All right, then. Let's deal."

As they retraced their steps through the club and up to the street, watched closely by a hundred young eyes, Dongfan Beisan throwing thumbs-up at friends, the whole thing struck Zhu as too easy. A man asking invasive questions about your wife simply walks out to the street with you, as if there were nothing to fear—a sign of innocence or stupidity? He leaned toward the latter.

The street was rain-streaked, dirty, and busy, people looking in shops and visiting bars, students everywhere in cheap button-up shirts and ironed jeans. At the sight of the black four-door Audi A6 that they had squeezed into this alley, Dongfan Beisan hesitated. Zhu opened the passenger door and sat down, his feet outside the car. He'd walked too much that day.

"So what are we talking about?" asked Dongfan

Beisan. "One, two records? Because I think we should discuss the lineup. I'm thinking about going solo. Mister Clean—that's my new name."

"Shut up," said Shen An-ling, his voice not unthreatening.

Zhu said, "Dongfan Beisan, do you know who I am?"

The musician's mouth worked the air; then he shook his head. "Not from Modern Sky, that's for fucking sure."

"I am the husband of Sung Hui."

He watched Dongfan Beisan's face as it shut down. The boy was removing all trace of emotion, first from the cheeks, then the eyes, and finally the twitching lips. Everything relaxed into that blank look that had been the salvation of so many Chinese. Finally, "I don't know her."

"Why, then, were you interrogating a girl about her?"

Zhu kept his voice light and measured, but Shen An-ling chose a different tack. From behind the boy, he whispered, "Because Dongfan Beisan wants to fuck your wife. That's why." He opened the rear door. "Get in."

"No," said the boy, still blank-faced. "I don't know what you're talking about."

Zhu exhaled and rubbed his face as a pair of men on bicycles rode by, keeping their eyes directly ahead. Zhu said, "Let's talk in the office," and Shen An-ling, taking it the wrong way, grabbed the back of Dongfan Beisan's shirt collar and pushed hard, so that the boy's forehead bounced loudly against the roof of the car. Pain ran through Dongfan Beisan's face; then he removed all expression again and submitted as Shen An-ling stuffed him into the backseat.

That single act of violence proved sufficient, for as they wound north through Haidian District, Shen An-ling taking the long way, sticking to dark streets and doubling back on himself occasionally, Dongfan Beisan abruptly broke the silence with "She's an American."

"You better not be talking about his wife," Shen An-ling said.

"No, no. Mary Caul. She works at the American consulate in Guangzhou."

Zhu lowered his sun visor to peer into a small mirror at the boy. "Go on."

"I met her at the New Get Lucky."

"The what?"

"Chaoyang District," Shen An-ling said. "They serve German beer."

"How long ago was this?" Zhu asked.

"When I met her? Five, six months ago. She's from New York City. Pretty. She liked me."

"Did you have sex with her?" asked Zhu.

He was surprised to see embarrassment break through the boy's mask. "When she was in town," he said, almost a whisper.

"At your place?"

Dongfan Beisan shook his head. "Never. Her hotel."

"Which one?"

"Crowne Plaza."

Shen An-ling whistled. "Must've thought you'd hit the jackpot."

The boy frowned but said nothing.

"And she asked you to check on my wife?"

"Last week. Thursday. Mary said that Sung Hui was an old friend of hers. She said she was worried about her, because she had . . ." He trailed off.

"Don't stop now," said Zhu.

"She said that Sung Hui had married a brutal man who kept her imprisoned. She had no way to contact her, unless she could meet her by accident. So she wanted to know what her daily schedule was."

"Bái chī," said Shen An-ling.

"He's not retarded," Zhu corrected. "He's just in love. The two are very similar."

Dongfan Beisan said nothing.

Zhu said, "How did you know to talk to a relative of my wife's seamstress?"

"Mary told me."

"She didn't know how to run casually into my wife, but she knew the name and family of my wife's seamstress?"

"I . . . I didn't think of that," he said. The kid really was an idiot.

Despite Shen An-ling's protests, they returned to the Blim-Blam and let Dongfan Beisan, stunned and wobbly, leave. Then they went to the office and learned from the files that Mary Caul was indeed attached to the American consulate in Guangzhou as part of the Foreign Commercial Service—or she had been, until last Friday, when she returned to the United States for good. She had left, Shen An-ling pointed out unnecessarily, the day after asking Dongfan Beisan to collect information on Sung Hui. Also unnecessarily, he reminded

Zhu that Leticia Jones's visit overlapped with Mary Caul's final days in China.

By then it was after midnight, so Zhu called home to learn from the maid that Sung Hui was asleep, then had Shen An-ling drive him to the Crowne Plaza. He spent the next three hours with the head of security, a round-faced Uighur who kept sending for pots of Long Jing tea as they sorted through audio recordings from rooms and video files from the public areas. Zhu had approximate days, and he knew one name for sure—Mary Caul—and had her file photo. The other—Rosa Mumu, a.k.a. Leticia Jones—had stayed at the Hua Thai, but he had her photo to guide his hunch. On a video file marked Tuesday, May 6, when the time code indicated 3:12 in the morning, they found it. Leticia Jones and Mary Caul sitting close together on a leather sofa in the lobby, talking animatedly, almost intimately.

"You have sound?"

"Apologies, comrade," said the Uighur.

Despite the extra care he took in making such decisions, Zhu made a mistake when, the next morning, Sung Hui asked what the rock and roller had been up to. After staring at the gray sky through the kitchen window for about four seconds, he decided on honesty and told her that the source of his questions was an American intelligence agent. Sung Hui moved slowly to the table and sank into a chair. She said, "They want to kill me."

"Why would they want to kill you?" he asked, reaching for her hand.

She didn't answer, just stared at his large hand enclosing hers.

"Because of your considerable efforts against them?" he asked.

She shook her head, smiling, knowing how funny that sounded. Since their marriage, she had ceased all Party work. She'd become, by her own admission, *a capitalist slug, yearning to live in a fashion magazine.* Finally, she said, "I don't know why they want to kill me."

"Because they don't."

She raised her head, the smile gone, clutching at his fingers with her other hand. "Then it's you they want to kill."

The problem, he knew, was that she'd lived and breathed radical Party doctrine too fully and for too long. For her, Western intelligence agencies sought only one thing—the destruction of Chinese communism—and would stack up as many Chinese bodies as they believed necessary in order to accomplish this.

"Maybe they don't want to kill anyone," Zhu told her, but she didn't look as if she believed that. He wasn't sure he did, either.

Zhang Guo had booked a private sea-view room at Yijing Lou, one of the top Qingdao restaurants, and before sitting down they toured the aquariums with the waiter and pointed out their preferences. "That one looks like Wu Liang," Zhang Guo said, nodding at a tired-looking gray eel on the floor of one tank.

Zhu bent to look closely into its black eyes, then straightened. "Close enough. I'll have him fried," he told the waiter, who bowed with exaggerated formality.

It was nine by the time their food arrived, and the table was already littered with four empty beer bottles that the waiter soon swept away. Through the open window they watched ships light the surface of the calm water and, above, the snuffing out of stars as clouds drifted in. "How did it feel?" asked Zhang Guo.

"How did what feel?"

"Wiping out the *Department of Tourism*," he said in his heavily accented English. "That's what they call it?"

"They don't call it anything now."

Zhang Guo snorted, then took another bite. "This trout is delicious. Want some?"

Zhu didn't answer.

"How's your eel?"

Zhu said, "They were the most terrifying two days of my life. Afterward, I slept for twenty hours."

Zhang Guo chewed thoughtfully, waiting.

Zhu said, "By the time I woke up, I'd lost my doubt. I'm not a maniac, you know. I knew as I sent out the order that what I was doing would be controversial. I knew why I didn't ask for permission—I would have been denied it. But we've sat back for too long, congratulating ourselves on our economic miracle and not ensuring its future. You well know that we have an agreement with the Chinese people. They will hold their tongues and allow us to do as we please only as long as they see progress. Steady progress in their daily lives. As soon as some agency like the CIA succeeds in its plots to undermine our progress, Chinese citizens will be faced with stagnation or, worse, a reversal of their fortunes. Unlike Jiang Luoke's deal with al Qaeda, this one is written in blood. A few bad years, and they will be out for ours."

"So you're thinking of the future. A young wife will do that to you."

"You're damned right I am!" Zhu said, louder than he'd said anything that day. He took a breath. "Think, Zhang Guo. One-child policy. In twenty years the average family structure will be one child caring for two parents and four grandparents. How are we going to support that if the Americans are picking at our economy? Think, too, of the fact that we have sixteen percent more boys than girls. How many millions of unmarried men will that make? Men with unsatisfied libidos, crippled by poverty. *That's* the next generation, Zhang Guo. Those are the disaffected men who, in twenty years, will hang us in the streets."

It had been a long speech, but Zhang Guo didn't need to spend much time digesting it; he'd heard much of this before. He sipped his beer from the bottle, emptied it, then set the bottle down. He said, "You've already lost this argument, Xin Zhu. Twelve years ago Jia Chunwang gave you a public throttling because you were trying to stop him from recalling our undercover agents in the West. You barely survived that. This year, you alienated the entire Ministry of Public Security with your unfounded mole theory. Now you're ignoring anyone who might oppose you. You're pretending they don't even exist. But they do exist, Xin Zhu. And they'll eat you alive."

Zhu sighed, reaching for his own bottle. "Did you know that, ever since he took the job, the director of the CIA itself had been lobbying to get rid of the Department of Tourism? They have as many backroom battles as we do. Quentin Ascot may be embarrassed by what I've done, but in the end he won't fight back because I've done what he's been unable to do."

"I doubt he wanted to actually kill the whole department."

"I saved him a lot of retirement packages."

"And now there's a Tourist poking around Beijing. Think that maybe your calculations were off?"

"How about these calculations, Zhang Guo? Imagine that I'm right about the mole in the Ministry of Public Security, and he reports to the CIA on Monday that Xin Zhu has been sacked. They learn that the only person willing to make them pay for what they did to us in Sudan was fired. Are you with me? Now run the math. How long before they try something like that again?"

Zhang Guo took out a cigarette. "Maybe, knowing you're not around to shoot them in the face, they'll try to make friends."

Zhu considered this, staring down at the remains of his fried eel. It didn't look like Wu Liang at all. "If someone is looking at me, it's not Quentin Ascot. I'm convinced of that."

"Then who is it?"

Zhu rubbed his face and reached for a fresh beer.

3

The only similarity between the fried eel and Wu Liang was the indigestion that struck him on the long train ride from Jinan down to Shanghai, making it hard to doze even in the deluxe soft sleeper cabin, with its private toilet and a view of the countryside blackness between stations. Nanjing was lit up like a landing field, even though the sun had risen by then, and it was afternoon by the time he reached Shanghai. Wobbly with fatigue, he stored his bag in a station locker, then took buses over to Fucheng Road and searched until he'd found, among the looming modern towers, a public phone booth. He called the Shangri-La and, putting on a slightly comical Hokkien accent, asked to speak to Mr. Xin Zhu. Two rings, then he hung up and called again, telling the clerk that he'd been disconnected. This time, it only rang once before a man said in a tired voice not unlike Xin Zhu's, "Wèi?"

"Mr. Xin Zhu," Zhu said, keeping up the accent,

"you called us regarding a date for this evening. We're sorry that your usual friend is not available, but perhaps we can send someone else."

"That may be acceptable," said the hotel guest, who was in fact He Qiang, a field agent he had twice before used to impersonate himself. It was a rare man who had the build to impersonate Xin Zhu, though He Qiang still required ample padding.

Zhu stifled a yawn. "She will need to know your room number, of course."

"Of course, it's 1298. But maybe, to start, she and I could have a drink in the hotel bar."

"An excellent idea," said Zhu. "Might I suggest an eight o'clock rendezvous in the Jade on 36?"

Zhu gave it another half hour, strolling down to the dock and finding, to his delight, a Häagen-Dazs shop, where he bought a scoop of Chocolate Chocolate Chip that he ate while sitting on a bench and gazing at the Huangpu River. He watched faces again, but these were a more developed version of the New Chinese he had seen on the train to Qingdao. The high-rises of Qingdao had their share of business elite, but Shanghai was their breeding ground. They sported suits like second skins, the women comfortable in Western fashions, all secure in the knowledge that their city, the most populous city of the most populous country on the planet, had a reach that stretched around the globe. He hadn't been lying when he told Zhang Guo that China was the superpower to be reckoned with, and though he could never feel comfortable with the economic policies that

Shanghai represented, its very existence proved that their country was now something completely different. Arriving here was like arriving at a future of perpetual motion, and it was part of his responsibility to make sure that nothing external slowed it down. Perpetual motion, perpetual revolution. He ate his ice cream slowly, feeling it cut through the eel that seemed to still slither in his stomach, and thought of speed.

He entered as any guest would, through the glassy front doors and into the packed marble lobby, knowing that whoever was watching—and whether they'd been sent by Wu Liang, the committee, or the Americans, *someone* was always watching—would think that he'd eluded them on the way out, and that was something no watcher would admit in a report. He breezed past a gathering of Japanese businessmen and shared the elevator with a Canadian couple who were plainly in love. A rare sight.

The door to 1298, though displaying a DO NOT DISTURB sign, was ajar. He pushed it open to find a clean, empty room, the blinds drawn, and a key card left on the foot of the made bed. He closed the door behind himself, heard noise in the bathroom, and found He Qiang, a thick, big-shouldered man in his forties with a small mole on his cheek, sitting on the toilet, smiling. Hanging from the curtain rod, dripping dry, was a padded undergarment—the "fat suit" He Qiang had arrived wearing.

They shook hands, and Zhu leaned close to his ear, whispering, "I'm going to sleep. Wake me at seven."

He Qiang nodded.

"She'll make it by eight?"

"You'll like her," He Qiang whispered. "Xinyang girl. Very nice, and she knows the town. If you like, she can show you a good time."

Zhu gave him a look, and He Qiang raised his hands.

"If you like, I said."

Zhu washed up, and by the time he lay on the large, hard bed it was just after two. He Qiang plugged headphones into the television, settled on the floor, and began watching a DVD that, Zhu realized before falling asleep, was from Bollywood. So He Qiang liked the music and melodrama of those sorts of movies. He'd never have suspected the man was a dreamer. Xin Zhu certainly was not, and his dreamless sleep proved it.

He Qiang woke him gently with a shake of the shoulder, then pointed at a cup of hot black tea on the bedside table, alongside a sheet of paper filled with childlike scrawl. As he sipped the tea, he read over what proved to be He Qiang's report of his time in the hotel. Who he'd spotted down in the street, how many calls (unanswered, of course) came to his room, and when, and the demeanor of the service staff that visited the room. Upon arriving, he'd changed his room but still found one camera in the overhead lamp, which he'd disposed of, and two microphones—he'd left one of them. No one had tried to replace anything. He Qiang's assessment, which tallied with Xin Zhu's, was that while there was no urgency to the surveillance, someone was certainly keeping tabs on him.

Zhu was able to verify this when he descended in the elevator, wearing one of the suits He Qiang had packed, and found, leaning against a wall outside the Jade, an athletic-looking young man working his way through a copy of *People's Daily*. He was dressed like a factory worker ready for a big night out—a peasant's idea of what the urban rich wear to gala events—but none of the hotel staff was kicking him out. Zhu passed him without a glance and found a place at the end of the Jade's glowing bar.

The girl was in her midtwenties, small boned with a wide, flat nose and pebbly eyes. She found him as he was finishing his second drink, and introduced herself formally as Liu Xiuxiu, then took the stool beside him. A Caucasian man in the corner was playing progressive jazz on a piano. Zhu ordered her a glass of Chardonnay, while he drank his Glenlivet. She, like Sung Hui, was from Xinyang, but that was where the similarities ended. This girl knew exactly what she was doing.

The conversation began with formalities, and he admired how she was able to ride the flow of topics and then control it without ever seeming to interfere. Like most conversations that week, Wenchuan and the whole devastated Sichuan province soon became its focal point. Liu Xiuxiu said, "Fifty thousand. I can't even imagine that many people, can you? If forced, I could count that high, but I can't picture it."

"After a certain number," he said, "the mind just balks."

"Exactly."

He took a sip of whisky. "Earthquakes are just scratching the surface. In three years, the Great Leap Forward killed at least twenty million from starvation. That's a number I've spent decades trying to grasp. I never will."

Appropriately, Liu Xiuxiu grew quiet and looked into her glass. A lesser escort would have said, *I don't know anything about politics*, but Liu Xiuxiu's silence suggested she knew enough to hold her tongue. Xin Zhu, however, was drinking on a ravenously empty stomach, and his judgment suffered. He said, "Back then, Xinyang was hit very hard. The political semantics are wonderful—we call it the Three Years of Natural Disasters. There was nothing natural about what happened. The food was there, sitting in the silos, but no one was allowed to eat it because the grain was needed to fulfill quotas." He smiled, raising his glass. "The Great Leap!"

Hearing his own delirious words, he expected her to set down her glass and walk out. Perhaps she would throw the Chardonnay into his face, but the glass remained in her hand, and she said, "Have you eaten?"

"No."

"Perhaps a restaurant would be a good idea?"

She was going to take care of him. He Qiang had done very well.

Though she suggested a place up Minsheng Road, he patted his stomach and told her that speed was of the essence, so they hurried to the Fook Lam Moon in another wing of the hotel. Zhu ordered shark's fin, while Liu Xiuxiu settled on fried rice with chicken and octopus. As he gorged himself on an appetizer of chilled shrimp they looked out over the Bund, where colonial-era European banks and customs houses cut through the high-rises. The sight filled him with the desire to discuss history, but he was starting to slide out of his idiocy and didn't want to push his luck. "How long have you been in Shanghai?" he asked, switching to English.

She smiled modestly and placed her hands in her lap beneath the edge of the table, and he noticed in this different light of the restaurant that her skin was like opaque glass. It made him think that, if enough illumination were applied, he would be able to see through the skin to her organs and blood vessels. In very competent English, she said, "I came six years ago, to study nursing at Jiao Tong, but . . ." She faded out. "Academics did not suit me."

"You have residence papers?"

She nodded but did not elaborate.

"And how do you know He Qiang?"

Another smile. "His cousin was a schoolmate in Xinyang, and when I came here I got in touch. He Qiang has been very kind to me."

Zhu wondered how kind, and how many rules He Qiang had bent for this pretty girl. He still hadn't gotten a proper meal, though, and until then he would continue to be magnanimous. "It must be difficult."

"It has been," she admitted, bowing her head. "Without friends like He Qiang, it would have been much more difficult. But now, I've . . ." Again, she faded out, then raised her head. "I've adjusted."

There was something piercing about that two-word sentence that, even in English, made Zhu want to weep. He understood why He Qiang had set them up together for this fictitious date. She was lovely, and she would, if asked, go to bed with him, but her true value lay in the fact that she had *adjusted* to the hard life of Shanghai. She could adjust to anything, even working for a man as problematic as Xin Zhu.

In addition to her fluency in English, which she had first studied and then perfected through her job, she knew a smattering of German. When he quizzed her about Shanghai, he found that she could recall the most insignificant details—the color combinations of shop signs, the names of most of Shanghai's doormen, as well as their wives—and that nothing he said was forgotten by her. Most importantly, she had—also, no doubt, because of her job—the uncanny ability of making him feel comfortable in his own skin, which was no small feat.

The food was delicious and restorative, but she barely touched her rice, though when he ordered the fruit platter for dessert she ate ravenously. She showed no hesitation when he suggested they go up to his room, but in the elevator, she seemed unsure about what to do, so she left her hands by her sides. He unlocked the door and let her in first, and it was she who first spotted He Qiang, standing in the bathroom doorway, gesturing for her silence. That, remarkably, did not throw her off. She walked to the dressers and, hands clasped in front of her stomach, waited. He Qiang smiled at Zhu.

Taking off his jacket, Zhu said, "You are a very beautiful woman."

Smiling now, too, Liu Xiuxiu said, "You're too kind." Then she said, "Let me help you with your shoes."

"Thank you," he said, but when she stepped forward, he waved her back and went to the bed, sat down, and took off his own shoes. "That feels nice," he said.

Seductively, she said, "Mmm."

"Come here," he said, then pushed himself onto the bed so that it squeaked. "Mmm," he groaned.

Liu Xiuxiu covered her smile with a small hand.

As if he were alone, Zhu fluffed a pillow and closed his eyes, then opened them. He gestured to Liu Xiuxiu, pointed at his watch and held up one finger, then waved her away. She nodded. To He Qiang he showed two fingers, then closed his eyes again. He Qiang led Liu Xiuxiu to the bathroom and quietly closed the door behind them.

As instructed, Liu Xiuxiu left at one in the morning, conspicuously holding her high-heeled shoes in her hand until she was outside his door, where she crouched and slipped them on. In the lobby, as she would later report, she noticed a few different men watching her but was unable to discern who among them had only professional interest.

At two, He Qiang woke Zhu and made him tea; then they sat together at the desk. Each had a sheet of paper and a pen, and they talked in the written word. Specifically, French. Zhu wrote in an elegant script, He Qiang in the block capitals of someone with far less education than he had. Zhu wrote:

The things one does to be unheard.

He Qiang smiled and nodded.

I like her. She's available?
Absolutely. Hates Her Job, Loves Her Country.
Relationships?
Ex-Husband, Criminal. No Problem.
Criminal class?
Green Gang. Collects Protection Money, Cuts Tendons.
Divorce?

He Qiang nodded.

I want her in Beijing tomorrow—Monday. Possible?

Another nod.

She's not coming back.
Understand.
You come, too.

He Qiang had begun to smile again. Since the killing of the American agents two months ago, he had been left to wander, which was no good for him. The call to fly to Shanghai and again impersonate his boss had been a welcome respite from his aimless days. Now he was being called back to the pit. He wrote, GOOD.

Zhu considered that word, *bon*, then wrote,

Tomorrow the committee will try to get rid of me.
I will hold them off, but in the meantime, you and
Liu Xiuxiu will work on another project. The Amer-
icans are preparing their retaliation.

He Qiang read carefully, then looked Zhu in the
eyes before writing again.

Against You?
Maybe. They're looking at my wife.

Another stare. He Qiang had only met Sung Hui
once, at an official gathering where he'd been assigned
protection duty, but he'd been visibly taken by the girl.

Makes No Sense.
It makes sense. We need to find out what kind of
sense.

Sung Hui had left the television on when she opened
the door for him that Sunday afternoon, and when he
settled on the sofa, he was greeted by images of a collapsed middle school in Juyuan that had trapped nine
hundred students. Government teams, with the occasional local, picked through the dusty crags, but a week
had passed, and the energy the whole country had witnessed just after the earthquake was fading. A female
commentator praised the resilience and strength of the
Sichuan people.

His phone rang—it was Zhang Guo. "Xin Zhu, I hope you had a restful time in Shanghai."

"Thank you, I did."

"I'm afraid I'm walking into walls, though. Concerning tomorrow."

"Well, it was worth a try," Zhu said and realized that even this failure told him something important. If Zhang Guo couldn't learn the details of a meeting that he, too, was scheduled to attend, it meant that Wu Liang was running it with an unusual level of secrecy.

"As for the other," Zhang Guo said, referring to Leticia Jones, "I'll need a few days."

"I'll see you tomorrow morning, then."

Sung Hui came in with a platter of pork dumplings, apologizing as she turned off the television and the images of disaster. "I know it does no good," she said, "but I can't help watching. It makes my own worries insignificant."

He didn't like to hear that, even if it mirrored his own thoughts. "You have no worries."

"Do you want to eat here?"

"I don't think I can make it to the dining room."

"Shanghai was difficult?"

He shook his head. "A weekend of reflection isn't easy for someone as slow-witted as me."

That provoked a musical laugh, and she settled next to him.

"The flight home was the problem. I should've bought two seats."

"Next time you will buy two seats. You'll bring me along. I'll help you with your reflection."

Like others, he had once been suspicious of this girl's affection for an old, obese man, but he'd slowly discovered that these were the very characteristics that she enjoyed most. Sung Hai hated the boastful men her own age, and his size gave her a feeling of protection. What, then, had she seen in Delun? This was a subject she had avoided so many times that he was no longer able to ask the question, no longer wanted to. Truth is not always the way.

She pulled her legs up beneath herself and lifted the platter. Using a pair of porcelain chopsticks, she guided a dumpling to his mouth. It was delicious.

As she fed him, she recounted the two days they'd spent apart, which had been filled with drinks and dancing at Vics with a couple of girlfriends, unsuccessfully shopping for new rugs for the foyer, and worrying about Sichuan schoolchildren. During the periods in between, she was reading *The Boat to Redemption* by Su Tong, a bestseller about a Party official expelled for lying about his revolutionary parentage. "Do you know what he does?" she asked.

"What?"

A pause. Her eyes grew. "He tries to *castrate* himself!"

"Unbelievable!"

"I believe it," she said. "You really should read it."

"When I get time."

"Have you ever had time?"

He exhaled, waiting for the inevitable.

"Time off," she said. "Someplace with clean air and sun chairs. You can sit by the water and read Su Tong."

Holding back a grin, he said, "I hear Trier is nice," then coughed when she punched him in the ribs. Package tours to Karl Marx's birthplace were advertised in agency windows all over Beijing.

"Oh!" She hopped up and went to a cabinet. "I forgot. I ran into Shen An-Ling at the store. He gave me this for you." She opened a drawer and took out an unmarked brown envelope. Shen An-Ling had scrawled his signature across the seal. It hadn't been opened.

Zhu kept a small office in the back of the apartment, and after thanking Sung Hui for the meal, he took the envelope, closed the door behind himself, and settled at the desk that overlooked the city from thirty floors up. It had been her idea to move into this Chaoyang District tower, and only she could have convinced him to willingly place himself so high up. He'd asked the most basic question—*What happens if the electricity shuts down?*—and she'd stared at him, as if she'd never experienced a power outage, which in Beijing was an impossibility. The problem was that she'd fallen in love with the apartment and, more particularly, the vision of the two of them floating above the city. How could he deny her that?

He tore open the end of the envelope and shook the letter into his palm. It was a short letter, written in an obscure naval code that dated from 1940, and after decoding it, he read it through twice. He paused, considering the revelations Shen An-Ling had assembled here, read it through again, then cracked open the window and used matches to light the envelope, the letter, and the decoded message. As they shrank, he placed them into an ashtray and lit a Hamlet, its strong scent filling the small room.

According to their sources, Leticia Jones changed to another name after landing in Cairo, then flew to London for a connecting flight to Dulles International in Washington, D.C. After two nights in the One Washington Circle Hotel, on Monday the twelfth, the same day as the earthquake, she went to a house in Georgetown owned by a real estate company called Living, Inc, and met with four people:

Alan Drummond, former head of the Department of Tourism;

Senator Nathan Irwin, Minnesota Republican;

Dorothy Collingwood, ranking officer in the CIA's National Clandestine Service, department unknown; and

Stuart Jackson, retired CIA, Directorate of Operations (which, by 2005, was absorbed into the National Clandestine Service), now a private consultant.

The meeting lasted nearly seven hours, and lunch was delivered by an aide of Dorothy Collingwood's. Shen An-Ling's sources had been unable to listen to anything. They left one by one, at twenty-minute intervals, first Senator Irwin, then Jackson, Collingwood, Jones, and finally Alan Drummond—the youngest of the ringleaders, only thirty-nine—who walked two blocks and took a taxi to Union Station, where he boarded a train to Manhattan, and his home at 200 East Eighty-ninth Street.

Shen An-Ling's assessment at the end of the note was, like Shen An-Ling, simple and to the point: *Something must be done, now. I await your orders.* You couldn't buy loyalty like that—not anymore, at least.

4

Fifteen minutes before his meeting, Xin Zhu ascended the steps in front of the Great Hall of the People. Twelve enormous columns slanted at him, and he saw schoolchildren in sun visors lined up at one of the entrances. Six wore facemasks against the dust that was predicted to rise throughout the day. Green-clad soldiers stood at the main door, watching him enter. Breathing heavily, he waited until he was inside the marble lobby to wipe the sweat off his cheeks with a handkerchief. A voice said, "Xin Zhu!"

It was Shen An-ling, he of the soft skin and thick glasses that magnified his puffy eyes. Unlike Zhu, Shen An-ling was burdened by a shoulder bag stuffed with thick folders.

"What's that?" asked Zhu.

"The background. Offer them this, and they'll get off of your back."

"For as long as it takes for them to read it all. How many pages?"

Shen An-ling, too, was covered in perspiration, but it was the sweat of anxiety, and it stank. "I have no idea. A thousand?"

"More, I'd guess. I'm not sure I want them looking at all that."

"Okay," he said, "but I'll bring it along in case you change your mind."

It was a fair enough proposition, and Zhu accepted it. "Where do we face our doom?"

The Beijing Hall was not far away, down a long corridor past bas-reliefs of glorious times that were either historical moments Zhu had never witnessed or hopes for the future. A guard stood outside the room itself but didn't check their papers, and inside they found fourteen low upholstered chairs arranged in a half oval, so that one side could face the other. Behind them were eight more wooden chairs, arranged in parentheses. Thick carpet covered the floor, pushed this way and that by the morning's vacuum cleaner, and though the walls had been meticulously cleaned, the green paint was fading in spots. Someone would be in trouble for that.

Sun Bingjun was already seated in a chair on the left side, which was a surprise. A known drunk, the frail, thin old man was usually late to meetings, if he attended at all. Zhu approached, and they shook hands. "How was Shanghai?" Sun Bingjun asked, red-faced and baffled-looking.

"I can't keep anything a secret, can I?"

Sun Bingjun smiled. Looking at him, it was easy to

forget he was a lieutenant general, a decorated veteran of Vietnam, and a Hero of the Cultural Revolution. Years and vice had undermined him, but his illustrious history, as well as a brief but successful tenure as the minister of state security, protected him and his current position in the Politburo from most attacks.

"Shanghai was a place to clear my head."

"That should be useful today."

"Absolutely."

Zhu bowed his head and retreated to the right side, settling in the center seat. Shen An-ling took a wooden chair behind him and began rummaging through his bag.

The Supervision and Liaison Committee had been formed in 1992 as an offshoot of the Central Committee's Political and Legislative Affairs Committee, whose six members had felt overburdened by the scope of overseeing the entire spectrum of Chinese law enforcement. So they created a separate committee, with a membership of twenty-six, to deal primarily with interministry conflicts, which had ballooned during the nineties. This year's secretary was a Central Committee hotshot named Yang Xiaoming, from Sichuan, who was usually more interested in his oil concerns than in attending committee meetings. It was his deputy secretary from the Ministry of Public Security, Wu Liang, who shouldered most of his responsibilities. Though he had been invited many times to face the committee's questions, Xin Zhu had never been invited to become a member.

Yang Qing-Nian, the youngest of this committee's

members, strolled in with tall, white-haired Wu Liang, who was the same age as Xin Zhu. Both came over and offered hands, and Zhu was surprised to find no hint of gloating in Wu Liang's behavior. Wu Liang had worked hard to set up this morning's meeting and keep its agenda secret, but by his demeanor, it could have been a gathering to discuss traffic lamps in Lhasa.

"How is Sung Hui?" Wu Liang asked.

"She's very fine."

"I'm glad to hear that. A lovely woman."

"And Chu Liawa?"

Wu Liang's wife was older than both of them, a storybook rear-guard tigress, or so the rumors suggested. She had pushed her husband up through the ranks, angling him against foes in Yunnan, then in Nanning, and finally in Beijing, where over the last decade he had risen to the top of the food chain while insufferable absolutists like Xin Zhu remained in their dusty outlying offices, collecting intelligence but little else. "Very healthy," Wu Liang said finally, and from his lips, it sounded like a threat. Yang Qing-Nian said nothing; he didn't have to. His face took care of the gloating his sage was too cultured to show.

Feng Yi came in next, shaking hands with everyone, beginning with Wu Liang and ending with Xin Zhu, following the correct sequence from political superior to inferior. Unlike the others, he was purely political, having gained entrance into the Central Committee by flattery and knowing how to keep his mouth shut, avoiding committed opinions at all costs. Recently, he'd been handed a ranking position in the Guoanbu's Second

Bureau, but he still remained the most reserved during discussions of any importance.

Zhang Guo, on the other hand, shook hands with no one. He came in clutching a file to his chest, like a schoolgirl, settled into a free chair, and started unpacking his cigarettes. He looked more tired than the others, or perhaps it was anxiety. When the waiter came around, delivering tea, Zhang Guo's cup shivered to his lips. His eyes were bloodshot, unlike when they'd met on Friday, and Zhu decided that it had nothing to do with what was occurring at this moment; Zhang Guo was learning how a young mistress, particularly the well-known Chi Shanshan, could wear out a man of his age. He was, Zhu suspected, entertaining second thoughts.

For whatever reason, Wu Liang had not asked them to meet in their usual building, but had reserved this spare Central Committee space, and as the meeting was informal only these five members of the committee arrived. Zhu had no idea how many had been invited, but he doubted that Yang Xiaoming, the committee's absent head, even knew it was occurring. If he'd been informed, though, the disasters in Sichuan, his old stomping grounds, would have kept him far away.

Once the waiters had left and the guard closed the doors, Wu Liang stood wearily and placed a digital audio recorder in the center of the floor, equidistant from all the participants. "Just in case," he said to everyone as he returned to his chair.

"In case of what?" asked Zhu.

"In case of disputes later on," Wu Liang informed him. "None of us are young men—except, perhaps, Yang Qing-Nian," he said with a smile. "I'd hate to run a security apparatus based on our memories."

"Perfect reasoning," Zhu admitted. "And I'd like to thank the committee for inviting me here this morning. I consider it an honor."

"Bullshit," said Yang Qing-Nian. "I suggest we skip the formalities. Can we agree to that?"

"Yang Qing-Nian speaks with the voice of youth," Wu Liang said with a calmness that proved they'd planned that outburst. "I'm agreeable to dispensing with formalities, as this meeting is intended to be unofficial . . . exploratory in nature. However, I do not want to steer this particular boat. Are there opinions?"

"Were the better rooms occupied?" That was Sun Bingjun, chewing at the corner of his mouth.

Wu Liang blinked at him. "Yes, Comrade Lieutenant General. It's a busy time, and my request was last-minute."

Sun Bingjun set down his teacup and nodded; Feng Yi said, "Dispensing with formalities is all right with me." Zhang Guo lowered his head in agreement.

Looking across the room with raised brows, Wu Liang said, "Xin Zhu?"

Zhu said, "I always agree with the masses. Please." Behind him, he heard Shen An-ling cough his amusement.

Wu Liang removed a sheet of paper from an open briefcase propped against his chair. "It is May 19, 2008, and . . ." He checked his watch. "Nine fourteen in the morning." He listed the attendees, then said, "Before we start, I would like to remind everyone that, at 2:28 P.M., there begins a three-minute moment of silence for the victims of the Sichuan Wenchuan earthquake."

There was no need for Wu Liang to remind anyone of this, but with a recording device nearby, he couldn't help himself. Feng Yi said, "Perhaps we could offer ten seconds of silence right now?"

Zhu looked at him, then at the others. He caught Sun Bingjun rolling his eyes.

Yang Qing-Nian said, "I second that motion. Vote?"

All hands, of course, went up.

Ten seconds later, Wu Liang cleared his throat. "Thank you, Feng Yi." He lifted his notes, finally coming to the point. "We're here to discuss recent actions made by Comrade Colonel Xin Zhu of the Sixth Bureau of the Guojia Anquan Bu. Two actions, in particular: First, there was the April 15 memo from Xin Zhu to this committee stating that intelligence from his office would no longer be shared with the Ministry of Public Security. His reasoning, as outlined in the memo, was that the ministry is no longer secure enough to contain such highly sensitive intelligence."

Yang Qing-Nian shook his head in disgust.

"The second item," Wu Liang went on, "which is perhaps more problematic, concerns the repercussions of Xin Zhu's ill-advised action, in March, against a small department of the American Central Intelligence Agency. Xin Zhu has already been reprimanded for his disastrous mistake, and the fact that he still holds his position in the Sixth Bureau is, I believe, a testament to his political prowess."

"May I speak?" Zhu asked.

"Of course, we're avoiding formality here."

Zhu looked at his hands resting in his lap, then at Wu Liang. "My ill-advised actions in March have been well documented by this committee. You now speak of repercussions. I wasn't aware that any of significance had occurred."

"Yes," said Wu Liang. "Yang Qing-Nian, I believe you have that information?"

Yang Qing-Nian straightened in his chair, glowing with pride; he certainly did have something. "Comrades," he licked his lips, "the Ministry of Public Security has received intelligence that a former member of the Department of Tourism—the department Xin Zhu effectively destroyed—was on Chinese soil two weeks ago. She made contact with an American consular officer, now returned to the United States, who used an intermediary to find out about Xin Zhu's home life. Information about his wife, Sung Hui."

The bomb had been dropped, and Xin Zhu read destruction in their faces. Sun Bingjun rubbed his weary eyes. Feng Yi turned his entire body to face Yang Qing-Nian. Zhang Guo, looking more exhausted than ever, stared hard at Zhu. That look seemed to say, *You're on your own now.*

Wu Liang, of course, kept his composure. He and Yang Qing-Nian had been fleshing out that narrative all weekend. Had they questioned Dongfan Beisan?

Did they know that Zhu had already visited him at the Blim-Blam?

Yang Qing-Nian reached into his own leather briefcase and took out a file. "The documentation is here. Though her birth name is unknown, we have two different names for this American agent. Leticia Jones is an old work name we learned from the files Xin Zhu released before he decided to close his doors to us. The passport she traveled on was Sudanese, name of Rosa Mumu. In addition to looking into Xin Zhu's life, she met once with Abdul Khalik—someone we all know as a leader of the East Turkestan Islamic Movement that wishes to turn Xinjiang Province into an Islamic cesspool, beheading all Chinese citizens who reject their God."

This new information hit Zhu in the stomach, threatening to turn to lead the breakfast of wheat noodles and pork fat that Sung Hui had lovingly cooked for him. Behind him, there was a heavy silence from Shen An-ling. He worried the young man might have fainted, but it wouldn't do to start looking around at this moment.

Old Sun Bingjun spoke first, and slowly. "Are you telling us, Yang Qing-Nian, that, because Xin Zhu killed some of their people, the United States is now going to support the Islamization of western China?" He pressed his palms together. "There's something highly insane about that."

Feng Yi, the perpetual moderator, said, "I see your point, Sun Bingjun, and it makes sense. However, this is not the United States government we're talking about.

It's the Central Intelligence Agency, which has a history of mad behavior. Further, we're probably not even talking about the entire agency, but a single small department that could conceivably be attempting to save face."

"A department that was disbanded after Xin Zhu's actions," Sun Bingjun reminded him. "It doesn't exist anymore. It receives no funding."

Wu Liang spoke up: "The Department of Tourism, as documented by Xin Zhu, has a tradition of finding funds through any and all means when its Langley paymasters have withheld money. Only a couple of months ago, it robbed an art gallery in Zürich to fund its nefarious actions." He paused. "A department exists when those inside of it agree that it exists. A department that knows how to fund itself can, arguably, live forever."

Heads turned—not to Zhu, but to Zhang Guo, who was staring at his knees. It was generally agreed that, on issues of financing, Zhang Guo was the most qualified in the room. Though he didn't look at them, he knew what the silence meant. He lifted his shaky teacup, saying, "Wu Liang is correct. One example is a man we all know, Yevgeny Primakov of the United Nations. He has not only been able to maintain a secret intelligence section within the UN without an official budget, but he was able to create and develop it outside the knowledge of the UN Secretariat and the general public. If a man can single-handedly do that, then a handful of people can certainly maintain a department that already existed."

Zhu stared at Zhang Guo, but his friend kept his eyes averted from everyone.

Sun Bingjun cleared his throat. "So. This Department of Tourism has resurrected itself. As an opening salvo, it is exacting revenge on Xin Zhu and, by extension, the People's Republic. That is the present theory?"

"You tell me, Comrade Lieutenant General," said Yang Qing-Nian. "The facts are here. One of their agents pries into Xin Zhu's personal life, then meets with one of the Republic's great enemies. Then leaves."

"To where?" asked Sun Bingjun.

"To Cairo. From there we lost her."

Zhu watched Yang Qing-Nian's features, trying to judge if this was truth. If it was, then he was ahead of them on at least one point. Sharing the information that Leticia Jones had gone to meet with the former head of Tourism, though, would do nothing to help his case.

Sun Bingjun drank his tea, musing over the facts in front of him. He was senior only in terms of age, and despite the glories of the past much of his actual power had been washed away, not only by his drinking but also by his early opposition to Hu Jintao's presidency, which had led him to speak too publicly during the SARS crisis of 2003. Since then, all the old veteran's public statements had been masterful balancing acts between saying much and saying nothing. Now, though, they were behind closed doors and, remarkably, he looked sober. Sun Bingjun exhaled. "In my experience of examining the actions and motives of the Central Intelligence Agency, its reasoning is never so simple.

Revenge as an end in itself is simply not part of the Americans' thinking process. They're not Mossad, nor are they adolescents."

Yang Qing-Nian, the closest to an adolescent in that room, said, "Revenge is not for the sake of revenge, Sun Bingjun, but for the sake of sending a message that they will not be treated as Xin Zhu has treated them. That is one motivation. The second is timing. With the Games nearly upon us, any disruption they can provoke—be it here in Beijing or in Xinjiang—will embarrass us on the world stage. Even if they fall short, the possibilities for success are too great for them to ignore."

"Of course you see it that way, Yang Qing-Nian," Sun Bingjun said in his bored voice, "because you still think in terms of revenge. But if a plan like this fails, it does not simply mean that the Americans won't disrupt our Games. It means the exposure of their plans to the world, which would damage them more deeply than anything they could do to us. Remember what happened last year? The CIA was caught funding those feral agitators in the mountains who call themselves the Youth League—a touch of irony, using our youth organization's name. The scandal and humiliation led to the fall of one CIA director and enormous cuts in its funding. They are unlikely to start supporting Islamic terrorism now—certainly not for revenge. The risks are too great. So, if the Americans really are taking such an incredible risk, then their reasoning goes much deeper than revenge, or *sending a message*. Not even a small, self-funded department would be so short-sighted."

Wu Liang spoke up. "So what do you suggest, Sun Bingjun?"

"I'm suggesting nothing. I'm only pointing out that, if the visit of this agent is really a sign that a CIA department is engaging in some operation on Chinese soil, then the reasons are far more complicated than a hatred of Xin Zhu here, or even of Chinese intelligence."

Silence again. Wu Liang seemed temporarily lost in the face of Sun Bingjun's flawless logic, and Yang Qing-Nian looked embarrassed. Zhang Guo said, "Is there someone we can consult on this? Someone within their agency?"

Feng Yi said, "The Second Bureau has a few CIA sources, but they're not ranking enough to know about this. Wu Liang?"

Wu Liang set down his teacup. "Possibly. I have one source that may be able to dig deeper." He took a long breath. "Xin Zhu may be the one to talk to."

Finally, they looked at him. He chewed the inside of his left cheek. He'd once had a wonderful source, but not anymore—James Pearson, aide to Senator Nathan Irwin. "I will ask," Zhu said, and bowed his head. "I thank the committee for bringing this troubling news to my attention, and I will do my best to make sure it is explained to everyone's satisfaction."

"I'm sure you will," said Wu Liang. "Further, I hope that when you receive information you will share it with all of us here in the committee. Which brings us to the other subject of this morning's discussion."

Yang Qing-Nian shifted in his chair, preparing to

speak, but Wu Liang shot him a look. The young man had botched one item already; he would take care of the other one himself.

Wu Liang said, "I think all of us here are familiar with Xin Zhu's April 15 memo, a copy of which I hold here." He waved a single sheet of paper. "In it, he stated that the Ministry of Public Security was no longer secure enough to contain his office's intelligence. Naturally, this committee—the whole committee—demanded more explanation, and on Friday, April 18, the committee received a twelve-page collection of specific pieces of intelligence that, we were told, resided in the files of the Department of Tourism. By triangulating these nuggets of information, Xin Zhu explained, he could reach no other conclusion than that the Department of Tourism itself was running a high-level source within the Ministry of Public Security. Thus, his intelligence would be withheld until the leak was plugged."

Everyone in the room watched Wu Liang, who continued, "Now, upon receiving the initial memo, I admit that I was skeptical. Xin Zhu and I have often resided in different rooms in the house of socialist philosophy. I saw this as further evidence of his paranoia. Then I examined the twelve-page report and felt less sure of myself. The ministry is, as you all know, close to my heart, and the facts Xin Zhu had collected, when viewed together, shook me deeply. I spent the weekend having very difficult conversations with ministry comrades, and I even viewed some of them with suspicion. Investigations were begun. I was—and I'm hesitant to admit this, but it's true—in a panic. What if Xin Zhu was right, and we were bleeding information to the Americans? Catastrophe!"

Zhu closed his eyes to listen better. He could feel where this was heading, could hear it in Wu Liang's exaggerated innocence and emotion. You build a tower in order to tear it down, and the tower Wu Liang was building was enormous.

"By that Monday, four weeks ago, I had a list of suspects. Nineteen. I worried so much, you see, that nearly anything could admit one to that list. Yang Qing-Nian and I began more intense interviews. We took them from their homes, placed them in separate cells on East Chang'an Avenue, and began talking. At this point, there was no reason to treat them as prisoners, so they kept their clothes and were fed and treated well—only their phones were confiscated.

"The interviews, though, were not going well. By Wednesday we had talked to each of them twice, and so I decided to visit Xin Zhu at his office in Haidian and share what little I had. I thought that, as good comrades, we could work together. I was, I now know, mistaken."

Zhu remembered that day. Wednesday, April 23, 2:00 P.M. Wu Liang and a hard-looking secretary filled the office with foul Russian tobacco smoke, going over his twelve pages one line at a time, fighting over veracity, asking for documentation and demanding the connections that had brought Zhu to suspect the Ministry of Public Security.

"What I learned that day, after hours of rigorously confronting each item in those twelve pages, listening to and then challenging each of Xin Zhu's explanations, was a simple fact. Each of these items—and there are one hundred and twelve in all—is simply that: an item on a piece of paper. Each is an item connected to a piece of information gathered by his agent, the American senatorial aide, James Pearson. For each he has either an e-mailed report with attachments or a handwritten one, accompanied sometimes by flash drives—all from James Pearson. But where, I found myself asking, is this golden source, this James Pearson? We know the answer. He was picked up by the CIA trying to flee the United States. He is unavailable. And the place where James Pearson found these so-called truths? That would be the office of the Department of Tourism, on West Thirty-first Street, in Manhattan. The department Xin Zhu so hastily destroyed, the offices of which have now been gutted by the CIA. I have photographs of the offices if any of you wish verification."

He'd talked a long time, but talking had always been Wu Liang's strong point. He danced with facts and manipulated them to showcase his modesty and erudition. With a mouth like that, and a wife like Chu Liawa, there was no end to what he could accomplish.

But he wasn't done yet.

"As I say, I entered his office convinced of Xin Zhu's honesty, ready to make our ministry secure again. I entered contrite, but I left angry. Furious, in fact. I had spent the previous days grilling good comrades on the strength of what now looked to me like a self-serving deception. My anger, however, had not reached its apex, for upon returning to East Chang'an, I was informed that Bo Gaoli, who some of you may know from his sterling history helping to run the counterterrorism department, was dead. Faced with the shame of this unfounded suspicion, he had used his belt to hang himself in his cell."

Wu Liang let silence speak for him now. The committee knew of Bo Gaoli's suicide, but the details had never been released. There had been a rumor of a sexual predilection, another of financial indiscretions. No one—certainly not Zhu—had known that he'd been in a ministry cell when he did it. Now that Wu Liang had shared this fact, everyone turned to examine Zhu's reaction, and he did his best to control himself. Was he successful? He wasn't sure. He thought that he could ask Shen An-ling later, but his assistant could only see the back of his head.

Xin Zhu wondered if anyone was going to ask the obvious, and obligatory, question: Was it possible that Bo Gaoli's suicide was an admission of guilt? He himself could not ask it—it was up to someone else, perhaps Zhang Guo. But no one asked anything, and Zhang Guo only stifled a yawn with his cupped hand.

Since no one else seemed interested in speaking, Zhu opened his mouth. "I certainly regret the death of Bo Gaoli, but it does not alter the facts as I read them. The intelligence listed on my report did, in fact, originate in the Department of Tourism, and the only conclusion I can come to is that its source was within the Ministry of Public Security."

Wu Liang sighed audibly. "This is like burning down a man's house and *then* accusing him of keeping illegal merchandise inside it. You burned their house down, Xin Zhu. You torched yourself in the process."

"I would like to think that my long service to the Party would justify a measure of faith."

Sun Bingjun set down his cup. "I would ask a question of Wu Liang, if I might."

Wu Liang nodded.

"Why," he asked, shifting in his chair, "do we hear about this now? The suicide of Bo Gaoli occurred nearly four weeks ago. If Xin Zhu is such a danger, then why have you left him a month to spread his plague?"

Zhang Guo smiled into his fist; Feng Yi raised his head, saying, "That's a good question."

Wu Liang lost none of his poise. Again, he sighed. "For the reason Xin Zhu brings up: his long service to the Party and the People's Republic. Though I was angry—though I suspected deceit in order to attack a rival organization, or perhaps to attack me personally—I wasn't about to institute disciplinary action until I could prove that Xin Zhu's accusations were false. That only occurred when we discovered the presence of the aforementioned Tourist, this Leticia Jones, on Chinese soil."

"I don't follow," Sun Bingjun said patiently.

"It's very simple, comrade, and at this point I would like to ask Xin Zhu a simple question, a question that we could only pose at this point in time."

Zhu looked at him.

Stone-faced, Wu Liang said, "If the CIA has a source within the Ministry of Public Security, then why would it send someone here to find out your wife's daily schedule?"

Zhu knew that the question was not finished.

"Why would they risk sending one of their own people—which, we agree, is a great risk to them—if they owned one of us? Your wife's schedule is not classified information. It's something that anyone within the ministry could find out with a simple phone call. If they have, as you contend, a source within the ministry, then getting one of their own people to ask questions in the middle of Beijing is not only stupid, it's incredibly redundant."

Zhu bit the inside of his mouth to stifle a nervous smile. The logic was beautiful, more so because he could not point out its one flaw: Mary Caul, the consular officer who had convinced Dongfan Beisan to pose his questions, left the country before she could hope to get any answers. She had never cared about the answers. Of course, to bring this up would be admitting that he had already lied about what he knew. So he said, "I don't know, comrade. However, I remain convinced that the Americans do own someone within the ministry, based on the evidence I submitted."

"What I think," said Wu Liang, "is that you are tenacious to a fault. You've embarked on a mission to smear the ministry with lies, and now that you've been caught with the lies in your hand you're pretending your hands are empty. I'm angry about this, but more than that I'm disappointed that someone with such a history of socialist endeavor would sink so low. When

Hu Jintao talks of the Eight Virtues and Shames, he reminds us to *be united, help each other; make no gains at others' expense*. Xin Zhu, I fear, has ignored that one with all the greed and ambition of a Hong Kong stock trader, and we should seriously consider bringing his dismissal to the entire committee for a vote."

Noticing how wet his palms were, Zhu couldn't help but admire the mouth on Wu Liang. Perhaps to remind himself of the insignificance of what was happening in this room, he thought, *Fifty thousand dead*. What could stand up to that?

He thought, *This, and you, mean nothing*.

5

Two hours later, along a tree-lined residential street north of the Haidian Theater, Shen An-ling opened the door for him, and he climbed out of the car. They'd both been silent during the ride, because Shen An-ling had left his car with the guards at the Great Hall, and there was no telling if someone had slipped a microphone into the cushions. *This*, Zhu now thought, *is getting ridiculous.*

The first barrier to their offices was an unassuming door behind which an old woman smoked at a foldout table, looking like a bathroom attendant. While in front of her lay a newspaper with more Sichuan headlines and an open Sudoku puzzle book, just under the table were an intercom, a cell phone, and a Type 77B pistol that was kept loaded with nine hollow-point rounds. He'd had to work to track one down, as the gun was made only for export, and his requisitions had gone unanswered; in the end, He Qiang stumbled across one in

South Korea. Now, the old woman put out her cigarette and smiled, her face full of involuntary winks, and took out the intercom, saying, "Seven and eighty-eight here."

From inside, two guards unlocked and opened the next door, a heavy steel affair that had been carefully painted to look rusty. In their white room, they manned an X-ray machine and a metal detector, both of which Zhu and Shen An-ling sidestepped. Finally, another guard opened the last door, which brought them to a long, semiunderground office gridded with desks and desktop computers, Ethernet cables winding like lifelines up narrow columns to the suspended ceiling panels. Seated at the desks were the twenty-six clerks of his department, sorting through the news events of the day, through agent reports and intercepted communications sent from the Fourth and Seventh Bureaus. Zhu's department, officially called the Expedition Agency (unofficially referred to as Xin Zhu's Pit), was an outpost of the Sixth Bureau that had over the years gradually expanded its mission to overlap at least four different bureaus of the Guoanbu. Like the Second, it recruited foreign agents; like the Seventh, it prepared policy reports based on gathered intelligence; like the Foreign Affairs Bureau, it developed relationships with certain foreign intelligence agencies. And as part of the Sixth Bureau, it kept an eye on foreign activity aimed at undermining the stability of the People's Republic.

This expansion had been gradual and purposefully quiet, and by the time it had been noticed in 2002 by none other than Wu Liang, Zhu had produced too many critical reports to be considered expendable. This had not been Wu Liang's first attempt to undermine Zhu's rise in power using the Supervision and Liaison Committee, but it had been the most explosive, bringing members of all the Guoanbu's bureaus into a fistfight that was only quelled by the intervention of the head of the Political and Legislative Affairs Committee, who held both men up for reprimands.

Since 2002, Zhu had doubled his staff and trebled his field agents, and until the massacre of the Tourists, he had felt nearly invincible.

"We're dead," Shen An-ling said once they were inside his office at the far end of the floor. "Wu Liang has been building up to this for a long time."

"Nothing's done yet," Zhu told him, lighting a Hamlet as he settled behind his desk.

It was true. Sun Bingjun had refused to settle on a course of action, and Feng Yi had agreed. Zhang Guo, disappointingly, had remained neutral during the discussion, which was perhaps an attempt to position himself as the crucial vote, or a way of hiding his association with Zhu. So within this microcosm of five committee members, there was a perfect balance of indecision, which led to Feng Yi suggesting that Zhu be given some time to present his rebuttal to the charges. "Five days" had been Wu Liang's immediate suggestion. Sun Bingjun, proving once again that rumors of his alcoholic decline were greatly exaggerated, had laughed at this.

"Give Xin Zhu a chance, however small."

"We only have two weeks," said Shen An-ling, dropping into a chair. "Two weeks to chase our tails.

We've lost our best American source, and whatever intelligence the Ministry of Public Security has isn't going to make it to us. We're fucked."

Zhu smoked and gazed past him at the blinds, through which his employees worked away at their haystacks of facts and half-truths and lies. He didn't even react to Shen An-ling's atypical cursing, for it only showed that the younger man saw the situation for what it was: a disaster. Not only were they stuck with two weeks, at Wu Liang's insistence they'd been saddled with daily progress reports to those five committee members. Yes, it was a disaster, but there was no time for emotional nonsense. He would give Shen An-ling another five minutes to compose himself.

He tried to hold the situation up before himself and see its interlocking parts from different angles. The ex-Tourist Leticia Jones, looking pointlessly at Sung Hui and more pointedly at an Islamic terrorist. The fact that there was a leak in the Ministry of Public Security. The fact that Wu Liang had long been waiting for such a chance to strip him down like a paper tiger.

What about Bo Gaoli? Had shame for an unproven crime really been that hard to take? Though they were only acquaintances, Zhu had met Bo Gaoli on many occasions and had been taken by the man's cool, businesslike attitude toward his counterterrorism work for the Ministry of Public Security. Had Zhu wanted to reach out to someone in the ministry for help, Bo Gaoli would have made his short list. Yet this same man—a respected administrator and a husband of forty years— had killed himself for something he had not done?

Or had he done something? Had he leaked to the Americans, or had he committed some unrelated crime that he feared would be exposed under interrogation?

Shen An-ling found a pack of Hongtashan and lit one up, waving away the pungent smoke. He said, "What if we were wrong? What if there's no mole in the ministry?"

"What if there are two, or five?" Zhu answered without looking at him. "The Americans got that information somehow. It was too varied to be from intercepted communication, or even from a single lower-level office. We agreed on that."

"How many times have you told me that dependence on beliefs is the ruin of intelligence?"

One of Shen An-ling's finest traits was his ability to throw Zhu's own words back at him. "If our belief was wrong, the fault was in assuming that all the information came from one source, which is why we believed—no, *concluded*—that the leak was high in the administration. Five lower-level sources could supply the same information."

When Shen An-ling said, "It feels like we're holding on to something because we want to believe it," Zhu wished he would shut up but said nothing. Again, this was the young man's great value, his constant agitation against Zhu's assumptions. It kept the dialectic in motion, never allowing Zhu to rest, and it reflected Chairman Mao's greatest maxim: the need for perpetual revolution.

"Okay," Zhu said, placing one hand on the desktop.

"What if we *are* wrong? What if there is no leak in the ministry? What follows?"

"It follows that we're fucked," Shen An-ling said behind a cloud of tobacco smoke. "It follows that we've ostracized an entire section of the government for no good reason, and that we can reasonably be held responsible for a man's suicide. It follows that you will be removed from the Pit, and either we'll be castrated and absorbed into the rest of the Sixth Bureau, or some friend of Wu Liang will appear to take over."

Patiently, Zhu said, "So if this is the case, and we're wrong, how did we end up at this point? What was the poor logic that brought us to this terrible end?"

Shen An-ling waved smoke away. "I suppose we were blinded."

"By?"

"By our dislike for Wu Liang."

"That doesn't explain how the Americans got their information. Where did it come from?"

"I don't know."

"Is this the only thing we don't know?"

Shen An-ling frowned, puzzled. "There are plenty of things we don't know."

"Such as?"

"Such as Bo Gaoli's reasons for killing himself."

Zhu nodded thoughtfully. "Yes."

"We don't know why the American was looking into your wife's life."

"But we do know that she met with Alan Drummond and his friends," Zhu reminded him. "That's something that Wu Liang does not know."

"But Wu Liang's question is a fair one, and I'm ashamed that I didn't ask it first—if they have a ministry source, then why did she ask questions?"

"There are more important questions," Zhu said, finally saying aloud what he'd been thinking during Wu Liang's extended monologue. "Why did Leticia Jones leave before she could get her answers? And most crucially: Why did she ask her questions so clumsily?"

Slowly, Shen An-ling lowered his cigarette from his face to his knee and said, "Talks to an unsecured consular officer, who talks to a deadbeat rock and roller, who talks to the daughter of a seamstress. Certainly she knew we would trace it back to her."

"Certainly."

"She wanted us to know. Yet did she want us to know that she didn't care about the answer? Did she want us to *know* that it was a ruse?"

They let that sit between them, each staring at separate points in the mid-distance, until Shen An-ling remembered aloud another of Zhu's sayings, "Do not always assume motive where human error will suffice."

The phone on Zhu's desk rang, and when he picked it up his gaze settled on the white box of rice balls Sung Hui had prepared for him. "Wèi," he said.

He Qiang's dulcet tones came at him. "Comrade Colonel Xin Zhu, I have returned from Xinyang."

"The family is in good health?"

"Yes, Comrade Colonel."

"You said you were bringing a cousin back to Beijing. Did that go well?"

"Yes, Comrade Colonel. She's staying with me until

we get her papers sorted. Shall I come to the office to-day?"

"No," Zhu said, because he had no doubt that Wu Liang and Yang Qing-Nian had stationed some street vendors outside the building, or were simply watching through one of the three hundred thousand surveillance cameras installed throughout the city under the Grand Beijing Safeguard Sphere program, which would one day ensure that no one could find solitude outside their own shower cabins. "You take care of your cousin, and we'll talk again tomorrow."

"Thank you, Comrade Colonel."

When Zhu hung up, Shen An-ling opened the office door to admit a new girl, whose name Zhu couldn't recall. She carried a tea set, but when she began to pour Zhu distractedly sent her away. Shen An-ling thanked her as she left.

"Before we proceed," Zhu said, "we must fill in as many of the gaps in our knowledge as possible. Let's make a list."

Shen An-ling half-stood, reaching out to grab a hand-sized notepad from the desk, saying, "We only have two weeks."

"Panic is one of the symptoms of belief, Shen An-ling. We will not be rushed."

He'd considered going out in one of his employees' cars, or taking one of the more obscure exits to hide his departure, but there seemed little point when his destination was one of the more watched areas of the capital. So, a little after four, he climbed into his Audi, which one of his people had helpfully collected from Nankai Saturday morning, left the underground garage, and drove north of the center, just inside the Fifth Ring Road. High above, sand was blowing in from the deserts of Inner Mongolia, hazing the afternoon sky, but it hadn't touched down yet. It hovered like a quiet threat.

It was on a long stretch that the traffic suddenly vanished, and only when he noticed the lines of cars parked on both sides of the road did he realize it was 2:28, precisely one week after the earthquake. He sighed and drew to the side of the road, parked behind a vegetable truck, and settled back in his seat.

At first, probably like most people, he fought it. His head was too full of panicked self-interest. Three minutes is a long time, though, and during that last minute his head was finally in the middle of the country, in the mountains, with the devastated homes, schools, factories, hospitals, shops, roads, and tunnels, and the many, many thousands of people whose lives had been irrevocably scarred at 2:28 P.M. one week ago.

He knew the silence was over because its end was marked by horns blaring long and low up and down the road. All over the city, all over the country, cars, trains, ships, and air defense alarms were screaming into the sky.

He waited until the sound faded and the cars around him had headed off before finally starting the Audi and driving on.

His destination, a kilometer north of the complex that had hosted the 1990 Asian Games, went by the name of Ziyu Shanzhuang, the Purple Jade Villas, a 160-acre resort of green fields, pools, forests, wildlife, and the superrich. It was one of more than thirty such walled compounds nestled in the green upper reaches of the capital, a world away from the Beijing that he knew most intimately. The guards at the gate seemed to sense his unfamiliarity, or perhaps it was just the clanking noise his car was making these days, and even his Guoanbu ID did little to scare them into submission, a fact that gave him serious pause.

He took the long drive to the villas at a leisurely speed, rolling down his window and taking in the cool air that was freshened by long stretches of trees cultivated to perfection. Across a field he saw women with children that ran wildly around baffled goats and peacocks, and it felt, until he raised his gaze above the tree line to take in Beijing's skyline of towers beneath the gathering dust storm, as if he were deep in the countryside, far from prying eyes and ears. It was a magical illusion.

The guards at the gate had called ahead, so when he climbed out of his car Hua Yuan was already opening the front door, squeezing her hands together in front of her stomach. Her hair was in an amateurish bun, and he got the sense that she'd dressed in a hurry, which immediately gave him the picture of an old woman stuck in a claustrophobic, dusty house, in perpetual mourning for the husband who had killed himself. Nevertheless, she smiled as he approached.

"Hua Yuan, thank you for seeing me. I'm Xin Zhu."

"*Colonel* Xin Zhu," she said, holding out a small hand that he shook.

"You know of me?"

"We met once at a Workers' Day event. Briefly."

"I'm honored you remember."

She seemed to want to say something else, but changed her mind and asked him to come inside.

He'd been wrong about the claustrophobia and dust. It was an immaculate home, cleaned no doubt by a legion of workers, and open in its architecture—modern, almost American. She brought him through the foyer into a sitting room with blocky but comfortable sofas, a closed television cabinet, long, low shelves full of plants and books, and a large square window overlooking the fields. The window was framed by ivy that was threatening to grow madly across the view.

"This is a beautiful place," he said as he sat down.

"Tea?"

"Yes, thank you."

She left him alone for a moment, then returned and settled across from him in a matching chair. "We didn't use this place very much. Buying it was a favor for a friend of my husband's, one of the original Purple Jade investors. We were usually in town or the countryside— the real countryside. I've come here because it's easy. That's something I appreciate now. Ease."

A teenaged girl in a white uniform arrived with a tray and poured chrysanthemum tea for them both. Beside Hua Yuan's cup, he noticed, was a white plastic drinking straw. Once the girl was gone, Zhu began,

"Hua Yuan, I was hoping to speak with you about your husband's death."

"His suicide."

"Exactly," Zhu said. "Over the last weeks the question of *why* has been troubling me. If it's something personal between the two of you, then it is certainly not my business, but if it had to do with his work, then I would like to better understand it."

She examined him, as if he had arrived wanting to sell her something, and placed one end of the straw into her tea. She took a sip. "Xin Zhu," she said, "you obviously know everything about that."

"About what?"

"About Bo Gaoli's work. He was very excited."

Zhu stared at her damp lips. "Excuse me, Hua Yuan, but I knew very little about your husband's work."

"He talked to you about it."

"No, Hua Yuan, he didn't."

Her head fell to the side, taking in this information. "He *wanted* to talk to you."

"About what?"

"About his work. You know, he had become so excited that I thought he had a mistress. He shaved his shoulders that day. He was very hairy, you know. I thought he was shaving for some young thing. Funny, no?"

Zhu stared a moment. "Bo Gaoli was excited about something to do with his work, and he wanted to talk to me?"

"Was I not clear?"

"Well, we hardly knew each other. We'd met a couple times, but we were barely acquaintances. I would have been surprised to receive a call from him."

"But he was preparing to meet you, Xin Zhu."

"When?"

"Before he . . . left." She paused, frowning. "He didn't see you?"

"I never heard from him. Are we talking about the week of April 14?"

She considered that, drinking from her straw. "We are talking about Sunday, April 20, Xin Zhu. That's the day he shaved his shoulders and went to see you."

"But he didn't come back?"

"Yes, he came back. He told me to stay with my mother. That's in the real countryside. I left the next morning, Monday."

Monday, April 21. That was the day Wu Liang picked up Bo Gaoli and eighteen others for interrogation. Zhu said, "Why did he tell you to leave?"

"He did that sometimes. He told me to stay with my mother if he had work to do. I'm a good wife, Xin Zhu. I didn't ask. He was a practical husband; he never shared." She frowned. "He didn't see you?"

"No."

"Then why did he shave his shoulders?"

"I couldn't tell you, Hua Yuan."

This seemed to disturb her more than anything else, and Zhu wondered about her sanity, wondered if anything could be taken as fact. Her husband had sent her off to her mother's, and by the time she returned he was a corpse. Reactions to such a turn of events, he knew, were as varied as the species of fish. She said, "The maid had to clean the bathroom three times just to get all of the hair."

"Perhaps he tried to get in touch with me, but couldn't," he said, then, suddenly remembering Sunday, April 20, nodded and said, "Yes. I wasn't in Beijing that weekend. I was in Xi'an, and my phone had no reception." It was a lie, for he had been in Beijing, in bed with his wife, and had allowed his phone's battery to die. He tried not to think about how things might have turned out had he not been distracted.

But Hua Yuan had started on a particular train of thought, and it would take more than his little lie to derail her. She said, "I wonder how young she is. Could you find out?"

"Hua Yuan, I don't think this is my business."

"Don't tell me what your business is, you ignorant shit," she said, her steady calm tone making it hard for him to process the actual words. Then her eyes went wide and she pressed a fist against her mouth. "Oh. Comrade Colonel, I'm so sorry."

"Don't be," Zhu said, hands on his knees. "I only want to help, if I can, to unravel the mystery of your husband's suicide."

"A girl might be an explanation," she said.

"Only if the exposure of an affair would be too much to bear." He paused. "Would it?"

It was a question that hadn't occurred to her. She thought about it, again catching the straw with her wrinkled lips. She released it and took a long breath. "Xin Zhu, I once met a man my husband had spent three days interrogating. It was here—our first stay in this place. This man was mad, you understand. I think it was the interrogation that had done it. I was here alone at the time, and he'd somehow gotten past the guards. He threw himself against our window, right there," she said, motioning toward the large square framed in ivy. "He kept running at it until his nose and lips were bleeding, and when security came I went outside to see. The knuckles of his left hand had been smashed to powder—the fingers flopped uselessly when he waved them at me—and he was missing three toes on his bare feet. He told me, as they were taking him away, that my husband had done this to him, and that he wanted to be killed now. That night, when Bo Gaoli had gotten home from work, I asked him what this terrible man had done. He just sipped at his soup and said, *He did nothing. It was a mistake.* A mistake?" She cleared her throat, staring hard at that clean, clear window. "No, he wouldn't have killed himself from shame, certainly not over some girl."

Zhu's hands felt too large. He pressed them together between his knees, then moved one to the arm of the sofa. "I see," he said. "Then you don't know why he would have killed himself."

She shook her head abruptly, then said, "Of course, there was the money."

"Money?"

"About three hundred thousand yuan. Kept in a shoebox right here, in this house. I found it when I was throwing out his clothes."

Nearly fifty thousand dollars in a box. "You have no idea where he got that from?"

She shook her head.

"Did he travel a lot?"

"Certainly."

"Alone?"

"Sometimes."

"Within the region, or did he go farther? To the West, perhaps."

Her gaze drew back from the window, and she focused on Zhu. "You don't have this information already?"

"It would take time to track down," he said, though the truth was that it would require requests to other bureaus that, by now, might not be willing to help a drowning man.

"He went to Chicago for a conference in November. We went to Paris together in June. That was the West. He visited Hong Kong a lot, for work."

It all sounded normal for a man in Bo Gaoli's position, even conservative. "Did Wu Liang ever talk to you about what happened?"

She smiled sadly. "He said my husband was one of the greatest administrators China has ever known."

"Perhaps he was."

She ignored that. "He told me that they found Bo Gaoli on Wednesday. He was hanging in the bathroom of our apartment on Wangfujing. One of his colleagues had come looking for him, and Wu Liang came by soon after—he was the first government official on the scene."

"Before the police?"

She shook her head irritably. "There was no *police*,"

she said. "For a man like my husband, suicide does not exist. In the newspaper, they called it a heart attack. Which now makes me wonder about everyone I've ever heard of dying of heart problems. Doesn't it you?"

"It certainly does," Zhu said with a sigh.

"They say that wives always want to know," she said after a moment. "Of course we do. You love your man, or at least you believe you understand him, and if he chooses to kill himself, then you want to know. Guilt settles in. You come to believe that *you* did something wrong. But that's not me, Xin Zhu. I don't believe I was ever important enough to Bo Gaoli for him to kill himself because of something I did or did not do. I'm sad that he's gone, but I'm old enough to remember a time when, in Shanghai, we avoided walking near tall buildings for fear that a suicide would land on us. You're not old enough to remember those early years of the Chairman, but I do. Back then, simple fear could kill you. People were shockingly fragile, and you didn't ask why someone stepped off a building. They simply stepped off buildings, and you made sure you didn't get in their way."

Zhu chewed the inside of his mouth to avoid replying, for if he began he feared the conversation would never end. He bowed his head to her and slowly rose, wanting to leave without another word, but a few slipped out. "Thank you, Hua Yuan, and I am nearly old enough to remember. However, times have changed, and sometimes asking questions leads, if not to answers, then to better questions."

"Or to a grave," Hua Yuan said, then offered her

hand, limp, like a Frenchwoman awaiting a kiss on the knuckles. He shook it briefly, then let it go. At the door, she pointed out across the field. "We're in a city of more than fifteen million people. You see how empty it all is?"

"Yes."

"Our people have always known the value of a good wall."

He stopped by the office to find that things were running smoothly, then drove home through the swirling sand of the descending dust storm and parked outside their tower. Most residents used the underground lot, but for the last week, since Monday, he had avoided it, full of the irrational fear of his car getting trapped under all those stories. He turned off the engine, and, instead of getting out, used his encrypted phone to dial a long number. The dust storm was thick now, and he could see very little—which meant that anyone outside the car would see very little of him.

It was just before seven, and, conveniently, Beijing was twelve hours ahead of Washington, D.C., which meant that his man in the embassy would be getting ready for the office. After three rings, he heard a man's lilting "Wèi."

"It's been a while, Comrade Sam Kuo," he said.

Silence. "Yes, comrade . . ." Sam Kuo faded, perhaps in the company of his wife. "Good to hear from you."

"I trust you and the family are in good health."

"Yes, I am, and they are, too. And you—you as well, comrade."

"Sam Kuo," Zhu said, "I'm in need of a little help. Do you think you could assist me?"

Later, when Sung Hui was telling him about a cousin on her mother's side who was pregnant, he got up from the sofa and, taken by a feeling that was all too rare for a man of only fifty-eight years, kissed her neck, and then her lips. She gave him a soft smile and led him to the bedroom. As she crouched on top of him, nails digging into his soft, expansive chest, he wondered if Hua Yuan's peculiar sadness had provoked this sudden desire, or maybe it had been that last minute of silence for the deaths in Sichuan.

No—it wasn't either of those things, he realized as his wife's long hair tickled his face. It was that he was fighting for his life again, sending out agents, plotting moves on the other side of the planet. He was engaged in the one thing he had ever had a talent for, and it filled him with anxiety, anger, sadness, and love—the entirety of human experience.

6

I n the morning, he sent word to He Qiang that Liu Xiuxiu should visit a photo booth, then had Shen An- ling personally buy tickets on two separate flights to Washington, D.C., under names connected to passports they kept in their floor safes. For the rest of the morning, they discussed the little that Zhu had learned from Hua Yuan and the information Shen An-ling had collected on Leticia Jones. The story of Jones meeting Abdul Khalik could not be verified by any of their sources, but Wu Liang had helpfully sent the details of their meeting in a barren workers' bar, originating from a low-level ministry informer: A black woman talking foreign- accented Mandarin to a long-haired man clutching tea, a man the source later ID'd from ministry mugshots.

Although Leticia Jones had evaded surveillance af- ter the meeting in Georgetown, since Friday Zhu's agents had been tracking the movements of Alan Drummond. There was little to report. On Friday, Drummond had lunch a block away from his Manhattan condo at the Parlor Steakhouse with a man named Hector Garza (that was the name he'd given the restaurant's maître d'). A single clear photograph had been taken of the man as he exited the restaurant, but no positive match had been made yet.

"On that same evening," Shen An-ling said, "he and his wife, Penelope, went to 203 Garfield Place."

Zhu chewed his lower lip unconsciously. The last time he'd heard that address, he'd been in Berlin, saying it aloud to a Moldovan man whose daughter had been killed by the Central Intelligence Agency. "You mean he met with Milo Weaver."

"It was a couples' dinner, but the two men went to the roof for a private talk. We have no way of knowing what they discussed."

"And Weaver?" Zhu asked. "How is he?"

"Remarkably well. Andrei Stanescu is a terrible shot. He damaged Weaver's small intestine, but not critically. A week in the hospital. He'll be fine."

Zhu thought about that a moment before voicing his thoughts aloud. "We can be sure that Alan Drummond is sharing his plans with Milo Weaver, but I don't think we have to worry about Weaver, at least not yet. If I read him right, he won't be interested in anything but convalescing in peace. I don't think he really likes his old employers."

"Still, we should keep an eye on him."

"Oh, of course! Not at the expense of Drummond or his coconspirators, though. What occupies him these days?"

Shen An-ling scanned the sheet in front of him. "Looking for a job, apparently."

"Good man," said Zhu. "Something quiet."

A little after ten that morning, Xin Zhu left the office in one of his employee's cars and took the Fourth Ring Road south to the G106, straight into Daxing District. He followed some basic evasive maneuvers along the way, changing direction by bumping over cracked medians and shuttling over to alternate routes before returning to the main streets, so that what should have been a half-hour journey ran more than an hour. Finally, he reached a street with rows of middle-class apartment blocks six stories high. He Qiang's apartment was on the top floor of one of the central buildings, and in the elevator, Zhu tried to decipher two thick-marker scribbles on the wall, graffiti tags. It was a relatively new phenomenon in Beijing, something he'd heard complained about at too many parties, but inside this rusting elevator he had the feeling that they brightened up the drab, functional machine.

When He Qiang let him into the apartment, he found the television playing another Bollywood tearjerker, and Liu Xiuxiu at a typewriter, practicing some code He Qiang had been teaching her. All the lighting here was artificial, for He Qiang had closed the blinds.

Liu Xiuxiu ceased her typing and came over with her head bowed, wearing jeans and a thin white blouse. She looked surprised when Zhu reached out to shake her hand. Then she relaxed, going to make tea as He Qiang shut off the television. Zhu, looking at his agent, pointed at the ceiling.

"Our first lesson," He Qiang said as he handed over four passport photos of Liu Xiuxiu. "We cleaned the whole place."

"Anything?"

A shake of the head.

"Good." Zhu settled on the sofa and waited until the tea had arrived, then watched Liu Xiuxiu serve it with the grace of a courtesan. "Please," he said when he realized she wasn't going to sit with them, and patted the sofa. She settled down beside him, and he spoke slowly. "Liu Xiuxiu, the first thing you should understand is that you are here because you are, I believe, of equal value to any of my agents. Or as soon as you've gained some experience you will be. So, thank you for the tea, but do not feel it's your role here to serve us. That is not how I run my section."

Submissively, she nodded.

Zhu turned to He Qiang. "You will follow her to Washington and act as her support. She will have to make decisions on the ground, and unless you know for certain that she's making a decision based on false information, you will back her up completely. Understood?"

He Qiang did understand.

"I'm going to America?" Liu Xiuxiu asked, then, embarrassed, bit her lips.

"You and He Qiang will be leaving tonight on separate flights. To Washington, D.C. A contact will set you up with a place to stay."

"Sam Kuo?" asked He Qiang.

Zhu nodded. "He's not ideal, but we're pressed for time." He turned back to Liu Xiuxiu and was pleased to find the doubt gone from her face. His instinct about this girl was not unfounded. "Once you're settled, He Qiang will go to New York to begin a second part of the operation, but you will always be able to call him for advice, and after a few days he'll return to Washington. By then, though, you should have made progress on your operation, which will be to seduce one of two men— both, if it's possible—and gain information from them."

She nodded but asked nothing. He wished that she would, because he preferred his agents to be curious, to demand to be completely informed, even when he was unable to tell them everything. He turned back to He Qiang. "You remember the Therapist?"

"Of course."

"You'll employ him full-time on this. Tell him it'll be at least two weeks' work, his regular payment plus a bonus if it goes well."

"He'll like that. The Therapist only speaks money."

"You'll get more details before your flight."

He Qiang nodded, satisfied.

"Comrade Colonel," said Liu Xiuxiu.

"Yes?"

"May I ask the purpose of this operation?"

"The purpose?"

She paused, her lips tightening. "I know the outline of my particular job, but may I know how it fits into your larger aims—and what those larger aims are?"

"No," he said, but was pleased that she had asked. "You'll focus solely on your operation. When He Qiang returns from New York, you will not question him about what he's done. Is that understood?"

There was no sign of insult when she said, "Of course, Comrade Colonel."

Zhu opened his briefcase, took out a folder with photographs, and spread them out on the table. Each was labeled with a name, some with more than one. "These are the players we know about. You'll remember their faces and names, memorize the biographical details typed on the reverse side, and before you leave here at seven o'clock you'll burn them."

Liu Xiuxiu pushed the photographs around, pausing on Leticia Jones/Rosa Mumu. Zhu said, "That woman is extremely dangerous. If you do see her, do not engage. You report her presence to He Qiang."

The other woman, Dorothy Collingwood, was lightly airbrushed in her official portrait, wiping away the soft wrinkles collected during her years in government service. The other two, Stuart Jackson and Nathan Irwin, sported large, false smiles. "I want you to focus on the men, of course. A week ago these three met with Jones and this man," he said, pulling over another photo, "Alan Drummond. He's the former head of a secret CIA office that we had a hand in destroying. What I want to know is the subject of their conversation. I know it concerned China, because Jones had just returned from a trip here, but I don't know the details. It's imperative to all of us that we find out."

Though she seemed to comprehend the difficulty of the assignment, Liu Xiuxiu showed no hesitation. "Are the two men married?"

"Yes."

"Good," she said. "Married men are generally easier to seduce than single ones."

He Qiang smiled at Zhu, as if to say, *See what I told you?*

"This man here," Zhu said, sliding over a sidewalk surveillance photo of Hector Garza, who was darker than the others, with a narrow face, a small mustache, and black eyes, "is a question mark. We know he met with Alan Drummond in New York, but we don't know who he is, or if he even has any connection to what we're doing."

"He could be a Tourist," He Qiang pointed out. "We never had their pictures, just their codes."

"Tourist?" asked Liu Xiuxiu.

Zhu wished He Qiang had kept his mouth shut, but it was too late. "Agents," he told her. "Agents run by Alan Drummond's old department. They called them Tourists. For a time, they were legendary."

Liu Xiuxiu acted as if this were the kind of conversation she had every day. "May I ask what happened to the department?"

"We destroyed it," Zhu said again, not willing to go into the details that might shake her faith in her new employer. He looked at He Qiang. "Your focus will be Drummond, and you'll use the Therapist for this. We suspect that Drummond is the epicenter, so to speak, and once you've learned what he's doing you have to be ready to act. I'll get five more people to help you out."

"Is Xu Guanzhong available?"

"I'll find out."

"Thank you."

Zhu reached into his briefcase again and took out two plane tickets, marked with new names. "Someone will meet you at the airport with your passports."

"Who's this?" Liu Xiuxiu asked, reaching for a photo that was close to sliding off the edge of the table. In it, a man of about forty stared back with heavy eyes, below, the names Milo Weaver, Sebastian Hall, and Charles Alexander.

"One more question mark," Zhu said. "Milo Weaver has been meeting socially with Alan Drummond, and he was another employee of the department. He was injured recently and should be out of the game, but given his close relationship with Drummond, we can't know for sure. He Qiang will have to look into that as well."

Liu Xiuxiu set the photo back down.

"Are you excited?" Zhu asked.

Liu Xiuxiu considered this, staring at Milo Weaver's gloomy face. "I'm sorting through my feelings, Comrade Colonel."

"How are they leaning?"

She smiled, then raised her eyes to meet his. "There is one thing I have no doubt of."

"What's that?"

"That I was right to change careers."

"Why?"

"Because I was tired of serving only myself," she said before averting her gaze.

Zhu let that sit a moment, then leaned closer, lowering his voice to a whisper. "Liu Xiuxiu, if all of China could speak such poetry as that, then we would be the greatest nation in history."

* * *

At the office, he and Shen An-ling assembled a list of five agents to assist He Qiang in Manhattan, and though Xu Guanzhong was engaged in a long-term operation in Toronto, Zhu decided to bring him in as well. Later, after Shen An-ling had left for the airport with the finished passports, Zhu went back over the files. He started with the surveillance reports on Alan Drummond, then moved gradually back, so that he saw a man in reverse. An unemployed man moving backward into an office on the twenty-second floor of 101 West Thirty-first Street and watching, on computer monitors, the systematic killing of thirty-three of his agents, his Tourists, in all the corners of the globe. In this reversed life, Drummond's misery fades as he watches the screen, so that after he's seen the massacre he is a new man, full of confidence and even a lust for life. Like Zhu, he is married, and, like Zhu, he's in love with his wife. Unlike Zhu, he has never had children, and that, perhaps, makes all the difference.

It was a year ago when Xin Zhu learned that his son, Delun, had been killed with other Chinese workers doing repairs on the Sudan pipeline from Leal to the Red Sea, and while he was barely able to comprehend his own emotions his instinct took over, and he began to adjust his sights. He aimed first at the wild riot of desert people who had attacked his son's truck. Questions were asked—specifically, *why*. Their answer: the murder of their beloved cleric, Mullah Salih Ahmad, who had been agitating against Chinese companies digging into Sudanese sand and taking Sudanese oil. Zhu was in a position to know that China had had no hand in the murder. Who had? Not the al-Bashir government, because it knew the wrath his death would provoke. Then, with information provided by a source he'd acquired a few years before in the office of Senator Nathan Irwin, he learned that one particularly nasty department of the CIA had killed the cleric, in order to turn the populace against Chinese oil development. This action led directly to the death of Delun, Zhu's only child.

Though he spent months taking aim, the actual shot was, like so many important things in life, not witnessed by him. He remembered sitting in his office, in this office, right under the portrait of Hu Jintao, wreathed in smoke from his Hamlets, waiting for word. Waiting for anything. The first word had come from Sam Kuo—"James Pearson has been caught." This sentence told him that all the cards were finally on the table, and there was no reason to hold back anymore. By then, he had learned the whole Tourism communications procedure and knew precisely how to use it to his advantage. He ordered most of his office staff home, and in the nearly silent office, he told the remaining ones to send the first wave of text messages. Thirty-seven in all, one to each so-called Tourist. A go-code followed by the instructions to travel somewhere and kill someone—in each case, another Tourist—and to maintain complete silence until the job was finished.

He couldn't depend on the Tourists to simply destroy themselves, though, so a second wave of messages went out to Zhu's own agents, who had been waiting for days in their respective cities. Throughout the world, men and women who worked for the Expedition Agency stirred.

He was later fed reports that he spent days reading and rereading, for he had asked his people to give him all the details so that his imagination would not feed him lies. It was a necessary part of perpetual revolution, the reassessment and self-critique.

After nearly two months of intimacy with those reports, Zhu saw a street in Phnom Penh, where He Péng waited on Sisowath Quay. He was a twenty-eight-year-old whose parents both died soon after his birth in the 1981 Dawu earthquake, crushed by a concrete roof. The infant was dug out of the wreckage and transferred to the care of the state. Another life, and he would have grown up a farmer and probably never set foot outside the ever-shifting Sichuan province. Now, he was a young man who had traveled extensively, a young man with education and sharp wits, a man of the world with a Cambodian hotel key card in his pocket and a pistol hanging by a shoelace against the center of his back, its long suppressor tickling the base of his spine.

Guided by the details in his text message, He Péng had identified the American they referred to as #1 as he had entered the Amanjaya Pancam Hotel, then followed him inside. He Péng's secondary target—#2—was on the second floor, waiting to kill #1.

He had tried to keep it simple for all of them. Each had a #1 and a #2. Each knew that his pair would initially try to kill one another, and each knew that his only job was to make sure that both Americans succeeded. Zhu had explained to some of them, "We are not committing the act, we are its midwives."

In He Péng's case, midwifery proved insufficient. When he reached the second-floor room, he discovered a closed door and voices behind it, speaking English. One, he could tell, was injured, while the other was tending the wound. He Péng waited. When a male voice said, "I'll get more water," and a faucet hissed loudly, he unlatched the pistol from under his shirt, then used the key card to open the door. Inside, he found a woman sitting on the floor, against the bed—Japanese, he guessed from her features, though all these people were in fact American—bleeding from the shoulder all over the carpet. She barely had time to register surprise before he shot her once through the neck, then once through the heart.

The faucet turned off, and the man he'd followed inside appeared holding a glass pitcher steamy with hot water. That was the first casualty, shattering as He Péng's initial wild shot went through it and into the man's liver. The man stumbled backward into the bathroom, and He Péng followed, catching him as he reached for a pistol on the wet counter. A shot to the chest threw him back against the toilet. Another to the head stopped him for good.

What did He Péng think at that moment? Did he only think of his service to the people, or did he, when faced with a man and a woman dead by his hand, think about Sichuan fields that could have been his to tend?

No, He Péng was a good boy, and that afternoon was

the natural culmination of his life thus far. Zhu had less conviction when it came to Liang Jia in Vancouver, who had left a man bleeding in the West End, to be picked up by a kind stranger and brought to Vancouver General. It had taken a stern call from him to get her to leave the airport and head to the hospital to finish her job.

There had been one loss, Wang Shi in Buenos Aires, a mistake that was either Zhu's or Wang Shi's—he still wasn't sure. All he knew was that while one target American, his #1, was found in a hotel room, his #2, whose work name was José Santiago, got out of Argentina. Wang Shi's body was found by the police, beaten and shot once through the left eye.

Nearly two months later, he couldn't help but picture them all again, hotel rooms and pistols in Phnom Penh, in Jerusalem and Buenos Aires, in Bern and Johannesburg and Delhi. He saw a drowning in Tehran, a hospital bed in Vancouver, another in Brasilia, and bodies in fields in Tashkent and Cairo and Moscow. He saw sudden falls from great heights in Mexico City, Seoul, Dhaka, and London. He saw dogs picking over corpses in Hanoi and Tallinn, and in Tokyo he saw a bloated dead woman in a sushi restaurant, killed after hours. He saw an explosion in Afghanistan. Each was its own story, and his curse was that he knew them all. Together they became a great, violent narrative, his hand guiding thirty-three murders across the planet.

Now, he worried as he got up from his desk and prepared to go home to Sung Hui, all those corpses were coming to find him. Yet he felt more alive than he had in months.

Part Two

BROWNSTONE JUNGLE

**FRIDAY, JUNE 6 TO
SATURDAY, JUNE 28, 2008**

1

"When the world ends, Milo, no one will even notice."

"You're drunk."

Alan set his Heineken can on the flat, pebbly rooftop, then stretched hands and smoldering cigarette above his head, yawning. "Not yet. I'm just saying that when all this finally collapses, it's going to smell sweet. There won't be terror in the streets. No blood, no starvation—nothing like that. Just the scent of peppermint."

"Peppermint?"

"Lemon, caramel, jasmine . . . peppermint—take your pick. The next day will look the same, maybe a little better. They'll have no idea that everything important has just died."

Milo had been drinking tonic water; his glass was already empty. He took a position along the raised edge of the apartment building, as if falling four stories weren't a possibility. "If you're trying to sound smart, you're failing spectacularly."

A rare breeze swept over them. Alan sucked on his Marlboro, looking like the new smoker he was.

"Here," said Milo. "Gimme some of that."

Alan passed the cigarette, and as Milo took a drag, they gazed over rooftops toward Prospect Park. Despite it being a little before midnight, they were forced to wear shirtsleeves. Alan's wife, Penelope, had dredged up the phrase "global warming" five times that night.

It was three weeks after Xin Zhu's visit to Qingdao, though neither man knew about that. Nor did they know that, downstairs in the Weaver apartment, their wives were discussing marriage. Later that night, Milo's wife would relate the entire conversation to him, while Penelope would tell her husband nothing, not for some days at least.

"You really should stop," Milo said as he handed back the cigarette and took a blister pack of Nicorette from his shirt pocket. He squeezed out a square of the gum and popped it into his mouth. "You're not even addicted yet. Just quit."

"Makes me feel in control of something. I haven't felt that way in a long time."

"And Pen? What does she think of the new Alan?"

"She says he's a moron."

"You guys having problems?"

"Oh, no. That's the one thing that's going right."

Milo didn't quite believe that. He'd noticed the slow progress of Alan Drummond's depression over the course of periodic couples dinners that had begun after Milo had returned from the hospital. Alan claimed that that initial invitation had been his wife's idea, but as soon as they met in the Drummonds' Upper East Side apartment with Stephanie in tow, Milo saw plainly that it had been Alan's idea, and he read their future conversations in his ex-boss's young but dreary face: endings. Their careers, the bloody full stop to the Department of Tourism, and, distantly, their own mortalities.

The truth was that Alan had initiated the dinners because he wanted to jointly lick wounds, but Milo's only troubling wounds had been physical. After nine weeks, the doctor had pronounced his recovery "remarkable," but he still wasn't allowed alcohol. Some gin in his tonic might have made these conversations more bearable.

Unlike Milo, the drunken man wandering his rooftop still saw his future entwined in the intelligence world. Unlike Milo, he hadn't been shot point-blank by the weeping father of a girl who had been killed by the intelligence world—that could wash away anyone's illusions about their industry's virtues. In fact, Milo hadn't even planned to follow up with his own dinner invitation until they got home that first night and Tina raved about Penelope—*She's* funny. *And smart as hell. See? That's the kind of couple friends I've been hoping for.*

Alan squatted again and lifted his beer. "Did you know that he's in trouble with his own people?"

"Who?"

"Who do you think? Turns out his little massacre wasn't even sanctioned. He's weak now."

"Who told you this?"

"I've still got friends, Milo. I'm out, but that doesn't end friendships."

Milo wondered who in the Company would be dumb enough to share secrets with someone as bitter as Alan Drummond. Unless he wasn't really out after all. "Are you still unemployed, Alan?"

"Unemployed, yes. Dead, no. I've had a wonderful idea."

"You've *had* ideas, remember? I vetoed them."

"Modified. It's radically modified."

Milo remembered Alan's feverish rant, from two weeks ago, about how he could lure Xin Zhu to Japan and assassinate him in his hotel room. Then another one, more ambitious, involving terrorists from the Youth League, who would converge on Beijing during the Olympics with explosives and long-range rifles. He, like Milo, was still a young man, but when he got to raving, he sounded like a man twenty years older, fighting madness. "They were bad plans, Alan. They weren't the kinds of things that could be modified."

"Then let's call it a new plan," Alan said, standing. "Leticia thinks it's an excellent plan."

"Leave that woman alone."

"I'm telling you, she thinks it's good."

"Who else have you been bothering with this? Zachary?"

Alan shook his head. "Zachary Klein has apparently found himself a civilian life. But you know he wasn't the only other survivor."

"José—"

"Let's not name names," Alan cut in. "But there's

also a third, who wasn't on the Tourism rosters when everything went down. You remember him. My point, though, is that they all agree that it's an excellent plan."

Milo turned to give him his attention. "It might be the best plan, but I'm not taking part. I've made that clear."

"Did you know he got married?"

"Zachary?"

"Xin Zhu. Last summer he got married to some sweet young thing and—"

"Stop it."

Alan stared at him, then wiped his mouth with the back of one of his red hands; it made him look like a drunk. His bare arm, Milo noticed, was dense with muscle; he'd been working out. "Sixty years."

"What?"

"Sixty goddamned years," Alan said. "The department chugs along. Complete secrecy. Complete freedom. I get control of it for two months—sixty *days*—and the entire thing's wiped out." He looked at his can, as if it might hold answers. "You have any idea how that makes me feel?"

Milo had no idea how it made Alan feel, so he said nothing. Besides, Alan wouldn't have heard him.

"I keep seeing those dots. Red dots turning blue. I have nightmares about those dots. Do you?"

"Sometimes," Milo lied. His own nightmares covered different territory.

"Well, I have them all the time. Damn near every night."

They didn't speak for a while, just turned back to the

vista of nighttime Brooklyn. Cars rumbled along Seventh Avenue, music drained from bars, and a couple argued somewhere up the street. Chewing hard and getting too much nicotine, Milo tried to suppress a hiccup, but it slipped out, and Alan looked at him as if he'd cursed. Milo said, "Look, it's not your problem anymore. Zhu played it better than we did. That's all."

"You think that was a *game*?" Alan flicked his cigarette off the roof; it glowed and arced slowly down to Garfield Place. "Thirty-three corpses—a *game*?"

"That's how we treated it when we ran operations."

"You're con*doning* him?" Alan said, slapping one of his red hands against his hip. "When we ran operations we had reasons. Security reasons. Xin Zhu killed thirty-three Americans for revenge. How can you not see the difference?"

"We don't know why he did it," Milo said quietly, hoping to calm the man down. "We think he did it for revenge, but we don't know anything for sure."

"You don't even know their names, do you? Sandra Harrison, Pak Eun, Lorenzo Pellegrini, Andy Geriev, Mia Salazar, John—"

"It's not your problem," Milo cut in, irritated. "Not anymore. You know what your problem is now? That woman downstairs. You need to find a job so you can keep your life running."

"This, from an unemployed man?"

"I've got an interview next week. What about you? You look like hell, you know. You're going to sit around in your underwear hatching some plan to—to what?

Wipe out all his agents? Kill his wife? Bomb his office? No, Alan. I'm not helping with your revenge."

"I wasn't planning to kill—"

"No!" Milo said, raising a hand. "Enough. I don't want to know. I've told you before—I've wasted too much of my life, and too much of my family's life, fighting losing battles. I looked into Andrei Stanescu's eyes before he shot me. I listened to his disconnected speech—the man is completely destroyed, and I'm not going to be part of the machine that does that to people like him. Not anymore."

"But Xin Zhu *sent* him to you," Alan said, not understanding a thing. "We can *get* that bastard!"

Milo rubbed his eyes and took a breath before speaking. "You're not listening, Alan. Killing the Tourists didn't bring back Xin Zhu's son, and getting rid of Xin Zhu isn't going to bring back your agents. This is nursery-school moral philosophy. It's time to get your priorities straight."

Alan seemed to be considering it.

"Come on," said Milo. "Let's go downstairs and talk about the primaries. Or our glorious president. Let's talk about Barry Bonds, for Christ's sake. And if anyone brings up China, all you have to say is that it's a shame so many died in the earthquake."

"How many at last count?"

"More than sixty thousand."

"A lot," Alan muttered.

"Yeah, it is."

They stared at each other a moment, Milo feeling a

dull throb in his gut, reminding him of the miles he'd trekked looking for a mole, the many ways in which Xin Zhu had fooled them all, and the disheveled, mourning Moldovan man who had tracked him here with a pistol.

Alan wiped his lips again. "Maybe you're right."

"I'm not far from it."

"Listen," he said, his voice lowered slightly. "I'm thinking about taking a vacation."

"What do you call what you've had?"

Alan blinked at that, as if fighting down a rising tide of anger, but then it was gone. "Take Pen away from the city for a while. There's a great place up in Colorado, cabins on Grand Lake. Totally secluded, totally off the grid. Grand Estes Cabins."

"You want to be off the grid?"

"It's useful," Alan said, then winked.

Milo patted Alan's hard, muscled shoulder. "Come on, let's go downstairs."

Alan stepped forward, then paused. "But if you do change your mind—if you suddenly feel the urge for vengeance—you just let me know."

"I won't."

"Or if I'm not available, contact Leticia. You remember how to do that, right?"

Milo turned to him again. "I'm not going to change my mind, and I'm not going to go through Leticia's Byzantine contact procedure."

"But just in case."

"Sure, I remember. Now let's go try to fool our wives into thinking we're just nice guys."

He led Alan to the access door, and as they descended, ducking to avoid hitting their heads, they heard music filtering up the narrow, rickety staircase.

"What is it?" asked Penelope.

"I don't know. I—" Tina leaned to squint at the screen of Milo's iPod, which was wired into their stereo. "Françoise Hardy. It's pretty."

"You said this is Milo's music?"

Tina returned to the couch and scooped up her wine. "Yeah. Weird, huh?"

Penelope rocked her head from side to side, as if she wouldn't be pinned down to an opinion. "You're right, it is nice, but I have a feeling you put that on to change the subject." She spoke with a sly smile, then leaned back, cradling her own glass in her palm.

"No, no—just gave me a moment to think. The answer's yes. We're getting along well, though we've taken a break from the marriage counseling."

"His idea or yours?"

"Both of us, really. Stephanie saw her father in a pool of blood. Our focus now is on her. She sees someone once a week, and she seems to be dealing well. I'm sure we'll get back to the marriage soon enough, though I'm not sure we need it anymore."

"But . . . ?"

"No but. Not really. As soon as he finds a job, he'll be happier. You don't just go from living your life in hotels all over the place to sitting unemployed in this dinky apartment—not without a little tension. I know I sound stupidly optimistic, but I have reason."

Penelope shook her head. "I'm not saying anything. You know me, discreet as a Buddhist."

They both laughed at that. "It's just this place," Tina finally said, motioning to take in the whole apartment. "I wouldn't mind moving. Every time I go downstairs my chest tightens."

"You expect to find a guy with a gun."

"It's ironic, really. Last year, Milo wanted us to run off with him, to Europe. I said no. Now, running off sounds great to me, and he's the one who, as he puts it, never wants to get on a plane again."

"Funny," Penelope said with no trace of humor.

"How about you guys?" Tina asked.

Penelope moved her free hand so that she was clutching the glass with both. That thin smile returned. "I'm thinking about divorce."

It had been said so pleasantly that Tina thought she must have misheard, but Penelope's smile faded, and she knew she hadn't. "Since when?"

"Who knows? You never know when these things start. But it's become more serious these last couple of months."

"Since the department closed down."

Penelope nodded, then looked into her empty glass. "You have any more of this?"

It was the same delay tactic Tina had used a moment before, and she couldn't argue with that. She went to the kitchen, and, as she worked on another bottle of Beaujolais, Stephanie appeared in her pink pajamas, clutching the PlayStation Portable that Milo had irrationally bought her a week before. "What is it, Little Miss?"

Stephanie looked surprised, then she glanced behind herself toward the living room. "Is there . . ."

"What, hon?"

It took another moment to get the question out, and Stephanie's tendency to block up when speaking seemed to be an aftereffect of seeing her father shot. *Whatever you do*, the therapist had said, *don't draw attention to it.* Finally, Stephanie said, "What's wrong with Pen?"

"Nothing. What are you doing up?"

"I'm thirsty. What's wrong with her?"

"What do you mean?"

"She's crying."

Tina turned to her daughter, whom she sometimes worried had seen too much during her six years of life. "Crying?"

"I think so." A pause. "I don't know."

"Don't worry about her. She's just got some problems."

"You'll help her out?"

"Yeah, Little Miss. I'm here to help her out. You said you were hungry?"

"Thirsty."

"So that's why you're awake?"

"Yeah."

"And that PlayStation just happened to be in your hand when you woke?"

Stephanie turned it over, examining the machine as if its presence were a surprise. The gears in her brain worked. "I just woke up and there it was!"

Tina set her up with a glass of water and sent her back to bed, then brought out the Beaujolais. There was no evidence of weeping on Penelope's delicate, sensual face, just an occasional twitch at the corner of her lips. "I think I scared Stephanie."

"She's seen me cry often enough," Tina said as she refilled their glasses. She placed the bottle on the coffee table, then decided to sit next to her on the couch. "Go ahead."

"With what?" Penelope asked. "All I can say is it's gotten worse. Men are . . . well, they *are* their jobs, aren't they? Is that sexist?"

"Don't think so. Patronizing, maybe."

"What I mean is, you're a librarian. But is that *who* you are?"

"No, I get your point."

Penelope drank, whispered, "Mmm, this is good," then looked directly at Tina with a newfound intensity. "Anyway, the job disappeared, and he became a different person. Starts smoking. Exercises like mad. When he drinks, he does it stupidly. He starts fights for no reason. He's acting like some washed-up jarhead, which I suppose is what he is. He—and this sounds weird—he spends the longest time in the *bathroom*. Goes off to take a crap, and I don't know when I'll see him again. And no, it's not medical—not self-abuse either. When he's not shitting he barricades himself in his office. It's like he can't stand to be in the same room with me."

As Penelope spoke, Tina instinctively compared these observations to how Milo had become since his unemployment. Since getting shot. She wanted to find similar things in him so that she could hold them up and say, *See? They all do it*, but she came up short. "What does he say?"

"He says there's nothing wrong. Just distracted. He's working on a project. What kind of project? Sorry—it's top-secret stuff. I point out that he doesn't work on top-secret stuff anymore, and he backtracks and says it's for friends."

"Friends like Milo?"

Penelope shrugged. "You'll have to ask him yourself."

They let that sit between them, Tina wondering if Milo was, despite his insistence that that kind of work was behind him, helping Alan with some lingering projects from the Department of Tourism. "Is it really that bad?" she asked. "Sounds like a phase to me—divorce is permanent."

Penelope raised the glass to her lips but before drinking let three words slip out. "He hit me."

"*What?*"

She finished her drink and set down the glass. "Few days ago. Just once. During an argument. Right here." She tapped her left cheekbone, just under her eye, and that was when Tina noticed the extra layer of makeup on that spot. "He apologized, of course. Cried. But that was when it really came together for me."

"Okay," Tina said. "Now I get it. When a man hits you it's time to go."

"No." Penelope shook her head. "You *don't* get it. I'm not worried about getting beat up—despite the signs, that's not the kind of man he is. It was afterward, when he was there on the floor, crying. Begging me not to leave him. That's when I knew."

"Knew what?"

"That I didn't love him anymore. It wasn't him striking me. It was the miserable mess he'd become. I realized that I didn't care if he drowned in beer and ended up living on the street. I didn't care if he had a heart attack and died right there. No—it wasn't anger. It was apathy. It was the complete lack of all those feelings I'd had when we got married."

Again, silence came between them. Tina was thinking of the few times in their marriage that she'd thought the same thing—that she had no love for Milo anymore. Those moments had occurred, but always as a question rather than a statement: *Do* I love him anymore? Just as she was preparing to ask Penelope if, perhaps, she was asking herself a question rather than answering it, she was drawn to nine weeks ago, when Milo was shot on the steps of this very building. When it occurred, all she could think was that she wanted him to be okay. She'd even lost track of Stephanie during those brutal minutes. If anything had convinced her that their marital troubles could be worked through, it had been that event. That, maybe, was the thing she had that Penelope didn't have.

Finally, Tina said, "I don't really know anything, but if you're asking, I'd guess that you're trying to convince yourself that the marriage is dead, when it isn't."

"What makes you think that?" Penelope asked, the signs of real interest in her face.

"You're still with him, and you came here to tell me about it. You're looking for a way out of this mess."

Penelope didn't answer, only stared at her, and that thin, sad smile returned. Tina really had no idea who this woman was. Then the door opened and the men came in.

Each pair was acutely preoccupied by its own silence, and both silences were so painfully self-conscious that not even Françoise Hardy's breathy singing could hide them. So they all went to it at once, four awkward voices laughing and muttering banalities. They just wanted to fill the living room with noise. Any noise; it didn't matter.

2

While Xin Zhu lived without dreams, or at least lost them by the time he woke each morning, Milo had been plagued over the last month by a repeating nightmare. Unlike Alan Drummond's dream of spots on a computer screen changing color as people died, it bore no obvious connection to recent events.

It took place in a park that, from one angle, looked like Prospect Park, but from another resembled the area around Lake Devin in Oxford, North Carolina, where he grew up. He was with Stephanie, who in his dream was two years old, maybe three, and they were discussing the film of *The Wizard of Oz*. The foliage around them thickened, and an approaching man gave Milo a raised eyebrow and a hand signal—three flat fingers over his heart—as he passed. Milo knew that sign, knew that it was telling him to do something, but he couldn't remember what he was supposed to do. He reached for Stephanie's hand as she said, "You no leave me, Daddy?"

and he tried to hurry her up, but she buckled her legs, sliding to the dusty ground beside a park bench, and laughed, playing with him. Her act of rebellion terrified and enraged him, because now he remembered what he was supposed to do. So he scooped her up and ran with her through the trees, trying to cut through the park to the exit, but every time they emerged from the low hedges they were on the same length of trail, and each time a different man sat on the bench. The men always wore oversized trench coats, but the objects in their hands changed. One read a newspaper, the next talked on a cell phone, and the last peeled an apple with a knife. Though they said nothing, they were all demanding the same thing—three fingers rose to their hearts—and time was running out. The unspoken threat was that if he didn't do as they demanded, neither he nor Stephanie would leave the park alive.

The hedges on either side of the trail formed a low wall, and he caught his breath behind one, squatting and setting Stephanie down. He was crying by then, doing everything to hide it from her, but knew he wasn't succeeding. Still, she pretended that everything was all right. She asked a question about Dorothy's clothes, but he couldn't figure out what she was asking. He said, "Daddy has to go somewhere, Little Miss." She repeated her question about Dorothy, the sentence streaming on with awkward pauses and unexpected half-words, so that he still didn't understand it. Choking on his tears, he said, "You wait right here. I'll be back soon." She nodded, wide-eyed, trusting him absolutely. He kissed her in a frantic way until she pushed him away, laughing.

As he stood, towering over her, he saw movement in the shrubbery, but the bench on the trail was empty. He whispered, "Stay here, okay, Little Miss?" She blew him a kiss with her fat-fingered hand.

He stepped around the shrubs to the trail and headed for the bench, but changed his mind and returned to the hedge, squatting on his side so that were he to reach through the impenetrable branches, he would touch Stephanie. He waited, hands pressed to his face. He heard, "Daddy?"—a light whisper. Then with concern, "Daddy?"

Movement. Heavy feet. Whispers in an indecipherable language that sounded like Latin with a Slavic accent.

"Daddy?"

He was weeping uncontrollably now, hearing and feeling the men converge on her, and her single repeated word grew louder and more hysterical, melting into a high wail of fear or pain that, until he broke, grew exponentially. He always broke in this dream, crashing back through the hedge, cutting himself on thorns and falling onto wet ground. Her imprint remained in the bent grass, but he was alone, writhing uncontrollably, tugging at his own chest and stomach, trying to excise himself of every organ.

He woke from these dreams to wet pillows, sometimes to Tina—who, irritated, would ask why he was waking her up. He'd mutter some excuse and wander to the kitchen and pour a glass of water, but he was seldom able to get back to sleep. Instead, he found himself picking apart the dream, trying to uncover the basic question of it: *Why* was he giving up his daughter to nameless thugs in the park? He understood that the alternative was death for them both, but why did they want her in the first place? He was asking for logic from his dream, and no matter how many times the dream recurred, a logical answer remained far away.

The more appropriate question was: *Why am I dreaming this?* He had a pretty good idea. Back in December, while still working as a Tourist, he'd been ordered to kill a Moldovan girl, fifteen years old, and had balked. He'd instead tried to save her but had failed. When, nine weeks ago, the dead girl's father put a bullet in him, Milo had felt no sense of injustice. He might not have killed the girl, but if people like him didn't exist, she would have lived—that was the undeniable truth. Milo was as guilty as the man who had actually broken her neck, and in his dream, the men whose language resembled Moldovan were exacting proper revenge. It was his eye for that eye, and no matter how much he despised the dream he knew it would probably visit him for the rest of his life.

A week after their dinner, on Friday the thirteenth, Penelope left a message on Tina's phone. Alan wasn't in town, and she was canceling dinner at their apartment. When Tina called back, Penelope didn't pick up, so Milo called Alan's cell. His old boss answered sounding unnerved, like a man desperate to hide his anxiety. "Where are you?" Milo asked.

"Well, I'm not in Manhattan. Don't tell me you guys are that hard up for a meal."

"Overseas?"

"You didn't want any part of it, remember?"

"I don't," Milo said, but he had a sudden urge to know what, exactly, Drummond was up to. He hadn't liked the man he'd talked to on his roof last week, hadn't trusted that he could keep himself out of trouble, and the things Tina had told him about the Drummonds' disintegrating marriage had just sharpened his worry. Alan Drummond was bound to rush things; he was bound to make a mistake. "Are you all right?"

"Of course I'm all right."

"How about next week?"

"Why don't you guys invite Pen over? I'm not . . . well, we're not together anymore."

"Since when?"

"It's nothing. As soon as I've taken care of some things we'll see if we can't patch it up."

Though Tina had prepared him for such a turn of events, he was still surprised. "When did this happen?"

"Couple days after your place."

"And?"

"And I'm not talking about my marital life on an open line. Got it? Just ask Pen. She's already told your wife all about it."

"I want to hear your side," Milo said, because it wasn't surprise he felt; it was fear. He'd seen how marital troubles could run like dominoes through social circles, bringing out the hidden fault lines in each friend's marriage.

"How'd the interview go?" Alan asked. He wasn't going to share.

"What?"

"You were about to join the ranks of the employed."

"I have a feeling they actually checked my references."

"If the department were still together we could've given you an excellent CV."

"Watch out for yourself, Alan."

"Invite Pen over, she's probably lonely."

Penelope was out of town for the weekend, visiting her brother in Boston, so she didn't come for dinner until Monday evening. Milo noticed that she did have the look of a lonely person, humorless and quietly desperate for their company. Having Stephanie around throughout dinner didn't help, and the girl's explanation for the lack of tomatoes in the salad Tina had rustled up—"Mom thinks we'll all die if we eat tomatoes. They've got fish in them."—only left Penelope confused.

"Fish?"

"Salmon," Stephanie said authoritatively.

"Salmon*ella*," Tina corrected, "and I didn't say we'd die. It's just not a good idea to take chances. Over two hundred people have gotten sick—did you know?"

"No," Penelope said into her lettuce. "I didn't hear that."

Conversation couldn't really begin until Stephanie was gone, so once she had been packed off to bed they took positions around their guest. Tina sat beside her on the couch, while Milo took the chair across from her. It reminded him miserably of the interviewer he'd faced off with last week, when he'd known from the second question that they wouldn't call him, yet stuck out the entire interview in order to seem *professional*. He slipped some Nicorette into his mouth, then said, "Where's Alan? I talked to him, but he didn't tell me where he was."

Penelope shrugged and began on her fresh glass of wine.

"You're not keeping in touch?"

"He hasn't called me, if that's what you mean. Maybe he's finding himself a girlfriend." She turned to Tina. "One can hope."

Milo felt at a loss, so he let that sit and waited for Tina to take over, but all she did was stare back at Penelope, smiling sadly. He was outside for the moment, these two women staring at one another like melancholy lovers, and he wondered if Tina really had told him everything about their conversation. Perhaps she had found something to sympathize with in Penelope's sudden lack of love for her husband.

Finally, Penelope turned to him. "I'm the one who did it. I kicked him out. That was . . . Sunday? Yeah. A full week ago. He told me he had to go on a trip, so I told him not to bother coming back. I'd had enough."

"Enough of what?"

"The secrecy. The moods. All the things you can put up with if you really love your husband."

Tina was staring at him. It was an indecipherable expression—did she want him to shut up? He saw no reason to stop, so he said, "Alan thinks he can set things right once he gets back. He told me that."

Penelope nodded.

"You think that's right?"

Penelope raised her glass to her lips.

It felt like a few interrogations he'd run. Coy silences, self-conscious smirks. In those situations, he'd felt the urge to slap the person in question, but now he simply felt confused. What, really, were they trying to get out of her? The key to a failed marriage?

Later, when the women had cracked their second bottle (Milo stuck to tonic water), Penelope turned the questions around. "You should tell me, Milo. What happened in March?"

"You know. The department was shut down. Alan blames himself."

"Should he?"

Milo seldom thought in terms of blame, or tried not to, and now he had to take a moment to go through the sequence of events that had led to that computer screen and its flickering dots. If the blame had to be put on any one person, he would hand it to Senator Nathan Irwin, but there was no reason to tell Penelope about that. He shook his head. "No. The failures were in place before he took the job, and by the time he arrived, there was nothing he could do. But Langley blamed him, which is why he's having such trouble finding a job."

"No," Penelope said. "That's his fault. He hasn't even tried. He's spent all his time in his office, or the bathroom, plotting the end of the world. So you tell me. What happened that screwed him up like this? He's not the same man he was before he took that damned job."

Milo wasn't sure how much Penelope knew, nor how

much she should know. He'd shared more than was appropriate, or even legal, with Tina, but Penelope . . . The fact was that she had gotten rid of her Company man, and who knew what she might decide to say in the midst of an acrimonious divorce? He knew far too little about Penelope Drummond.

So he kept to the minimum of facts. "The department wasn't made redundant, and it wasn't closed down. It was liquidated. In the space of two days, nearly all of Alan's field agents were killed. The way Alan puts it, the department had been running well for sixty years. He took over, and it was wiped out in sixty days."

As he spoke, he watched her face for signs, and by the time he finished he was sure that she'd known none of this.

"How many?" she asked.

He hesitated, but saw no reason for evasion now. "Thirty-three."

Her face went slack. "Thirty-*three*?"

"Yes."

"Oh. Well."

Tina sat in silence, picking at her fingernails. She knew the story. She also knew that their deaths had been orchestrated by a Chinese intelligence officer, though he'd never told her his name.

Penelope finished her wine, then unconsciously wiped at her lip, reminding him of her husband. "That's why he's obsessed."

"Yes."

"And . . ." She frowned at the coffee table, then focused on Milo's eyes. "And are you helping him?"

Tina was watching him again, expectant.

"I'm trying to get him to let it go."

"Thirty-three people? Is that something anyone can let go of? Could you?"

He shook his head. "There's nothing to do. There's nothing Alan can do about it. There's nothing I can do about it."

"Someone should be arrested," Penelope said.

"It doesn't work that way."

"Tell her," said Tina.

Milo blinked at her. "What?"

Tina sighed, then grabbed the open wine bottle between them and began topping off their glasses. "Tell her what you told me. About China."

"I'm not sure—"

"Please," Penelope cut in. "Tell me about China."

Tina knew what she was doing, but she didn't care. Things like national secrets and government bureaucracies, for her, paled in comparison to a woman sitting on her couch being ruined by her husband's deterioration. He wondered what Alan Drummond would do in his position, then knew: Alan would become rude and sullen, climb to his feet, and leave. If Milo did that, Tina would simply turn to Penelope and tell her everything she knew. He could at least make sure she didn't mix up the facts.

He stood up. "Come on, Pen. Let's go to the roof."

"Roof?"

"I had to do the same thing," said Tina.

Penelope wasn't ready to go anywhere yet. "Why?"

"Bugs," said Tina. "My husband is paranoid."

3

"Where do you see yourself in ten years?"

Milo scratched his freshly shaven cheek, took a long, unsettling look at Redman Transcontinental Human Resources Administrator William J. Morales—*just call me Billy, all my friends do*—and settled an ankle on his knee. An afternoon headache had struck, like a bad reminder of the previous night's wine with Penelope, even though he hadn't drunk anything. "How do you mean?"

"You know," said Morales, waving a hand around to signify a word he couldn't find. "Where are you at? Family life, work life. Financial security?"

"How should I know?"

Morales blinked at him. "It's an imaginative exercise, Milo. No one's going to come back to test you in a decade. You just say where you'd reasonably like to be."

It wasn't Morales's fault—these sorts of questions

were preordained. He'd heard them so many times over the last month at so many private security consultancies, and had even answered them with his vanilla line—*Well, I see myself in a more secure position, in a job I love, but with time on the weekends to spend with my family*—but so far that hadn't made a dent in his employment prospects. So he would try a new tact: honesty.

"You never know. Someone might show up in ten years. Ask how your life measures up to your plans. These tests come up all the time. You fail, you get pistol-whipped and two bullets in the back of the head."

William J. Morales let a twitchy smile slip into his face, then pushed it away. He moved some papers on his desk; he glanced at his open laptop. "Look, if you don't have an answer, that's fine."

"I've got lots of answers, Billy. I just tend not to dwell on them, because I know how easily they can disappear. These days, I worry about the next step. It's hard enough keeping that straight, much less thinking ten steps, or ten years, ahead."

Minutes later, as he left the building, popping a Nicorette and taking the corner under the Manhattan Bridge, Brooklyn side, he noticed a small man in a denim shirt on the opposite sidewalk. The man glanced at him and put away his phone. Milo tugged his tie loose, considering his numerous failures in that interview, and tried to ignore both the man and the swelling of gas in his injured gut; he needed to find a toilet.

Milo expected him to cross the street to meet him, but the man in denim just walked parallel, pretending to have no interest, and perhaps he didn't—perhaps, Milo thought, it was just his famous paranoia. That was when another man—thin, dark-skinned, wearing a full suit that had to be uncomfortable in the heat—fell into step beside him and said, "Milo Weaver?"

Milo didn't slow down, just waited until the newcomer had repeated himself before saying, "Yeah?"

"Can I have a word?"

"I've got an appointment."

"It'll just take a minute."

"I'm already late."

The man did an extra skip to keep up. "This is important, Mr. Weaver."

"So's my appointment."

"It's about your friend, Alan Drummond."

Milo slowed, taking a better look at his shadow. Young, thirty or more. Mixed South Asian ancestry, maybe Indian. Sideburns. Fashionable-geek glasses. "What about him?"

"We should probably talk in private."

Milo stopped. In the distance he could see the York Street subway stop that would lead to home. "I don't have time to go to your office. Talk to me here. Start with who you are."

"Oh, of course," the man said, patting his pockets with a bony hand until he found a leather badge wallet. He opened it like a book. On one side, an eagle-topped badge told Milo that this man was a "special agent"; on the other, a laminated Homeland Security photo-ID gave the holder's name as Dennis Chaudhury, Immigration and Customs Enforcement. "Will that do?" Chaudhury asked as he folded it again.

"You can buy those things online."

Chaudhury looked briefly confused, then smiled. "Christ, you people don't trust anyone, do you?"

"What people?"

"Company people."

As they spoke, the man in the denim shirt crossed to their sidewalk and lounged in front of a pharmacy. Milo pointed down the street. "You have between here and that subway station."

"But Mr.—"

"I'll walk slowly."

With the first few steps, Dennis Chaudhury was left behind, but he jogged to catch up and said, "Your friend is gone."

Milo stopped again, feeling the sun beating down on him. "Gone?"

"Disappeared. In London. From the Rathbone Hotel."

"That's called missing, not disappeared. How long has he been missing?"

"Since Saturday."

Milo's stomach grumbled, and he wondered if this guy could hear it. He said, "Alan leaves your sight—well, not *your* sight. MI-5's sight?"

Chaudhury shrugged.

"He escapes his minders for three lousy days, and you call him *gone*?" Milo started walking again. "You're really hard up for work, aren't you?"

Chaudhury's voice followed him. "We think he's been kidnapped."

"What makes you think that?" Milo asked without looking back.

"I don't know. Maybe that someone turned off the hotel's surveillance cameras. By the time they were on again, he was gone."

Again, Milo slowed to a stop and turned back. Chaudhury was some distance behind him, hands on his hips, oblivious to the people passing him on the sidewalk. He said, "We're waiting for more from Five, but it's hard getting anything out of them."

"Why?"

"Because they're assholes, Mr. Weaver."

It was an unexpected answer, and Milo caught himself smiling.

"Truth is," said Chaudhury, "it was Scotland Yard that initially figured out something was weird. Disappearance was one thing, but he was using a fake name that they had already tied to a crime. Kind of ridiculous, using a blown name, kind of crazy."

"What was the name?"

"Sebastian Hall."

Milo bit his tongue to control his lips. He felt the urge to scream, but said, "Who do you think has him?"

"We don't know," Chaudhury said as he walked up to Milo, "but you might—you're a friend of his."

"What makes you think that?"

He was close enough to whisper. "Dinner parties."

Milo bit deeper into his tongue, then said, "You've been watching me?"

"Him, not you." A pause. "Should we be watching you?"

"What about Penelope?"

"The wife?" he asked, shaking his head. "You're the first one we've approached about this. I was hoping you'd have a simple explanation for us."

Milo looked past him to the one in denim, who'd moved to a newspaper dispenser. "Listen. I do have an appointment I have to keep. Can we talk this evening?"

"As you like, Mr. Weaver."

Once he was underground, squeezed in among warm bodies and holding on to a metal loop, feeling the grumble of his bowels, he let his sore tongue go and cursed sharply. That Alan had gotten himself kidnapped was one thing—it was bad but, given his state of mind, almost inevitable. That he'd done this using the name Sebastian Hall was something else entirely. He had used Milo's old work name, in order to force Milo's involvement.

Here, then, was the evidence. Alan had truly gone mad, and it had begun with specks on a computer screen, tracking individual murders across the globe. Red dots turning blue. Thirty-three Tourists going from hot to cold.

While helping Alan piece together evidence for the final report, he had learned that most had gone surprisingly quickly, perhaps even painlessly, their executions from unexpected gunshots to the face, surprise knives and wires slicing through windpipes and carotid arteries, and, in a few cases, hit-and-run automobile accidents. Only one went out in flames when the car she was driving down an Afghan road was struck by an Alcotán C-100 antitank missile.

Some—perhaps six or seven—didn't enjoy a quick exit. They were shot in the stomach and left bleeding in foreign streets for hours or poisoned badly and left suffocating in their hotel rooms. A woman in Mexico City and a man in Vancouver were discovered by generous strangers and carted to hospitals, but within twelve hours, they received visitors who ended their fights.

Of the four who survived, Leticia Jones and Zachary Klein had been on an under-the-radar job with Milo, out of the range of Xin Zhu's elaborate scheme to make Tourism wipe itself out. In Buenos Aires, José Santiago lived because his phone had been ruined by falling into a sink full of his shaving water, and when his assassin arrived, he was quick enough to kill him. In Hanoi, Tran Hoang was lounging in an opium den in Long Bien. He was the off-the-roster Tourist Alan had mentioned—meaning that Xin Zhu hadn't even known of his existence.

By then, Milo had resigned from the department and could return home, but Alan had had to travel to Langley. Though Director Quentin Ascot claimed to be too busy to attend the meeting, his assistant, George Erasmus Butler, the director's iron gut, arrived carrying a folder thick with failure. It wasn't just Alan he'd come to skewer but the entire Department of Tourism.

The fall had made Alan simple, obsessed with revenge. Now, it had gotten him abducted, possibly killed. And it was drawing Milo into something he wanted no part of.

At the Seventh Avenue stop, he took the stairs to the surface and tried Alan's number. His phone, a voice explained, was no longer in service. As he walked, he called his one contact in Homeland Security and left a message. He continued through the heat to where he waited under a birch tree not far from the loitering nannies chatting among themselves and giving him significant looks outside the Berkeley-Carroll School. A father was a rare enough sight at that hour. One nanny, a recently arrived Swiss girl who'd spent other days flirting with him, wandered over. She was in her mid-twenties and painfully blond with wide lips; she enjoyed talking to him in German. "Hallo, Milo."

"Hallo, Gabi."

"Letzter Tag, huh?" she said, and it took him a moment to remember that this was, in fact, the last day of school Alan Drummond was already interfering with his life. Gabi squinted at his face, then began to laugh. "Hast du es *vergessen*?"

"Of course I remembered," he muttered in German.

She said, "The only problem is that now I have to be with the brats all day long. I don't know how I'm going to survive."

"Day camp," he told her, now remembering more about Stephanie's life. "It's not far from here, and it's nearly the same hours. Tell their parents that all the brats' friends will be there."

She brightened visibly at the suggestion as Milo's phone began to ring.

"Entschuldigung," he said, and she watched him check the number and take the call.

"Did you call me from jail, Milo?" said Janet Simmons.

"From the unemployment line."

Self-consciously, Gabi turned back to look at the school, but she didn't walk away.

"Thank God for little mercies," said Simmons. "Is it true that someone put a bullet in you?"

"Is that the rumor?"

"It was on the wire a couple months ago."

"I'm nearly back to normal."

"And *normal* for Milo Weaver would be what, exactly?"

"Why don't you tell me about your life?" he asked. "I'll lay odds it's more interesting."

It wasn't. In part because of her failed pursuit of Milo a year ago, Simmons had been reassigned to border duty in Seattle. Though the demotion had been rough at first, she'd grown fond of the city.

"You sound happy," he said.

"Being engaged will do that to you."

"Well. Congratulations."

"We'll pretend that's why you called me out of the blue," she said, then added, "Why don't you tell me why you called me out of the blue?"

"I've got an ICE agent asking me questions. Can you check his name and verify he is what he says he is?"

"What does he say he is?"

"A special agent, just like you."

"Nobody's just like me, Milo. You should know that. What's the name?"

She promised to get back to him by the next day,

then asked about Tina and Stephanie. As he was trying to answer, children spilled out onto the sidewalk, weighed down by fat backpacks. Gabi waved long fingers at him and gave a wink as she went to meet the two boys she called her brats. In his ear, Simmons told him not to break Tina's heart, or else she'd be on the next plane to New York with her SIG SAUER. He promised to try his best. Stephanie waved for his attention.

At home, he and Stephanie ordered pizza, briefly assessed the academic year (*okay* was her opinion), and while she talked online with Unity Khama, a friend from Botswana she had met through a class project (even though it was after 10:00 P.M. in Gaborone), Milo used his own computer to search for *Sebastian Hall*. The first hit was dated yesterday, Monday, June 16.

An anonymous employee of the Rathbone Hotel had told a *Guardian* journalist that an American had vanished from his room on Saturday. Nothing particularly strange there, but Scotland Yard had been called in, which was odd. Further questions to hotel management had confirmed the disappearance, but, according to the police, the name was being withheld until the American's family had been contacted. By Monday, though, a Scotland Yard leak had let the name slip: Sebastian Hall.

Armed with that name, the *Guardian* journalist had found gold: an Interpol arrest warrant for one Sebastian Hall, dated 25 February, charged with involvement in the notorious E. G. Bührle art gallery heist in Zürich.

As was well known to *Guardian* readers, the mystery of the heist had been solved at the beginning of

April when, in Munich, Theodor Wartmüller, a ranking member of the German Federal Intelligence Service, the BND, had been caught with the missing paintings in his apartment.

So what, the journalist asked, was Sebastian Hall—assumedly a coconspirator with Wartmüller—doing in London? What had happened to him? Also why, the journalist continued, was New Scotland Yard remaining so quiet on the issue?

Beside the article was a police sketch, from the Interpol Web site, of Sebastian Hall. A face that, when set beside Milo's, was a nearly perfect match. Without his face to go by, it could have been anyone.

Milo said, "That fucker," and closed his eyes.

"What fucker?" asked Stephanie. She was standing in the kitchen doorway, clutching a can of Sprite with a straw in it.

"Oh, no one, hon, and don't ever say that word again."

Stephanie sipped on the straw, staring at him.

"Something wrong?"

She shrugged, eyes big.

He closed his laptop and came over, squatting to her height. He stroked some hair off her face. "What is it?"

"Nothing, I . . ."

"Are you worried about me again? Because I'm fine."

"What's going on with Pen?"

He thought a moment. "Nothing important, she's all right, too."

"But she's getting a divorce, right?"

"Who said anything about divorce?"

"I heard her talking last night."

"I thought you were asleep."

She pursed her lips on the straw so that they turned white. "I couldn't help it," she said finally. "She's loud."

"Come here," he said and pulled her closer. "They're having problems, yes, but that doesn't mean they're getting a divorce. People just fight sometimes. Like you and Sarah Lawton. Look at you now! Best friends."

She grinned up at him, then lowered her voice to a whisper. "I don't know, Daddy. Sarah's starting to get on my nerves again. Maybe I'll divorce her."

4

A little after eight, he found Dennis Chaudhury at a window table of the Twelfth Street Bar & Grill, a placement that struck him as sloppy. "Where's your friend?" Milo asked as he sat down.

On Chaudhury's plate lay the remnants of a burger and fries, and he tapped the corners of his mouth with a napkin as he spoke. "Prior engagements. You want something to drink?"

Milo gazed out the window at the busy evening street; there was no way to know if some other shadow had been brought in, and there was no point asking. He felt a strong desire for a vodka martini, wondering just how much damage it would really do to his insides. "Tonic water."

"Straight?"

Milo shrugged.

They didn't start their conversation until the waiter had collected Chaudhury's plate and delivered tonic water and a Beck's. Until then, Chaudhury asked about the neighborhood; he had never been to Park Slope before and was surprised by how genteel the place was. "Expensive, though, right?"

"Like you wouldn't believe."

"Life in the brownstone jungle."

Milo smiled.

"But you make ends meet."

"My wife does well."

"Lucky man."

Though there was no real justification for it, Milo didn't like Chaudhury. Perhaps it was just that he'd been the bearer of bad news, the same bad news he'd had to deliver to Tina right after their dinner, the same bad news he knew he would have to deliver to Penelope before this man got to her. Or perhaps it was only that, knowing the extent of Alan's madness, he felt in everything around him the weight of omens. He felt as if the settled life he'd finally achieved was going to be ripped from him.

Once they were sipping their drinks, Chaudhury leaned forward. "We're assuming his trip to London was connected to everything he's been doing over the last month or so. Correct?"

"I don't know. What's he been doing over the last month?"

Chaudhury settled back again and regarded Milo. "You're not really going to play that card, are you?"

"Alan didn't share."

"You were his only regular friend in town."

"He knew better than to open his heart to friends."

Again, Chaudhury examined him from a distance. "We're talking about an unbalanced man trying to take revenge on the Chinese. Can you at least tell me about his feelings?"

Milo let those words sink in before saying, "How's any of this Homeland's business, Dennis? He disappeared in the U.K., and now you're bringing up the Chinese. You walk and talk like a Company man."

Chaudhury shook his head at Milo's evident stupidity. "Do you really believe everything you read in congressional documents? Sure, this isn't our main line of business, but in this case we're helping out our friends."

"Friends?"

"Your former employers."

"Since when did Homeland and CIA become friends?"

Chaudhury raised his palms. "Since forever." He joined his hands. "In this case, the Company thinks it's not a terrific idea to appear to be investigating the disappearance of a man they buried so deep that it drove him nuts."

It was a fair enough point, and well within the realm of possibility. Whether or not he liked Chaudhury, in the end they were both interested in finding out the same thing, so Milo relented. "Some people thrive outside the Company. Others fall apart. I think Alan's been falling apart. To keep from blaming himself, he— and not without reason—blames the Chinese."

"He blames Xin Zhu."

That was a surprise. "Homeland knows about Xin Zhu?"

"Yes, we know about Xin Zhu. We know about Tourism. We know how the one killed the other."

"I'm impressed."

"Just your tax dollars at work—a lot of them."

Milo smiled.

"How well do you know Gwendolyn Davis?" Chaudhury asked.

"I don't. Who is she?"

Chaudhury reached inside his blazer, pulling out a stack of five or so photographs. Quickly, he shuffled through them and turned a passport shot around for Milo to see. A sensual-looking black woman gazed back at him.

"Gwendolyn? Really?"

"So you do know her," Chaudhury said, putting the photos away. "Gwendolyn Davis is the name she used in London. Last month in China, she used a Sudanese passport with the name Rosa Mumu. She also goes by Leticia Jones."

"Jones was her work name. Before."

"Tourism?"

Milo shrugged a noncommittal answer. He still wasn't comfortable speaking such things aloud.

"Well, we know Alan met with her in D.C. Then we find out she's in the Rathbone Hotel at the same time he is. By the time the hotel staff realized Alan wasn't around to pay his bill, though, she was out of the country."

"You're not blaming her for this, are you?"

"Like I say, Weaver, we don't know anything."

"What was she doing in China?"

Chaudhury exhaled, considering the limits of what he could share. "We don't know much, but she was meeting with people. Talked with a consular official, talked with a known terrorist connected to the East Turkestan Islamic movement."

"Really?"

"I'm not lying, if that's what you mean."

There was nothing hopeful in any of these details. Was Alan now using Leticia to support Uighur revolutionaries who wanted to kick China out of East Turkestan and establish an Islamic state? Last year, these people had shot up cars full of Chinese in Pakistan and sent the videotape to Beijing. In Dubai, one of their cells was caught planning to attack an entire mall that sold Chinese products. There were perpetual rumblings that they might commit atrocities during the Beijing Olympics—which, of course, had the Chinese terrified.

All this just to hit back at Xin Zhu? It was beyond stupid, beyond crazy.

Chaudhury said, "If you know how to get in touch with Jones—"

"I don't," Milo lied.

"Well, I'd love to have a chat with her sometime."

"I would, too." Milo felt a wave of despair at the dismal knowledge that was growing inside of him. The knowledge of what this was leading to, and what he would have to do as soon as he left this restaurant. Then he said, "Look, Dennis, I don't know what Alan's plan was, or why he was in London with Leticia. That he was doing *something* is not a surprise. But this is . . . well, it's a bit much."

"Maybe you'd like to help us figure it out."

"You don't need my help."

"Don't overestimate us, and don't underestimate yourself. You knew the department better than most people. If he was using old resources, you'd be familiar with them. You might even be able to track them down. Someone like Gwendolyn—Leticia, I mean. I don't think she'd open the door if I came asking questions. If you did, then maybe."

Milo sipped at his tonic. He had the uncomfortable feeling that this man was reading his mind. "How many people do you have working on this?"

"Not many. I'm liaising with someone from Five, and we've each got a small staff. At this point, we've just got questions, and no one's going to sign off on a full-blown op just to figure out why someone walked on his hotel bill. So I really could use your help."

Milo thought about that, wondering how modest Chaudhury was being. Or maybe it was the reverse, and Chaudhury was stumbling around on his own, exaggerating his resources. "I can make some calls, but that's it."

"It's a start."

"And an end. I'm too busy here."

"Trying to find a job," Chaudhury said, smiling, "to afford this wonderful lifestyle."

Milo was sure not to mirror that smile. "No, Dennis. I'm too busy keeping my family out of Alan's mess, and you're just making it harder."

Despite the truth of this, once he left Chaudhury with the bill and was walking down Seventh, he did call the Manhattan-area number Leticia Jones had given him a week after the massacre. She'd slipped it into his pocket and whispered, "Baby, for a good time just call." He wasn't sure it was still in use until, after five rings, there was a click and a computerized female voice said, "Please leave your message at the sound of the tone." Even then, he still wasn't sure.

Milo said, "Hi, this is Milo Weaver calling for Alan Drummond. I'm not sure if I've got the right number, but if I do please ask him to call me." Then he hung up and checked the time on his phone. It was 10:07.

The message itself was irrelevant to the contact procedure; only the time and the phone he called from mattered.

He had an hour to kill, so he walked over to Flatbush, down toward Grand Army Plaza, and took an outdoor table at the Burrito Bar & Kitchen. He felt out of place among the mixed crowd of young professionals trying to decide if they really wanted to get drunk on a Tuesday night, and sipped at the Coke the pretty-but-cool waitress brought him. It burned his throat.

Though he knew what he was doing, he found it agonizingly difficult to predict much further than this moment, for he was acting on obligation, not desire. Yes, he was calling on Leticia, and, yes, he would sit down with Penelope to break the news—such as it was—to her. Anything else was speculation. He did not want to help Alan and Leticia with their plans, because Alan was ruled by his pride now, which—if he was still alive—made him unpredictable and dangerous. That he boldly used Milo's own work name in London, a name with a criminal investigation attached to it, proved that he had believed he could coerce Milo into his elaborate web.

How far would he help Chaudhury? That was something he didn't know. He might not like the man, but if Homeland and CIA were simply trying to find out what Alan was up to, it was a legitimate aim. What he wanted was a reason not to help, and the only justification for washing his hands of it would be if Alan's operation had crashed and was now finished. There was only one person who could tell him if it was over, and she was just one more step away.

It was as he was finishing his Coke that he noticed, across the street, Chaudhury's denim friend outside a Duane Reade, keeping watch over him. It didn't matter.

He paid, then continued up the busy street toward Grand Army. He didn't look back, just waited at the curb for the light to change, then walked down the west side of the oval and crossed beneath it to reach a grassy triangular island between the Soldiers' and Sailors' Arch and the Brooklyn Public Library. Again, he checked his phone—11:04—and pressed it to his ear, faking a conversation. Around him, cars continued their loud, congested parade as he waited the required three minutes, trying to think of nothing.

He gave it an extra minute, and at 11:08 returned to the sidewalk. Somewhere above his head, he knew, was the public webcam he'd been unable to spot, and if Leticia checked her phone messages as frequently as she had told him, she would be on a computer or smart phone somewhere in the world watching him leave its frame. It was all she needed to know—he wanted to talk.

At home, Tina was on the couch reading an enormous novel; he saw she hadn't gotten far. "So?" she asked.

He settled next to her and placed a hand on her thigh. "They don't know anything."

"Of course they know something."

He leaned close and kissed her. "You're wise beyond your years."

"So?"

"I told them I'd make some calls, see what I could find, but that's it. I'm not doing their job for them."

She didn't reply, only stared at him, the paperback shut around her index finger.

"What?" he asked.

"Do you think he's dead?"

"No idea."

"But you have a feeling?"

"I seriously doubt it."

She finally put the novel on the coffee table, and he saw that it was *Infinite Jest*, by David Foster Wallace. "I wonder how we're going to break it to Penelope."

"There's no news to break. Not yet."

"Well, we're not leaving her in the dark."

"Why not?" he asked, because on the walk home he'd wondered this. Why talk to Penelope when, for all they knew, Alan could show up at her door tomorrow, clutching flowers?

"Because I've been there before," Tina said, "and I'm not going to let it happen to her."

She was serious, and it was a detail he should have predicted. Only last year, she had learned a lot of things he'd kept her in the dark about, and the realization of his dishonesty had nearly killed the marriage. Of course she'd insist on keeping Penelope informed. "Okay, I'll take care of it."

She shook her head. "No. She doesn't trust you."

"She doesn't?"

"Don't take it personally. She just trusts me more."

"Then you tell her."

"*Christ*," she said to no one in particular.

Milo looked in on Stephanie, who was snoring with her PlayStation aglow beside her pillow, then he showered and joined his wife in bed. She'd turned off the lights, and once he was under the covers she wrapped a bare leg around him. "Maybe you should," she said finally.

"Tell Penelope?"

"Help them figure this out. Alan was a friend."

"*Is* a friend. And he's off his rocker." He turned to look at her, but her face was hard to make out in the darkness. "The man's trying to take on the Guoanbu— China's entire foreign intelligence service. Does that sound balanced to you? I don't know what he did in London, but it's possible he provoked the wrong people and got himself killed. You really want me to follow his trail?"

"When you put it that way," she said, but he knew her too well to believe that he'd convinced her of anything.

5

The next morning, Tina called Penelope and insisted she come for dinner, then asked Sarah Lawton's mother if Stephanie could stay the night. The previous year, Stephanie and Sarah had been archenemies, but as with many children's relationships it only existed in the extremes, and when things warmed between them they became—despite occasional mentions of divorce—best-friends-forever.

Milo's only responsibility was to take care of the food, which he mistakenly chose to cook himself. Chicken fajitas with fresh salsa, guacamole, and sour cream. When Tina returned home from work, she snuck a bite of the meat and made a face. "Did you taste these?"

"I don't remember."

"You forgot the salt."

It was true, and his impressive-looking meal had little flavor. He powdered everything with salt after the fact, but it wasn't the same, and he could see the measured surprise in Penelope Drummond's face when she took her first eager bite. She and her husband were well-known foodies, spending large chunks of their income on new restaurants and following specific chefs' careers. Still, Penelope ate, as they all did, until she frowned at them both and said, "Is something going on?"

"What?" Tina said.

"There's something weird here." A pause. "You're not planning a ménage à trois, are you? Because I may be single, but I'm still a decent girl at heart."

They laughed at that, a little too loudly, and Milo wondered how Tina was going to do this. She had insisted on breaking the news herself, but how does anyone pass on the news that a husband has gone missing? Probably not in the middle of a meal. Before dessert? he wondered, then realized with frustration that he'd forgotten to pick up ice cream.

"No, really," said Penelope, holding a guacamole-smeared fork above her plate. "Something's going on."

That's when Tina's eyes, despite the innocent smile on her face, glazed with tears, and Milo knew that whatever she'd planned was history now. Penelope put down her fork and stroked Tina's wrist. "If it means that much to you, then, sure, I'll sleep with you."

Tina laughed again, pitifully, and shook her head. Milo said, "It's nothing like that."

Not letting go of Tina, Penelope raised her eyes to him. "Well, then, Milo. Maybe you should tell me."

She'd said it very coolly, and Milo answered, "In a sec." He mopped his lips with his napkin and went to the kitchen for another bottle of wine.

As he worked on the cork, he heard whispers from the living room, then a loud, "*What?*" That was Penelope. By the time he returned, Tina had dried her tears and was holding on to Penelope's wrist, though she wasn't crying either; she was staring at her flavorless food. Then she glared at Milo. "Tell me."

"I don't know much," Milo said, clutching the bottle and staying well away from the table. "London, the Rathbone Hotel. If he'd just disappeared, that would be one thing, but someone shut off the hotel cameras. Anything's possible."

"Anything?"

"Kidnapping is the theory."

"Or murder?"

He hesitated.

"Well?"

"It's possible, but there's no sign of that."

She held onto his eyes. "Who?"

"No one knows yet. People are working on it."

"You?"

"I'm looking into it."

She stood then, and Tina, still leaning forward, watched her. Penelope seemed to want to say something as her cheeks flushed, but nothing came out. She walked to the foyer, hesitated, then continued and, after collecting her purse and figuring out the complicated locks on the door, walked out of their apartment.

She returned an hour later. By then, Milo had packed the dishes into the dishwasher and the leftovers into the refrigerator, while Tina remained at the table drinking half the bottle of wine. She kept saying, "I did it all wrong," and each time Milo said, "There's no right way to do it."

Penelope buzzed from the street, saying only, "It's me," and when she arrived with her blond hair cowlicked on one side, it was obvious that she'd been drinking. "Can I come in?" she asked but was already walking past Tina into the living room. When she saw Milo, she said, "Hi," and dropped onto the couch. She took a long, loud breath. "I don't have any other friends I can talk to about this."

She didn't talk about it at first, though. She threw her purse onto the floor and stretched out, putting her feet up, her soiled heels resting on a pillow.

"I like this neighborhood," she told the ceiling lamp. "There's a terrific bar down the street. I forget the name. You know it?"

"It's great," Milo said as he went to one of the chairs.

Penelope remained fixated on the lamp. "I could sell our place and get something here. How much would a one-bedroom cost?"

"A lot."

"I should be able to get that much for ours."

"You know," Milo said, "he could be all right. Could be just fine."

"He might be," she agreed, "but he wouldn't come back to me, would he? I kicked him out."

"He told me he thought he could patch things up."

"You said that before."

In the silence that followed, Tina found fresh glasses and poured wine for everyone, forgetting that Milo wasn't drinking. Penelope placed hers on the floor beside her purse. "Milo," she said. "I forgot to ask why."

"Why?"

"Why did someone kidnap my husband from a London hotel room?"

"When we find out who, we'll know why. And vice versa."

"It's the Chinese, isn't it?"

"Maybe. No one knows."

She slowly sat up, looking groggy, muttering, "The Yellow Peril. Is that racist, Tina?"

Tina sat next to her without bothering to reply.

Penelope tried to fix Milo with her gaze, but she seemed to have trouble focusing. "You're going to London?"

Milo shook his head. "Better people are working on it."

"Alan said you were the best."

That didn't sound like Alan Drummond. "He was exaggerating."

Penelope chewed on her lower lip, then looked over at Tina as if she'd only just noticed her. She gave a small smile and turned back to Milo. "You do have some idea. I can see that. I can't see much, but I can see that."

"Maybe," he admitted, because what he could see was that he had a small window of opportunity. She'd gotten over her shock, and she was at least tipsy. "You can help, though."

"Me?"

"Tell me everything you know about what he was working on."

She looked again at Tina, perhaps wanting assistance, but Tina remained in her corner of the couch, waiting. Penelope said, "You don't want to go to the roof?"

"If the Company's listening, I won't have to repeat it to them later."

"And the Chinese? What if they're listening?"

When he didn't immediately answer, Tina said, "Ironically, Milo only worries about the CIA."

Penelope nodded at that. "Well, I already told Tina—right in this room, so I guess *you've already heard it*," she said to the walls, grinning conspiratorially. Then she sighed. "Alan wouldn't tell me anything—secret, you know. He was obsessed; I know that. He made a lot of phone calls and worked off of his desktop."

"Calls from the landline?"

She shook her head. "One of his cells."

"Can I take a look at his computer?"

"I'll give you the keys and you can go get it now. The password is 'intrepid.' With ones in place of the *i*'s."

"You didn't overhear any of the calls?"

"Just one. But he was speaking German. I don't know German. He knew that."

Milo waited.

"He went to D.C. on day trips."

"Often?"

"Once that I know of, but he hid that from me, so if I discovered one used train ticket there were probably more. Back in the middle of April, he was gone for three or four days. Wouldn't say where."

"You didn't hear any more of his calls?"

"He was very good at closing his office door," she said. "But there was a visitor."

"When?"

"Beginning of the month?" she wondered, shaking her head, then nodded. "A Wednesday. I'd gone out for groceries, but our local place was closed—inventory, or renovations; I don't remember which. I came back, and he was having Scotch with a Latino-looking guy. Alan was flustered, I could tell, but he introduced us. Hector Garza."

"Did he have an accent?"

Penelope shook her head. "Sounded midwestern to me. When he left, Alan said he was giving Hector a work reference."

"So Hector used to work in the department?"

"Computer technician. That's what Alan said."

"Young? Old?"

"Early thirties, maybe. Not tall—my height."

Milo rubbed at his face as if taking all this in, but he was running through his memories. He knew of no Hector Garza from the old office, even though, in the aftermath of the department's demise, he'd gone over the list of administrative employees with Alan to help figure out transfers. One of the four surviving Tourists, José Santiago, might fit that description. "Anyone else?"

"He didn't have a lot of friends. Not anymore. Just you."

Thirty seconds passed, then Tina said, "Did you get ice cream?"

"What?" said Milo.

"Dessert."

"I forgot."

Penelope said, "Wait a minute."

"What?" said Tina.

Penelope shook her head, and a lopsided grin appeared on her face. "He told me. He *told* me."

"Told you what?" asked Milo.

She settled her clasped hands over her stomach and said, "I'd forgotten. I mean, it was something like two months ago—just after you were shot," she said to Milo. "When he was fired. He asked me—*Christ*, how come I forgot this?"

"Just tell us," said Milo.

"Well, he told me that he knew about something that was a danger to the country, and he said that he thought he knew how he could neutralize it."

"Why did he tell you that?"

A sad smile crossed her face. "He was asking permission. He asked if me if he should work on it or not."

"What did you say?" Tina asked.

The smile disappeared. "I told him I was all for it."

"And you never connected that to how he'd been acting?" asked Milo.

"He never mentioned it again," she said, staring into his eyes defensively. "Two months ago he brought it up, late in the night— he'd woken from a bad dream—and then never again." She shook her head. "We were on vacation. I forgot about it."

No one spoke for a few moments, until Penelope said, "Don't you think you owe it to him?"

Both looked at her, but she was speaking to Milo.

"You really were his only friend."

He rubbed at his nose. "I'm doing what I can."

"But you're still here."

Milo slowly got to his feet. "Give me your keys, then."

As she dug through her purse, Milo's phone let out the *chirp-chirp* of an incoming message. He dug it out of his pants. It was from Janet Simmons, and once he'd read it he cursed beneath his breath, then read it again.

NO SIGN OF YOUR FRIEND IN OUR RECORDS.
LET ME KNOW IF YOU NEED THE CAVALRY.

"Something wrong?" asked Tina.

He deleted the message and gave her a smile. "I just wish life was simpler."

Penelope, her index finger through a ring laden with keys, let out a contemptuous snort. "Maybe you should have chosen a different career path."

His stomach was acting up again as he walked to the subway, but it wasn't the old bullet wound; it was anxiety, the fear that the Chinese, who had until now been on the other side of the world, were now *here*, in his backyard, for who else could Dennis Chaudhury be working for? He hated himself for his stupidity, for having spoken openly with a complete stranger. A stranger he'd met with, just down the street from his *home*. This was what happened when you began to enjoy life outside the Company. You forgot that no one is above deception. You became as naïve as all the other civilians. Now, Alan had drawn the Chinese right into the middle of his life.

Rumbling underground in a half-full car, though, he realized that he couldn't even hold onto this conclusion. A Company agent might pose as a Homelander, or perhaps the NSA was following up on signals intelligence it didn't feel like sharing with the Company. Even the FBI could be running Chaudhury, wanting to cover its tracks by posing as Homeland Security.

What about Britain? Alan had disappeared in London, and MI-5 would be interested in knowing why an ex-CIA man had disappeared on its turf. If the Company was staying quiet, then Five might send someone over, or ask Six to do so.

Once he'd opened himself up to that possibility, he considered the Germans, who had once been hunting Sebastian Hall. The overbearing Erika Schwartz of the BND had learned that Hall was in fact Weaver months ago and would certainly be interested in his reappearance in London. Drummond, he remembered, had been speaking German on the phone . . .

Without knowing what, exactly, Alan had been working on, he had no idea what other countries could be added to the list. Trying to figure out whom Chaudhury worked for was an exercise in confusion.

Because of the weekly dinners, the doorman at 200 East Eighty-ninth, the Monarch, recognized Milo's face. He tapped the brim of his hat and let Milo in, but said, "I'm sorry, sir, the Drummonds are out."

Milo held up the keys. "I know. I'm picking up something for Penelope."

"Can I help, sir?"

"Probably not, but thanks. I'll let you know if I need anything."

He took the elevator to the sixteenth floor, then paused in the carpeted corridor to work his way through the ten keys Penelope carried everywhere. He got it right on the third try and slipped inside.

It was a huge place, easily three times larger than his apartment, and fitted out in a vaguely retro style that Milo had always admired. He went to the open-plan kitchen and poured himself a glass of flat tonic water, then passed the Bauhaus sofa on his way to the office, a leathery affair with an old, lumbering Dell computer beneath the oak desk.

The first thing he noticed was that the computer was unplugged, and the Ethernet cable had been taken out. The simplest security—if it wasn't attached to the Internet, no one could hack it without first breaking into the apartment. Without electricity, Penelope wouldn't be as tempted to use it. So he plugged it in and, as it powered up, browsed the shelves that ran the length of one wall. History books—military, political, and cultural. American foreign policy. Napoleonic battle tactics. Soviet expansionism. The funding of Islamic terrorism. There were a few hundred titles here, organized fastidiously by author. On the bottom shelf, laid flat because of their size, were books on design.

It was a remarkably tidy office—the office, perhaps, of an unemployed man—and the opposite wall was decorated with framed pictures. Old family photos: grainy, some ripped and pieced back together, of Boston socialites going back to the 1920s. Mixed in were recent black-and-white close-ups of leaves, fruits, and tombstones—he remembered that Penelope had taken up photography. In the corner was an elegant drinks cabinet full of bottles. Throwing caution to the wind, Milo added vodka to his tonic.

When the computer asked for a password, he typed *Intrep1d*, and the hard drive began to click and whir. He opened the desk drawers but found only pens, a stainless steel letter opener, a few blank Post-it pads, and a ream of printer paper. The computer went quiet, and on the monitor, he saw a blue, empty desktop. He opened the C-drive and found only system folders and a few basic applications. Drummond had either cleaned the computer before leaving, or everything was right there, but hidden. He turned it off again, unplugged it, then dragged the computer case out from beneath the desk. It took about three minutes to figure out how to pop open its front, and he removed the hard drive. In the kitchen he found a Ziploc bag and sealed it inside, leaving it on the counter.

For the next two hours he went through the office again, slowly, pausing only to sip at his drink. He went through the books one at a time, fanning them to find loose slips of paper, which were always bookmarks or receipts used as bookmarks. He turned around each of the photographs on the wall. He pulled apart the desk, checking inside its shell with his hands and beneath the drawers. He went through the printer paper, then disassembled the laser printer. He used the letter opener to unscrew the back of the computer case and looked inside. He pulled up the throw rug, checked the floorboards, and broke open the seat of the chair, then went to the light fixture in the ceiling. He returned to the photographs and opened each frame. Nothing. Then he checked each of the three electrical outlets.

It was when he began unscrewing the outlet beneath the window that he found a hair-thin wire leading from behind the panel, up behind the curtains to the curtain rods, where it powered a camera. It was a small thing, like a webcam, but built to order with an antenna and a clip that attached to the end of the curtain rod. There was no manufacturer's name or serial number. From its position, the camera witnessed the entire room, but it wasn't so small that Alan wouldn't have noticed it. He had to have known of its existence. Milo unclipped the camera and peered into the wide-angled lens, then ripped out the power cord and pocketed it.

Though he'd tried to put each item back together after taking it apart, by midnight the office looked different. The chair sagged, its seat hanging open; the computer gaped at him where he couldn't put back the front panel. It was as if, by searching for a few hours, he'd aged the place prematurely, but he was too tired to keep at it. He grabbed his empty glass and returned to the living room, then stopped. In an armless chair Alan had once told him had been designed by Mies van der Rohe sat Dennis Chaudhury, his heavy eyelids very dark, but there was a smile on his face. "Hello, Milo."

"How long have you been here?"

Chaudhury rocked his head from side to side. "Half hour? More? I didn't want to interrupt your work. It's always a nice surprise to find out someone's doing your job for you."

"You're alone?"

"One friend in the lobby, another in the hall. I thought you and I could talk alone."

As Milo came around and settled on the couch, he noticed that the hard drive was gone from the kitchen counter. "This your first visit?"

"Penelope wouldn't leave the place. When we found out she'd gone to visit you, I was upstate. Took a while to get back. She there for the night?"

"Probably. She's had a rough time of it."

Chaudhury nodded as if this were sad news. "So what did you find?"

"You've got the hard drive. That was it."

"Anything interesting on it?"

"It's either wiped clean or encrypted. I don't really know my way around computers."

"Don't worry—we've got plenty of people who do. What does Penelope say?"

"Whatever he was doing, he kept it from her."

Another nod. "Took it hard, did she?"

"Did the Brits get back to you?"

Chaudhury considered his reply. "They say they'll have something for us later."

"Sounds like they're being uncooperative."

"A kinder word would be 'careful.' "

"Anything else?"

"Nothing important," Chaudhury said, then picked at the knee of his slacks. "You planning on going?"

"To London? No."

"Good. I've already sent someone, and I don't want you getting in the way."

"Isn't that overstepping your bounds? Sending field agents to London?"

Chaudhury's self-satisfied smile faded, then he rocked his head. "You really think the Department of Homeland Security has any boundaries, Weaver?"

"Maybe not, but the better question is whether or not *you* have boundaries."

"How's that?"

"You're not a Homelander. I'd just like to know what you really are."

Chaudhury blinked, only briefly thrown, then touched his hands together. He sighed. "I'm on the side of the angels. Isn't that enough?"

"That would make you the first one I've ever met."

Chaudhury rubbed at a nostril, placed his hands on the seat of the chair, and pushed himself up. When he spoke, his voice was lowered. "I'm Company, Weaver. That's all you need to know."

"Why the pretense?"

"Because my bosses thought you might not want to help us. They seem to think you have a beef with the Company. Maybe because we stuck you in a jail for a while. We brought you back, of course, but you chose to leave the nest again. Maybe you don't like us anymore."

"I don't hold grudges."

"They'll be so pleased to hear it."

"Section?"

Chaudhury stuck his hands in his pockets. "What?"

"What's your section?"

"Counterterrorism."

"Under Bill Ferragamo?"

Another pause. "No."

"Who?"

"I'm not playing twenty questions. You want to help me find out who abducted your friend, then great. If not, then fuck off. It's all the same to me."

"I'll fuck off, then," Milo said and walked out of the apartment. On his way to the elevator, he passed a thickset hood that looked less like CIA than like Balkan mafia.

At home, he found Tina dozing on the couch, her head in Penelope's lap. Penelope was watching a late-night talk show in which an actress with a new film out was showing off her platform shoes. Penelope gave Milo a tired smile as he settled on a chair. "I'm sober now," she said with something like pride.

"Good for you."

"Did you uncover all?"

He shook his head, realizing that Tina was wrong—Penelope did trust him. She'd learned her husband was missing and wasn't rushing off to the police; she was leaving everything to him. "Alan left the place clean," Milo told her. "He knew what he was doing."

"He always did."

"What kind of security did he have in his office?"

"Security?"

"Motion detectors, cameras, that sort of thing."

"Should he have had something?"

"I'm just asking."

She grinned. "Well, I hope he didn't have a camera. You know that great leather chair? We used to have sex on it all the time." The grin faded. "Before he turned into . . . well, before he started pushing me away."

Milo stared at her, wondering. "When was the last time?"

"That we had *sex?*"

"In his office."

She didn't look like she was going to answer, but finally arched a brow. "Nearly a month ago. I actually remember the date. May 23, a Friday. We finished just minutes before you guys showed up for that roast lamb. Any more intimate questions?"

Milo shook his head. There was no way that Alan would have missed that camera, which meant either that he knew who was watching him or that he had installed it himself. Either way, three and a half weeks ago, on the evening of May 23, the camera wasn't there; it had arrived after that date.

6

Tina took a vacation day on Thursday, and Penelope showered before joining them for coffee and leaving with Tina, who was off to pick up Stephanie. After they'd been gone a half hour, Milo's phone rang. It was his father, Yevgeny Primakov. "Misha! Do you know what Monday is?"

Milo had no idea.

"Public Service Day. Every June 23 the United Nations celebrates the value and virtue of public service to the community. It'll be a festive day."

"Are you kidding me?"

"Spare me your cynicism, my boy. The true joy of Public Service Day is that I'll get a rare chance to see your ravishing wife and breathtaking daughter. Perhaps even my infuriating son."

Milo resisted a smile, though it was difficult. "Okay, I'll let them know. We'll have dinner."

"Not your food. We'll go out. My treat."

"Of course it's your treat, Yevgeny."

"Listen, Misha, I have an appointment with a foreign minister. I just wanted to make sure you would be there."

"I try not to travel these days."

"Not even to London?"

His father seldom wasted a call for purely familial reasons. "You heard?"

"About the Sebastian Hall that wasn't you? Of course I did. And I made sure you were in good health in Brooklyn before forgetting about it."

"It wasn't me, but it was a friend. Can you find out anything?"

Yevgeny hummed a moment, considering this. "Which friend?"

"Alan Drummond."

"I see."

"It's important we find out the details."

"Who's we?"

"Me. His wife, Penelope. Tina."

Another hum. "No one else?"

"A few other people."

Silence, but Milo didn't feel up to explaining Dennis Chaudhury. Background voices on his father's side were speaking French. "Okay, Misha. I'll bring what I can on Monday."

"Thanks, Yevgeny."

Milo ran an online search for miniature cameras, hoping to stumble across the make of the one he'd gotten from Alan's office. While it looked similar to many, it matched none.

He heard Stephanie stomping up the stairs, and went to open the door for her. He was surprised to find his daughter's upper eyelids completely black. His first thought was that she'd been beaten. His knees went weak. She was smiling wildly. "What do you think, Daddy?"

"I think you look like someone's punching bag."

Her smile vanished. "Well . . . it's pretty," she said as she walked past him, ignoring his attempt at a kiss.

Behind her, Tina came slowly up the stairs. "Did you see?" she asked.

"Makeup?"

"Magic fucking Marker," Tina grumbled.

Milo grinned. "Sarah, too?"

Up on their floor now, Tina leaned against the banister and raised an eyebrow. "You'd think so, wouldn't you? Sarah thought Stephanie needed to bring out her eyes a little more."

"What did her mother say?"

"She said, *I think it looks cute.* And laughed. Stef's not staying there ever again."

While Tina made more coffee, he found Stephanie in her room, examining herself proudly in the mirror. When Milo hovered in her doorway for too long, she said, "You really think I look like a punching bag?"

"Now that I've had a moment, no. It's kind of interesting."

"In a good way?"

Milo stared at her, as if thinking this through. His daughter's disheveled hair, her pudgy nose, her big ears, her habit of double-blinking when she wanted a serious answer, her pursed, thin lips—all of this was absurdly beautiful to him. It was a face, like his wife's, that he would never be able to see objectively. "Good, sure, but maybe it was a bad idea to use a marker."

"It'll wash off."

"I don't think so."

She turned from the mirror to frown at him; she looked nothing like a six-year-old. "It's *water* based. That means it'll wash off."

"Good," he said. "Why don't you wash it off so that when we go out for lunch people won't think we're abusing you?"

She didn't laugh.

He wandered back to the kitchen and found Tina sulking in the corner with her cup. "So you didn't find anything at Alan's?"

"Not much. The computer was blank, but there was a camera."

"A camera?"

"It's been there less than a month."

He showed Tina the device, and as she turned it in her hand she said, "You're sure someone else didn't put this there?"

"It was out of the way, but it wasn't hidden. If someone else put it there, it wasn't a secret from him."

She handed it back. "So he put it there in case someone came to search his office?"

"Maybe, but that doesn't make much sense. Anyone searching his place would run across it as easily as I did."

"He should've used a nanny-cam. They put them in clocks now, so babysitters have no idea."

"Do they?"

"How can you not know about these things?" she asked.

"What about Penelope?"

Tina came out to the living room; he followed. "She's messed up. The last time they talked, she was kicking him out of the house. She needs to know what's going on."

"I'm working on it."

"Does that mean you're going to London?"

"I don't need to. Yevgeny will be in town on Monday, and he's bringing information."

"Little Miss will be happy. She likes him. I do, too."

"Don't bring all this up to him. I'll take care of it."

"Why can't I ask him?"

"Because he's not supposed to know what he knows, and you'll put him in a position of having to lie to you. There's no reason for that."

"I bet I could get him to talk."

"I bet you could, too, but don't."

They both looked up as Stephanie walked in, her face red and wet from washing, but the black coins of her eyelids hadn't lightened at all. "Sarah *lied* to me," she told them. "This isn't water based at all!"

It was over pizza at La Bruschetta that Milo noticed Chaudhury on the opposite side of Seventh Avenue, under the awning for Rite Aid, staring through the window at him.

"Sorry, ladies," Milo said, patting his lips with a napkin. "There's someone I need to talk to. Be right back."

As he rose, Stephanie craned her neck to peer out the window. "The dark guy?"

"Yeah."

"He's got eyes like mine."

It was overcast but still warm out on the street when Milo waited for the traffic to ebb and jogged across to join Chaudhury, who first said, "You haven't been beating up on that kid of yours, have you?"

"She said your eyes look like hers."

"Maybe it's because my dad *did* beat up on me."

Milo stared at him, wondering if it was a joke. There was no way to tell. "You find anything on the drive?"

"I'm not here about that. I need you to give me that camera you took."

"Is it yours?"

"Everything's mine." In answer to Milo's look, he softened and said, "No, man. I just want our technicians to take a look at it. See if we can find out who was spying on your friend."

"You want to tell me how you knew it was there?"

"No," said Chaudhury. "How about two o'clock? Give you time to eat your pizza. I'll drop by your place to pick it up."

"You don't come near my place," said Milo. "We'll meet here. And in the future, if you want me, call me. Don't ever show up when I'm out with my family."

Chaudhury opened his hands, patting the air. "Calm down, tiger."

"Are you going to tell me about the drive?"

He rubbed the side of his nose—one of those awkward, obvious signals that amateurs think looks natural—and Milo noticed Chaudhury's denim friend crossing the street to their side. "There's nothing to tell. It was wiped clean. Zeroed out."

"So what are you going to do now?"

Chaudhury shrugged. "I'll see what my man in London can find."

"You're done with me?"

"Yeah, Milo. I'm done with you. But if you come across some hot tip, I'd appreciate hearing about it."

"See you at two," Milo said.

As he returned to his seat, he saw that Chaudhury and his friend had left, and that Stephanie was sucking through a straw, stealing his Coke. "Give that back, kid."

Smiling, she puffed her cheeks and blew noisy bubbles into his glass.

"Ah, forget it," he said.

"Was that the Homelander?" Tina asked.

"I'm not sure."

She stared at him.

"Now he says he's Company."

She nodded at that but frowned. "So? Anything new?"

"About who?" asked Stephanie.

"Nothing," Milo said to Tina. To Stephanie, he said, "Alan."

"What about Alan?"

Tina gave him a look, and he realized that they hadn't discussed what they were and were not going to tell her. Procrastination was evidently Tina's only plan. That, or absolute secrecy. "The fact that someone keeps stealing his Coca-Cola," he said. "It's a big mystery. They're going to have to bring in the army soon, shut down the city, and search each house until they find the person who did it."

Wide-eyed, Stephanie blinked at him and, very seriously, said, "It wasn't me."

When he met Chaudhury on the sidewalk at two, there was no sign of his denim-clad friend. Milo handed over the camera in a paper bag. Chaudhury seemed to want to talk, but Milo didn't. "Take this," Chaudhury said, reaching into a back pocket. He produced a blank, white business card with a D.C. 202 phone number and the name "Director Stephen Rollins" handwritten on it. "It's the office number. I strongly suggest that you leave it alone, but if you find you can't put down your paranoia and you absolutely must verify that I work for who I say I work for, call that number."

"Who's Director Rollins?"

"My Lord and Master." Chaudhury grinned. "Though I prefer to call him by his proper name. God."

"Will you get in trouble if I call?"

"Me? I'm a survivor, Milo, I've no worries. I just think you'd probably like to stay off my boss's radar," he said, then raised a hand in farewell.

At home, Milo found Tina cleaning up the living room. "Looks like we're getting a permanent guest," she said.

"What?"

"Penelope. Someone ripped up her apartment."

"I put everything back," he said quickly.

"The bedroom?"

"What?"

"Did you slice open her mattress and tear out the springs?"

"Oh."

"I told her to pack a bag and come back."

Penelope arrived two hours later, and Milo carried her large, heavy suitcase up their narrow stairs. She seemed more put out than scared, and while Milo grilled chicken breast for a Caesar salad, the two women drank wine in the kitchen doorway and berated the Central Intelligence Agency. "It was them, wasn't it?" she asked Milo.

"I think so."

"They could have just asked me. Knock on the door, say, *Mrs. Drummond, may we please look around?* I would've said yes."

"They don't always think so directly."

"What does that mean?" Tina asked.

At first, he wasn't sure what he had meant. Then he knew. He turned to face them. "The Company spends as much time anticipating disaster as it does collecting intelligence. If someone says, *Let's go ask Mrs. Drummond if we can look around*, someone else at the table certainly says, *She's upset. What if she says no?* Then they all have a think—okay, if she won't let us in, what happens next? Because operational planning is about staying five steps ahead. If you aren't, then things go wrong. If Mrs. Drummond is upset, and says no, maybe she'll be sure not to leave the apartment so that no one can come in to look around. Or maybe she'll hire some-one to keep the place secure."

"But I wouldn't do that. Christ, Alan worked for the Company. He loved the bastards."

"You would do that if you had something to hide. You would do that if you thought Alan had something he was hiding from them. That's what they're thinking. So, logically, the only thing they can do is break in when you're not there, then get out as fast as they can. Which means leaving a mess."

There was no point telling either of them that a man named Dennis Chaudhury had worked all night rip-ping the place apart. She knew what she needed to know—that the Company had done this, and that she should not pretend to herself that the Company was her friend.

"I should write a letter," she said finally.

"By all means," he said, turning back to the hissing chicken. "Just don't expect an elegant apology. Not on paper, at least."

7

Some families thrive by being open to the world, absorbing visitors into their daily routines, while others hold themselves always at a distance, in voluntary exile, as if bringing in some third party might blemish their particular joy. The Weavers were part of this latter group. When friends and family visited, they used their too-small apartment as an excuse and put them up at the nearby Park Slope Inn—it kept the intrusions within a predictable, manageable bracket of time.

Penelope, though, crashed like a boulder in the middle of their living room, taking their couch for her bed. It was awkward for everyone except Stephanie, who seemed energized by the disruption. On Friday, Tina went to work, leaving Milo and Stephanie to deal with their guest. Penelope, perhaps to get out of their hair, left at noon for "errands" and didn't come back until after five, carrying a large bag full of metal containers of steaming Thai food from a restaurant called Sea. By then, Milo and Stephanie had spent a couple of hours browsing at BookCourt, shopped for groceries, and bought tickets for Sunday's international puppet festival at the Yeshiva University Museum. Penelope held the bags aloft and said, "No more of Daddy's unsalted food!" Stephanie cheered.

Saturday began with a surprise, for Milo had forgotten his own thirty-eighth birthday. He woke to Tina and Stephanie piling on top of him with kisses and happy wishes. Everyone ate chocolate cake for breakfast, even Penelope, though she criticized the quality of the chocolate the baker had used. Stephanie gave him an aluminum box for pens that she had painted with unintentionally abstract dragons, while Tina gave him a set of Waterman pens. Tina had apparently told Penelope about his birthday, for she, too, handed over a heavy wrapped present, which turned out to be both volumes of Julia Child's *The Art of French Cooking*. "Salt, you'll find, is a very common ingredient."

They all seemed to enjoy most of Saturday, going out for a movie Stephanie chose, *Kung Fu Panda*—the title seemed to say it all. By Sunday morning, though, Penelope's mood had taken a nose-dive, and when Stephanie got out of bed at nine to sit in her pajamas and watch cartoons, Penelope pulled a pillow over her head and groaned. Over breakfast, she told them, "Alan and I always agreed that not having children was a lifestyle choice—we simply wanted to keep some style in our life."

Tina, who depended on her Sunday morning quiet

time with the arts pages, grew noticeably irritated when Penelope kept interrupting her to bring up Alan's virtues and flaws. When Penelope was washing up, Tina said, "Christ, she does test one's nerves, doesn't she?"

They all piled into the subway to reach the Yeshiva University Museum on West Sixteenth for the Jewish, Greek, Czech, and Chinese puppet festival. It was something Tina had read about the previous weekend, and Milo was excited to show Stephanie something that wasn't transmitted through a television screen. Watching her laconic reactions to the puppets on the lit stages, though, he worried that she'd been warped too much already. Despite the historical curiosities of Mitzvah Mouse, the herky-jerky illuminations of the Greek shadow puppets, and the strangely lifelike Czech marionettes, Stephanie remained entirely unmoved—until the Chinese hand puppets.

Though the first show, concerning a married couple arguing over how best to cook an eel, did little to raise her interest, when during the second show Wu Song came on wearing his red kimono against the black velvet background, tinny music rising behind him, she settled down and focused. Then came the tiger, an elaborate, large-headed monster with wide, flat teeth, twisting with anger and hunger. Milo didn't know the story, but it seemed pretty basic—Wu Song, while passing the Jingyang Ridge, kills a tiger with his bare hands, an act that makes him famous. Still, it was a masterly show, a dance between Wu Song's martial arts and the man-eating tiger's artful lunges, and by the time the tiger had been dispatched, Stephanie was leaning forward, pinching at the fabric of her jeans. Penelope, beside Tina, muttered, "So that's what they do."

Only later, at a coffee shop on Union Square, did she elaborate over a dish of vanilla ice cream. "They didn't tell the rest of his story, which doesn't surprise me. Old Wu Song was a real killing machine. He later avenged his brother's death by poison by decapitating his brother's wife and killing her lover."

"*Really*?" asked Stephanie.

"It's one of those lovely stories about loose women sliding easily into murder, then getting what they deserve." She winked at Stephanie. "Let that be a lesson to you."

On their way back to Brooklyn, Milo's phone chirp-chirped, and he found an invitation from his father—*Byblos Restaurant, 11:00*—and texted back *Yes*.

"Who was that?" Tina asked over the rumble of the subway car.

"Yevgeny. We're lunching tomorrow."

"Grandpa?" asked Stephanie, brightening.

"First me, then you two can have him for dinner," said Milo. "Tomorrow or Tuesday."

"Well, I'll be off your couch by tomorrow," said Penelope. "The new bed's being delivered, as well as some new furniture."

"You can stay," Tina said, a little too quickly. "If you want. I mean, if you're not comfortable there."

"Thanks," Penelope said, seeming to believe her, though the truth was that both Tina and Milo couldn't wait for her to be out of their home.

* * *

On Monday morning, otherwise known as Public Service Day, after Tina had left for work and he'd walked Stephanie to the Camp Friendship facility on Sixth Avenue and Eighth Street, Milo returned slowly home and dialed the Washington number Chaudhury had given him. Partly, he was preparing an answer to the question he knew his father would ask—*How do you know who this Chaudhury character is?*—but more, his curiosity was growing, and he wanted to find out who, exactly, was looking out for Alan these days. After three rings, a female voice said, "Director Rollins's office."

"I'd like to speak to Mr. Rollins."

"Your name?"

"Milo Weaver."

"And this is concerning?"

"An employee of his."

"Name?"

"Dennis Chaudhury. Want me to spell it?"

"No, thank you, sir." She paused, perhaps typing it all out, and said, "Director Rollins is out of the office today. Can he reach you at this number?"

"Yes. You have it?"

"Yes, sir. Will eleven o'clock tomorrow morning be all right?"

"I think so," he said, trying to sound friendly. "What's the name of the director's section?"

"You don't know?"

He paused. "I've forgotten."

"Well, Mr. Weaver, this section is like an expensive restaurant. If you have to ask . . ."

* * *

Running late, he met his father at Byblos, a crowded upscale Lebanese restaurant not far from the United Nations Headquarters. Yevgeny was already pushing hummus and pine nuts around a small oily plate with a piece of grilled pita bread, and Milo noticed him lick his fingers and wipe them on his pants as he rose to greet his son. It was an unlikely gesture from a man who had, for the decades Milo had known him, prided himself on his gentlemanly demeanor. Once he'd sat again, he brushed at his cheek as if swatting away a fly, a tic he'd been developing for years. The man was sixty-seven, and though he'd seen signs of his father's gradual decline, this was the first time Milo had really seen the decades in him.

To move things along, Yevgeny had decided on entrées for them both—a spicy Kafta Koush Kash for Milo, and a fried fish entrée called a Sultan Ibrahim for himself—and once the waiter had left he offered the hummus dish to Milo. Milo declined, so Yevgeny scooped up more and took a bite, then, in Russian, spoke through a half-full mouth—another inconsistency. "I don't think your friend is dead."

"Neither do I," said Milo. "The question is: Where is he?"

Yevgeny shrugged. "Who's to say? A little before four in the morning, on Saturday the fourteenth, someone sabotaged the hotel's security cameras. The staff got them working again after about fifteen minutes, then they went down again. There's a half hour or so of dead time."

"Anyone could have come in and taken him."

"But no one took him."

"What?"

Yevgeny smiled. "The city of London is as thick with cameras as that hotel."

Milo rubbed the bridge of his nose—he'd forgotten that Yevgeny, or Yevgeny's friends, would have access to the police cameras. "So he walked out on his own?"

"He left and took public transport to Hammersmith before getting to a street without cameras. From there, he vanished."

It was something, and Milo felt the relief in his back, the sudden release of tension he hadn't known he was holding on to.

Yevgeny swatted at his cheek. "Your friend, he's a curious one."

"I know."

"Guess how he got to London."

"Plane."

"Five planes. New York to Seattle. Drove to Vancouver and then flew to Tokyo. From there, to Mumbai. Mumbai to Amman. Amman to London. Each plane, another name. His own only on the first flight to Seattle."

Alan had circled the planet to reach London. "How long did this take?"

"Four days. In Mumbai and Amman, he left the airports briefly; in Tokyo, he stayed in the international terminal and waited for the next flight."

"You got this from MI-5?"

"Some of it. They knew he flew in from Jordan; I filled in the rest."

"What else do they know?"

"Arrived in London very late on Thursday the twelfth. Checked into the Rathbone and on Friday made a single call from his room, to a third-floor room registered to one Gephel Marpa. Want me to spell that?"

"Please." Once he'd done so, Milo said, "Tibetan?"

"Very good. Long-standing member of Free Tibet. London resident, which means Mr. Marpa came to the hotel on purpose."

"So they met?"

"Maybe—no one knows. At least, Five isn't saying yet. Saturday afternoon, after Alan Drummond disappeared, Marpa left the hotel and returned to his home in South London."

"What did Alan do for meals?"

"Room service."

"So he flies there Thursday, spends Friday in his room. Maybe talks to Marpa, maybe not. Someone shuts off the security cameras, and he walks out."

His father nodded.

"Why sabotage the cameras in the first place? He knew the street cameras would get him."

Yevgeny took a deep breath. "Who's to say?"

"Leticia Jones," Milo said after a moment. "She was in the same hotel; she turned off the cameras."

His father shook his head. "It wasn't her."

"How do you know?"

"Can't I retain a little mystery?" he asked, some of his old charm coming through. "Trust me, son: Your alluring Tourist didn't turn them off."

Milo frowned at him, wondering if his father knew

who had turned off the cameras but didn't want to share. There could be any number of reasons for his reluctance, ones that, perhaps, had no bearing on Alan's situation. Milo said, "If it wasn't to hide Alan leaving the hotel, it was to hide the movements of someone who went in to speak to him first. Alan might have walked out on his own, but I'll lay odds that someone else convinced him he had to leave. Threat, or whatever."

Brows raised, Yevgeny said, "One of many possibilities."

Milo stared past his father a moment, to where a waiter stood near the register in the back, talking on a cell phone. "I don't get it," he said finally. "Alan flies around the world to get to London, arranges to meet a Tibetan dissident in the hotel, then never goes to the man's room. Then he walks. I want to see that video footage."

"You'll have to get it yourself. My contact has seen it but can't smuggle out a copy."

Their food arrived, wreathed in a pleasantly pungent smell, and Milo noticed with dismay that his father's lips soon became damp and littered with flakes of fish. He felt the urge to reach across with his napkin and wipe it for him, but no matter how far gone he was Yevgeny would never allow that.

"How's your work?" Milo asked.

Yevgeny chewed and considered the question. He raised his utensils in a half-shrug. "It goes on and on. I've never told you the details of my days, have I?"

Milo shook his head. Though he knew that, for the

past six years, his father had been running a secret intelligence-gathering department within the UN, he had no idea what his job actually demanded. Milo knew he ran agents, but not how many or how often.

"It requires a lot of travel. Not as much as a Tourist, of course, but a lot for a man my age. These days, there's all that security to deal with—my UN credentials aren't as ironclad as they used to be. And the work's expanding; I've even had to bring on an assistant to keep everything organized. I would retire, but I don't know who to pass it on to."

"Your assistant," Milo suggested, "let him take over, and you can stay in touch in case problems arise."

"*Her.* And, no—I know that she doesn't want the job. This is why I keep suggesting you give up this idiotic employment search and just come join me."

"I've had enough of traveling," Milo said. "Besides, I really don't want to work for my father."

Yevgeny folded his hands beneath his moist chin and stared. "Perhaps you're right, Milo. I'm not entirely sure you'd have the stamina for the job."

"Reverse psychology hasn't worked since I was sixteen."

Yevgeny reached forward and patted Milo's hand. "Everything is worth a try."

Before leaving, Milo ordered some to-go baklava and waited by the front door while Yevgeny put the lunch on his card. As they walked eastward, they settled on dinner with Tina and Stephanie the next evening; then Milo told him about Dennis Chaudhury, likely of the Central Intelligence Agency. Yevgeny frowned at the story, then took out a handkerchief and wiped some grease from his lips. "He sounds very ignorant, this Mr. Chaudhury."

"I'm sure he knows more, but it's done now. He thinks he's gotten all he can get from me."

"Have you verified he is who he says he is?"

"I've got the number of his boss."

"A number he gave you?" Yevgeny said doubtfully.

"I'll talk to the guy in the morning, then run the information myself. It doesn't matter, though. The Company will run its investigation, and either they'll share results or they won't."

Yevgeny paused, turning to get a good look at his son, then shrugged and continued walking. "I'm surprised you can let all this go so easily."

It wasn't as easy as his father suspected, but now it was easier. Alan had walked out of that hotel on his own two feet. Alan had been running an operation—perhaps still was—and London had been part of a ham-fisted attempt to draw Milo into it. It had been clumsy and stupid, and that was argument enough to keep his distance from Alan Drummond.

"Happy birthday, by the way."

On the local 4 train, heading home, he worked to ignore some fresh pain in his gut, a mixture of lunch and the old bullet wound, as well as Alan Drummond—who, he'd decided, no longer deserved his attention.

As so often in his life, however, his own desires were inconsequential. History moves forward, and none of us live alone, no matter how hard we try. The desires of others manipulate our hours and days to their own obscure purposes.

He knew this as truth as he raised his gaze from the white foam box of sweets in his lap and saw, sitting opposite him, a sensual, fresh-skinned black woman with a broad smile on her face. She wasn't looking at him, but he was the only thing on the train she was interested in.

8

It was instinct, reaching into his pocket and, with one hand, popping the battery out of his phone. Not looking at her was instinct, too, as was the sudden attention he gave to his peripheral vision as he climbed to his feet and disembarked at Union Square. As he crossed Fourth Avenue to the park, to his left the enormous Metronome gushed white clouds, the time reading 13:54.

There was no point looking back. Leticia—or Gwendolyn, or Rosa—would approach him after she'd made sure he wasn't being tailed. So he followed the edge of the park north, past some huge outdoor party full of young people and patrolling police, to East Seventeenth, where he popped a Nicorette and headed down into the W Hotel's Underbar. After the sunlight, his eyes had to adjust to the darkness to take in the couples scattered throughout. He headed directly to the bar. A distractingly attractive bartender asked how he was doing; he told her he was doing well. He'd noticed no real problems after Wednesday's vodka tonic in the Drummond condo, so he decided to take another step. "Ketel One martini, please. Dry. Straight up. Two olives."

"A man who knows what he wants," she said as she turned to find a glass.

"Actually, make it two. I've got a friend coming."

Leticia arrived five minutes later and took the stool beside him without saying a word. She wore a light indigo blouse that, in better light, showed off the brand of her brassiere, and her hair hung in loose loops to the top of her neck. Milo slid one of the martinis to her.

"Gosh, mister. Isn't this rather forward?"

"I like your hair, Gwendolyn."

She leaned in and kissed his cheek, smelling of almond oil. "Baby, I'll always be Leticia to you."

The bartender was giving them a smile, so they moved to a small table near the wall and settled close to each other. "You didn't see anyone, did you?" he asked.

She took a sip and crinkled her nostrils. "Mmm. That's good."

"Was there somebody?"

"Male. Five-six. Hundred eighty pounds, give or take."

"What did you do to him?"

"Was he Company?"

"Probably."

"Good. He'll live."

He felt an urge to lecture her, but it was beyond repair now. She was still acting like a Tourist—reckless and definitive. "You want to tell me?"

"It was easy." She raised her left hand, fingers flat,

her long painted nails reflecting the low lights. "See the side of my hand?"

"Alan. Tell me about Alan."

Leticia dropped her hand and, as she took another sip, scanned the dim bar. She set down her drink. "That wasn't my fault. It wasn't my job to be his bodyguard."

"Leticia."

She touched the stem of her glass. "He told me you were out."

"I was never in."

"Well, he thought he could get you in."

"By using my name? He was wrong."

"But now you want in."

"No, I don't want in. I just want to know what's going on. He's not dead; I know that."

"That makes one of us," she said.

"What do you mean?"

"What I *mean*, baby, is that him disappearing wasn't part of any plan I knew of."

Milo considered that for a moment, sipping his martini. "Then why don't you tell me about the plan you did know of?"

She blinked slowly at him; her eyes, he realized, perhaps for the first time, were enormous. "He came to me about a week and a half after the massacre . . . a few days before you were shot. He didn't have it together yet; he wanted to bounce ideas off of me, see what I could add."

"He wanted revenge."

"He didn't know *what* he wanted. Not yet. Then you were shot—he blamed himself for that. *Then* he got reamed by Langley and lost his job. Later, he started fighting with his wife. You see? This Chinaman closed down his life. Not just Tourism but the whole shebang. So, yeah. He wanted revenge. Wouldn't you?"

"There's a difference between what I'd want and what I'd do."

"You don't have to tell me that," she said and, beneath the table, stroked his knee with one fingernail.

He pulled his leg away. "Go on."

"You need to lighten up."

"Just tell me what's going on."

She shrugged, leaning back. "Second week of April, he calls me. He'd learned some new things. One: Xin Zhu got married last summer. Two: What he did to us was completely unsanctioned by Beijing. Three: Xin Zhu is teetering on the edge of dismissal. *He's weak*, says Alan. *He's weaker now than he'll ever be.*"

She took another drink, and Milo waited.

"You know me—I'm no genius. I don't get it. The man's weak now; what's that to us? So Alan goes on, as if to a child, and tells me that with this information we know what is on Xin Zhu's mind. Once you know someone's obsession, you know what he's going to do."

"He thought that was enough of an edge?"

"It was something."

"So Alan was going to run an entire operation against him with . . . what? A few Tourists? You and—who? I know Zachary Klein was out. José Santiago? He, or someone like him, met with Alan before he disappeared."

Leticia blinked again, more slowly. "Tran Hoang came in, too."

"So Alan had three people, and he expected to bring down a colonel with a private department in the Guoanbu's Sixth Bureau—someone who, despite his troubles, might be one of the most powerful people in Chinese intelligence?"

"He's got three *Tourists*."

"You're not Tourists anymore."

"Don't underestimate us, Milo. You of all people should know better."

"I'm just trying to understand. He has no network, no signals intelligence—more importantly, no open-ended budget."

"He has more than you'd think."

"Like what? Turkestan militants?"

Leticia's face went cold. "Where'd you hear that?"

"The Company guys you beat up." He leaned closer. "Would you really be that stupid?"

"We're not doing anything with the Uighurs."

"What about the Youth League? Alan was interested in them. After all, the Company's already supplied them with weapons."

"Nobody's talking to them either."

"I hope not. They'll go for any plan, no matter how half-baked, just as long as it involves fire." Milo paused, waiting, but she offered nothing more. "So, if it's not them, tell me how he was going to bury Xin Zhu."

She took a longer drink this time, until all that was left was a puddle of vodka. She pulled out the wooden skewer and bit off an olive. As she chewed, she scanned the bar again but only said, "You in or out?"

It took a moment to wrap his head around that question. "You mean it's still on?"

She arched a brow. "When did we ever drop an operation because someone stepped out for a minute?"

"You don't know where he is anymore."

"Reminds me of my ex—when he left, my friends thought I should stop everything."

She was being coy, and he didn't understand why. The man who had been coordinating the operation had disappeared, yet she felt confident enough to keep moving forward. It wasn't blind loyalty—Tourists were seldom afflicted by such a thing, particularly when their department didn't exist anymore. He said, "Alan wasn't running this, was he? You?"

She shook her head. She was enjoying his confusion.

"Who?"

"In, or out?"

"Out. Definitely out."

She shrugged as if this were no surprise, then ate her last olive.

"Alan suggested he still had Company contacts. Does that mean it's a proper operation?"

"If you're in, you get the information, and we can call on you when we like. If not, then not."

"He used my Tourist name. I think that entitles me to a few answers."

Looking at the puddle in her glass, she considered his request. Again, she sighed. "You know why he did that."

"Because he wanted to force me to help. A pretty cold move."

"He knows you're the kind of person who needs a fire under his ass to get moving."

Milo felt his good humor draining away. "He uses a name Interpol has on its lists, a name that both the Germans and the Chinese can connect to me. That puts my family in danger."

"You and that damned family. Milo, the Chinaman doesn't give a rat's ass about your family. That's why you ended up with a bullet in your belly, and they didn't."

Milo rubbed his face. The fact was that all that had come before—Xin Zhu's elaborate operation to kill thirty-three men and women around the globe—had been provoked by the murder of his son, an event Tourism was only distantly responsible for. Xin Zhu *shouldn't* care about Milo's family, but he had long ago proved himself unpredictable.

None of this concerned Leticia. Despite losing the title, she still thought like a Tourist. He guessed that she would think that way until she died—which, given her current trajectory, could be anytime.

He opened his wallet, counted out three tens, and placed them on the table. "Nice to see you again, Leticia."

She watched him stand and take his box of baklava. "Well, you know how to get in touch with me."

He didn't reply; he only walked out of the bar.

Outside the Camp Friendship facility, as he felt the martini eat at his insides and thought about what he'd learned and not learned while drinking it, Gabi broke off from a trio of nannies to join him. "Hallo," she said.

"Hallo, Gabi."

In German, she said, "I'm proud of myself. Took one day to convince my masters that their brats should be in day camp. I don't know if I could have taken a summer of them every day."

He smiled at that; then she pointed at the nannies she'd been talking to. "Malaysian, French, and Romanian, I never thought I'd be in a place so international in my life. I picked up dry cleaning from a Greek woman, bought groceries from some Vietnamese, paid bills to an Indian clerk, and was just now getting chatted up by a big Chinese father."

"Chatted up?" he asked.

"Ja," she said, then turned, scanning the spare crowd on the sidewalk. "Well, maybe he wasn't a father, after all, and just wanted . . . well, you know."

Milo, too, found himself scanning the street, looking for a Chinese man posing as a father, trying to convince himself that it was nothing to worry about. The possibility of the famously large Xin Zhu hanging out in Brooklyn was too unbelievable even to consider.

Over dinner, Tina complained that, now that she was back home, Penelope wasn't answering her phone. "Was I too much of a you-know-what with her?"

"I don't know what," said Stephanie, her eyelids now a pale purple.

"You were fine," said Milo.

"I said I don't know *what*."

Though he made no mention of Leticia Jones, in bed he told Tina that a little more information had come his way, and it only reinforced his belief that not only was Alan engaged in a foolishly dangerous plan, he had also been trying to manipulate Milo into taking part. "He used one of my old names," he finally admitted.

"What do you mean, used it?"

"He used a passport with my old work name to check into the Rathbone Hotel."

She shook her head in an expression of irritable confusion, as if he'd just spoken backward. "But . . . why?"

"Just that. To pull me in."

"He thought that would work?"

"It almost did," he said, for during dinner, watching his daughter's discolored eyes, he'd been overcome by the feeling that he'd sidestepped a bullet. "But it was reckless," he told her. "What pisses me off is that people can connect the name to me, thus, to you and Stef."

"Really?"

He nodded.

"The Chinese?"

Again, he nodded.

She went silent, then turned to look at the foot of the bed. "I could kill that bastard."

There wasn't much more to discuss, but that didn't stop Tina from prodding him throughout the night with irritated questions, most of which he couldn't answer. At one point, as he was drifting off to sleep, she said, "They train you to do that, right?"

"What?" he groaned, raising his head from the pillow.

"Sleep. Sleep when things around you are falling apart."

"Sure," he said after a moment. "It's important."

"It's inhuman," she said.

9

In the morning, he got up early and made coffee, then helped Stephanie work on her eyelids; they were nearly ink free, but her ego was still bruised. He didn't see Gabi at Camp Friendship, but as he was leaving he saw a large Chinese man, standing alone on the other side of the street—big boned, with a mole on his cheek—that might have been Gabi's admirer. He wasn't looking at Milo, though; he was looking at the grounds, where children were gathering around a teacher. Though there were similarities, this was not Xin Zhu—he was thirty years too young.

Despite his desire to abandon it entirely, when he got back to the apartment he began to research the path that Alan had taken from New York to London, via Seattle, Vancouver, Tokyo, Mumbai, and Amman. He wasn't sure what he was looking for, but he checked the week of Drummond's travel, beginning June 9, searching in vain for public events along the route that might shed some light on his purpose. The best theory he could come up with was that the path was entirely evasive and Alan was trying to shake a tail.

His phone rang at precisely eleven, shocking him out of the claustrophobic world of the Internet, and when he checked the number he noticed the Washington, D.C., area code before remembering that he'd been expecting this call.

"Mr. Milo Weaver?" said Stephen Rollins's secretary.

"Yes, yes. That's me."

"I have Director Rollins on the other line for you."

"Right. Thank you."

There was a snap, then three clicks. Then silence. Milo waited but heard nothing from Mr. Rollins. "Hello?" he said.

"Mr. Weaver," said a man's voice. It was heavy and tired-sounding, and there was an accent he couldn't quite place. "You wanted to talk to me."

"Yes, it's about someone named Dennis Chaudhury. I wanted to verify that he's one of your employees."

A pause. "Yes, I can verify that. Mr. Chaudhury works for me. Was there anything else?"

"Well, yes. I would like some evidence that you, Mr. Rollins, are actually working for the Central Intelligence Agency. Where's your office?"

Another pause. Milo wondered if the man had someone else in the room with him. "One oh one West Thirty-first Street, Manhattan."

Now, it was Milo who paused. Until two months ago, that had been the address of the Department of Tourism—

which had been shut down. Had it reopened? Was Dennis Chaudhury a new Tourist? He doubted it—hardly anyone had wanted Tourism to continue; it had been shut down with glee. More likely, the building had simply been reassigned. "Does the department have a name?"

"Of course it does, Mr. Weaver," Rollins said. His voice was different now, relaxed, the odd accent heavier. As if he'd given over a small piece of his secret and now felt free to share anything. "But I'm not sure you could pronounce it."

"Try me."

"Guojia Anquan Bu," said Stephen Rollins.

To stop himself from slipping off his chair, Milo shot out a hand to catch the edge of the table. Guojia Anquan Bu; Guoanbu; the Chinese Ministry of State Security. He was finally able to place Rollins's accent. He tried to speak, but it was difficult. He cleared his throat. "Who is this?"

"I think you know, Mr. Weaver, but I think that perhaps you're too proud to admit that you know."

His hand felt the fear first. It took the phone away from his ear, holding it at a safe distance, and the thumb stretched over the keypad to hang up. He stopped it, though, and forced the phone back to his face. He said, "What's going on."

Xin Zhu said, "Mr. Chaudhury believes you only know what you've told him about Alan Drummond's plans, but I'm not convinced. I asked him to give you my phone number. I knew you would call eventually."

Milo remembered Chaudhury saying, *I just think you'd like to stay off my boss's radar.*

His dry mouth made his words hurt in the back of his throat. "I don't know anything else."

"What about Leticia Jones? She certainly knows more than either of us do."

"She wouldn't tell me."

"She beat one of my people senseless on her way to meet you. She knows enough to make sure no one is listening. What did she share with you?"

"She told me that they're going to bury you."

Another pause. "How?"

"She didn't tell me, because I don't want any part of it."

"But she would tell you if you did want to be part of it."

Milo said nothing. There was nothing to say.

"I have a proposition, Mr. Weaver. Once in the past you said that you admired my work; now is your chance to be a part of it."

Milo had said that once, but it had been a long time ago, and said in confidence. He tried to remember if he'd said it in front of the man had who turned out to be Xin Zhu's mole, but he couldn't focus. "I was delusional," Milo said. "I've gotten over it."

Xin Zhu made a noise, either a wheeze or a laugh, and Milo noticed a faint digital echo, the kind that sometimes accompanies transatlantic calls. "You must understand my position," he said. "I am here, attempting to the best of my abilities to do my job, and then it comes to my attention that someone wants to do me harm. Not just me, but harm to my country—to the security of my country. What do I do? What would you do?"

Milo didn't answer.

"You would do the same thing I've done. Try to find out who wants to do you harm, and how."

"Not why?"

"I know why. Because Americans are obsessed with revenge."

"That's a joke, right?"

"Is it?"

"You killed thirty-three people to avenge your son's death. That's shockingly vengeful."

"Simply because Americans are obsessed with revenge does not mean that I am not. One does not contradict the other, does it?"

Milo stood and shook out a leg, trying to ease the tingling, "What does Alan Drummond say? You have him, of course."

"I wish I did," said Xin Zhu. "Ms. Jones doesn't have him?"

"Maybe he's dead."

"I don't think either of us believe he's dead. Your father certainly doesn't."

Milo wondered if they had been following him or following Yevgeny, or if they had simply read the SMS his father had sent, arranging lunch. That would've given them a full day to wire the Byblos table and fill all the other tables with customers. He said, "I don't know either way."

"Another thing for you to discover. I never had any plans to touch a hair on Alan Drummond's head."

"I find that hard to believe."

"It's true, Mr. Weaver. He decided to break our agreement. Had I chosen to reprimand him for this, I would have killed his wife, not him."

"Penelope?"

"It was her life he was risking by doing what he did."

"What did he do?"

"He ignored my instructions."

"I don't understand."

"You will. But for now let's discuss how you can uncover the facts."

"No," said Milo. "First, you'll tell me why you think I'll help you."

"Maybe because you once helped a dead man, who also happened to be your enemy, to uncover the identity of his murderer. Mr. Sam Roth, otherwise known as the Tiger."

"Get yourself killed, and I'll be happy to find the murderer."

"That joke is in poor taste, Mr. Weaver."

"Tell me about your relationship with Alan."

"Simple. I discovered he was engaged in a plan to, at the very least, smear my reputation. I convinced him of the error of his ways. He began to work with me to undermine the plan."

"Why didn't he just stop it?"

"Because he was not the only person involved. Leticia Jones, for example. Senator Nathan Irwin."

"Irwin's involved?" Worse and worse. A year ago, Irwin had tried to have Milo killed.

"As I told you, Americans are obsessed with revenge, none more than politicians. There are two more conspirators from your old employer. A retired Directorate of Operations officer named Stuart Jackson, and Dorothy Collingwood, who works in the National Clandestine Service. Perhaps you know them?"

Milo didn't, and said as much.

Xin Zhu sighed. "But you understand now. Alan Drummond could not simply tell these three powerful people that the plan was canceled, therefore his job was to make sure it failed."

"He double-crossed you?"

"You could say that."

"The camera was yours. The one in Alan's office."

"Of course. Upon our instructions, he placed it there himself. It turned out that he did very little work in his office."

Enough time had passed so that the shakes had lessened, and Milo had lost the feeling that he was under a great weight. He said, "Listen, Zhu."

"You call me by my first name. Very intimate."

Milo hesitated, realizing that Xin Zhu was right. Chinese names end with the given name, yet Milo, Alan, Nathan Irwin . . . they had simply fallen into the rhythm of calling him Zhu. He had no idea why. "Xin Zhu," he said. "I wasn't going to fly around the world for Alan, and I'm not doing it for you. You've got plenty of people to take care of this."

"I don't think Leticia Jones or Nathan Irwin would trust my employees. No, Mr. Weaver. It has to be you."

"Well, it won't be."

"Please," said Xin Zhu, "open up your computer."

Milo's laptop was already open in front of him. "Okay."

"Now go into the browser and type the following IP address."

Milo typed the four numbers, separated by periods, that Xin Zhu dictated. The computer stalled a second on a white screen, working to load two videos. "What is this?"

"It will just be a moment," Xin Zhu said, then, to someone else, spoke a short phrase in what Milo suspected was Mandarin.

As the elements of the videos appeared one after the other, two 4×3 rectangles lining up horizontally, he saw that both were streaming videos, live feeds. Then, nearly simultaneously, both loaded and began to play.

On the left, the camera moved with the motion of a body; it was hidden on someone around chest-height, filming the interior of a large library Milo knew well. Columbia's Avery Architectural and Fine Arts Library, where Tina was the director. The person who wore the camera walked past the service desk, past rows of computers occupied by students, and into a short corridor of offices to the furthest door on the left. The cameraman's hand appeared and knocked beside the label identifying the office of the library's director. There was no sound, just a second's pause, and then the hand opened the door to reveal Tina inside, behind her desk, reading glasses low on her nose over a stack of forms, looking at the cameraman inquisitively. She spoke her side of a conversation.

On the right, the camera did not move. It was attached to something in the corner of a room. There were books here, too. Children's books. There were toys, and sitting in a circle with a woman in her forties who clapped her hands while singing were fifteen children obediently singing along. Surprisingly, he noticed Sarah Lawton first, with her prim blond hairdo and a ballerina outfit, before seeing, two children away, Stephanie. She looked bored and irritable.

Xin Zhu's voice said, "You see now?"

Milo could feel nothing. His hands, legs, and even his head had gone numb.

"This is not how I like to run things, but you should keep it in mind as you do your work."

Milo whispered, "This is what you did to Alan."

"Alan thought he could get out of it by leaving his wife. By driving her crazy with his bad behavior, then running. He was wrong."

Remembering Tina's unanswered calls, Milo said, "You have Penelope."

"No," Xin Zhu answered quickly. "Harming her will not make Alan Drummond reappear. Remember, though, that I've learned a lesson about being too generous, and I won't repeat my mistakes. Remember that we can get to them anytime we like. Please don't force us to do anything so radical."

Milo remembered Chaudhury saying, *I prefer to call him by his proper name. God.*

* * *

After vomiting in the toilet and washing out his mouth, he felt as if everything had been purged from his body. His organs, his fear, his soul, and even his love. His emotions weren't actually gone, just shoved into a little box in some far corner of his psyche, put out of the way, to be dealt with later. The surprise was that he could, after months, achieve this so quickly. He wanted to tell Tina, *They train us for this as well*, but he would tell her nothing. He would renege on the oath of honesty he'd given her, and while his excuses might be valid, he knew he was placing himself on the slippery slope back to complete deception.

Though he didn't know from where, he knew that he was being watched or listened to as he called Leticia's special number and said, "It's Milo," and hung up. It was 11:46. He put on a light jacket, then left the apartment.

Walking north on Seventh toward Flatbush, he tried to find his shadow, but it was a busy time of day, the stores open and full, and he found himself succumbing to racial profiling anytime an Asian face passed. There was no reason to think that Xin Zhu would be using his own people for this; he could hire whomever he wanted. Someone like Chaudhury, or the black man in the too-heavy coat who was trailing him on the other side of the street. Anyone, he realized, could be wearing a camera in his or her shirt or blouse.

Was he frightened? Certainly, but that was packed away, too. Was he without hope? No, but he couldn't know if it was true hope or the artificial hope Tourists manufacture to fuel their forward movement. He needed to put pieces together, to turn them around in the light and understand exactly where he stood and what his options were. It had been months since he'd called himself a Tourist, but the simple clarity of Tourism had not yet left him.

As it stood now, he had no choice. Xin Zhu did not engage in empty threats, nor did he take a step without having thought five steps ahead. Milo could not walk away from this, nor would he be able to collect his family and escape. Xin Zhu would have planned for those possibilities.

The cell phone in his pocket buzzed. This time it was a private number. "Yes?"

"Where are you going?" Xin Zhu asked quietly.

"To get in touch with Leticia."

"You can't do that from your home?"

"Afraid not."

"How is it done?"

"Your people can watch and learn."

"I'd rather know now."

Milo told him.

"Like the other night," Xin Zhu said.

"Yes."

"You have an hour," he said. "Why are you rushing?"

"Because I need a drink."

Xin Zhu hung up.

On Flatbush, he watched for busy restaurants and bars and noticed that Mooney's Pub, which was scheduled to be demolished at the end of the month, was packed. A rarity at noon, but he supposed that nostalgia was hitting everyone at once, so he squeezed in, nodding at a couple of faces he recognized from the neighborhood, working his way to the bar, waving a hand and calling for a vodka martini.

Mooney's was by all outward appearances a dive, but it was an institution that was now a victim of gentrification. There was a mix of old hands and hipsters here, mostly white, and as he carefully carried his drink away from the bar, he used his right hand to touch jacket pockets. By the time he reached the wall, he had someone's iPhone in his palm and was sliding it into his own pocket.

As he drank, he watched the crowded entrance, half-listening to Johnny Cash and June Carter singing of Jackson. The black man didn't appear again, but a single Caucasian woman in her thirties wandered in, looking subtly out of place. Perhaps it was her, perhaps not; she gave no sign.

Contrary to his training, he thought for too long about blame and realized that he'd done this to himself. It was he who had made the call to Director Stephen Rollins. Chaudhury had even warned him to leave it alone. Told him he didn't want to be on the man's radar. Now he was.

Could he have let it go? Could he have just accepted that Chaudhury was CIA? No, and Xin Zhu had probably known this. Milo imagined the sequence of events: He confronts Chaudhury about not being a Homelander, provoking the next layer of the story. He works for the Company. Chaudhury passes this information on to Xin Zhu, who says, *If he presses, give him this number.*

One of Xin Zhu's talents was knowing when to flex and bend to accommodate unexpected twists, like Milo's curiosity. Xin Zhu was the ultimate pragmatist. He arranged it so that once Milo made the first call, he had a full day to plant his shadows, and then by the time he called back Milo was trapped.

He had no way to know if Xin Zhu would have let him be if he hadn't called, and that was what helped fuel his self-doubt. It was why reflecting on blame was anathema to good Tourism.

Halfway through his drink, he pushed off the wall and worked his way back to the toilets. He didn't look back, nor did he hesitate, for hesitation is like wearing a sign on your back. He pushed through to the small, dirty bathroom as an already drunk guy was pushing out, then leaned against the door and used the iPhone to dial the number he'd been repeating to himself ever since ordering his martini.

After three rings, Janet Simmons said, "What?"

"It's Milo."

"Are you in a bar?"

"I need you to arrest my family."

"What?"

"Tonight, if possible. They'll be at home, and I want you to take them into custody. They're in danger."

"From whom?"

"You wouldn't believe me."

"Where are you?" she asked as Milo felt pressure against his back; someone was trying to get in.

"Brooklyn," he said. "Get here and take them. That's

it. I'll let you know when it's safe." A fist banged against the door. Milo called, "Just a sec!"

"You've got some crazy ideas about my authority. Remember all those tricks you played on me? You didn't earn me any bonuses."

"Then fabricate something. If you don't, they'll end up dead. When they're safe, call me, but not before."

"Does this have to do with Dennis Chaudhury?" she asked.

"Yes."

"Company?"

"Chinese," he said, and when she answered with silence, he said, "I have to go. Just do it. Please."

"You're serious."

He hung up and opened the door, apologizing to a six-foot man with a mustache, then worked his way back to the front, passing the single woman on his way to his drink, which was still where he'd left it. For verisimilitude, he paused to check his zipper, and perhaps it was that which provoked the attention. The single woman glanced at him—briefly, the way one takes in a whole room—but it was a definite look.

He finished his drink and, leaving the iPhone behind his glass, walked out. At twelve forty-four, he faced the busy network of traffic on Grand Army Plaza. He didn't look back, just waited at the curb for the light to change, then crossed streets until he'd reached the triangular island. He stood completely still. Around him, cars continued their loud, congested parade as he waited, trying to think of nothing.

10

On the walk home, he decided he hadn't done enough. Though he trusted that Janet Simmons would do her best to help him, he didn't know what was and was not possible for an agent in her position. The other alternative, though, made him queasy. The last time he'd asked his father to hide someone, it had been a fifteen-year-old girl who, in the end, had escaped the old man and was killed on the side of a French mountain road.

The circumstances now were different, but he still felt unsure as he developed his second strategy, beginning with a visit to the grocery and buying materials for a Vietnamese noodle soup. He took the items up to the apartment and julienned the vegetables, and before storing them in the fridge grabbed a ballpoint from the counter and slipped it into his pocket. He unwrapped the paper covering the chicken breasts and, as he put the paper into the trash, ripped off a rough square and slipped it into his other pocket. Then he pounded the chicken, seasoned it, and slipped it into the oven to grill while he went to the small bathroom behind the front door.

As he undid his pants, he took a look around the small space—toilet and sink, a mirror and an overhead lamp. He found no signs of surveillance, but in fact, he worked less from observation than from the hope that, while the apartment might be full of cameras, Xin Zhu's men had no interest in watching this space. He sat on the toilet, took out the pen and paper, and began to write in Russian.

He picked up Stephanie from camp, putting on a happy face, and listened to her complaints about Sarah Lawton, who'd had the audacity to wear a ballerina outfit to school without informing Stephanie first. When they got home, she smelled the air. "You're cooking?"

"Noodles. You like my noodles."

"I thought grandpa was taking us out."

"It'll be more comfortable here."

She sighed, heading off to her room.

When Tina arrived at five thirty, she asked the same thing and seemed equally disappointed, and when Milo went down to meet Yevgeny's chauffeured car, the old man was more than disappointed; he was angry. "They don't give these reservations to just anybody, you know."

"Don't be an ass," said Milo, trying on a smile. "Tell your driver to join us if he likes."

"Francisco doesn't like home cooking," Yevgeny said as he leaned down to the open window. "Do you, Francisco?"

"Despise it, sir," said Francisco, a beefy, dark man with a South American accent. "You will call when you need me?"

"I'm afraid I will," Yevgeny grumbled before turning to follow his son into the building.

Milo didn't pass the note on the street or in the stairwell. Though he didn't trust his own apartment, he was even more wary of anything in the public realm, which was why he had vetoed the restaurant. It wasn't until they were inside, and Stephanie was running up to him, that Milo grabbed his father by the waist, shouting, "Watch out for the maniac!" and slipped the paper, folded around the spare apartment keys, into Yevgeny's rear pants pocket. The old man certainly felt the move, but he played along well, making a loud noise of terror as his granddaughter barreled into him.

Milo patted him on the shoulder. "Drink?"

"Immediately," said Yevgeny, then pinched Stephanie's cheek so hard that she yelped.

As they settled into conversation, Milo realized that he was now in Alan's shoes, the Alan he had talked with on the roof two and a half weeks ago, the Alan who was agonizingly preoccupied by a matter of life and death but unable to communicate it to anyone. Now, here, Milo had to pretend to listen to Yevgeny's description of Public Service Day, and all the wonderful things the United Nations had done to celebrate it. Why, Milo wondered, hadn't Alan slipped him a note? Why hadn't he shared more on the roof? Because Alan didn't trust that which he did not personally control, even if it meant not trusting Milo. Because Alan didn't believe anyone other than himself could rescue Penelope.

Or was Milo wrong? Had Alan dropped clues that he was too dense to have noticed? He thought back. *I keep seeing those dots . . . there were other survivors . . . cabins on Grand Lake—Grand Estes . . . he got married to some sweet young thing . . . I wasn't planning to bomb . . . You don't even know their names, do you?*

Nothing pointed to anything. Or it all pointed to everything.

For the moment, none of this mattered. What mattered was Homeland Security and his father's people, and what they could do for him. Each time he heard footsteps in the stairwell, he waited for the banging on the door, then the inrush of agents. How would they do it? Would Simmons be with them? Would they take Milo and Yevgeny as well?

Yevgeny leaned close to Stephanie—who, wary of another pinch, pulled back—and said, "You've got something here."

"It's Magic Marker on her eyelids," Tina informed him.

"No," he said, and pulled something out from behind Stephanie's right ear. He opened his hand to reveal a rather beautiful bracelet made of five rows of polished agate stones. "How could you hear a thing?"

"Wow," said Stephanie, taking it carefully. She wasn't sure what to think.

"I heard you were making friends in Botswana," he told her. "So I told their ambassador that I knew a girl with a burgeoning interest in his beautiful country. I asked for advice on a gift. He made some calls and had this sent over in the diplomatic pouch, direct from Gaborone."

"Wow," Stephanie said again. "Thanks."

Milo thought, *I never told him about Stephanie's Botswana friend.*

She latched the bracelet onto her wrist while Milo brought out the serving bowl full of noodles and broth, to which he had added the chicken. Then came smaller dishes of vegetables, and another of a fish sauce concoction. "It looks good," Yevgeny admitted, before examining his hands and saying, "I had better clean myself."

"Use the small bathroom," Milo told him.

While his father was gone, Tina helped with silverware and asked if he was feeling all right.

"Sure, why not?"

"You're a little distant."

"I'm fine," he said and kissed her on the lips, thinking mawkishly that this could be their last kiss in a long while.

Once Yevgeny returned and gave Milo a significant nod, verifying that he would, according to the instructions in the letter, take Tina and Stephanie away tomorrow evening, he actually did feel better. He reminded himself again that the old man's failure with the fifteen-year-old really had been a different situation. This time, Milo was being smarter. He'd admitted to Yevgeny that he was under constant surveillance and told him to not speak of this until his girls were absolutely safe. He'd said only that the Chinese were involved but refused to go into details until he knew Tina and Stephanie could not be touched. Yevgeny seemed to understand everything, and the only sign of anxiety was the now more frequent swiping at his cheek.

The noodles went over remarkably well, and halfway through the meal Milo's phone bleeped a message. It was a single word from a private number: ROOF. He deleted the message, patted his napkin against his mouth, and rose. "Sorry, I've got to make a call. Be right back," he said and walked out of the apartment.

He found Leticia Jones standing in the center of the roof, smoking a menthol cigarette. It was a blessedly cool evening, and she wore a long black linen jacket that reached her calves, which were covered by leather boots. "Hey, baby," she said.

"Come on downstairs. My noodles are a hit."

She smiled, then stepped closer. "Sorry, I gotta see a guy about a thing."

"That's always the way."

"You are *cute*," she said, touching his cheek with her long, painted nails, knowing exactly how to keep a man off balance—or some men. To Milo, she was only growing more wearying. "But let's be serious, okay? I'm assuming you're in, or else you wouldn't have called."

"Yes."

"Would you like to tell me why?"

"Because I don't have a choice."

"I hope you don't think I'm forcing you into anything, Milo."

"You don't need to," he said, "Alan's already done that."

She nodded, perhaps understanding, then exhaled. "Well, it's this way. You'll go to Georgetown tomorrow for a two o'clock meeting with some people who want to talk to you."

"People like Nathan Irwin?" he asked, remembering what Xin Zhu had told him.

Leticia seemed to consider ignoring the question, but then cocked her head. "Somebody's been doing some thinking." She paused. "Unlike me, Irwin doubts conversions. Unlike me, that man don't like you. See what I mean?"

"Sure."

"You'll be there?"

"With bells on."

"Something for the imagination," she said, then gave him an address. She came closer and kissed his cheeks. "Take care of yourself, okay?"

Milo turned to open the roof-access door for her, but she was already walking off, stepping up onto the raised edge, and leaping down to the next rooftop. He wondered how many buildings she had to go before reaching a jimmied access door that would take her to the street.

When he returned to the table, Yevgeny was quizzing Tina about where she would like to live. "Anywhere in the world. Forget your job. Forget about money entirely. Where do you imagine is your ideal home?"

The question seemed to fluster her. "God, I don't know."

"Hawaii," said Stephanie.

"Excellent choice," said Yevgeny.

Milo said, "How about—"

"Not you," Yevgeny cut in. "You've seen too much anyway. I'd like to know what a sophisticated American woman dreams of."

Tina took the question seriously, pouring wine as she mulled it over, then said, "Costa Rica? That's supposed to be wonderful."

"Interesting," Yevgeny said approvingly.

"No," Tina said, shaking her head. "Geneva."

"Even better. You've never been to my apartment there, and I think that should be remedied."

"We're moving to Switzerland?" asked Stephanie.

Yevgeny smiled, looking at Milo, who didn't smile. He didn't like the idea of them hiding out in Yevgeny's Geneva home. It was *known*.

After dinner, Tina asked a question that, strangely, she had never posed before, "What do you *do* at the UN?"

"Milo knows this. I work for the financial section of the Security Council's Military Staff Committee."

"Which makes him an accountant," said Milo.

"Which makes me an administrator," Yevgeny said. "I'm a mess with numbers."

"So that's what you do?" Tina pressed. "You manage a team of accountants?"

"Something like that, but they're an excellent group, and they hardly need my attention. I have an enormous amount of free time."

"That's it? You check in with them occasionally, and travel in leisure the rest of the time?"

"Anyone would be lucky to have my job," Yevgeny said, aiming his words at Milo.

"I'm jealous," Tina said.

Yevgeny leaned across the table and placed his hand on hers. "Then leave this fool and run off with me."

"Can I bring Stef?"

Stephanie went to bed wearing her bracelet, and all three adults had a hand in tucking her in. Afterward, Milo brewed coffee, and Tina told Yevgeny about Alan and Penelope. She told everything she knew, which was little, and added that that afternoon she'd gone by their apartment on her lunch break.

"Why?" asked Milo.

"I still can't find her." To Yevgeny, she said, "But you know all this, right?"

Yevgeny looked at Milo, then shrugged.

"And?"

"And I'm in contact with people in London, looking into this. I don't think he's dead."

"Milo doesn't either."

"He walked out of that hotel."

"He used one of Milo's old work names," she said after a moment. "Why would he do that?"

"I don't know."

"Maybe he really has gone crazy."

Yevgeny considered that, as if it were an angle that hadn't occurred to him, then shook his head. "No, he's just American."

Tina blinked at him as Milo set down the cups. She said, "What does that mean?"

"Nothing really," he said. "It's just that Americans . . . well, they're distinctive in the developed world, aren't they?"

"Are we?"

Yevgeny smiled. "Of course. Your people still believe in Utopia. Maybe because it's part of your founding myth, the search for the perfect home. In the twenty-first century, Americans still think it's possible to have a society in which a level of civility is constant, where a perfect balance of control and freedom can be maintained. It's quaint. Try a few hundred years of war and civil strife on your own land, and see how much of your faith remains." He paused, but they were still waiting. "Alan Drummond's failures have shown him the flaws in his own utopian dreams, and that's a terrible thing to face. Traumatic. When it happens to America—when, for example, a small band of desert lunatics brings down two enormous towers, proving that America's sense of security was always an illusion—the country lashes out. It snaps. There's an irrational side to it, something wild. No one likes to be shown that their core beliefs are wrong, particularly when those illusions fuel their only happy dreams. So when America's dreams have been bruised, the nation comes on like an express train. God help anyone standing in its path."

Yevgeny reached for his glass, looking suddenly embarrassed. Milo remembered similar speeches from his teenaged years, living with him and his family in Moscow. Back then, he'd been adolescent and angry enough to fight the old man on every point. Now, Milo only said, "Well."

"As for Alan Drummond," Yevgeny said quickly, then cleared his throat. "I can only imagine that he's lashing out in a similar fashion, and believes in his fight so deeply that he's willing to drag others, like Milo, into it."

Milo tensed when he heard crashing footsteps on the stairs, but then he heard the voice of their neighbor, Raymond, coming home drunk. "Christ, that guy's loud," Tina said, reading half of his mind, then looked at Yevgeny. "That sounds a bit harsh."

Yevgeny blinked, confused.

"About America. Do you really think we're that naïve?"

"Maybe," he said, shrugging. "Milo's sister, Alexandra, thinks America is full of xenophobes. That's something I'd never suggest."

"It's the stupidest thing I've ever heard," Tina said definitively.

"Maybe you should invite her here. Show her what she's getting wrong."

Though she'd never met Milo's younger Russian sisters, Tina seemed to like that idea. Milo didn't. He'd spent too many years keeping that other life under wraps to be comfortable, even now that it was in the open, with Alexandra, the sharp London lawyer, invading his home. Alexandra had tried to insinuate herself a few years ago, meeting Milo at a restaurant and staking out her claim: She deserved to know about his life. Milo had done his best to make it clear: You're part of my old life; this is my new life. To her credit, she took it with good humor, even confessing, *Sometimes I wish I could do the same thing to our family. Kudos*. There was no antagonism—he had no fight with Alexandra or the younger Natalia—but he found the prospect of complicating his life by the addition of more family members unbearable. Having Yevgeny around was enough of a chore.

Now, though, he could tell that Tina needed this—she needed to know more about her husband's family—so he said, "Maybe I should give her a call."

Later, Milo walked Yevgeny down to Seventh Avenue, where Francisco was waiting. All Yevgeny said as they shook hands was "I know you didn't mean what you said up there, but you really should call your sister. She would appreciate it."

Milo just nodded.

In bed, he told Tina that he would have to go to D.C. in the morning, and that she would have to pick up Stephanie from camp. "Is that doable?"

"I'll find a way," she said quietly, then placed a hand on his chest. "Why D.C.?"

He'd considered saying that he had a job interview, which would have been easiest, but he was sick of lying to her. By being partly honest now, he could temper his guilt over the bigger lie she would discover once either Janet Simmons or Yevgeny appeared the next night to take them away. He said, "It's just a day trip, and it's to find out some more about Alan."

"Someone in D.C. knows?"

"I think so."

"Then he wasn't just crazy, was he? He was working with someone."

Though he admired the connection she'd just made, he wished she hadn't made it. "Anything's possible," he said. "Did you enjoy Yevgeny?"

"He's an oddball, but I like him. And I *do* like the idea of taking a vacation in Geneva. Don't you?"

"Who wouldn't?" he asked, though the last time he'd been in Geneva he'd fought another Tourist and tied him up in his hotel room. That same Tourist later killed fifteen-year-old Adriana Stanescu, and was then killed himself during Xin Zhu's annihilation of the department. Geneva was the last place he wanted to return to.

11

Milo took the subway to Penn Station and boarded the 10:00 A.M. Acela Express for D.C., thinking not of his destination but of the street corner he'd come from, where he'd taken Stephanie to day camp. Had she felt his anxiety? Had she noticed the lingering hug he'd given her, the one she'd had to push to escape from? He'd wanted to leave something for her, some small gift or word of warning, but anything out of the ordinary could lead to disaster, and so he'd plastered the smile to his face, kissed her, and sent her on her way.

The two-hour-and-forty-seven-minute journey was delayed by unexpected congestion around Philly, so that he arrived at Union Station at one thirty. He had to rush through the crowd for the Massachusetts Avenue exit. His taxi made good time until a forced detour around a demonstration along Virginia Avenue, and he reached the small, unassuming colonial on Potomac Street NW by ten after two.

The name on the front gate was Washington, and when he rang the bell, the gate was unlocked electrically without a word from inside. He walked up a small parcel of overgrown yard to the front steps and waited a moment to see if he needed to ring the doorbell—he didn't. It clicked and was pulled open by a small, tired-looking man he'd last seen—in the flesh, at least—looking ill as he came to terms with the fact that one of his aides had been a long-term agent for the Chinese, and that that single oversight had led to the deaths of thirty-three people—thirty-four, counting one of his other aides. This same man had also been responsible for the murders of two of Milo's friends: Angela Yates, CIA resident in Paris, and Tom Grainger, former Tourism Department head and Stephanie's godfather. He'd attempted to have Milo killed. Yet here he stood—Nathan Irwin, Minnesota Republican—still breathing and looking healthy. Perhaps sensing what Milo was thinking, Irwin said, "You're looking in remarkably good health."

"Well, I'm not dead."

"Get inside," said the senator, looking over Milo's shoulder in a nervous, awkward way.

The interior was modest, with a staircase directly in front of them, and a living room that looked like it had been decorated by a firm of elderly women with a love of art nouveau, but without the budget to achieve their dreams. "We're alone?"

Irwin shut the door. "Cut the bullshit, Milo. What's your game?"

"Are we alone, Nathan? Or are some of your aides floating around?"

Irwin winced—it was a childish jab, and cruel, considering how defeated Irwin had been after the discovery—but he recovered. "Of course we're not alone. We're never alone. Now, what are you up to?"

Milo wandered into the living room, stroking an elaborately printed chair, catching dust on his fingers. It was an unclean safe house. He said, "I want to know what happened to Alan, and Leticia says the only way I can learn that is to help you out."

"But you said no to that."

"Have you never changed your mind?"

"Never," Irwin said, but when Milo looked at his face, he was smiling. Then the smile went away. "What I want to know is why you changed your mind. We've got you pretty well profiled, Milo. You're as simple as any putz on the street. You like your comfort. You like your family. Now that you've finally got both of those things again, I don't think you would throw them away. Because throwing them away is precisely what you'd be doing, at least temporarily."

Milo said nothing for a moment. He had reached a china cabinet and found a collection of ceramic pigs from around the world staring back at him with a broad variety of expressions. "Why does any of this matter?" he said finally. "I'm here to help. It's not like you have an army behind you anymore. It can't be easy putting something this big together."

"It matters," said Irwin. "First of all, you have no idea how big or small this operation is. Maybe Leticia's our only asset."

"You've also got José Santiago and Tran Hoang."

A loud exhale. "She tell you that?"

"You've got three Tourists, but now Alan's gone missing. You're in a bind. What you could really use is a new administrator, and I've got the experience."

"So now you don't just want to help out. You want to run the operation."

"Do you have someone else on hand? Do you have someone else who has experience dealing with Xin Zhu?"

"You never actually met the man."

"Are you working with anyone who has?"

Irwin still hadn't moved from the entryway but was leaning against the banister leading up to the second floor. He looked older than he did on television, but Milo expected that this was true of everyone. The lighting here wasn't advantageous, and there was no makeup team. The truth was that Irwin looked terrified—which, Milo thought, he should be.

"The problem," Irwin said, "is that for you to run the operation, you'd have to know its whole scope, and I'm certainly not ready for that."

Milo had expected resistance—in fact, he'd expected more. Yet he knew from Xin Zhu that Irwin was just one of three players with a hand in this operation, and so Irwin's vote was not definitive. Milo said, "Tell me, then. What role did you imagine for me?"

"I imagined nothing. Leticia brought you in. You're here now so that these sorts of decisions can be made."

"By you?"

Another smile cracked the senator's features; then he nodded at the stairs. "Come on."

It was a narrow staircase, and along the wall were three framed photographs of small children, black-and-whites from the late fifties or early sixties. Milo wondered who they were, but didn't ask; he doubted Irwin knew. At the top, they turned left and entered a small bedroom in the rear of the house, but there was no bed, just a table and four wooden chairs, and tightly laced curtains covering the window. There had been a bed—an imprint remained in the carpet—and there was a dresser and an old vanity, but he noticed all this later. Upon entering, his attention was taken by the well-dressed middle-aged woman sitting at the table with a plastic bottle of Evian. Her hands were crossed in her lap. She watched Milo enter, then stood up, offering a hand. "Hello, Mr. Weaver. My name is Dorothy Collingwood."

Of the National Clandestine Service, he thought as he took her small hand, but he said, "You're not a senator, too, are you?"

She laughed lightly. "Please! I wouldn't take Nathan's job for all the gold in Christendom."

"Then you must be Company."

"I must be," she said, smiling, and returned to her chair. "Actually, I'm NCS."

He felt odd, standing in a dusty Georgetown bedroom with a well-regarded politician and a Company official. Irwin had been in Washington for nearly fifteen years, and he imagined that Collingwood was relatively new to her job—he'd never heard her name before. He wondered if she'd gotten in over her head.

"Is this it?" asked Milo. "Just the two of you?"

"There's a third," said Collingwood, "but he couldn't make it."

Stuart Jackson, Milo thought.

Collingwood waved at the chairs, and Milo sat to her left. Irwin sat across from Milo, to her right. Milo said, "I'm here to help. With Alan gone, you've got to be hurting."

"Do you think we're hurting?" Collingwood asked, but she was looking at Irwin, who shook his head. "Nathan thinks we're doing fine. So you can go home."

Milo looked at her a moment, then at Irwin, who stared passively until, unexpectedly, his left eye twitched. It meant nothing beyond the fact that this was a man under a lot of stress. Milo said, "Leticia thinks differently."

"People on the ground always do," said Collingwood. "You've been around long enough to know that." She took a long drink of her Evian.

"She asked for my help."

"Without consulting us," said Irwin.

Milo was no longer sure why he was here. He knew why *he* was here, but not why they had bothered to meet him. "It's up to you," he said. "I'm just puzzled. I understand Alan. He was personally humiliated by Xin Zhu, and he became obsessed with revenge. You, too," he said to Irwin, "to a degree. Xin Zhu planted someone in your office, so you can't feel very good about that. But you," he said to Collingwood, then paused. "I may be wrong, but I doubt you also have a personal gripe with Xin Zhu. You're approached by a man—Alan, I assume—who's been made unstable by his desire for revenge and . . . and what? You actually decide to go along with it?" He shook his head to show how ridiculous that was. "I don't know what you're doing here."

"So that's your narrative?" she asked after a moment. "A simple tale of revenge, a boy's game of tit for tat?"

"An eye for an eye," Irwin suggested.

Neither said anything for a moment, waiting, until Milo said, "So it's a lot bigger than revenge."

"Of course it is," said Collingwood.

"And you're not going to tell me."

She shook her head. Irwin just stared.

Collingwood said, "Listen, Mr. Weaver. What you see here—a couple of bureaucratic monsters running some agents from a dusty room—that's only part of the story. We didn't originate it; we inherited it. Now we're here to help wrap up the storyline. Do you understand?"

"Not really," he said. Irwin, he knew, had come into the world of espionage via his position on the Senate Committee on Homeland Security and Governmental Affairs. However, senators and ranking CIA officers didn't sit around in dusty safe houses—they hired other people to do that. The people who populated safe houses were there to protect the identities of politicians and ranking officers who were pulling the strings; in this case, the situation was reversed. Whatever was going on here, these people were desperate to keep it to a select group, which didn't yet include Milo.

"Sorry for the mystery," she said, "but that's all you're getting. Now it's your turn to explain yourself."

Milo had spent most of the train ride going over his own narrative, because that's all this was—a narrative. As with any interrogation there needed to be a surface storyline and an underlying one. Ideally, a third one would make it more convincing, but he didn't think he would need that. "I didn't want to get involved," he said. "I think you both know that. Alan tried to bring me in before he ran off. Then, when I talked to Leticia, she tried as well."

"And you said no both times," Irwin pointed out.

"Of course. I don't like this world. I haven't for a long time. Nevertheless, I didn't realize Alan would be so persistent. He made sure the decision was out of my hands."

"The name," said Collingwood.

Irwin said, "What name?"

"The one he used in London before he disappeared," Milo said. "It was my old work name, in Tourism."

Irwin looked over at Collingwood; this was news to him.

Milo said, "He used a name that is known to both the Germans and the Chinese, known to be mine. Eventually, one or the other country is going to start pointing in my direction."

"Then take a vacation," said Collingwood, matter-of-factly. "Pack up your family and rent someplace in

Florida for a few weeks, until this blows over. I can give you some phone numbers."

Irwin rocked his head. "It's an idea, Milo."

Milo smiled grimly. "Sure. I'll skip town and leave it to the two of you. To Leticia and José and Hoang. I'm sure that, after a couple of weeks, you will have bent over backward to make sure I'm not part of the fallout when whatever you're doing explodes."

Collingwood said, "Nathan, I do believe he doesn't trust us."

"If I'm in," Milo continued, "there's a chance that I can control the damage so that my family remains untouched."

Milo waited while Irwin bobbed his eyebrows and Collingwood took another drink of water. After a moment, she said, "So you'd like us to bring you in, simply so that you can protect yourself?"

"And his family," said Irwin. "Never forget his family."

"That's part of the reason," said Milo. "The other part is that I can help you."

"Of course he can," Irwin said, a little loudly. "He's the finest Tourist ever produced! A prince among men!"

Milo gave him a look, then turned back to Collingwood. "I know Xin Zhu better than anyone on your team. I've had access to reports you haven't seen. I know how he thinks."

Irwin said, "That didn't save all those Tourists, did it?"

"That was a lack of information. I wasn't told that his son had been killed in Sudan. Had I known, we could have saved them."

"What about these reports?" asked Collingwood. "Why haven't we seen them?"

"Because it's not American material. I got them from my father."

"Yevgeny Primakov," Collingwood said to Irwin. "He runs that UN department we were talking about."

Milo blinked at her. His father's intelligence arm was, or was supposed to be, completely secret. Was it a surprise that they both knew about it? He wasn't sure.

"Could we use your father?" asked Collingwood.

"I could ask," Milo lied.

Irwin exhaled loudly. "This is idiotic," he said to Collingwood. "We both know Milo's a bad seed."

Collingwood smiled. "Did you really say 'bad seed'?"

"The child of a KGB officer and a Marxist terrorist? The very *definition* of a bad seed."

"Right," Collingwood said, still smiling.

That they knew about his father was one thing, but Milo, perhaps naively, was surprised that they knew about his mother.

His face must have been an open book, for Irwin said, "Come on, Milo. That's never been a secret from the Company. Hell, it's why you were recruited in the first place, right out of college. I've seen your file. You had lying in your genes. They wanted to make sure you lied for us, not for someone else. Isn't that right, Dorothy?"

Collingwood shrugged. "That's what the files say."

He tried to hide his growing surprise. He shook his head, desperate to change the subject. "The point is that, liar or not, we all know that I could help make sure this is a success. I just need to know more about what's going on."

Collingwood brushed a strand of hair behind her ear. "Well, what do you want to know?"

"What happened to Alan."

"Nathan?" she said.

Irwin shook his head. In the dim light his cheeks looked flushed, and Milo finally understood that Irwin was not the alpha in this room. Collingwood was. She was calling the shots. Revenge truly was not the point of their plans.

"It's a problem," Irwin said finally. "We don't know."

"You don't know what happened to Alan?"

"He's off the grid. He walked. We don't know why."

"What was he supposed to do?"

"Meet with someone, then reconnect with Leticia."

"Meet with who?" Milo asked, though he knew the answer was Gephel Marpa.

Irwin looked at Collingwood and said, "I'm *not* telling him that. Not yet."

"Fair enough," she said.

Milo said, "If you want me to ask my father for information, I'll need to have a story for him. You can't keep me entirely in the dark."

"You have your story already," she said, looking at him. "Revenge. It's not unheard of, you know."

"So I get nothing? I work entirely blind?"

"Consider Leticia your seeing-eye dog," she said. "Although I'd like to believe you, I know what excellent liars you Tourists are, and I'd be a fool to take you at face value. Leticia knows as much as she needs to know, and she'll share what's necessary. You'll meet her tomorrow at JFK, Terminal Three. Eight in the morning, and you come as a blank slate. Can you do that?"

He nodded.

Collingwood said, "Tonight we'll decide on the depth of your involvement, and by tomorrow she'll know how to use you. What are you going to tell your family?"

"Flying to San Francisco for an interview."

Collingwood raised her eyebrows. "You think your wife would want to relocate?"

"She's amenable."

"Tomorrow, then," she said and stood, offering her hand again. Milo took it.

Irwin walked him downstairs and, at the door, said, "Don't fuck us on this, Milo. The bricks will fall directly on your head."

Replies to that awfully mixed metaphor occurred to him, but he pressed them down, stuffing them into that box in the back room of his head. He trotted down the front steps and flagged a taxi that was cruising down the street. He climbed into the back, saying, "Union Station," as he pulled the door shut. It wasn't until the taxi was moving again that he noticed the driver's face. It was Dennis Chaudhury.

"Shit," said Milo.

"Just transporting today," Chaudhury said as he took a turn onto another street. "I told you not to call him, didn't I?"

"Yes, you did."

"Sorry, then," he said, "but you're supposed to tell me what happened at the meeting."

Milo watched colonial houses pass by. "Well, I'm in. Tomorrow I meet up with Leticia Jones at JFK."

"To go where?"

"I don't know."

"Really?" he asked, peering in the rearview.

"Really."

"Don't tell me that's all you know."

"I know what happened to Alan."

"Aha!" said Chaudhury, sounding pleased. "Do tell."

"He was supposed to meet with Gephel Marpa on another floor, then meet with Leticia. He didn't do either. He walked out. They don't know where he is."

Chaudhury exhaled, frowning at the road. "That's odd."

"No, it isn't."

Chaudhury looked at him in the mirror, waiting.

"Alan had only two options. He could continue to work for Xin Zhu, or he could remove himself completely from the equation. He assumed that, without having him in hand, Xin Zhu wouldn't touch his wife, which was the only thing he cared about."

Chaudhury stopped at a traffic light, staring ahead and saying nothing until the light changed and they were moving again, and then it was only to ask the details of the meeting. Those in attendance, which room it occurred in, and if it was recorded. Milo answered everything honestly—he had no idea about the recording, though he suspected it hadn't been. When they were close to Union Station, Chaudhury said, "What's your take?"

"Whatever they're doing, they're terrified of it getting out. It'll be a while before I'm let in on the secret, if ever."

Chaudhury tossed an iPhone over the seat; Milo caught it. "Keep this on you," he said, passing over a charging cord as well, "and when he calls, you had better answer."

Milo caught the 4:00 P.M. return train, and a little before five, as they were approaching Wilmington, he called Tina, who was at home with Stephanie. They'd ordered delivery Chinese, with an extra dish of kung pao chicken for him. "It'll be clotty and cold by the time you get here."

"Just how I like it."

"You find out anything about Alan?"

"Not much. I'll tell you when I get back," he said, though he doubted he would tell her anything, because she and Stephanie would not be there. They would either be with Janet Simmons, or—and, preferably, he realized—with Yevgeny. They would be safe, and he could finally be free to do whatever he needed in order to assure their continued safety. One thing at a time, though. "Have you found Penelope?"

"No," she said.

"And the eyes?" he asked.

"Eyes?"

"You know."

"Oh, right. I see traces," she said, and in the background, Stephanie said, "Stop looking at my eyes!"

He fully expected his new phone to ring sometime during the ride, but it was his old one that rang a little after six, with an unlisted number. Hesitantly, he answered it. "Hello?"

"Milo! It's Billy. I've got some good news for you."

"Billy?"

"Billy Morales. Redman Transcontinental."

He didn't know if laughing would be appropriate, so he just said, "Right. Hello, Billy."

"Now you've got it. Listen, if you're still on the market, we've got an attractive offer on the table for you. It may require a little more travel than you were interested in, but if you take a look—"

"Billy," Milo said. "Do you mind if I call you back tomorrow? I'm kind of busy now."

"Well, sure," Morales said, sounding vaguely confused. "Listen, if you're getting offers elsewhere you can be up front about it with me. You know that. Redman knows how to negotiate."

"That's not it, Billy. Trust me. Tomorrow?"

"Roger," Morales said, and Milo hung up.

Milo reached Penn Station at six forty-five. He took the subway to Park Slope, rocking monotonously with other passengers-of-many-nations, thinking of Gabi's excitement over the international face of this city. She was right to love it.

At Garfield Place, he checked the street for watchers, found none, then climbed the stairs. Though he heard the quiet murmur of a television from Raymond's door, at his own he heard silence. No television, no talking, no walking. The door was unlocked. He shut it behind himself and said, "Girls?" There was no answer. It was twenty minutes before eight o'clock.

He took a breath, leaning against the door as he locked the bolt. This was what he had wanted, what he had planned for, but there was no satisfaction. No matter that they knew their captor, and that they knew Milo had arranged their abduction, they had to be scared. That was normal; it was *human*. Now, he could move forward. He could be open with the senators. He could—and this seemed the only option—play a double game against Zhu.

It was during this momentary rush of optimism that he smelled it in the air. Mixed into the fragrance of soy sauce and his kung pao chicken, a vague odor of shit and, beneath it, sulfur. He let go of the front door and stepped slowly forward. As he left the foyer, the living room opened up, coming into view. Everything was correct—the television, the tables, the chairs—but in the middle of the room, lying with his head turned to the side in a pool of blood soaking into the gray rug, was his father, a look of surprise on the visible half of his face.

His throat closed, hardening, and he couldn't swallow. He waited, forcing the air into his lungs, holding onto the wall. Closed his eyes; opened them. The old man was still there.

Before approaching the body, Milo ran without noise to the bedrooms and bathroom, checking behind doors and under beds until, sure that the place was empty, he returned to the living room and gingerly touched Yevgeny's neck. Ignoring the stink from his postdeath bowel movement, he slid his hand down the back of Yevgeny's shirt to check his temperature; there was still a trace of warmth. The Tourist part of him thought, *This happened minutes ago.* The human part of him was back in a claustrophobic Moscow living room, at the beginning of his stay, listening to a KGB colonel laugh at a joke his teenaged son had just butchered in his grammar-school Russian.

Compartmentalization was failing him; he could feel it. He got to his feet and stepped back and stood straight against a door frame, as if the building could support him, and wiped away the tears. He didn't want to sit because he feared he would never be able to rise again. He took out his cell phone and looked at it through blurred vision, then put it away again. There was no one to call. If Janet Simmons had collected his family, then she would call when they were safe. Was waiting the only option?

No. He could assemble facts. That's what you did in situations like this—you gathered facts from witnesses.

He carefully stepped out into the corridor and went to Raymond's door. The television was still on. He knocked three times, then did it again, louder. He listened, wondering if his neighbor was passed out drunk again, then checked the door—it was locked. Milo withdrew. Even if Raymond had heard something, he wouldn't have heard enough to tell Milo who had them.

He shoved two pieces of Nicorette into his mouth and returned to his apartment, chewing vigorously. He skirted past Yevgeny's body and went into the kitchen. There was vodka, but he limited himself to a single shot to take the edge off. By the time he set the empty glass down, his eyes were drenched again. He wiped at them, trying to remember his training, thinking that if he had to try to remember it, then it was of no use to him anymore.

Yevgeny had come to take them away. That much he understood. Had he gathered them, only to be attacked by Zhu's men? Or had he come late, after Simmons had removed them, and stumbled upon Zhu's men picking over the place, wondering what had happened?

He dialed Tina's number. A melody cut through the silence, and he found her Nokia on an arm of the sofa. Then, unsure why, he called Penelope Drummond. Her phone, he was told, either was outside the network range or turned off.

That's when he heard another phone ring, and at first he thought it was Yevgeny's. He took two steps toward the corpse before realizing it was coming from his own pocket. He took out the iPhone and, without checking the display, answered it. "Where are they?"

A pause, then Xin Zhu's voice said, "Out of the way."

"Do you have them?"

"They're not with me right now, if that's what you mean."

Milo opened his mouth, but forced himself not to say the words that had formed in the back of his throat: *You're a dead man now.* Xin Zhu seemed to understand his position, for he said, "Now, please don't engage in outrage, or threats, or anything you'll later regret. You've only brought this upon yourself, Mr. Weaver."

Dizziness set in, and the sickness he'd been holding back spread through his body. "This wasn't necessary."

"It was, and you know it. Mr. Drummond proved that. All you need to know now is that the orders I give you are to be followed without hesitation. Are we clear?"

"Yes."

"Good," Xin Zhu said. "Now get rid of the phone and go do your job."

12

He arrived at JFK's Terminal Three, with its distinctive flying saucer roof, just before eight in the morning. He was a blank slate. He'd left behind all his papers, his wallet, his phone, and cut the tags out of his navy suit. All he carried was a folded stack of cash and two blister packs of Nicorette. When he climbed out of the taxi, he had to pause to avoid getting hit by porters, uniformed police, and fellow travelers. It took him a moment to get his bearings because airports, where he had once felt at home, were now anathema to him. Leticia Jones was already approaching with a sultry smile.

"Hey, baby," she said, kissing his cheeks. She looked perky in her striped business skirt as she led him by the elbow through the initial security check and into the airy but crowded terminal.

"Where to?" he asked, though he had trouble finding the breath to speak.

She walked him to one of the departure screens, full of the world's cities. "You choose."

"What?"

"How about Vegas?" she said, noting a nine thirty flight.

He turned to stare at her. He knew how he looked—knew that his eyes were a mess—but didn't give a damn.

"Boston, then?" she suggested. "Cancún?"

"What the hell's going on?"

"No," she said after a moment. "I think Mexico City will do quite nicely."

They stood in line at the Delta counter. Behind them, a family chatted merrily about terrorists, while ahead of them a trio of Mexican businessmen exchanged occasional words in Spanish, but Milo and Leticia said nothing to one another. Milo watched faces. It didn't take long to spot Chaudhury, clutching a newspaper beside a family camped around their luggage. There might have been more, but his vision wasn't cooperating; it blurred over every few seconds. The same was true of his thoughts, and he found himself thinking that, had he known then what he knew now, he would have killed Chaudhury in D.C.

When they reached the counter, Leticia opened her small purse and took out two well-thumbed passports. "Two for the nine thirty-five to Mexico City."

"You have reservations?" asked the clerk, a diminutive brunette with olive skin.

"It's under Frederickson," she said and nodded at Milo. "That's him." She leaned across the counter, and in a high whisper added, "*He's in a mood today.*"

Like you wouldn't believe, he thought.

The clerk suppressed a grin, then checked their passports—Gwendolyn Davis and Sam Frederickson—and printed out boarding passes. "Any luggage to check?"

"Just us," said Leticia, then grabbed Milo's arm. "Come on, honey."

While they waited in the winding line for security, he saw Chaudhury with a cell phone to his ear, calling in their status. Leticia seemed to notice him staring, so he said, "You reserved the tickets."

"You gotta reserve," she said. "This plane's always full."

"What if I'd said Cancún?"

She smiled. "Mr. Frederickson made a lot of reservations for this morning."

They made it smoothly through security, and as they were slipping their shoes back on Milo said, "Should I be confused?"

"Well, I hope so."

They reached Gate 5 a little before nine, but there was no space for them to sit, so they leaned against a column. Milo's damaged intestine was speaking to him in the coagulated voice of despair, and he was sure he couldn't pull this off. He couldn't sit in a plane with Leticia Jones and fly to Mexico. The only thing he could conceivably do was lie on the hard floor, close his eyes, and die. Would that save them? He didn't know, but he suspected it might. Then Leticia said, "Chill out, baby. You act like you've never been on a plane before."

"I'd just like to know what's going on."

"So you can report it to your masters in Beijing?"

It was a sign of his utter incompetence that he stared at her hard for a whole second, shocked, and he read in her face the slight turn in mood that told him it had been a joke that, perhaps, was no longer a joke. She was wondering if she was going to have to kill him. He said, "What are you talking about?"

"Lighten up and just play along," she said, then again looked down the busy corridor.

"You're waiting for someone."

"Maybe someone will come, maybe not."

When boarding began, they joined the cattle-rush of passengers, stuck somewhere in the middle of the sweating horde, and once they were a couple of passengers from the front Leticia tugged his sleeve and said, "Time to go." Docilely, he followed her out of the crowd and to the other side of the terminal, where they stood in another line at Dunkin' Donuts and bought coffees and croissant sandwiches. He picked at his food, knowing that he wouldn't be able to keep it down, for it just reminded him of the scent of Chinese food in the apartment, and then everything else.

They sat at Gate 12, which was mostly empty, and ignored the announcement calls for their passport names. Finally, the Mexico City flight took off, and they left through security. There was no sign of Chaudhury. They waited at a taxi stand, and when they got into a cab Leticia asked for Union Square Park. The driver, a light-skinned North African, turned on the meter and called in the ride, but when they reached Queens Boulevard Leticia handed him a fifty and asked him to take them instead to Port Morris, in the Bronx, but to keep it quiet from the dispatch. It took him two seconds of reflection to accept her proposal.

Though buses were the obvious next mode of transportation from Port Morris, it turned out that Leticia had left a hybrid Ford Escape a couple of streets inland. It was just after eleven.

Only once they were driving did she decide to relieve the tension. "We're not flying out until after seven, so don't worry yourself, but I hope you saw those shadows in the airport. You did, didn't you?"

"An Indian guy," said Milo.

"And . . . ?"

He blinked at her. "Is this a test?"

"There was a white chick with him. I doubt I lost them—at least, I hope not—but I think we're being pretty convincing."

"Who are they?"

"Chinese, probably, but maybe Homeland's gotten wind of something." She sniffed, and he wondered if that was a pointed remark. Had his call to Janet Simmons been heard by everyone? But she only said, "It's best we assume the Chinese."

"Leticia?"

"Yeah, baby?"

"Where the hell are we going?"

"We're going for a bite and a drink. Couldn't you use one?"

She drove up the Major Deegan Expressway and

then across the Hamilton and Washington bridges to reach New Jersey, where she took Bergen Boulevard down to North Bergen, full of heavy redbrick buildings and shops. She turned off the main drag beside the park and finally pulled up at a corner Mexican restaurant called Puerto Vallarta, which was busy with a lunchtime crowd. She'd called ahead and reserved a seat under the name Jenny.

As they were seated, Leticia asked for a pitcher of margaritas. "Smile, baby," she told Milo, but he thought he might explode. He thought that if she made another joke he would smash his head against the table until he bled. Maybe that would cut through the black, dizzying funk that had invaded him as he sat beside his father's body in his living room. He drank two more shots of vodka from the bottle, looking at the old man's matted hair and the loose skin on his fingers, trying to escape his memories and regrets and focus on what this meant, and what it required of him.

When the pitcher came, she filled his glass and said, "Drink up now. It's gonna be dry as hell where we're going."

He raised his head at that. It was a hint, but he didn't bother speculating aloud. He sipped his margarita, then, like a man just out of the desert, poured it down his throat until it was nearly empty. Either it would help him or it would kill him. That was how he was starting to see the world.

"I think your doctor would frown on that," she said, slipping a straw into her glass.

He took a long look at her, his first sustained gaze that day. He'd been a Tourist himself, and knew that everything she showed him—the cool exterior, the impeccable beauty, the style and the humor—was simply for show. There was another woman just beneath the surface. A killer, yes, but someone who had been born to a home and been a child and a teen and a young adult, someone who had ended up in a world that most people would run from. She'd had her chance to leave when the department had crumbled, but she hadn't taken it. He said, "Why'd you come back?"

She didn't have to ask what he was talking about. "What else am I gonna do?"

"I've seen you in action—you could do a lot," he said. "And don't tell me you haven't thought about it. Every Tourist keeps an escape plan on ice. Somewhere, you've stashed another name and a bundle of cash."

She wasn't going to deny it; there was no point. A Tourist without an escape route wasn't much of a Tourist. "Maybe I'm afraid of boredom," she said finally. Then she asked, "You know what I did before this?"

"Tell me."

"I was teaching English, if you can believe it. In Hong Kong."

"You know Mandarin?"

"That must have been on the recruiter's mind."

"But that's not enough," he said after a moment, and it felt better, just a little, to think about this and not himself. "Something in your history tipped them off. Did you murder someone?"

"Nearly," she said, thinking briefly about whatever story lay behind that one word. "No, no corpses littering my past. But I was involved with some . . . *ladies* in the Bay Area. I think I made my character clear there—I tried to get them to go militant. One of them, it turned out, was from the Company."

That answer demanded more questions, but he only said, "You've got other talents. You should walk away from this. Go figure out what you really want to do."

She seemed to seriously consider that, then said, "What happens if, after a few months, I realize that *this* is the only thing I want to do?"

"Well, it means you need to see a shrink."

"Has that helped you?"

It was a jab at his and Tina's couples therapy, and he wondered how and why she knew about it. "It's a way to pass the time," he said.

"And keep the wife off your back."

The impulse to smash his head into the table swelled again.

He had known from the start that he would have to move his father. A corpse in the middle of the living room would, within days, attract attention, particularly in that heat wave. Like a Tourist, he'd thought in terms of time and decomposition, not in terms of parenthood.

He first searched the body, wallet with credit cards, frequent-flier cards, and hundreds of dollars and euros, which he pocketed. There was a passport, two phones, restaurant receipts, and a small sheet of paper with a single typewritten line, in capitals:

THEY ARE SAFE

Which, of course, was the note that Yevgeny had planned to leave for Milo, the note that never even made it out of his pocket.

It took a while, for though Yevgeny Primakov had lost weight in recent years, and more from blood leaked from the holes in his heart and his right lung, he had died a solid man with a barrel chest; he was heavy. Grunting, Milo finally got him into his arms and, like a groom with his bride, carried him into his and Tina's bedroom. The springs protested from the sudden weight. Milo sat on the edge of the bed a moment and then, inexplicably, lay down beside his father's corpse. He wanted to think clearly, to wash away all the distractions that provoked panic, for panic was what Xin Zhu was depending on. Panic was what stuttered his thinking, interrupting it every forty seconds with an image of two more corpses on this bed, scattering his thoughts into the stratosphere.

That image came back to him now, over his pork enchiladas, but in his brief vision their bodies were not in a bed but in a forest, or a park, mangled and twisted among branches. He pushed his plate away.

Leticia was halfway through her own enchiladas, which were filled with refried beans and cheese. She frowned at him. "You don't like them?"

"Had a big breakfast," he said, then refilled his glass with margarita.

They left at three thirty and took the traffic-clogged

Route 1 to Newark Liberty International. Leticia parked in the short-term lot for Terminal C, and as she used a spare T-shirt to wipe off the seats and the dashboard and the steering wheel, Milo sighed. "Someone got their car stolen, just so we could get some Mexican food?"

His comment seemed to annoy her. She tossed the keys down by the gas pedal, got out, and shut the door with her elbow. She walked on, not bothering to check if he was following.

Once they were inside, she gave him another nugget of information about their dry destination. "We're going to Saudi Arabia."

"Okay," he said after a moment. "Can you be more specific?"

"Jeddah, okay? We've got a meeting. That's all you're getting now."

They stood in line, and again Leticia took over, handing over passports. Rosa Mumu, Sudanese, and John Nadler, Canadian. They already had reservations for the 7:25 Continental flight to Frankfurt, landing the next morning at 9:15, as well as the 12:30 Lufthansa flight from Frankfurt to Jeddah, and upon learning this Milo felt a brief tingle of possibility. Three hours in Frankfurt could be very useful.

In the line for security, they compared notes—there was no sign of Chaudhury or the "white chick" Leticia had seen at JFK. She seemed disappointed by this, and when he pressed, she let out a little more. "Well, you know, it just bothers me. To think we're going through all this, and whoever they are might be so stupid as to assume we actually went to Mexico."

"If it's Homeland, they don't need to follow us. They just watch from the cameras."

"Yeah. *If*," she said. "Anyway, there's time. Once they realize the plane landing in Mexico City doesn't have us, they've got four hours to figure out where we are. If they can't get the job done in that amount of time, then they're not worth wasting our time with."

He waited for more, but there was nothing she wanted to add.

It wasn't until they were waiting at the gate, Milo nearly passing out, that he felt her elbow nudge his ribs. She was smiling. "You see *that*?"

He did. It was Dennis Chaudhury, strolling up the aisle with his newspaper. He settled in another chair at their gate, as if he were a complete stranger.

"Oh, *well*," she said as Chaudhury opened a copy of the day's *Times*. "The cojones on that man."

"Want me to get rid of him?" Milo asked, stifling a yawn.

"Certainly not." Then, giving him a look, she added, "Baby, I don't think you *could* get rid of him if you wanted. You've had one too many margaritas."

"As you command," he said, then climbed to his feet. "I'll just be a minute."

He knew she was watching him, half expecting him to approach Chaudhury. Yet he didn't have to approach the man to have a chat. He walked directly to the bathroom without looking around and, just inside, waited. A bald man was washing his hands, then left. Ten seconds later, Chaudhury entered, the newspaper folded under his arm.

That Chaudhury had no idea what awaited him was apparent in the fact that he wasn't ready for Milo's lunging kick into his stomach. It took all his failing strength, but the shot was true, hitting him squarely in the stomach, his toes perhaps even bruising the man's ribs. Chaudhury stumbled back, and Milo snatched one of his floundering hands and swung him deeper into the bathroom, where he stumbled and slid across the floor, on his back, gasping. Milo also stumbled but regained his balance and dropped onto Chaudhury with his elbows down, one in his stomach, the other in his face, connecting with his jaw. Milo ached all over, but Chaudhury was bleeding now, disoriented. Milo climbed up, straddled him, and sat on his chest, then pounded a fist into his temple. He did it a second time before Chaudhury got out a single word: "Stop!"

It was a word Milo wasn't able to conjure up himself, but once it was out in the air he realized, even running solely on adrenaline, that it was the only thing to do. Kill him, and everything would evaporate, including his family. Milo breathed heavily, staring at the tiled walls, as if the man between his legs didn't exist. His mouth hung open, saliva dripping down his chin. He climbed to his feet and walked to the tile wall and leaned back against it. He watched Chaudhury slowly, achingly, climb to his feet and limp to the sinks. As the noise of running water filled the bathroom, Chaudhury said, "You made a fucking mistake, Milo Weaver."

"He'll understand."

"Pretty presumptuous."

Milo watched him wash his mouth and face and stare with dismay at his reflection. "You don't have any idea, do you?"

"About what?" Chaudhury asked, angry.

"He's got them."

Chaudhury had a finger in his mouth, massaging his gums. He looked in the reflection at Milo, confused. "Who?"

"And my father's dead."

Chaudhury drew his finger out of his mouth; it was wet and pink. "You're talking about your family."

Milo didn't answer. He walked over to the urinals, unzipped, and began to pee.

"Look, Milo, that wasn't me. He Qiang—that's the guy who would've done it."

Milo stared at his clear stream. "You're telling me his name?"

"What the fuck do I care? I'm a private contractor. He's one of Xin's men. He's the one with the philosophy."

"Tell me more," Milo said as he put himself away and zipped up.

"Can't tell you what I don't know." Chaudhury leaned close to the mirror, touching the side of his eye. "He Qiang brings the orders and pays the fees. I know of the man I'm working for—Xin Zhu—but I've never met him. And I like it that way."

Milo left the urinals and ran water in the sink beside Chaudhury, rinsing his hands. "Description?"

"He Qiang? Big guy, heavy but not fat. How do you describe a Chinese face? Round, slant-eyed. Mole on his cheek that needs trimming."

Milo used paper towels to dry his hands, then walked out.

Leticia was watching him intently as he crossed back to the gate, yawning into the back of his hand. The adrenaline was fading, leaving him wasted. He crashed down beside her.

"*So?*" Leticia asked.

"So I peed. Where's the guy?"

"He's in the bathroom, you idiot!"

Milo widened his eyes, then pointed at where he'd come from. "*That* bathroom?"

"What the hell are you up to?"

Milo shook his head in feigned surprise, then nodded. "Oh, look. There he is."

As a flight attendant announced that Continental Flight 50 to Frankfurt would soon commence boarding, Chaudhury walked swiftly and purposefully out of the bathroom, and though his skin was dark, there was a definite redness on the left side of it. His eyes were watery and bloodshot, and he was pressing a wet paper towel to the side of his mouth. The red spots on the white paper were visible from where they sat. Then he did something that Milo hadn't expected—he left. He turned away from the gate and walked away.

"That's weird," said Milo.

Quickly, Leticia snatched his right wrist and raised it, turning his hand around to better see the bright red, slightly swollen knuckles. With a disgusted sound, she threw it down again. "Idiot."

"You want them to follow us, right?"

"That's the idea."

"Well, now they'll be sure to have someone waiting in Jeddah. And just so you know, they are Chinese."

She gave him a look that suggested—what? That she was impressed? That she was about to kill him? He had no idea, but in the tired euphoria that followed what he'd done he didn't care. He had a name, He Qiang, that went with a face he'd seen outside his daughter's summer camp, and he had a new possibility in Frankfurt. He felt more like a Tourist every moment.

13

He had eight hours to think. It was, objectively, plenty of time to find answers, or at least to reorient himself and place things in their proper perspective. However, by the time they landed at Frankfurt at ten in the morning, forty-five minutes late, nothing felt *better* in any sense of the word. Clearer, perhaps, but no better.

As they had begun to soar up the Atlantic coast, Milo had taken a short nap, because by then it was required. He'd gotten no sleep with his father's corpse lying beside him on his bed, and a day of skipping around the metro area with Leticia and too many margaritas had pummeled him no less than the final exertion of beating Dennis Chaudhury. As Leticia plugged into the airline's entertainment system, he closed his eyes and was soon asleep. And in a park. Holding his daughter's hand, then running with her.

"You need another drink, baby?" Leticia asked when he woke with a start, swinging his hands.

Airplane. Leticia. Atlantic far below. A drink was the last thing he needed. He closed his eyes again and tried to think rationally. Like a Tourist.

His most urgent goal was to divide everything into what he did know, what he suspected, and what he did not know at all. From those things, hopefully he could come up with a plan of action.

He knew, for instance, that his family was no longer under his protection. He suspected that they were being held by Xin Zhu, though he only had the man's word for that—he'd seen no objective evidence of it. Yet at the same time, he could not afford to decide it was *not* true, for to do that and be wrong would be a disaster.

Among the things that were beyond his knowledge was how far Xin Zhu would go to make sure Milo remained under his power. Obviously, the last thing he would want to do would be to kill Tina and Stephanie and let Milo know about it—in that case, he would lose control of Milo completely. However, death is only one sort of threat. Xin Zhu could easily hurt them or mutilate them and feel free to let Milo know about it, for Milo's only recourse would be to work harder.

With this in mind, there was only one plan of action concerning his family: He had to play along, and if he had the chance to undermine the man, it would have to be done in such a way that Xin Zhu would never find out.

It was important to settle this first, because his terror over his family's situation was blocking him up. He could think of nothing else. Even after he'd dealt with it, though, it still took a while and an airline sandwich to begin to move on.

He said to Leticia, "Is anyone looking for Alan?"

"The whole world's looking for Alan," she said without hesitation.

"Is that why we're going to Jeddah?"

She shook her head. "We've got more important things to do than look for that turncoat."

"Why do you call him that?"

Leticia sighed, then leaned closer and lowered her voice. "Milo, Alan Drummond made himself a threat as soon as he walked out of the Rathbone Hotel. And he knows it. But he doesn't care. Since then, we've had all our red flags going for him. MI-5 has his vitals. Embassies are listening. Not a whisper. He's good, it turns out. You know he got the Medal of Honor in Afghanistan?"

"No, I didn't."

"He's more than just an administrator," she said after a moment, "and he's no idiot. He's got enough spy craft to elude us all."

"To what purpose?"

She shrugged. "All I know is that his operation is running counter to *my* operation, and that's a problem."

"And what happens when he's finally found?"

"That depends on him, doesn't it?"

"Are you going to kill him?"

"You're very sensitive, aren't you?" she asked, then smiled. "No, I'm not going to kill him. If I'm ordered to, I'll have to be given some pretty persuasive evidence. Like, that he's actually working against us. Or for the Chinese."

"I doubt that," Milo said.

"You never know." She tapped his forearm with a long nail. "Any of us could be."

For all of her elusiveness, Leticia was at least verifying the story Irwin and Collingwood had told him. While a plan of attack may have originated with Alan, some sort of schism had occurred between him and Collingwood, Irwin, and Jackson. The disagreement had been so strong that Alan had felt the need to disappear completely, jeopardizing not only the others' operation but also his wife and Milo's family.

Once the trays had been taken away, Milo said, "How do you know that it's better to work for Irwin than for Alan?"

"Excuse me?" she asked, turning to get a better look at him.

"There are two plans here," he said. "Irwin and Collingwood's, and Alan's. You said you don't know the scope of either one. So how do you know that it's not better to throw your lot in with Alan?"

She licked her lips, thinking a moment. "Milo, have you taken a good look at Alan lately?"

"He's unbalanced."

"That's a nice word for it. Don't get me wrong—I *like* Alan—but would I put my life in his hands?" She shook her head. "Look, Milo, you're giving yourself a headache with all this thinking. I suggest you go back to sleep."

Two plans, he thought as she put on her headphones again. He knew—or he suspected—that Alan's plan was built on revenge, while the others had something else in mind, perhaps hidden in the obscure folds of foreign policy. Whatever Alan was up to, it was problematic enough that Collingwood had sent out a worldwide alert for him.

Here, he tried to separate himself from his prejudices. No matter how mad Alan had become, Milo leaned naturally toward his side, for on the other side was Irwin. Though Milo tried to keep his distance from terms like "good" and "bad," he knew that he was naturally putting such labels on these opposing sides. Then, of course, there was Xin Zhu.

The problem with this—with taking sides at all—was that their fight was not his concern. His only concern was getting his wife and daughter back, and all of his efforts had to be focused on that. He was no longer an employee of the federal government.

He needed help, he thought as he slipped a blue ballpoint with the airline's logo into his pocket. He was caught between too many sides, Chinese and American, each of which had its own interests that, eventually, could cost him more than he was willing to lose. So far, he'd asked two people for help, and in each case it had failed, but that didn't mean that he shouldn't continue to try.

As they entered Frankfurt Airport, he watched for security cameras, which were easy enough to spot. They were everywhere. He and Leticia cut through the crowd of travelers toting bags and dragging children and, among the shops in the main terminal, found the toilets, each with a security camera watching the entrance.

"Don't make us late," she said as she wandered into the women's bathroom.

Inside the men's, he took out the airline's ballpoint and ripped a paper towel from the rack. He pressed it flat against the wall, thought a moment, and then wrote in large, clear block letters:

> To Erika Schwartz, BND-Pullach—
> We Need To Talk. Keep Your Distance.
> —JOHN NADLER

He folded the note into his pocket, then stepped out of the bathroom. Leticia was still inside, and he turned quickly, pulling out and unfolding the note, to look directly into the lens of the security camera above him. He held out the note for five seconds, counting, then ripped it in half, and again into quarters as he returned to the bathroom. He continued to tear at it until only small fragments remained, which he flushed down a toilet.

It was Leticia's idea for them to sit separately on the plane to Jeddah. "They'll have had time to put someone here to watch us, so we might as well pretend to be elusive," she said. However, during the five-and-a-half hour flight, neither saw anyone obvious among the thoub suits and white shumaggs and black abayas and hijabs. They landed at 8:00 P.M. and left separately, and after a smooth entrance through passport control, where he stated his intention was tourism, he found Leticia haggling with a limousine driver along the brightly lit ring of Al Madinah Al Munawwarah Road. The night air was warm and full of the Red Sea.

It took fifteen minutes for the limo to deliver them to the Jeddah Hilton, driving through a nighttime cityscape of banks and shopping plazas identified in Arabic and English, and new, clean hotels. He noticed an illuminated billboard with the face of a smiling man in a red shumagg, a mustache, and a wide black goatee—King Abdullah Aziz, Custodian of the Two Holy Mosques—keeping benevolent watch. By the coast, the hotel towers rose, and between them he caught glimpses of beach, glowing with lamplight. Jeddah was the largest port on the Red Sea, the most cosmopolitan of Saudi cities, and a perpetual resort and convention town. The religious police, or mutaween, held little sway here, though upon arriving at the hotel they heard the nighttime Isha prayers broadcast from speakers in the distance.

Though he hadn't seen her visit any exchange desks in the airport, Leticia paid for the ride in riyals, and in the hotel she produced two new passports, booking them into a room as Mr. and Mrs. Greene. As they took the elevator up to the tenth floor, where the hotel's modern lobby rose airily to the roof, she said, "Don't get comfortable. We're checking out in the morning."

"I didn't see anyone on the ride here."

"Neither did I," she said, leaning forward to peer down to the ground floor, "but there was a couple in the airport. They certainly noticed me."

Milo couldn't remember any couple, but he knew he could have missed anything. "Locals?"

"White."

He hoped that they were from Erika Schwartz.

Their room had an expansive view of the beach, the land low and flat, sinking into the sea, and the ships' lights were like fallen stars floating between them and Sudan. "What time?" he asked.

"Soon." She began to unbutton her blouse. "I need a shower."

He took a can of Pepsi out of the minibar.

"You want to join me?"

Despite fourteen hours of travel, she didn't look worn out at all. Unlike him, she was still living the Tourist life, but looking that alert just wasn't possible. "What are you taking?"

"That doesn't sound like a yes to me," she said, smiling. When he didn't reply, she said, "Why? You want some?"

He did. Back when he lived her kind of life, Dexedrine had been his stimulant of choice, but right now he would take anything to keep from crumbling. With her shirt hanging open, revealing a lace-edged black bra, she went through her bag. The last Tourist he'd done drugs with had produced excellent cocaine, but Leticia took out a small brown bottle and tossed it over. "Just one. I don't have many."

It turned out to be Adderall, used to treat ADD and narcolepsy, and the prescription was for Gwendolyn Davis, the name she had used in London. By the time he'd swallowed one with a mouthful of Pepsi, she was down to her underwear, pretending he wasn't there, folding her clothes neatly on the corner of the bed, then bending at the hips for no apparent reason. She looked at him over her shoulder with a smile.

"I'll be in the bar," he said, taking the soda can with him to the door. "If they lost track of us, my face should help out."

Unfazed, she straightened. "A face like that never helped anyone."

14

I n the elevator, he pressed his forehead against the glass, watching the lobby floor rise to meet him, noting faces that turned upward, but none looked familiar. When he got out, moving slowly past businessmen in robes and suits, escorts in Western fashions, and tourists of all nations and attire, he headed first to a lobby sofa and settled down. He didn't bother looking around, but he made sure he was visible, examining a brochure floor plan of the hotel. After two minutes, he headed downstairs to the Manhattan Sport Diner. He stood at the door, moving his gaze gradually around the place, taking in all the kitschy American memorabilia and the three plasma televisions showing the same soccer game. When a woman with a pen in her pocket asked if he was dining alone, he told her he was just looking for his wife; she must be in another restaurant.

There were plenty to look at: the Vienna, the Al Safina, the Al Khayam Iranian Restaurant, and two terraces—La Terrace restaurant, and the bar at the pool terrace. Only once he'd displayed himself at all these locations did he return to the basement level and, close to the Manhattan Sport Diner, enter a men's bathroom and go to sit in one of the stalls.

It took three minutes for the door to open and a man to walk past all the stall doors and, finally, choose the one beside Milo. He locked his door, sat down with a stifled groan, and quietly said in what sounded like a local accent, "You've got something to tell me?"

"I don't know who you are."

"And there's no reason to know, sir. I heard that the last time you knew someone you nearly killed him in a bathroom. I'm just here to pass on your messages."

It was enough of an answer. This man was working for Xin Zhu. "Do you have any messages for me?"

"Just a request that you keep your hands off of innocent people such as myself."

"Tell him," Milo said, "that tonight I'm meeting someone. I don't know who."

There was a pause. "May I ask when you will know this?"

"After the meeting."

"Yes, of course," then, "Oh, I forgot. I do have a question for you."

"Yes?"

"In the Frankfurt airport, what was on the paper?"

"What paper?"

"I do not know. Yet this is the question."

Milo took an involuntary breath. "Tell him he will have his answer as soon as I speak to Tina."

"Tina?"

"He knows who that is. In fact, tell him I demand to speak to her in the next twenty-four hours."

"To this Tina."

"Yes."

Milo heard the *scratch-scratch* of a pencil on paper. Finally, the man said, "This is an ultimatum?"

"Yes."

"And so what is the *then?* If this is not done, then . . . ?"

"I don't know yet, but I have a rich imagination."

Scratch-scratch. "Is that everything? I was prepared for a longer report."

"I'm sorry to disappoint you. Tell him that I'm not trusted yet."

The man went silent, and Milo waited for more scratching, but he only flushed his toilet, unlatched the door, and left the bathroom. Milo flushed his own toilet and went upstairs to the pool terrace, feeling the Adderall tweak his blood flow and brighten his eyes. The fresh sea air was inviting. He took a lounge chair away from the pool and ordered apple juice from a waiter. Now, after ten thirty, the terrace was only sparsely populated. Most of the guests were having late dinners or turning in, and so when the European couple arrived they stood out. He saw them whisper to one another and make their way to the opposite side of the pool and talk briefly to the waiter. They settled down, the tall blond woman in a slim gown, wrapped in a shawl to protect her bare shoulders from the night breeze, the shorter dark-haired man in a semiformal suit with casual shoes. The man made no pretense of not knowing who Milo was, watching him carefully as he took a pack of cigarettes out of his jacket and lit one. The woman was typing intently on her BlackBerry. Finally, she sent her message and laid the phone on the tiles beside her.

He had done it, had gained some small measure of control, and this little victory pleased him. He thought of Alan, also under Xin Zhu's thumb, taking control by starting to smoke, and this reminded him that he hadn't had a Nicorette in over a day, but he felt no withdrawal. Control, again.

He was starting to get up, to return to the bathroom for another meeting, when Leticia leaned down to kiss his cheek. She was wearing a long summer dress and flat shoes, along with a black fabric shoulder bag. He felt envious—his own clothes were feeling stiff and unclean. "You missed a glorious shower," she told him.

He raised his apple juice as an offering. She leaned down and took a sip as he tilted the glass, his hand twitching from the rush of amphetamines. She straightened, licked her lips, and said, "Well, we wouldn't have had time for much more than a quickie. Come see the water with me."

She reached a hand to him, and he took it, climbing to his feet. Together, they left the pool area, and she reached an arm around his shoulder, pulling him close. "You saw them?"

"I did."

"There's a reason I don't know the word 'worry.' "

On the way out of the hotel, she stopped in the lobby bathroom and reemerged covered in a long abaya and hijab, all black. She gave him a wink, and they headed out. Together, they went down to the beach and then north, past couples and groups of young men sitting in their robes in the sand, toward a tall obelisk of spheres topped by a crescent moon. They remained on the beach, though, and from the folds of her clothing Leticia pulled out a touch-screen cell phone and watched the scrolling numbers on it as she walked. Her GPS led them to a section of sand above the tide line, where she said, "Dig, boy."

It didn't take long to uncover the plastic oar and the wide, flat piece of folded rubber that was an inflatable raft. To his relief, there was also a small, battery-powered air pump. He carried everything down to the water, and while Leticia performed lookout, he filled the boat as quietly as possible and pushed it, bobbing, into the sea. The warm water soaked his pants. Leticia took off her shoes and raised her abaya to her hips, then walked into the water and rolled, on her back, into the boat. He pushed it out until the water was at his chest before climbing in beside her and taking the oar.

When they reached the darkened fishing boat forty minutes later, he was exhausted again. It was a cabin cruiser, about thirty feet long, humbly rusted. The captain was an old Egyptian named Ibrahim Fekry who had first helped the CIA as a teenager, during the Suez Crisis of 1956—Milo learned this in the first few minutes of their acquaintance, listening to his singsong French. He had scarred features, skin blackened by decades of sunburns, and a face that was in a perpetual state of animation. He looked younger than his seventy years. Most importantly, though, he had papers to allow him to fish freely in this part of the Red Sea.

He was immediately taken by Leticia, calling her "my Nubian princess," and she warmed to the attention. Quietly, Fekry asked Milo if he had slept with her yet, but Leticia's hearing was sharp. "He refused," she called from the bow, "even though I offered."

Disbelief spilled into Fekry's face, followed quickly by disgust. He didn't speak to Milo again for the rest of the journey.

Again relying on Leticia's phone, they reached a spot from where they could see, in the clear blackness, lights from two countries. There was the myriad of colors from Saudi Arabia, and only occasional dim white clusters from Sudan. To the north and south, they spotted boats moving gradually along, as if no one were in a hurry. As they waited, Leticia told Milo to keep his mouth shut. "You're here to look like my boss, and that's how I'm going to spin it. I don't know how they would deal with a woman on her own, and I'm not interested in finding out. We'll be talking in English, but you won't say a word. Ibrahim?"

Fekry worked open a crate and handed Milo a 9 mm Bernardelli pistol. Milo checked the safety, put a round into the chamber, and slipped it into his jacket pocket.

Her contact arrived late, just after two thirty, in a bright red speedboat that shook the peaceful night. Three men, two in simple robes, the driver had a Kalashnikov strung over his back, while a heavyset man beside the motor held his Kalashnikov up to his shoulder, aimed at their boat. Between them sat a man in dark brown

Sudanese robes, a jelabiya, hands crossed in his lap, waiting as they killed the engine.

All three were richly black, and as they approached Milo could only see eyes and the occasional flash of teeth as they spoke to each other. In English, the driver called, "You're in Sudanese waters!" His syllables pounded like hammer blows.

Fekry muttered something that sounded like an Arabic curse as he backed to the far side of his boat. Milo didn't like this either.

"I'm in Sudanese sand," Leticia called back—it was a recognition code. "Put those guns away."

"You," said the driver, pointing a long finger at Milo, "you're not supposed to be here."

"If he's not convinced," Leticia said, "you get nothing."

The man in the brown robes cocked his head, then spoke to his men in Arabic, and they both relaxed. Then he stood up without faltering as the speedboat rocked beneath his feet and, with a voice nothing like his driver's, said, "Aasalaamu Aleikum."

"Wa-Aleikum Aassalaam," Leticia answered. Milo said nothing.

"Do we remain in our places?" the man asked. His accent had a touch of London to it.

"I'm not going down there," said Leticia.

"So be it," he said and settled down again. "You are interested in helping us push out the Chinese who support our enemy's government. Is that correct?"

"Yes," said Leticia. She was leaning forward against the gunwale, speaking quietly.

"It's an interesting proposition," he said thoughtfully. "We've discussed it—in a limited way. Our primary issue is that it would take place outside of our country. Khartoum is our natural enemy, not Beijing."

So there it is, Milo thought. *Out in the open.*

Leticia said, "Beijing is supplying Khartoum with weapons and money. Chinese advisors are teaching the Janjaweed how to better kill your people. The UN arms embargo means nothing to Beijing."

The man just stared at her, waiting.

She said, "Without Chinese support, al-Bashir will fall. You know this. An attack on Khartoum might wound him, but it would never crush him. This way, you can deliver a greater blow without laying waste to Sudanese people."

"Which is the very point," he said, beginning to sound exasperated. "We know this—it's why I'm talking to you now. The risks, though, are immense."

"Bigger than the long-term risks of losing this war?"

"We'll be heading back to the negotiation table soon."

"Only a fool believes what that government signs."

The man looked from Leticia down to his hands in the folds of his robe. "I have one question for you before you have our decision."

"Please."

"Why did you ask to meet here, in the middle of the Red Sea?"

"I explained that before. My associate here wants to see the face of the man who will help carry this out. He believes in faces more than words."

"Is that why he does not speak?" the man asked, looking hard at Milo.

"He's a politician," Leticia said quickly, perhaps too quickly. "He knows that speaking aloud makes him part of something."

"I do not believe you," the man said, and as he said the words, his driver and the other man raised their rifles. The sentence had been a prearranged code. Milo's hand was in his pocket, clutching the Bernardelli, but Leticia spoke calmly.

"If you don't believe me, then turn around and go. We'll find someone else who's not so afraid."

"Someone who's more stupid," he said, almost phrasing it as a question, and they stared at one another for about ten seconds before the man raised a hand from his robe, flat, fingers together, and the men lowered their guns. The driver started the engine, filling their world with noise again. "Ma'a salaama," the man called to Leticia, but did not raise his hand again.

She answered in kind.

Once they were gone, leaving frothy waves in their wake, Milo gave the pistol back to Fekry and went to sit beside Leticia at the bow. She watched the black water, then looked at him. "What?"

"You're trying to panic the Chinese. You're trying to panic Xin Zhu."

"Look who's the smartest boy in class," she said, but the joke seemed to give her no joy.

Remembering that she had also met with Islamic militants in China, he pushed further. "Information overload. You're diverting his attention from the real attack. Just one or two diversions and he can ignore them, but five or six, and he has no choice but to pay attention."

She looked satisfied by his astuteness.

"Alan's idea?"

"Originally, yeah."

"Are you going to tell me what the real attack is?"

"I wouldn't tell you if I knew."

"You really don't know?"

She shook her head, and when he asked if this didn't bother her, she said, "I'm just happy I haven't been shelved. They'll tell me when it's time."

"Irwin and Collingwood."

"The IRS," she said, finally grinning, "but I'm getting the feeling that this isn't going to work."

"Whether or not these people accept it is beside the point," he said. "The important thing is letting the Chinese know that you're trying to do something. That you're talking to Darfur rebels."

"Sure," she said, "but we've misjudged a lot here. I talked to the Uighurs, and they weren't interested. I talked to the Tibetans after Alan disappeared—they wouldn't even listen to me. I hope the others are having more luck."

"The two other Tourists."

"One."

"What?"

She sighed loudly. "In Frankfurt, I got the news. They got Tran Hoang in South Korea. So it's *serious*, kid."

She leaned back on her outstretched arms as Fekry

started up the engine. Milo found her lack of confidence unnerving, and it made him think of his own irrational confidence, the one that kept telling him that he could gain the upper hand and turn events to his advantage. As a Tourist, Milo had once believed that the only way to deal with failure was to treat it as if it were success. To Tourists, success and failure are the same thing.

As they headed back to shore, beneath the engine's grumble they heard a haunting sound rolling over the water. Leticia checked her gold wristwatch. "Four fourteen. Hijri prayers."

He wasn't a Tourist, not really, and there was no reason to think he would ever gain the upper hand in any of this.

15

Leticia woke him a little after noon with a kiss on the nose as more prayers floated through their open window, and after he showered, she presented him with clothes. On three hours of sleep, she'd spent the morning on Tahlia Street, where she'd found a light Ralph Lauren suit with a green silk tie. Once he was dressed, she used a hotel comb to pull at his hair. "We should get rid of that gray," she said fussily.

"I like my gray."

She stepped back, judging his appearance, then said, "You know how a little gray makes a man distinguished? Well, that's only true for some men. On you, it just looks old."

"I'm only thirty-eight, Leticia."

"Making it all the more sad."

She modeled her own purchase, a black sleeveless drop-waist dress from Prada, with a pair of leather boots that reached to just below her knees, leaving most of her thigh bare. He wondered where she was getting this money. Those bottomless Tourism credit cards were a thing of the past.

It didn't matter, though. None of these people mattered anymore. He'd had a night to reflect on everything, to truly grasp his helplessness, and had come to a decision. As soon as he talked to the Germans, it would be settled, and Alan Drummond, Xin Zhu, Nathan Irwin, and even Leticia Jones could go to hell.

"So?" Leticia asked.

"Very nice."

"You know, we've still got time."

Milo briefly considered it, for what did any of those old rules mean now? If you cut yourself free, you're free of everything, even selfishness. He gave her a wink and collected his cash. "I'll be in the lobby."

"No questions?" she asked. "Not interested in where we're going next?"

"You'll tell me eventually," he said and left.

Though her partner didn't appear, the tall German woman crossed the lobby soon after he arrived. She gave him a significant look, then headed to a counter lined with in-house telephones and lifted one. He followed, grabbing another phone two down from her. He put the receiver to his ear, listening to the *beep-beep* of the dial tone as she said, "Take the stairs to the first floor," then hung up and walked away.

He followed her instructions, and in a long corridor of identical doors he waited until, halfway down, one opened but no one came out. He approached quickly, because Leticia would be in the lobby soon, and when he stepped inside, he found a small, mustached man sitting on the corner of the made bed, hands resting on his knees. It was Erika Schwartz's assistant, whom Milo had only known as Oskar, a happy participant in Milo's torture a few months ago. Milo closed the door behind himself. In German, Oskar said, "Tell me one reason I should be sitting right here, talking to you."

"I don't know, Oskar. You're the one who's sitting here."

"That's my boss's decision. Strangely, she feels like she owes you."

"For the cigarette burns?"

Oskar wiped at the corners of his mustache. "Something else, apparently." He stood then, and though he tried, he couldn't quite manage a threatening stance. "She helped your idiotic father, and we nearly got ourselves busted for the favor."

"My father?"

Oskar just stared.

"When?"

Oskar shrugged. "He asked for help extracting your wife and daughter, and—guess what? No wife and daughter. Me, I'm of the opinion you killed your old man. So why don't you try to convince me I'm wrong?"

Milo blinked at him, feeling as if a remarkable coincidence had occurred. His father had gone for help to, of all people, the woman he was now asking for help. But was it a coincidence? Not really. Erika Schwartz had already been looking at Milo because of the Sebastian Hall name, and would probably have discussed him with Yevgeny. Who else would Yevgeny have gone to? Milo rubbed his face and said, "The Chinese have them. My family. A colonel named Xin Zhu."

"Why did he take them?"

"He warned me he would do it," said Milo. "It was my mistake. I thought I could outsmart him."

Oskar nodded, as if he saw some truth in this, but said, "Now that you've summoned me, I assume you have something to ask."

"Find my wife and daughter. And if you can't find them, I want you to have me killed."

After a momentary frown, Oskar laughed. "Kill you?" He covered his mouth with a hand, then waved. "Please! Is it my birthday?"

"I'm serious."

Oskar shook his head, his smile still large. "Absolutely not, Weaver. As much as I'd be happy to pull the trigger, you're not going to convince us to enter the assassination business. Talk to Mossad. Hell, talk to the CIA."

"She owes me this."

"I don't think she owes you *that* much, Weaver."

"She has her job because of me."

Oskar's smile faded. While Milo had stolen the four paintings from the E. G. Bührle in Zürich, he had given two to Erika Schwartz, which she then planted in her predecessor's apartment. Of course, a three-hundred-pound woman would have had trouble sneaking into an apartment with two large canvases—she would have needed help—someone small, about Oskar's size.

Oskar said, "Here's something you might not know, Weaver. The same evening your family was taken, your next-door neighbor was attacked in his apartment. He was knocked out with drugs, then tied and gagged. He didn't see anything that we know of, but . . ."

Milo stepped back involuntarily as those words sank in. He ran into the dresser. Raymond Lister, the drunk. "They were there."

"Yeah, Milo. While you were crying over your father, your wife and daughter were right next door. In your defense, they probably weren't calling for help— they would've been drugged, too. But, still."

Milo flashed on that night with his father's body, and his imagination, in a vain attempt to change history, walked him out his door and to Raymond's, where he kicked hard, shattering wood, and found . . .

"And now," said Oskar, "the surprise."

"You've got something else?" Milo whispered.

Oskar walked past him to the bathroom door. He opened it and looked inside, saying to someone, "Your turn now," then stepped back.

A woman walked out. Not Erika Schwartz, not Janet Simmons, not Tina Weaver. She was tall, long in the nose, with dark hair that hung past her shoulders. Everything about her was long, but unlike when she was a girl, all elbows and knees, none of this was awkward on her. Like Milo, and like Yevgeny, she had heavy eyes, the flesh around them bruised and serious.

"Alexandra?" he asked, letting the shocked smile come into his face.

His sister didn't smile. She walked up to him, standing a couple of inches taller, and said, "You'd better talk, Milo. Or I swear I'll kill you myself."

Part Three

THE HOUSE OF GOOD DEEDS

**SATURDAY, JUNE 14 TO
SUNDAY, JUNE 29, 2008**

1

Alexandra was too tired and, she felt, too old to be dealing with this, though she was only thirty-two. It was three thirty on a Saturday morning, she'd left Freddy, a man she'd only met two days before, in her bed, and the night's ridiculously priced cognacs at Zebrano's were still washing through her scattered thoughts. Bloody family.

She climbed out of a taxi at Goodge Street, then took the Charlotte Place pedestrian lane past shuttered stores to the elbow of Rathbone Street. To her right, the Duke of York was closed, but its smell remained from the sidewalk littered with cigarette butts and spilled beer; to her left, smoky lights glowed from inside the lobby of the Rathbone. She wore a gray hoodie pulled down over her forehead, so that from a distance she looked like a chav at the end of a rowdy night—it was a useful illusion, particularly for the CCTV cameras.

Room 306, he'd said. *Go see if your brother's in.*

Half brother, Milo, the one who'd grown up American and never answered her e-mails. Last Christmas, though, his wife had sent a "hello, you might not know me but" letter, which Alexandra hadn't bothered to reply to.

Francisco was straight ahead, waiting just past the hotel and making no move to approach her. She guessed he was in a blind spot, so she went to him. His hands were stuffed deep into his jacket pockets, and his Spanish face, beneath a black baseball cap, looked muddled and sleepy, making her think of his code name, Hound. Her father named his agents after dog breeds, as if by this he could assure canine loyalty. Once they were close, she said, "He woke you, too?"

"Your father thinks no one sleeps."

"How much time do you need?"

"Five minutes. I'll send you a message."

"What am I supposed to do for five minutes?"

"Don't fall asleep," he said and left her on the sidewalk. He ducked into an open garage on the side of the hotel and, after a moment's pause to work with his tools, opened the locked service entrance and went inside.

It was too chilly to stand still, so she continued down Rathbone Street, past the Newman Arms, to where it bent to turn into Percy Street, then walked back, thinking all the time of the world of opportunities that could be her's, if she would only quit working for family. For two years now, he'd called her his "assistant." She still wasn't sure what that meant. A certain amount of communications, of keeping track of her father's agents and appointments, of going into the field when he couldn't make it or when, like now, the worries were personal in nature. Her job description read like a secretary's.

Sasha, all I know is that someone using his old work papers checked in Thursday night. I didn't know about it until I got a call from a German associate.

Erika Schwartz?

He didn't answer.

Openness, Nana. Remember our agreement?

Yes. Erika Schwartz.

The one who tortured Milo.

A pause. *She believed at the time that she had reason.*

She thought he had killed a little girl, Nana. I would've done the same thing. I'm just wondering why she's telling you about this.

Because we're old adversaries, Little One. It's the same thing as old friends.

Then call the room, Nana. Ask who's there.

I did. No one answered. The only people we have in London now are Hound . . . and you.

Her phone vibrated. She took it out and read, *M'LADY*—Francisco's sense of humor.

She hurried her pace, rounded the corner across from the Duke of York, then ducked through the Rathbone Hotel's entrance. In the empty lobby there were no rock gardens—her father's term for teams of sedentary watchers—and the front desk was empty. She pulled back her hood to show how harmless she was and nodded pleasantly to a bellboy as she continued to the elevator. She stepped inside, pressed number 4, and watched as the doors closed—there was no sign of anyone, rock gardens or otherwise.

The fourth floor was empty, and, thanks to Francisco, the camera at the end of the corridor was dead, so she found the stairwell and trotted down to the third floor, where she found another dead camera. Room 306 was halfway down.

Though she had one in her apartment, she hadn't brought a gun, because she fully expected to find her brother dozing in the room, and even if it wasn't him she could cover easily enough. She would just be another woman with alcohol on her breath, knocking on the wrong door in the wee hours. London was full of girls like her.

She knocked three times, loudly, and waited. "Charlie!" she said, putting on a Yorkshire accent that, despite a youth in Russia, she'd mastered pretty quickly. "Charlie, I know you're in there!"

There was movement on the other side of the door, and she knocked again. "Charlie, I can hear you! I'm not leaving until you let me in."

More movement, then the door opened. A haggard-looking face stared back at her. Tall man, late thirties, handsome in a military sort of way, wearing boxer shorts and a T-shirt that showed off a well-muscled body.

"Oh. You're not Charlie."

"No," he said, his accent acutely American. "I'm not Charlie."

He looked innocent enough, but he was using one of Milo's names, which meant that innocence wasn't the right word to describe him. She leaned closer, one hand on the door frame, and dropped the Yorkshire. "You're not Sebastian Hall, either, are you?"

He blinked, stifling a yawn as he covered his mouth with a hand that was flushed and red. She picked up on a paler ring of flesh where a wedding band no longer resided. He said, "Who are you?"

She lowered her voice now, letting the Russian accent come through. "All I'm interested in is knowing why Milo Weaver didn't open this door."

There was movement to her right, and both of them looked to see Francisco standing in the corridor, hands in his jacket. He would have a gun. Her father would have insisted.

"Who's he?" asked the man.

"Friendly. May I come in?"

He stepped back, pulling the door further open to reveal a tidy room. He walked to the television and opened the minifridge beneath it. Francisco was next to her now, and she asked, "How long do we have?"

"Seven, eight minutes, more if I go back down."

"Wait here five minutes, then go down."

He nodded, and she went inside, then pushed the door until it was almost closed.

"Is he staying outside?" the man asked.

"Shall we start with your name?"

He handed over a tiny bottle of cognac—he'd identified her scent—and took whisky for himself. "I'm not going to be an open book, lady. Let's start with your interest in Milo Weaver."

She didn't see the point in being coy with only a few minutes available. "He's my brother."

He raised his brows, legitimately surprised. "I knew he had two sisters, but . . ." He unscrewed his bottle. "Natalia?"

"She knows better than to get involved. I'm Alexandra."

"Are you here as your father's emissary?"

She shrugged.

"I'm Milo's . . . well, I was his boss. Now we're just friends."

"Alan Drummond, then," she said. "And this is what Milo's friends do? Stir up international interest by traveling on a passport that ties him to an art robbery?"

"Christ, you're well informed." He threw back the whisky.

Alexandra unscrewed her cognac and drank it down as well. It delivered a pleasant punch. She said, "Except I don't know the *why*. Are you trying to get him arrested?"

Confusion flickered over his features—confusion, or pain, or guilt. She'd never been particularly good at reading faces; body language was what she picked up on. He said, "I don't have a choice. Other people are pulling strings."

"They're watching you?"

"Yeah."

"No one's in the lobby."

"There are cameras throughout the hotel."

"We've shut them down—for the next few minutes, at least. If you want to walk, now's the time."

"It's not that simple," he said, but she could see from his hands that he was considering it.

"You'd be surprised how simple most things are, Mr. Drummond."

"Alan, please."

"We can get to know each other later. Right now, you can walk. That's good for me—after all, if you disappear, all the authorities have is a name. I suspect it would be good for you as well. If you want, we can make it look like a kidnapping."

He stepped back, set down his empty bottle, and turned back to her. She was losing him.

She said, "Who are they?"

"It's complicated."

"One they? Two theys?"

"You make three," he said, smiling. "Listen, I can protect Milo's family. His wife and daughter, I mean. I've already planned for that."

"Who's protecting your family, Mr. Drummond?"

She'd grown used to these conversations, ones in which central subjects were left vague or entirely anonymous. First, as a litigator, she'd sat with the guilty talking circles around actual crimes, and later, working for her father, she'd engaged in conversations in which nothing, it seemed, was even said. This was nothing new. However, it irritated her when half-empty sentences led to radical decisions, for without the details she couldn't be sure what she was talking Alan Drummond into. Now, he was falling into embarrassed silence. She said, "You have to give me a crumb, so I know how to help you."

"Why would you help me?"

"Because it's nearly four in the morning, and no bars are open. I've got time on my hands."

Drummond turned slowly, looking around the room, taking in the open bag and the folded clothes and a magazine—the *Economist*—on a bedside table. On its cover stood two men, American presidential candidates John McCain and Barack Obama, under the headline AMERICA AT ITS BEST.

"Unless it's necessary for your purposes," she said, "I'd leave everything. No need to draw attention to yourself when you walk out."

He nodded, then went to the clothes and began to dress. "You have a car?"

"My friend does."

"I'll walk out of here on my own, but you can pick me up somewhere else that's convenient. By convenient, I mean a dead zone."

She thought a moment, remembering various streets that hadn't yet been equipped with Transport for London CCTV cameras, then told him an intersection in Hammersmith.

Later, as she and Francisco sat in his chilly Toyota, waiting for the man who would never come, it would occur to her that Alan Drummond knew from that moment in the hotel room that they wouldn't see each other again. He'd come around too quickly. The question, though, was: Why had he come around at all? She hadn't threatened him, and she'd had no intention to. All she'd wanted was to know if Milo was there or not. Much later, when she knew most of the story, she understood that she'd simply arrived at an opportune time, and Alan Drummond was smart enough to know when to change his plans; he was brave enough to make immediate decisions.

She texted Francisco, asking for another ten minutes for the cameras, then left Alan Drummond and went through the lobby, nodding agreeably at the tired bellboy, pulled up her hood, and walked back down Charlotte Place. She took a right on Goodge before Francisco, breathing heavily, caught up with her. "So?"

"So let's go to Hammersmith and wait for him."

"It's not your brother."

"It's someone who doesn't give a damn about my brother."

A moment or two later, Francisco said, "I never gave much of a damn about my brother, but after he died I felt differently. That's the tragedy of human love."

He sometimes did that, taking some stray statement as an excuse to reveal a sentimental piece of personal history, and she'd always understood this as an attempt to draw her into a closer relationship. She'd heard enough of Yevgeny's warnings about his agents to know better. She said, "Where did you park your car?"

By five, when they were both yawning incessantly and knew that Alan Drummond wasn't ever going to show up, Francisco started to drive, and she called Yevgeny in Geneva, taking him through the chain of events and semirevelations. "Two possibilities: Either he walked on us, or someone picked him up. I'm pretty sure he walked."

"But what was he doing there?"

"Wouldn't say. He knows what he's doing to Milo, but it doesn't seem to bother him."

"Is he an imbecile?"

She'd considered that possibility as well. "He claims there are two parties watching him, though he wouldn't say more. Other people, he says, are pulling his strings."

"What the hell does that mean?"

She didn't bother answering. Nana was touchy this morning.

He said, "We've got a lot of other things to deal with now, but let's keep an ear to the ground about this."

"You're going to call Milo?"

"No need to trouble him yet."

"But he's causing *us* trouble. It's only fair."

"Fair?" he said, as if the word were new to him.

2

Erika Schwartz didn't believe that the man in London was Milo Weaver—it was just an identity, after all, but it was an identity that had been used by the disbanded Department of Tourism, and so it demanded investigation. She'd placed a flag on the name months ago, so on Friday, the day after Sebastian Hall checked into the Rathbone, BND-Berlin notified her that the identity was in London. She requested a photo and was told they would work on it.

Her first impulse was to call Milo Weaver directly and clear this thing up. While he probably didn't know all the answers—who, really, ever did?—she might be able to strike him off the list of possible players. If, of course, he was interested in ever speaking to her again.

Possible players in what? She had no idea, but after the games she'd played with Leticia Jones and Hector Garza in April, she felt sure that this was connected.

Instead of Weaver, she placed a call to someone she

contacted so rarely that she had to dig through her notebooks to find the number. The old Geneva phone was out of service, so she checked through the database until she found the current personal mobile number for Yevgeny Aleksandrovich Primakov of the United Nations.

This, too, was a Geneva number, and she was lucky to find him in—the man, she knew, traveled more than most of her agents, bouncing from country to country according to the UN's whims. "'Allo," he said, but didn't bother stating who he was.

"It's your oldest girlfriend, Yevgeny," she said in English.

"By how long we've known each other, or by the year you were born?"

"Both," she said, not bothering to hold back her smile. She'd never succeeded in any of her schemes to trap him during the Cold War, though their occasional safe house meetings had been entirely cordial. After the war, they periodically met up at German-Russian friendship conferences, drank wine together, and shared war stories that were, by then, a little less classified. Despite all she knew about him and the things he had done, he was an incredibly charming man. "You sound healthy," she said.

He laughed at that. "Well, my voice is my one asset. The rest is for science. You still sound like a lovely little girl."

From their first meeting, he had teased her about her high-pitched voice, which had never matched her girth. "Just as long as you keep your eyes shut."

"Congratulations, by the way, on your promotion."

"Can we talk over this phone?"

"I should hope so," he said. "My boys spent an entire month tinkering with it."

"Which boys would those be?"

"Neighborhood kids."

She said, "Did you hear about the little mystery in London? Someone named Sebastian Hall. I think the name's familiar to you."

"At my age everyone's an acquaintance."

"You know, of course, who the name was once used by?"

"Actually, that hadn't come across my desk yet."

"Your son," she said.

"My son?"

"Milo Weaver."

Yevgeny paused then, perhaps wondering if he should deny it, for though they had discussed his murdered wife, Ekaterina, and his two daughters, Natalia and Alexandra, Milo Weaver's name had never been uttered, nor had the name of Milo's mother, Ellen Perkins. Still, she wouldn't make such a stab if she didn't know the facts, and he was aware of this. "How long have you known?" he asked.

Since 1979, she wanted to say but couldn't. One advantage to never mentioning Milo Weaver had been that she could hide the fact that she had been the last person to interrogate his mother before she killed herself in a German prison. So she said, "I'm not calling to dredge up history, Yevgeny. I'd just like to know what you know about this. Sebastian Hall was one of

Milo's known work names, and I'd like to know why someone is using the same blown identity when all it's going to do is point fingers at your son."

She could hear his labored breaths before he spoke, and briefly—irrationally—she worried that he was having a stroke. When he finally spoke his voice was clear and composed. "I'm sorry, Erika. I don't know much at this point. You're right, though—its connection to Milo is . . . well, it's curious. I can keep you updated as I learn more."

"Thank you. And I'll do the same."

"Doubtful, but I live in hope."

She didn't receive a photo of Sebastian Hall until late Saturday, many hours after he'd disappeared from the hotel, and when she opened her e-mail from Berlin she was surprised to find the face of Alan Drummond staring back. Then she learned that he was gone, and that the hotel cameras had been sabotaged.

By Monday, Sebastian Hall's disappearance was a subject of public inquiry in Britain, and on Wednesday, a report came in from New York. It turned out that Alan Drummond's wife, Penelope, had had dinner with Milo and Tina Weaver. They were social. Also on Wednesday, and more importantly, Oskar finally received the Rathbone Hotel's guest list from his English contact, a list that made her tooth ache. Gwendolyn Davis, a.k.a. Leticia Jones, had been in the hotel at the same time. As had Gephel Marpa of Free Tibet, but she didn't understand the importance of that until Oskar said, "Marpa *lives* in London. Why was he at the hotel?"

When Yevgeny called her late Thursday afternoon,

she brought up the interesting hotel guests and got the irritating feeling that none of this was news to him. Then she shared what she had been able to learn about Alan Drummond's movements around the world, from New York to Seattle, to Vancouver, to Tokyo, Mumbai, Amman, and London. It turned out that Yevgeny had known about Mumbai, and he told her that Drummond had been seen exiting the Mumbai airport, though no one had followed him. Eventually, he said, "I talked to Milo on the phone today. He doesn't know anything about this."

"You asked him directly?"

"He asked me to look into it. I didn't tell him we already were."

"You could probably share with him."

"On Monday, I'll be in New York. We'll talk then."

"Yevgeny?"

"Yes?"

"Would you like to tell me about Xin Zhu?"

A long pause. "He's a colonel in the Guoanbu, isn't he?"

"The CIA is after him. I suspect that Alan Drummond was in London for that reason. If the enemy of our enemy is our friend, Gephel Marpa might be a good choice for a collaborator."

"You've put a lot of thought into this, haven't you?"

"I'm a big administrator now, Yevgeny. You know how much free time that gives you."

"What are you interested in knowing about Xin Zhu?"

"What did he do to the Americans? In particular, what did he do to the Department of Tourism?"

That department was another topic they had never discussed before, but she had no doubt that, with a son who had worked there, Yevgeny knew plenty about it. He said, "That department doesn't exist anymore, so you don't have to worry about it."

"I'm not worried about it, Yevgeny. I asked a simple question."

"He wiped it out, Erika."

"Literally or metaphorically?"

"Literally."

She sucked in air—her suspicion back in April had been right. "Why?" she asked.

"I don't know."

"Do you know who's running the CIA's retaliation?"

"I don't know that there *is* a retaliation."

"Are you withholding, Yevgeny?"

"Of course I am, but I'm not hiding anything that would help you."

"Maybe I should be the judge of that."

On Friday, Erika's people in New York sent a set of photographs, from Thursday, of Milo Weaver speaking on a Park Slope sidewalk with an unknown man. He had stepped out of a pizza restaurant with his family in order to meet the man, then met him in the same spot a couple of hours later. He handed over something small, and the man gave him what looked like a business card. The man was dark (Northern Indian, an analyst noted, maybe Kashmiri), but they had little else on him. He'd left the second meeting by public transportation, but no one had thought to follow him.

On Monday, she read a report from New York noting that Penelope Drummond had spent the weekend with the Weavers before returning home—someone had broken into her apartment and torn it apart, assumedly searching for something. She had a frustrating conversation with a contact in the CIA's National Clandestine Service Counterintelligence Center, who played dumb whenever she came near the topic that was on her mind, though in the end she decided that he wasn't playing at anything—whatever was going on was above his clearance.

She spent Tuesday on other matters—matters that actually concerned the security of the Federal Republic of Germany—and was taken off guard when, at six the next morning, her phone woke her from a deep sleep. Six in the morning, Wednesday—midnight, New York time.

"Did I wake you?"

"Of course, Yevgeny."

"Do you have anyone in New York, watching Milo?"

She considered lying, but perhaps she wasn't awake enough because she said, "Yes."

"How many?"

"Five."

"That could be enough."

"You sound hysterical, Yevgeny. Are you all right?"

"I need a favor. Do this for me, and I'll tell you whatever you like."

"Anything?"

"Anything, Erika. I mean it."

She sat up in bed, staring at streetlamps through the crack in her curtains. "Something's wrong."

"Yes, but he's not telling me enough."

"Milo?"

"I need you to perform an extraction tomorrow night. Tonight—Wednesday. Two people, perhaps three."

"A willing extraction?"

"Once I talk to them, it'll be willing."

"I'll need more people. Five isn't enough. Do you have more?"

He thought a moment. "I can get three more."

She tried to shake her head awake but was still fuzzy, and she didn't like to make compromised decisions. "Can I call you back on this? After I've had my coffee?"

"I'd prefer an answer now."

It was in the way he made that statement, his voice hard yet with an undercurrent of anxiety, that she understood that this was emotional for him. Whatever it was, he hadn't thought it through objectively enough, and there was only one possible answer she could give him. Perhaps because of the lingering fuzziness, she didn't see this, nor did she hear the voice inside her that kept saying, *This is none of your business.*

"You'll tell me everything?" she asked after a moment.

"No walls."

"Then of course I'll do it."

3

Words have a nasty habit of catching in the imagination; they spread like hepatitis. This is why, from the beginning, her father had resisted any attempt to name his secret department. Most of the United Nations member states didn't even know—officially, at least—that it existed, particularly America and Russia, both of whom had threatened to veto his 2002 draft proposal for an independent UN intelligence agency. So Yevgeny hadn't proposed it at all. Instead, he'd tracked a few like-minded diplomats from Germany, Kenya, Luxembourg, Iceland, Bangladesh, Portugal, and Ghana. They found bureaucratic loopholes to fund the anonymous department, and when he passed them important intelligence, it was up to them to take it to the floor of the General Assembly.

Upon hiring Alexandra, he opened up his records to her and answered every question she posed to the fullest of his ability. For example, he explained that, from the very beginning, organization had been a problem. The Icelandic ambassador to the UN wanted him to use a Brussels office that his country had corralled for its own use. The Portuguese representative countered with his own office in Geneva. As others made their own suggestions, it quickly became apparent that each diplomat wanted personal oversight, and probably planned to bug the prospective office. So Yevgeny had to take care of it himself.

He had always had a greater enthusiasm for, and a far better grasp of, technology than his children, and in 2003 it came to his rescue, allowing him to decentralize the fledgling department. He hired two secretaries and gave them laptops. Each month they moved separately to different apartments within a network of safe houses spread throughout Europe, traveling by car or train, so that no one would have to run a computer through security checks. The two secretaries synced their laptops daily via two encrypted remote databases, sharing reports culled from agents with whom they were in continual contact. Yevgeny remained physically separate from the secretaries, though he received daily reports through his BlackBerry, and with that information made decisions he could relay back.

According to Yevgeny, it had been an agony to set up, but once the system had been established, it ran smoothly enough. Reports were fed to him, and he decided what to do with the information. A report, say, on the Portuguese dispute with Spain over the borders of Olivença could be given to the Bangladeshi representative to put before the General Assembly, while a report concerning the hazardous Bangladesh-India border region could be handed to Portugal. In the ideal workings of his anonymous agency, all information could be made public simply by giving it to the country with no stake in its release.

By 2006, however, he was overwhelmed. It was inevitable, as his staff of primary agents grew from fifteen to twenty-eight, and his secretarial pool doubled to four. His BlackBerry beeped with fresh information throughout the day, and he was soon faced with a backlog of sensitive information he could no longer keep track of. This was why he approached Alexandra.

She'd been divorced for four months, and though her career in the London office of Berg & DeBurgh, specializing in intellectual property, had been going well ("rising star" had been used to describe her), she'd never made a secret of the fact that the job, like her marriage, hadn't been satisfying in a long time. *I've been running in place for five years, Nana.*

So come work for me.

She'd taken a week to make her decision, and her yes came with one stipulation. *No manipulation, no dishonesty. I'm an equal partner, or I'm not there at all.*

Of course I'll be honest with you, Little One. You'll take over when I'm gone.

Don't bet on it, she warned, then tested him. *Why did you come to the UN?*

When others had asked this question—when she, too, had asked—he'd always replied with idealistic vagaries. *It was the new millennium, you understand? It was time to stop serving one nation's petty interests and turn to the world at large.* Alexandra knew him too well to have ever believed that public relations line. Now, he looked sadly at her and said, *I did it to save my life. My life was the reason. That, and your brother.* A pause, and then slowly he began to tell her the story.

When Milo came to them, he was fifteen years old and American to the core. His foster parents had died in a car accident, and Yevgeny brought him to Moscow to live with them, provoking weeks of family chaos. Alexandra and Natalia—and even their mother, Ekaterina—hadn't even known of his existence. *Remember what he was like?* Yevgeny asked. *A holy terror, but if I'm going to be honest, I'll have to admit that those three years he was with us, from 1985 to 1988, marked the beginning of my move away from Mother Russia, toward the UN.*

That caustic American teenager, in perfect Russian he'd picked up in no time at all, had called their father a KGB hypocrite. *What are you—blind? You're a criminal. You talk about the proletariat, but all you do is oppress the proletariat. You're not even aware of your crimes. You're stuck in a smug, petit bourgeois cocoon.*

He sounded just like his mother, Yevgeny admitted.

Only once the boy had returned to America for college could Yevgeny ask himself if any of it was true. Even Ekaterina admitted that the boy wasn't entirely wrong.

So, said Alexandra, *based on a teenager's sense of hypocrisy you changed your life?*

Oh, no. It was a start, but it took more.

During the nineties, as the KGB transitioned to the FSB, Yevgeny retained his colonel's rank and pay by playing all sides. The Yeltsin government wanted him out, but the other old men in the ranks wanted him to stay, because if he went, they were sure to follow. Then, in a fit of self-serving pragmatism, he made a deal with the young government to tie his old comrades to the 1991 coup attempt against Gorbachev. By 1998, his position in the FSB was secure, but he had gained a clique of enemies who, in early 2000, placed a bomb under his car. That day, Ekaterina decided to drive herself to the GUM shopping center.

Alexandra had been in London by then, a few years into her law career. She heard the news by telephone, then read it on the BBC World News Web site.

You were devastated, she said.

Of course I was. But this is the part you don't know, so listen.

It took Yevgeny four months to track the five men responsible for her murder. Two he arrested, and the other three he killed himself.

She recoiled before catching herself—he was being honest, after all. *I had no idea.*

I made sure you had no idea.

That should have finished things, and for a while Yevgeny convinced himself that it had, but slowly, week by week, he grew sicker. The doctors found nothing wrong beyond his continual intake of vodka and whisky, but by the end of the year he could hardly leave the house.

Where was I then? she asked.

You were busy. And I wasn't going to trouble you, because I knew something that the doctors didn't know. I knew that my prodigal son had been right. Remember what he said? You're not even aware of your crimes. *He was right. I wasn't aware of them, but my body was, and it was committing slow suicide.*

The United Nations had been a remedy of sorts, and though his old colleagues sniggered about the quicksand of bureaucracy that would certainly engulf him, he felt himself, with each successful move, becoming stronger.

With each good deed? she asked cynically.

Good deeds are a matter of perspective, Little One. If you can convince yourself that what you're doing is good, then all of you will believe it, and maybe it will be good.

So Alexandra joined her father's house of good deeds, a shadow organization lacking even a name (though for convenience they sometimes called it the Library among themselves), and shared duties with her father. Her job lay at some crossroads between the four secretaries, the now forty-two field agents, and Yevgeny himself, for she sometimes helped him decide to whom to deliver nuggets of information. This unstable job description had been his idea, because she needed to learn about all aspects of the craft if she ever, eventually, had to step into his shoes. That she didn't want to step into his shoes seemed beside the point.

On the Monday that Sebastian Hall's disappearance became news, Alexandra called on Deputy Assistant Commissioner Meredith Kaye in a Hampstead pub. Earlier in the year, Yevgeny had brought sensitive information to the Metropolitan Police concerning a smuggling ring, information that the Albanian government hadn't been interested in sharing. So when Alexandra pressed about the disappearance, Kaye hesitated only a moment before telling her about Gephel Marpa of Free Tibet, and that he'd had no reason to be staying at a hotel in a city where he lived.

"What does he say?" asked Alexandra.

"That he was escaping an argument with his wife."

"You think he was there to meet with Sebastian Hall?"

"Maybe," Kaye said, sipping rum and Coke, "but if so, there's no sign they ever met. There is, however, every reason to believe that Sebastian Hall is a false name."

"It is, Meredith. His name is Alan Drummond. American."

The deputy assistant commissioner leaned back, wrists pressed against the edge of the bar. "Well, I'm glad I acquiesced to a drink."

Alexandra pretended to be surprised by surveillance camera blackness around Drummond's escape and listened with some trepidation to the CCTV chronicle of his walk and subway ride over to Hammersmith, but Kaye never mentioned the young hoodlum who wandered into the hotel—perhaps she knew it had been Alexandra or, she thought hopefully, the street camera had just been malfunctioning. They did that a lot. All Kaye said was "We're checking license plates—assumedly he grabbed a car."

This told her that Drummond had, in fact, followed her directions to Hammersmith before finding his own route out of the city.

Kaye said, "One more odd thing. Another guest in the hotel, a woman named Gwendolyn Davis, arrived on Friday, then checked out Saturday morning, even though she had reserved three nights. That in itself isn't so strange, but as a matter of course we ran her papers and came up with . . . well, with nothing. Her American passport looks legitimate, but we've got no record of her entering the country. If she's been living here a while, we have no record of her renting a place, driving a car, or anything."

Freddy didn't sleep over again, but they talked regularly, carefully avoiding promises. When she left town on Wednesday, though, she made the mistake of promising to call him when she got back to town. "When'll that be?" he asked, but she didn't have an answer for him.

From the Marylebone apartment in London, and, from Wednesday, the fourth-floor El Raval studio in Barcelona (where she'd come to talk with an agent who'd bought information from a Basque turncoat), she gathered source intelligence on New Scotland Yard's investigation into the disappearance of Sebastian Hall. She also listened to her father share occasional tidbits from his old sparring partner, Erika Schwartz.

On Saturday morning, she took an express train to Geneva and used spare keys to get into her father's apartment, five floors above the BHI bank on the Quai du Mont-Blanc, overlooking the harbor. She spent only a few weeks a year here, shuttling more often between Library-owned residences in London, Hong Kong, and Mexico City. Before going out again, she showered and changed, then did some work, first sending orders for two agents—one in Tokyo, the other in Kampala—to withdraw from their jobs. Each was being watched by the local police. She directed them to the Lisbon and Bologna safe houses, so the secretaries could debrief them fully.

She'd arranged dinner with an intelligence officer from the U.S. consulate who had, in the past, been friendly. Over plates of salad and foie gras de canard at the Brasserie Bâloise, however, she watched the signs of his friendliness contract.

"So I asked around," he said finally. "This guy, Drummond, was canned months ago. Whatever he's doing, you can't pin it on us."

"I'm not trying to pin anything on you, Steve. I just wonder why Scotland Yard is looking for him, and why he was traveling on a passport connected to an art heist."

Steve popped a liver-smeared toast into his mouth and chewed loudly. He was one of those Americans, the ones who couldn't help but do everything loudly. "I wish I could help you, Alex. Really." Then he leaned back, laying one arm over his stomach.

His face said little, but his body had spoken volumes from the moment he entered the restaurant, and she knew that while what he was saying might be technically true—he really might wish he could help her— the bigger truth was that there was an elephant in the room that he was desperate not to draw attention to. She said, "They told you to stay away from it, didn't they?"

He suddenly noticed his defensive posture and turned his hands palms up. "They? Is that the conspiratorial *They*? I asked about him and just came up cold."

There—the skin pulling back at the temples—now he was lying. "Okay, Steve. Forget about it."

He smiled, perhaps from relief, and grabbed another toast. "Alex, don't tell me this has to do with United Nations fiscal oversight. Every time we talk, you're asking about something that has nothing to do with your office."

"Of course not," she said, winking. "I work for al Qaeda."

Afterward, when she reported to Yevgeny, the old man said, "I think it's time to talk to Milo. I'm flying out tomorrow."

"It was time to talk to Milo a week ago. I don't know why you waited."

"You should come. Just a few days. Public service, and a little time with Milo's family. I know Tina would love to meet you."

"Another time," she said.

"Did you know he's looking for a job?"

"No, Nana. I didn't. Have you made your pitch yet?"

"I wouldn't have to if you'd just take the position," he said, so she hung up.

I t was, of course, a disaster from the start. On that
Wednesday morning, Lester, one of Erika's five-man
team watching Weaver, woke with chills—he'd picked
up a summer flu. Worried that it would spread, she ordered him left behind as the remaining four met with
Yevgeny's men—only two: Francisco, a Spaniard, and
Jan, a Czech. That made six, when Erika had wanted
eight, minimum. She made sure that Gilen, her most
experienced, led the team as they sat in a double room
of the Kings Hotel on Thirty-ninth Street in Brooklyn,
settling on the details. Yevgeny came and went, apparently forced to keep to some UN-related dates. He
seemed, Gilen reported, petrified of discovery—and
old. Gilen asked Erika more than once if she really
trusted this frail, trembling man's intelligence, "because if we fuck this up, someone's bound to trace it
back to us."

"Then don't fuck it up."

Was the risk worth it? As the hours crawled along, she wondered. What, really, did "everything" mean to Yevgeny? Certainly, it didn't match the dictionary definition, but it meant a lot. It meant answers to old mysteries that had plagued her, answers that could turn up some bad eggs in the BND. It meant an eye into Yevgeny's own UN department, and its secretive operations. It meant, perhaps, an eye into the mystery of Yevgeny Primakov himself.

Was all that worth the embarrassment of a failed extraction? What if Tina and Stephanie Weaver put up a fight? Even if Yevgeny was there to explain it to them, how much did they trust Milo's father? How much did Milo trust him?

By 1:00 P.M., New York time, Gilen reported that they had settled on the extraction route from the Weavers' home on Garfield Place, as well as the method of transport—the trunk of a Chevrolet Malibu station wagon, and then the rear of a laundry van—and the approach and withdrawal from the premises. Yevgeny wanted the Weavers taken to a house in southern Connecticut, and from there he could manage the next leg of their escape, though he refused to share details with Gilen. Erika told him not to force the issue.

She did, however, call Yevgeny after listening to Gilen's summary. Why, she asked the old Russian, did the Weaver family have to be taken by force?

"Because speed is of the essence."

"Then go up and tell them to put on their shoes and follow you outside. You do have enough sway with them for this, don't you?"

"They won't be alone. They're being watched."

"By whom?"

Hesitantly, Yevgeny said, "The Chinese."

It wasn't often in her line of work that situations laid themselves out in parallel lines and then started to converge, but whenever that happened she felt that rare rush of aesthetic pleasure that reminded her why she had devoted her life to such an unrewarding career. Patriotism perhaps played a role—she wasn't sure—but it paled in comparison to the joy of seeing puzzle pieces fit together. She said, "Alan Drummond was after Xin Zhu, and now Xin Zhu is after Milo. You aren't going to keep pretending that Milo is an innocent in this, are you?"

"I don't know what his role is, Erika, not really. But he needs my help. I owe him."

"You owe him for what?"

"For my shortcomings as a father," he said, and from the tone of his voice, she even believed him.

"Is this really just a story of revenge, Yevgeny? Alan Drummond sets out to take vengeance for his department? He drags Milo into this, and then Xin Zhu has no choice but to protect himself by . . . by what? By threatening Milo's family?"

Again, he remained silent, his way of saying *yes*. Or *probably*.

"I would do the same thing as Xin Zhu," she said. "You would, too."

His silence now wasn't an affirmation of anything, she knew; it was his inability to think of an answer. She was reaching for a moral point, which was of course irrelevant. Yevgeny wasn't interested in arguing who was right and wrong. If pressed, he probably wouldn't know. Yevgeny was acting entirely on loyalty, which seldom served anyone well.

As when Xin Zhu sat in his office, waiting for word from his agents as they dispatched thirty-three Tourists, Erika Schwartz remained in her office long after other people had cleared out. She stared at the phone, waiting. It rang, finally, a little after midnight, by which time she had finished her evening Riesling, a plate of delivery gyros, and two Snickers bars. Gilen talked first, and then Yevgeny.

From three that afternoon, two of Gilen's agents had been watching the Weaver home. They saw Tina Weaver arrive just after four thirty with Stephanie. At five twelve, a Chinese-food deliveryman arrived toting two bags of food. He buzzed the Weaver home as another male walked up, and both men entered at the same time. The deliveryman, Hanna noted, was Asian, likely Chinese; the resident who entered with him was also Asian, origin unknown. Of course nationalities, particularly in that city, meant little.

Less than five minutes later, the deliveryman was gone, and it wasn't until five forty-eight that Yevgeny got out of Gilen's Chevy a block away and began his walk to the apartment. By then, Yevgeny's men, Francisco and Jan, had reached the apartment's roof via a building three doors down. If anyone reported suspicious activity on the street, the roof was their Plan B.

Yevgeny did not ring before going into the building but used the key Milo had given him. He climbed the stairs to the third floor, found the door unlocked, and then, thinking better of it, continued to the roof-access door, which he unlocked. Jan and Francisco joined him, no one saying a word. "The place was quiet," Yevgeny explained, "except for some neighbor's television." Silently, they entered the apartment, which was empty. They found remnants of dinner, an unopened box of kung pao chicken, and, beside the food, a typed note that read,

THEY ARE SAFE

The place had simply been vacated.

Jan and Francisco searched the rest of the building, looking for a laundry room or some other place they might have gone. They were nowhere.

The three men left the building and sat together in Gilen's car, sharing their discovery and discussing what could have happened. That's when Gilen called Erika in Pullach, and she heard the misery in Yevgeny's voice as he insisted that Xin Zhu now had them. At one point he even said, "I've failed him again." She tried to persuade him that there were other possibilities, but he was immovable. "While we were sitting there, watching the front door, they went by the roof. Francisco and Jan must have just missed them."

There was no point remaining on Garfield Place. Erika agreed that they should terminate the operation and told them to leave by different routes. Yevgeny, however, remained behind. "Milo will be home soon, and someone has to explain it to him."

"I can leave someone with you," she told him, but he wanted no one, not even his own agents, to witness the confrontation he predicted he would have with his son.

"Xin Zhu has played his hand," Yevgeny pointed out. "He'll never come back to this address."

Within the next half hour, Yevgeny was dead.

They knew this approximate time frame because, earlier, Erika had asked her sick agent, Lester, to take a heavy dose of Tamiflu and wait at Penn Station. From there, he followed Milo Weaver back to Garfield Place, where he arrived a little after seven thirty and sat outside while Weaver went upstairs. Weaver did not leave until the next morning—seven o'clock—alone. In the meantime, Gilen had taken over Lester's watch, and after Weaver left he broke into the apartment. He called Erika as soon as he stepped into the foul-smelling, cold bedroom. It was after one o'clock in the afternoon in Germany, and Erika was sitting in front of another untouched salad when he called with the news. Gilen didn't believe Weaver had done it, and Erika didn't believe it either, which meant that there was a half-hour window, between seven and Milo's arrival at seven thirty, when Yevgeny had been killed. Milo had spent the night with his father's corpse, then left on that warm Thursday morning and disappeared.

So this is how it ends, she thought after hanging up. She remembered the early seventies, when the KGB kept in touch with those idiot children with too much Marx and too many guns, who ineptly tried to overthrow capitalism in West Germany. She caught glimpses of Yevgeny Primakov on the periphery of the action.

Eventually, they met in safe houses for discussions of mutual benefit. He began bringing bottles of white wine to their meetings, giving her detailed vineyard histories that were lost on her. Beer had been her drink, but Yevgeny insisted that wine would help her live longer. "We kill ourselves with vodka. Your people do it with beer. Let's try to outlive our people." She remembered her own depression when he was recalled to Moscow suddenly, likely because of an affair he'd had with an American girl who'd joined those Marxist revolutionaries. It only deepened when she met the coarse KGB man who took his place, a man who had no interest in wine, beer, vodka, or anything that did not directly relate to the International Struggle. Now, all that charm and culture lay rotting in a too-small apartment in Brooklyn.

She considered what to do with Yevgeny's body, finally deciding that nothing was to be done besides the obvious—remove his phones and all signs of identification. Weaver had thoughtfully turned the air conditioner to full blast to slow decomposition, and the most important thing was to make sure that her own people made it out of New York unassociated with any of this. Once they were gone, she went through the files and uncovered a number that she had never dialed before, one that she didn't want to dial even now, but it was important that the news come from someone who at least had an inkling of what had happened. It was 6:00 P.M. Thursday, Pullach time.

"Yes?"

"Alexandra Primakov? Hello, my name is Erika

Schwartz. We met once years ago, but you probably don't remember."

A pause. "I know who you are, Miss Schwartz."

"Oh. Good. Where are you now?"

She heard wind through the line; then Alexandra said, "I'm at Geneva International."

"You're not flying to New York, are you?"

"Actually, yes. I'm looking for my father, and I'm having trouble reaching him."

"That's what I'm calling about, Alexandra. Your father."

Alexandra changed her flight and reached Munich's Franz Josef Strauss Airport by eight thirty. Erika was waiting for her at the curb, sitting in her gray Volvo, and by the time they parked at her house in a leafy Pullach neighborhood, she had shared the entire story.

"And where the hell is Milo?" Alexandra asked. It was one of the few things she'd said, and the words seemed to contain all of the anger she'd been holding back.

"We don't know."

"Then I'll find him," she said and climbed out of the car. She walked through the trees that sheltered Erika's house from the road and took out her cell phone. Erika felt a pang of worry—not for Alexandra but for Milo Weaver. There was no telling what this woman would do to him.

Inside, they ate roast chicken and drank Riesling. Alexandra gradually relaxed. "I don't really know him," she said. "Milo. As a teenager, sure, but then he left, and I could count the number of times we've seen each other in the last two decades on a couple of hands."

Erika had relatives she could say the same about. "He's unlikely," she told Alexandra.

"What does that mean?"

What did it mean? The word had just come out of her, perhaps because of the wine. She said, "He's never quite what he seems to be. He's very easy to underestimate."

"And what about his family?"

Erika shrugged.

"Alan Drummond seemed to think he could protect them."

"When did he say that?"

Alexandra didn't answer.

"Well," Erika said, "it wouldn't be the first time an employee of the CIA got something wrong."

Then an odd thing happened. Around four in the morning, Erika's phone rang, and Oskar related a report they'd picked up over the news wire. At eight o'clock on Thursday night, New York time, a team of ten Homeland Security agents, in a flurry of loud, boisterous activity, invaded number 203 Garfield Place. Terrified residents attested that they went directly to the third floor and after knocking and shouting commands broke down the Weaver door. The agents removed a corpse on a stretcher, but since it was covered no one could say for sure who had died, or how. Homeland Security certainly wasn't sharing. They did, however, interview the residents about the events of the last couple of nights. No one knew of anything out of the ordinary. No one except a man named Raymond Lister, the Weavers' next-door neighbor, whom they found tied to his bed and gagged. The journalist writing the story did not learn what Mr. Lister had shared with the agents before he was bundled off in a government SUV, because the head of the Homeland Security team, Special Agent Janet Simmons, cut him off with a "national security" excuse.

Francisco and Jan had not missed Tina and Stephanie Weaver's kidnappers, because, before their arrival, they had not left the building.

She woke Alexandra in the guest room to share this information, but it didn't tell them much more than they already knew.

They had coffee together in the morning, and Erika offered to bring her into the office. "If you don't mind," Alexandra said, "I'd rather stay here. Is your place wired?"

Erika shook her head. "Not that I know of."

"Then I'll stay, and we can compare notes at noon, and again at five. Is this agreeable?"

A lawyer, Erika remembered. She spoke just like a lawyer.

Just before noon on Friday, Oskar walked into her office. She was already on the phone with Berlin, dealing with one of her agent's deaths in Paris. France had sent the body back but was growing irate at what it saw as a territorial infringement. In seven different ways, Erika could only assure the BND president that the man had been on leave. "Are we not allowed to take foreign vacations anymore?"

She tried to wave Oskar away, but he drew an index finger across his neck to get her to hang up. When she didn't respond immediately, he held up a printed CCTV image of Milo Weaver staring directly up at the camera, holding out a paper towel with a note written across it in English, beginning,

To Erika Schwartz, BND-Pullach

As the president said, "The problem, in their eyes, is—" she hung up and said to Oskar, "Where?"

"Frankfurt Airport. Right now."

She took the printout from him and read the brief note again, then looked up at Oskar. "He really is quite mad, isn't he?"

5

What she saw when she stepped out of that bathroom surprised her. It had been . . . four? No, *five* years. She'd come to New York for a Berg & DeBurgh corporate retreat, and one of the American lawyers, a loudmouth named Patrick Hardemann, had over drinks mentioned his daughter, Stephanie, and miserably admitted that "of *course* she doesn't carry the Hardemann name; she goes by her stepbastard's name—*Weaver*." Intrigued, Alexandra quietly fished for the stepdad's given name, then asked where they were living—Park Slope, Brooklyn.

She'd found him easily enough and called to suggest they meet for dinner. "I'd love to see your wife and daughter. Really, Milo, we *are* family." Instead, he'd come alone to the restaurant and after minutes of evasion finally admitted the truth: His wife and daughter didn't know that he had a sister, not even a half sister.

They didn't know about Yevgeny. They knew nothing about his Russian side.

She took the hint and later decided that the world had not become a smaller place because of this, not really, for she hadn't had him in her life to begin with. After leaving for college, Milo Weaver had for all purposes dropped out of the Primakov clan. She convinced herself that she was satisfied to find him relatively happy and healthy— that would have to be enough. Besides, there was a certain poetry to it. For years Yevgeny had kept him a secret from his wife and daughters, and now Milo was keeping them a secret from his own wife and daughter.

Now, here he was again. He'd gotten himself involved in something, and whatever he'd done had killed their father.

What surprised her was that Yevgeny had ever considered giving him the reins to the Library. Who was this anxious-looking man with gaunt cheeks and flakes of gray? The one who had said to Erika's assistant, *If you can't find them, I want you to have me killed*, and meant it? This was the kind of man you used in order to get at someone worthy; a man like this was never the final goal.

Yet it *was* he, her brother, Yevgeny's "holy terror."

He's very easy to underestimate, Erika had said.

"Alexandra," Milo said, his voice breaking.

She walked up to him. This was the reason Yevgeny was dead. She thought she might cry, for she hadn't cried yet, so to stop herself she said, "You'd better talk, Milo. Or I swear I'm going to kill you myself."

His hands had already started to move forward, perhaps for an embrace, but now he pulled them back, palms out. "Okay." He retreated a step. "Wait. What are you *doing* here? Don't assume you can trust these people."

It was an odd thing to say, but then, Yevgeny wouldn't have told Milo what her job was these days. "I'm here on my own," she told him. "They're assisting me."

He blinked. "Jesus. You worked with him?"

"If by *him* you mean our father, then yes. Now, speak."

Milo rubbed his forehead. "He was there—in Brooklyn—to take care of my family."

Christ, he was slow-witted. "I *know* that, Milo. Remember, I've been talking to Erika Schwartz."

"No *names*," Oskar said, irritated.

They both ignored him. Milo nodded, thinking. "Right. I hadn't known he'd brought her into it."

"Sounds like there's a lot you don't know."

Again, he nodded some silent agreement, then frowned. "It's about Alan Drummond."

"*Mein Gott*," said Oskar.

"And Xin Zhu," she said. "But your precious CIA is really at the core, isn't it? Look, Milo, maybe you don't know what happens at this point in the story, so I'll explain. This is where you tell us exactly what they're up to."

"I can tell you what I've seen, but I don't know why they're doing it all."

"They want revenge against the Chinese."

"Apparently not," Milo said, checking his watch. "This has to be quick."

"Then talk."

He sat on the edge of the bed, where Oskar had stationed himself before, and told her in a quick, efficient manner what he knew and how he knew it. It was a story he'd obviously repeated to himself endlessly, pruned of extraneous details, and she imagined that he'd been working it over in order to better understand it himself. Did it make her more sympathetic, knowing how Xin Zhu had threatened him? Not really. When he finished, she said, "You've got to have some opinion by this point."

"The only thing that makes me think this is not a revenge operation is what I was told during one conversation with Irwin and Collingwood. Maybe that was only for my benefit. Maybe they know I'm being run by the Chinese, or perhaps they suspected the safe house was bugged. All I know for sure is that what I'm doing with Leticia is a ruse to distract the Chinese from something else. Leticia thinks it's another attack, but they're not keeping her in the loop."

"Where is Alan Drummond?" she asked as Oskar's phone rang. He answered it.

"No one knows," said Milo. "That's what I've been told."

Oskar said, "Jones is heading for the elevators."

Milo stood but didn't leave. He seemed to be waiting for something, so she said, "I talked to Drummond," then wondered if she should have said anything.

Milo looked at her, frowning again.

"Before," she said, "when he disappeared. He told

me very little, but he did say that your family would be safe. He'd made sure of it."

Milo's eyes grew but then relaxed, the light gone from them. "Everyone makes mistakes," he said and walked to the door. Before leaving, he turned back and spoke to Oskar. "An attempt. Try an attempted kill. That would help clear me with Jones. And if you slip and accidentally get me here," he said, tapping the center of his forehead, "then no hard feelings."

Before either of them could answer, Milo was gone.

"What do you think?" she asked.

Oskar took his tote bag from under the bed and looped it over his shoulder. "I don't believe a word he said."

"He sounded convincing to me."

"He always does, but without knowing exactly what he wants, there's no way of knowing the truth of anything Milo Weaver says. Even then, you can't be sure."

It was the highest compliment she'd heard applied to Milo, even higher than Yevgeny's admission that the teenaged Milo had been right about his corrupted soul. Maybe there really was more to him than met the eye.

Oskar was listening to his phone again. He hung up. "They're taking a taxi to the airport."

Francisco was already at King Abdulaziz International, and he called Alexandra while she and Oskar were on the road, heading there. "They got tickets to Hong Kong," he said, "one stop in Dubai."

"Are they at the gate?"

"Not yet."

"Call back when they are," she said.

Francisco verified that they were at the gate for the Hong Kong flight as Alexandra was entering the airport, but it turned out that Cathay Pacific's Flight 746 was full. She and Oskar booked themselves on a Qatar flight, four hours later. Oskar called for someone to watch Dubai, in case Milo and Leticia left the flight during the layover. Alexandra had two agents in Hong Kong, and she called them to head to the airport. Oskar insisted on sending two of his own. "That's overkill," Alexandra told him. "Jones will see it immediately." They settled on one of Alexandra's and one of his.

She remained in phone contact with Francisco before and after security, and once he reported that Milo and Leticia had entered the jet bridge leading to Flight 746, he told her, "It's real, but I'll wait to be sure."

Alexandra and Oskar were in the air when the call came from Dubai—Flight 746 had landed and taken off again. One of Oskar's people, a Swede named Gunnar, was able to get on board and had verified that Milo and Leticia were sitting together in coach, above the wing.

They stopped briefly in Doha, Qatar, by which time Flight 746 was over India, and by the time Alexandra and Oskar were nearly out of Indian airspace, Flight 746 had landed in Hong Kong at six in the morning, Sunday. Oskar followed Gunnar's reports of their progress to the taxi ranks, while Alexandra's phone bleeped messages from an agent named Dachshund of their progress outside the airport, heading toward town. It didn't take long before a heavily made-up stewardess leaned over Alexandra and Oskar and whispered threats if they didn't turn off their phones. She pointed at the back of the seats in front of them, where two radiotelephones were embedded into the rear of the headrests. "That's why we have these," she said. Neither Alexandra nor Oskar, however, wanted to use a credit card. Not for this trip.

Their solution was to creep back to the toilets, one at a time to avoid suspicion, and squat in the cramped space, typing out messages and reading replies, and by the time they were approaching Hong Kong International they had accumulated enough of a narrative to begin speculations.

Upon landing after their eleven-hour flight, Milo and Leticia had taken a taxi directly to the grand Peninsula Hotel. Leticia paid the driver—she was the only one carrying a bag. They entered the hotel, one of Oskar's men following. He reported that they made it almost to the elevators before Milo placed a hand on Leticia's arm and whispered to her. There seemed to be a disagreement, for Leticia clearly wanted to reach the elevator, but Milo kept squeezing her arm to restrain her. Finally, Leticia acquiesced, and they left the hotel. Outside (from here, Alexandra's man, Dachshund, reported), rather than asking for a taxi, they walked around the corner to Nathan Road, then back to the next hotel at the intersection with Middle Road, the Kowloon, where they checked into a room under the names Gwendolyn Davis and John Nadler.

"They saw something they didn't like," Alexandra said as their plane descended toward the island.

"You mean your brother saw something he didn't

like. Jones wasn't sure. The lobby was full—somebody there spooked Milo."

"Maybe it was your guy."

"Impossible," Oskar said, then chewed his upper lip, stretching out his thin mustache.

"They weren't checking in," she pointed out after a moment. "So who were they there to see? Alan Drummond?"

"Maybe Xin Zhu."

"Can your people access the hotel records?"

Oskar winked and took out his phone again.

Sure enough, by the time they were in their taxi, riding down the highway skirting the green, mountainous edge of Lantau Island and watching the arched backs of green islets sticking out of the water, Oskar's phone bleeped and informed him that, as of yesterday, one Sebastian Hall had been checked into room 212.

They crossed the Lantau Link and on Tsing Yi headed south to Stonecutters Island's walls of colored containers and stacked highways before diving deep into Kowloon's dense metropolis of skyscrapers and harbors. Signs in Chinese and English pointed them toward Victoria Harbor, and with so many signs and faces to look at neither bothered to talk any further about their purpose in being there. It wasn't the paranoia of Xin Zhu or Milo Weaver; it was the sensory pleasure of being faced with such a richness of colors.

Once they got out in front of the Peninsula Hotel's classic European façade along Salisbury Road, a white-gloved doorman opening the door for her, Alexandra immediately spotted Dachshund, a tall Malaysian with a mustache. He gave her only a cursory glance, signifying that things were normal. Inside, Oskar pointed out his agent, a short, heavyset woman talking loudly with what appeared to be a plainclothes security guard, distracting his attention from their entrance.

Alexandra handed Oskar her passport. "You check in for both of us. I'm going up."

"I'm coming," Oskar said, his smile disappearing.

"I've talked to him before. We have a relationship. Call me when you've got the room."

He stared at her a moment, hard, then headed back to the front desk.

She shared the elevator with an elderly Chinese woman who got out on two, which gave Alexandra a chance to see that the second floor was empty of human surveillance, as was the third floor. It was after nine in the morning, and some doors had newspapers like mats in front of them, others soiled room service trays. She took the stairwell back down to the second floor. By then, the elderly woman was inside her room, and Alexandra was alone. She found 212 quickly enough, and took a breath. She tapped on the door. Silence. She banged with knuckles and, just as before, laid on a thick Yorkshire. "Charlie? I know you're in there!" Pause. Nothing. She'd expected him to at least say something, given their rapport. Three more bangs with the side of her fist. "Charlie, I'm not leaving! I—"

The door to 212 clicked and, almost simultaneously, swung open. Light from the hall made only minor work of the darkness in the room, where the blinds had been pulled tight, and all she saw of the man was what was visible from behind the door frame. The toe of a patent leather shoe. A grayish hand pointing a SIG SAUER 9 mm at her. Half of a face.

"Oh," she said. "You're not Charlie."

"No," said the man. "Now go back to where you came from. *Now.*"

Part Four

PERPETUAL REVOLUTION

**MONDAY, JUNE 2 TO
TUESDAY, JULY 1, 2008**

1

Among the surprises that came at Xin Zhu over those weeks, Liu Xiuxiu's stellar performance was perhaps the greatest. He'd brought her on with confidence, sensing in her a natural-born operative, yet he'd known her so briefly that, as soon as she and He Qiang had flown to America, he began to experience doubts. As with the killing of the Tourists, once things were set in motion, doubts only served to interfere with his work, so he set them aside as he dealt with more immediate problems.

Time, for example. He'd been given two weeks to take care of the American problem, but by the second committee meeting on June 2, three weeks before Yevgeny Primakov's death, he'd only just gained control of Alan Drummond, and Liu Xiuxiu's seduction of Stuart Jackson was still in its initial phases. When asked how much more time he needed, Zhu made a show of thinking about this, and said, "For progress? Two more weeks.

For a definite end? A month, hopefully. Perhaps a month and a half."

No one spoke for a few seconds. The men examined their laps, the walls, the carpet. Only Sun Bingjun watched Zhu, a light smile playing in the corner of his mouth, as if he were musing over a morning spent with the bottle. This possibility terrified Zhu, for Sun Bingjun had turned out to be his greatest ally.

Wu Liang raised his hands in mock exasperation. "I suppose it's time for a vote, but beforehand, I would like to remind the committee what Xin Zhu has done when given an abundance of freedom. He has murdered wholesale, and he has saddled good men with such a level of suspicion that one chose to end his own life. I have to wonder how many more corpses we'll be faced with after another month."

Sun Bingjun shifted in his chair. "I, on the other hand, have to wonder how many Chinese citizens will become corpses if Xin Zhu is *not* allowed to continue his investigation. I would happily trade the lives of a few Americans for the safety of Olympic crowds." He paused to let that self-evident truth sink in. "We all know how intelligence works. Xin Zhu may have nothing for three weeks, and then the next day it could all come in a great flood. Let's not handcuff Xin Zhu."

The vote was split along predictable lines, 3–2 for giving Xin Zhu whatever time he needed to complete his work unhindered.

This success filled him with pleasure, though the feeling was short-lived. Hector Garza, a.k.a. José Santiago, was spotted in Moscow, and at the same time the Tourist named Tran Hoang entered South Korea—at least, his passport crossed the border—and then disappeared. Then, on Monday, June 9, on his way to Cambodia to meet with Uighur exiles to further the conversation Leticia had begun with them the previous month in Beijing, Alan Drummond skipped his connecting flight in Seattle and vanished in a rental car. Cursing himself, Zhu called Drummond throughout the day, realizing that if he simply *disappeared*, there would be nothing he could really do. You can't threaten a man you can't find. So it was a surprise when, the next day, Alan Drummond answered his phone. "What?"

"Where are you?"

"Tokyo. I'm heading out again within the hour."

"What are you doing in Tokyo?"

"There was a change of plans. Get to Vancouver and start another path. I'm heading to London to meet with some Tibetans."

"You should have told me."

"Sorry, comrade," Drummond said, sounding pleased with himself. "I told you these people are tricky. They'll keep me in the dark until your head is on a stick. Even then, they probably won't tell me what happened."

Then, in London, he did precisely what Zhu had worried he might do—he vanished, leaving only one clue: the name Sebastian Hall. A disaster. He needed good news, and he needed it quickly, for Wu Liang and the committee were waiting for his progress reports.

The day after Zhu spoke for the first time to Milo Weaver, the good news finally came.

As per his request, from the moment of her arrival

in Washington Liu Xiuxiu had been sending reports every four days, and perhaps out of a desire to please she wrote at length, giving not only the facts but her reflections on them, putting her inner world on display. Through these reports, he had watched her steady progress and, more importantly, how she gradually settled into her new world. Liu Xiuxiu had arrived on May 20 with He Qiang, and together they had met Sam Kuo, the embassy attaché, in a Dupont Circle–area club. There, Sam Kuo handed off keys to a nearby apartment and gave them a list of forthcoming events—charity dinners, political rallies, cultural nights—that would have a higher percentage of Washington movers in attendance: people like the senator, Nathan Irwin, and the retired CIA officer, Stuart Jackson, who kept his hand in the political pool. Decisions were made, and Sam Kuo arranged invitations for Liu.

Her public face had begun with a dinner for a charity funding research into leukemia, where she arrived as the guest of the embassy's chief doctor. Neither of the targets were in attendance, but she mixed as best she could. Two nights later, though, on May 27, when she joined Sam Kuo himself at the Kennedy Center for a performance of the opera *Elektra*, they were both pleased to find Stuart Jackson in attendance, and without his wife. Jackson was the only one of the three conspirators that Kuo had a personal acquaintance with. "Luck is already on our side," Liu Xiuxiu wrote. "He's a tall man, stiff, white-haired, but proud of it. He's intimate with religion. Not to presuppose too much, but this should not be difficult. Those with the most barriers don't drop them in pieces; when they weaken their walls crumble completely."

Xin Zhu worried at first that Liu Xiuxiu's confidence was too expansive. She had, after all, built her reservoir of experience within the confines of mainland China. Only a rare bird would be able to master the nuances of another country in such a short time. Nevertheless, he had forgotten that most of her clients had been foreigners, and he had forgotten that she, like the rest of the world, already knew so much about American love and lust from the cinema. In a particularly philosophical report, she wrote, "I don't imagine that Hollywood produces a perfect reflection of American relationships any more than some of our own films perfectly reflect the lives of working people. However, as with our own films, American audiences witness what they take as the proper rhythm of romance, and are changed by the experience. I've seen it in my clients; they think of real sex as something they saw in a pornographic film, something that has always been denied them, and only them. Likewise, Americans feel disappointed when serendipity and little cinematic miracles do not fill their relationships. It goes a way toward explaining the high rates of divorce in this country."

She'd obviously spent a long time thinking about these things, and now she had a chance to put her theories to practical use. To make life easier for Jackson, she had given herself a Western name, Sue. To bring out his curiosity, she claimed to be a painter and filled her apartment with large, unsigned abstracts rented from an artist Sam Kuo knew.

Two days after the Kennedy Center, she ran into Jackson at a coffee shop near his Georgetown house. A smile, a modest laugh, and during their brief talk a hand on his arm—once, and briefly. A slipped confession: "I go weak in the presence of powerful men." A note for the future: "My girlfriend and I are going to the Flashpoint next Wednesday to see a play—I don't know what it is, but she swears it'll be interesting." Then, as she was leaving, "Sorry—I must have sounded stupid." It was a statement that demanded his denial— but before he could protest, she fled the store, leaving him with the desire to see her again and clarify that she hadn't sounded stupid at all.

That he actually showed up at the small theater on Wednesday, June 4, was almost too good to believe. Liu Xiuxiu had come with a Chinese American dancer, Sam Kuo's mistress, and in the lobby, she pretended not to see Stuart Jackson until he was standing right next to her. He smiled and offered his hand. She took it and then leaned forward to accept his kisses on her cheeks—something Jackson had not planned to do, but could not deny her. She introduced her friend, who knew to smile and remain distant until, during a pause, she suggested that they have a drink after the show. "From what I've read about this play, we'll need one."

Jackson pursed his lips, considering this. "I may have to juggle some things to make it work."

"Oh, *please*," Liu Xiuxiu said, full of childlike eagerness.

The Bridge of Bodies turned out to be a one-woman play about an immigrant's return to her birthplace in

Haiti, involving numerous costume changes, political commentary, and moments of magical realism that, as Kuo's mistress had told them, required a postshow drink to digest properly. On their way to a bar, the friend's phone rang, and she had to bow out—her boyfriend had returned early from Canada, she claimed, and was demanding her presence. "Tell him to come out and join us," Stuart Jackson said, perhaps worried where this was heading.

"Oh, no. When he's in this mood, he's a bore." As she backed away, she gave Liu Xiuxiu a significant wink.

Liu Xiuxiu did not broach any subjects of significance that first evening, and being, if not a politician, then of a political demeanor, Jackson knew how to charm a woman with questions rather than statements. She gave a story of her life involving immigrant parents who brought her, at ten, to Los Angeles, the strictures of a traditional upbringing, and her attempts to break free and swim in the currents of American life. "Optimism," she said, smiling. "This is America's gift to the world."

Though she made it clear that she lived alone, she made no attempt to bring him back to her place. "If someone is sitting on a fence," she explained to Zhu, "pushing never helps." So the night ended chastely, them sharing a taxi to her place and her standing on the sidewalk, waving as the car took him home. He had her phone number, though she had made it a point not to ask for his.

Jackson called her on Monday the ninth, the same

day Alan Drummond left for Seattle, and asked if she would like to have dinner with him on Wednesday. A quick check told Zhu that Jackson's family was out of town for the week, and he passed that information back to Liu Xiuxiu. "This is good," he told her during one of their rare telephone conversations.

"Yes," she answered, then paused.

"What is it?"

"It's too fast."

"You said he likes you. You said you got along."

"He does like me, but he's also careful. He's from the world of intelligence. I expected to have to run into him at the coffee shop again."

"His family's out of town. He sees it as his only chance."

"Maybe," she said, and he liked that, despite her confidence, she was suspicious of her successes. She was going to develop into an excellent agent.

It was on Wednesday, after dinner at a small French restaurant outside the Beltway, that she invited him up to her apartment for a drink. He seemed amused by her small place and confused by the paintings, which she refused to interpret for him. "Art is communication," she told him, "and if it doesn't communicate on its own, it's a failure." However, she could sense his excitement, having been welcomed into the bohemian art world, and when she poured him a second Scotch he said, "Would it be all right if I kissed you?"

She laughed at this, and when she saw the dismay in his face she said, "I've been waiting for you to kiss me ever since *Elektra*."

He left in the morning with a bounce in his step. She could tell that this was new for him; he hadn't realized how freeing it would make him feel. When she wrote out her report, she even noted that he was generous in bed, ensuring that her orgasm was taken care of before focusing on his own. Despite himself, Zhu thought of his own sex life with Sung Hui, wondering how she would report on him.

Jackson was busy all Thursday, but on Friday, after attending a reception, he arrived at her apartment at one o'clock in the morning, slightly drunk. They spent much of Saturday together, until he had to leave for rural Pennsylvania to join his family. On that same day, in London, Alan Drummond disappeared.

It was going amazingly well. Liu Xiuxiu had not yet broached the target subjects with him, but Zhu trusted her, and knew that this was an area that she understood better than he ever would. Jackson had, however, discussed some of the projects he was working on with various politicians and congressional committees. His role was adviser, he told her, for he had a breadth of experience "that these youngsters can't even fathom. Sometimes I think that they'd sink if I wasn't there to plug up the holes in their boats." Then he mentioned that he even used his vast experience to advise on some project "that deals with issues related to China."

Instead of pressing, she turned it into a taunt. "So you're an expert on China, are you?"

"I know a thing or two about a thing or two."

"Is that so?" she asked, tugging off the panties she had just squeezed into.

Jackson and his family returned from Pennsylvania on Tuesday, and when he called her the next day he sounded upset. "I can't stop thinking about you. When can we meet?"

This time, she delayed. Her uncle was in town, staying with her until Friday. The uncle, of course, was He Qiang, who was only staying the day to check on her and to liaise with Sam Kuo. On Saturday, June 21, as Milo Weaver celebrated his birthday, Jackson arrived mad with sexual excitement, and they ignored the bed, ending up on the old hardwood floor and tearing one of the paintings in their tussle. Afterward, the talking began. He was under incredible stress, he explained elusively. The family? she asked. "Yes, but no. Not that. Work." Some extremely difficult maneuvering was going on with that project he had mentioned before.

"Something to do with China?" she asked and immediately kicked herself for being so obvious.

But he didn't hesitate. "Yes. It's . . . look, I'm not young anymore—you can see that. Once, I was able to deal with these things, but that was a long time ago. Now, I'm more of a politician than anything else. I know how to charm, I know how to lie, I know *people*. But when these sorts of things happen, you realize how little control you really have over your world."

"I don't understand."

He paused, stroking her arm, perhaps wondering how much he could say. "I'm not a spy, not anymore."

She sat up at that, because it was the only plausible reaction. "Who says you're a spy?"

"No one, no one," he said, waving it away. "Forget it."

She pretended to forget, her only reference to it being the additional kindness she lavished on him when he returned for two hours on Monday afternoon, and again on Wednesday, June 25, the same day Milo Weaver went to Washington to meet Nathan Irwin and Dorothy Collingwood. What Liu Xiuxiu didn't know was that Jackson had chosen to spend the afternoon with her rather than sit with his coconspirators as they vetted Weaver, though Xin Zhu put this together easily enough. It certainly meant something important, but even more important was what he told her. He again brought up his work-related anxieties, and Liu Xiuxiu posed the question, "Why do you feel like a spy? It's none of my business, but I hate to see it tear you up."

He labored over his answer before saying, "Because I'm sitting there looking at information we're getting out of China, and it's obvious that this isn't just regular intelligence. It's too good to be that. We've got someone right in the Chinese government giving us reams of excellent information."

According to her report, she kept her composure, but who knew what the truth was? She asked, "So what's the problem with that? That's good, isn't it?"

"Sure, but it's too much information, too much and too good. I'm told all this is because our source's wife, some ferociously ambitious bitch, is getting him to sell off as much intel as possible before they disappear from China with their financial security blanket. So our guy is being reckless," Jackson said, stroking her bare hip.

"That's his problem," she said after a moment. "You'll benefit from his mistakes, won't you?"

He stared at her, maybe wondering about her level of cynicism, and said, "The *real* problem is someone else, another official who's onto him. With the amount of intelligence we're getting it's just a matter of time before this bastard catches our man. You see?"

She nodded.

Jackson took his hand from her hip. He rubbed his eyes and sighed. "Xin Zhu, that's what they call this bastard, and when he catches our man he'll string him up and gut him. We'll have nothing, and our one friend in their government will be dead. *That's* the problem. These young guys only care what intelligence they can get out of him right now, but what about next month? Next year?" He shook his head. "Xin Zhu," he said, his repetition of her boss's name making her quiver, "is our problem, and we've got to get rid of him."

That there was a threat against him was not news, but three words—*ferociously ambitious bitch*—told Zhu more than he had hoped for. He only knew of one high-ranking ministry official whose wife matched that description.

2

Xin Zhu had come into the office at five in the morning to decode and read Liu Xiuxiu's report, and he felt he needed more sleep to be able to understand its ramifications. Instead, though, he sent out for breakfast. He had just ordered a bowl of congee with duck eggs when his cell phone began to chirp with incoming messages. These were from He Qiang, but they were forwarded reports from his favored agent, Xu Guanzhong, who had been assigned to watch the Weaver home.

Xu Guanzhong had taken a room across the street from the apartment, just over the Garfield Farm Market, listening to the microphones they had installed. He listened to Tina Weaver order Chinese food, receive it from a deliveryman and, around five, speak to her husband on the phone. Light, unconcerned.

After the call, they heard a television sitcom. Then, a few minutes later, there was a knock on the door. Tina

Weaver said to her daughter, "Don't break that," as she walked to the limit of the microphone's range and opened the door. *"Hey,"* was the last word she said. There was the soft thump of a body hitting the floor. Stephanie Weaver's voice, "Mom? Who is it?" A grunt.

Movement. Heavy steps out to the front door. Silence. The footsteps returned, paused, then left again. Silence. Footsteps crossing the apartment, then the television was silenced. Back to the front door. The catch of the door being shut.

He Qiang called to discuss the sounds, and they considered options. He Qiang felt the only option was to send Xu Guanzhong over to the apartment, but Zhu was unsure. That was when He Qiang said, "Hold on. He just sent a message—someone's going in. I've got a picture here. It's Milo Weaver's father."

Zhu listened to this live, for by now Xu Guanzhong had patched his microphones through to He Qiang's laptop, and He Qiang had turned his phone so that Zhu could hear everything. Yevgeny Primakov knocked on the Weavers' door, calling, "Hello? Ladies?" Nothing. He tried the door, found it unlocked, and then left. After some seconds he returned with what sounded like two more men and walked inside quietly, moving through the whole apartment. A single Russian curse—*"Sukin syn"*—and then, in English, "Anything. Any sign."

After a minute, a South American accent said, "It was quick. No struggle."

"Here's a note," said an Eastern European voice.

Another Russian curse from Primakov. They left, and Xu Guanzhong saw the old man exit the apartment building with two younger men. A Chevrolet Malibu station wagon pulled up to the curb, and Primakov got inside with the other two, while a man and a woman took positions outside, as if keeping guard. Within ten minutes, it was over. Primakov and his men got out, the car drove off, and Primakov's men left in separate directions, as did the man and woman. Yevgeny Primakov, however, reentered the apartment building.

On the microphones, his distress was recorded. He poured himself a drink from the refrigerator, then walked from room to room, muttering to himself, sounding like the confused old man he must have been. Walk, stop, walk. Finally, a longer stop, and louder muttering in Russian. All Zhu could make out was the phrase ". . . if not here . . ."

A glass set down. Heavier steps out the front door and, distantly, banging. Hand against a neighbor's door. In English: "You're in there! I know you're in there!" Silence. More banging, then silence.

When Yevgeny Primakov returned to the apartment, closing the door behind himself, what he said in Russian was clear. "Idiot. Old, damned idiot." He was angry with himself, ashamed. He went to the bathroom and turned on the water in the sink. Splashing.

From the angle of the microphone, Zhu and He Qiang and Xu Guanzhong were able to hear what Yevgeny Primakov could not: namely, the front door opening and closing again.

The water was shut off, and muted grunting came from Primakov, the sound of someone muttering into a thick towel as he walked into the living room.

Then the unmistakable *thk-thk* of a suppressor-equipped pistol. The thud of a body hitting the floor. The front door opening and closing again.

"Xu Guanzhong is not going in," Zhu told He Qiang as soon as the sounds ended. "Someone over there knows exactly what he's doing, and I'll not have any of you killed. Not today, at least."

So they waited, and as they waited Zhu thought about Yevgeny Primakov, feeling an overwhelming sadness, not unlike the sadness Erika Schwartz felt, that this man had ended his days in a Brooklyn apartment. Unlike Schwartz's, however, Zhu's sadness was less for Yevgeny Primakov—who, really, he hardly knew—than for himself. Would Xin Zhu end up dead on some foreign floor? Or might his death be even less noble, the slow deterioration of political squabbles—or, eventually, the easy escape that Bo Gaoli had chosen?

Xu Guanzhong reported Milo Weaver's arrival at seven forty, not long after Zhu's steaming bowl of congee arrived. Together, they listened to Weaver in the apartment. Zhu had no idea who had taken his family and killed his father, but he knew there was only one possible move for him now if he didn't want to end up like Yevgeny Primakov—if not dead, then dead in the water. He picked up the phone and dialed.

"Where are they?" was how Milo Weaver answered the call, making this easier for him.

"Out of the way," Zhu answered, which was technically true.

Shen An-ling arrived a little after eight, and Zhu

began by talking him through Liu Xiuxiu's revelations. "Our philandering conspirator has admitted that there's a mole."

Shen An-ling stared hard at him. He looked as if he, too, hadn't gotten much sleep, his hair matted and dirty. Perhaps realizing this, he ran fingers through his strands. "Just like that?"

"Just like that."

"Well."

"Yes?"

Shen An-ling stared at the desk, then raised his eyes. "Do you believe him?"

"It fits our theory. Additionally, there was one clue the senator mentioned. He referred to their mole's wife, calling her . . ." He lifted a piece of paper from his increasingly disordered desk. "Here. He called her a 'ferociously ambitious bitch'."

Again, Shen An-ling stared. Of the five members of the committee that was making their lives difficult, only Wu Liang's wife truly matched that description. Chu Liawa was more famous for her ambition than she was for her powerful husband. For once, though, Shen An-ling didn't bother stating the obvious. He only said, "Is she really that good?"

"Liu Xiuxiu? I think she is."

"But *that* good? Good enough that a CIA man would share such classified information with a Chinese girl?"

"I don't know," Zhu admitted, then, to change the subject, told him about the rest. Milo Weaver's meeting with the conspirators, then the disappearance of his family and the murder of his father. That left Shen An-ling—again, uncharacteristically—speechless. "This changes a lot," said Zhu.

"There's another player."

"Two other players," Zhu corrected. "Yevgeny Primakov came with others, probably his United Nations people, assumedly to take the family into custody. Yet someone else actually took the wife and daughter, and then killed Primakov. It's extremely messy."

By then, an e-mail had delivered all of Xu Guanzhong's photographs, which included clear shots of three men and one woman who had helped Yevgeny Primakov in Brooklyn. They ran the faces through the system, coming up with three matches. One, presumably the South American accent they had heard over the microphones, was Francisco Soto González, a Chilean who had worked for three months in Yevgeny Primakov's financial section of the UN Security Council's Military Staff Committee, before being let go for no apparent reason two years ago and dropping out of the records. The woman and the man who had lingered on the street were known field agents for the German Federal Intelligence Service, the BND.

By seven that evening—seven o'clock Thursday morning, New York time—He Qiang reported that Milo Weaver had left the apartment for his meeting with Leticia Jones. He Qiang asked for permission to go into the apartment, which Zhu denied. "Consider the place radioactive," he said. "We don't know who's watching it."

They tracked Jones and Weaver, despite the Mexico City evasion, and Zhu was back in the office the next morning when he learned of Milo Weaver's attack on the Therapist. Despite his growing anxiety, Zhu laughed at the news. "How is the Therapist?" he asked.

"His ego's a mess," He Qiang told him. "He believes that we kidnapped Weaver's family, and he's angry that we didn't warn him."

"Let's keep it that way. We'll put someone in Frankfurt and someone else in Jeddah. I'd like you to go back to Washington, meet with Liu Xiuxiu, and then pack up."

"We're going home."

"She will stay another week. Let's not blow her cover too soon."

"A vacation."

"She's earned it."

"And the Therapist?"

"Give him a bonus and tell him he should be happy Weaver let him live. We're done with him."

He Qiang paused for a moment too long.

"What?"

"I just wish we knew who took the family."

It was Saturday, noon, when the call came. He was at home, having just finished a late breakfast with Sung Hui, who was turning on the television. He had spent so long looking westward that when the clerk from the Third Bureau, which dealt with the territories of Hong Kong, Macau, and Taiwan, said, "Comrade Colonel, we've come across one of your foreigners," Zhu assumed he was calling about someone in Germany or Saudi Arabia. Perhaps it wasn't even that he'd been looking westward, but that he'd spent the morning watching

Sung Hui, wondering about Milo Weaver's missing wife over in America. Either way, it was a surprise when the clerk on the line said, "You put a flag on Sebastian Hall, American. He's about to land in Hong Kong. Would you like us to hold on to him?"

A gift from heaven. Alan Drummond was coming to him.

"Let him pass through, but put at least six men on him. Don't lose him."

"Understood."

Two hours later, he was told that Sebastian Hall—a Caucasian man who fit Alan Drummond's description—had checked into the Peninsula Hotel, room 212. He was dwelling on his pleasure when he received another call, this one from Sun Bingjun. "Xin Zhu," he said slowly, sounding like he already had a few drinks in him, "Wu Liang just gave me some interesting news."

"Yes?"

"He tells me Alan Drummond is in Hong Kong."

How information traveled. "It's true, Comrade Lieutenant General. He's in a room in the Peninsula."

"So you'll be arresting him?"

"I'm not sure I will."

"Good. I was going to suggest we take care of this more quietly."

"Not that either," Zhu said, for he didn't want Alan Drummond dead. Not at this point, at least.

"Then what are you planning to do, Xin Zhu?"

It took him a moment to think it through, watching his wife smiling vaguely at something on television, but Sun Bingjun was waiting. He hated making decisions like this. "Alan Drummond expects us to detain him, or to attack him. Thus, we will do neither."

"Are you sure, Xin Zhu? This could be your only chance to clean up your mess."

"I understand that, comrade, but if we kill him, nothing will be cleaned up. If we arrest him, we'll be forced to play the game the way he wants us to play it. No. The only solution is to wait and watch."

"Maybe he wants to talk."

"In that case, he can pick up the phone. He knows how to get in touch with me."

Sun Bingjun said nothing.

"I've already recalled some agents from America. They're familiar with the situation. In the meantime, I'll send Shen An-ling with some men to assist the Third Bureau's surveillance."

"I hope you know what you're doing, Xin Zhu."

"So do I, Sun Bingjun."

"And if you need anything, anything at all, do not hesitate to call on me."

"Thank you, Comrade Lieutenant General," Zhu said, thinking that things, finally, were turning his way. "Let's hope I don't need anything."

3

Using the passports from the hotel, Milo and Leticia took a Cathay Pacific flight that left Jeddah at two ten, landing in Dubai to let off and take on more passengers before continuing on to Hong Kong International. While they sat on the tarmac in Dubai, Leticia checked her phone, read a message, then walked to the rear of the plane to make a call. When she returned, she had removed her abaya, and Milo got the sense that something else had changed as well. It wasn't until they were a couple of hours from Hong Kong, nine hours into their journey, that she said, "By the way, Milo. Your father's dead."

She'd chosen an ideal moment, when his eyes were closed and he was starting to fade into sleep, but he used that to deflect, moaning, "Huh?"

"Your father," she said. "Yevgeny Aleksandrovich Primakov. He's dead."

He snapped open his eyes and pulled back from her,

glaring. It was the only thing he could think to do. "What the hell are you talking about?"

She was watching him so closely. "Milo, I don't know how many ways I can keep saying it."

"Says who?"

"Says Dorothy, that's who. Homeland Security knocked down your door on Thursday night and found your dad's body."

He blinked. "What? In my—*wait*. What about Tina and Stephanie? Were they there when this happened?" He was trying to measure out the hysteria in his voice. "Did they see this?"

Quickly, Leticia shook her head. "No, they're fine. Don't worry about them. They were at a restaurant."

Relief—just a touch for show—then confusion. "I don't get it. Homeland was there? Why?"

"You tell me."

"And who killed Yevgeny? Why was he in the apartment?"

"How'm I supposed to know?"

He put on his thinking face. "Call her back. Now. Tell her she has to protect my family."

"Already done, Milo."

"What does that mean?"

"She told me that they moved your ladies to a safe house uptown. They're fine," she said, and he marveled at how easily she could spin a lie. "What they don't understand is who offed your dad. Any ideas?"

"Let me out."

"What?"

He began to stand. "I said, let me out. Now."

She got up so he could step into the corridor, then settled back down, looking up at him. He played up his anxiety, for it was the one true emotion he needn't hide. He said, "You can thank Alan Drummond for it. Alan Drummond and Dorothy Collingwood and Nathan-fucking-Irwin. Even you, Leticia."

"Ain't none of us pulled that trigger," she said, a touch of insult to her voice.

"We both know who pulled the trigger," Milo said, "and he wouldn't have done it if it hadn't been for all of you." He looked as if he were going to spit on her, and, at that moment, talking himself through the emotions all over again, he nearly did spit on her. He held back, though, and decided to push her into a corner. "Call her back. I want to talk to them."

"To your family?"

"They'll want to hear from me."

Leticia shrugged. "I'll call, see what I can do," she said, but for the rest of the flight, she didn't take out her phone.

By the time they landed in Hong Kong it was six o'clock Sunday morning, and they'd spent eleven hours on the plane. Milo had taken some of Leticia's Adderall—she'd gotten a refill in Jeddah—and he was alert as he showed his Canadian passport to a uniformed man with quick, efficient movements. Leticia went through a different line, and as Milo walked alone through the glittering airport, speculating on everything, he noticed a short man in cheap civilian clothes approaching him, catching his eye. As he neared, the man turned his left hand to reveal a cell phone nestled in the palm. Milo opened his right hand. As they passed each other, he accepted the phone and slipped it into his jacket pocket.

The phone didn't ring, and by the time he met Leticia under the futuristic awning over the taxi station, where a steady South China Sea breeze cleared away cigarette smoke, he felt a pressure in his chest waiting for a call to come. Leticia grabbed one of the red taxis that went into the city center, and he climbed in after her, sitting behind the driver. "The Peninsula," she told the driver. He hoped they were being watched, for a call from Zhu while sitting beside Leticia Jones would be worse than a disaster.

It didn't ring, and as they crossed bridges and passed expanses of water, finally sinking into the knot of claustrophobic towers, he tried to get straight in his head the various people he was dealing with here. Zhu, watching from a distance. Leticia and, by extension, Collingwood, Irwin, and Jackson, were close enough to touch. Somewhere, Erika Schwartz's people were working with Alexandra and her United Nations people. In a crowded city like Hong Kong, with so many hands on the wheel, things could go very wrong.

He wondered what Leticia really knew. Had Collingwood told her the truth about his family, that they had disappeared, or had she lied to Leticia? Was it possible that Leticia believed what she'd told him?

He thought of his sister. *Sister.* He still couldn't quite believe he'd faced off with Alexandra, nor that

Yevgeny had had the gall to hire her for his agency. She, he suspected, was the assistant that their father had said did not want to take over his job. Who would?

And then a part of him, the tiny, wiggling, panicked mortal who lives inside all of us, even Tourists, wondered what would happen if Leticia's phone rang and she said to him, "Here you are, Milo—you can talk to your wife." What if Leticia was on the side of the angels?

The Peninsula Hotel, with its looped drive that in itself seemed a luxury on this crowded island, was bustling with activity when they got out of the taxi. Leticia smiled at the doorman who let them in, and it was in the creamy colonial lobby that Leticia finally leaned close to Milo's ear and said, "Alan's in 212. We're here to get him."

"Extract him?" Milo asked, looking around the bustling space. Faces of many colors and shapes floated around.

"Something like that. He's been a pain in our asses for too long," she said, striding toward the elevators.

Milo felt frustrated by her rush, and by the mix of nationalities. What did he really expect to see? Men hiding behind newspapers? Women waiting for dates who were never going to come? Perhaps, but the most useful way to approach any entrance was to begin by suspecting everyone and everything. Then he saw it, against one of the many squared columns.

Milo caught her arm. "Wait."

"What?"

There, a large Chinese man, big boned, a black mole on the cheek, sitting in one of the thronelike chairs scattered throughout the lobby, actually thumbing a newspaper. "Not now," he told her. "We're being watched."

"We're always being watched," she said, and pulled out of his grip, heading forward.

He jogged to catch up and grabbed her elbow. "Brooklyn," he whispered. "I recognize one of them from Brooklyn. At my daughter's school."

That got her attention. "Well, it's a popular hotel."

"No," he said. "He was only there a couple of days. Said he was a father, but no one saw him with a child."

Leticia stared a moment into Milo's eyes, then relaxed. If the Chinese had brought someone over from America who had already been watching Milo, then they'd likely do more than just watch the two of them take Alan away. "Okay, baby. Let's go somewhere else."

The modern Kowloon Hotel sat on a crowded stretch of the Middle Road, opposite the rear of the Peninsula. They installed themselves in a seventh-floor room, and then Leticia brought him into the bathroom and turned on the shower. Quietly, she asked him to explain himself one more time, which he did. Why did he remember this man's face? "He was suspicious." Did he think this man was connected to the murder of his father? "I strongly suspect it," Milo said coldly, not bothering to mention that the man's name was He Qiang and that he had kidnapped his family, the family that Leticia had told him was safe. Instead, "Are you planning to kill Alan?"

She took a breath, and the moisture from the shower made her skin glisten. She said, "A few days ago, he was spotted in upstate New York. Got away, but he's definitely up to something. It's our job to find out what, and for whom."

"No suspicions?"

"Well, his wife's disappeared, too."

"We were looking for Penelope before I left."

"By we, you mean you and your wife."

"Yeah. Collingwood can ask Tina herself."

She nodded at that, then bit her lower lip—that was a sign of . . . of what? What did she really know about Tina and Stephanie?

"And while you're at it," he added, "remind her to let me talk to them."

"You might want to get some rest," Leticia said after a moment. "I've got to go see a guy about a thing. We'll be having a guest soon."

"Who?"

She turned off the shower and used a towel to pat her face dry.

Seven minutes after she left, a phone rang; it was the one he'd received in the airport.

"Yeah?"

Xin Zhu said, "What are you two doing in Hong Kong?"

"I've already made it clear that I want to speak to Tina. Is she with you?"

"I remember your demands, but I won't be pushed into anything, least of all that. You'll have to take my word that they're in good health, but if you don't work with me, they won't remain that way."

"A photo, then."

"Mr. Weaver, they've only been gone three days—for you, four, because of time zones. There's no need to crumble yet. Imagine that they've gone on a trip to see their family in . . . Austin, Texas, right?"

Milo didn't answer.

"It'll make you feel better. Trust me."

It didn't, but there was no point arguing. "We're here to see Alan Drummond."

"To what end?"

"To get him out of here."

"Why?"

"Because he's gone rogue."

"You actually use words like that, don't you?"

"It's accurate," Milo said.

"Do they know that he was once my agent?"

"I wouldn't call him your agent, any more than I'd call myself your agent."

"That doesn't answer my question."

"No, I don't think they know about that."

"Why is Alan in Hong Kong?"

"That's what we're here to find out," Milo said. "His wife is missing. If you don't have her, then he's put her somewhere safe. I suspect he's here to kill you."

"That would be a feat," Zhu said.

"So is evading both the Guoanbu and CIA for two full weeks, while skipping around the world."

"Point taken, Mr. Weaver. Please get rid of the phone, and I'll be in touch again. Your friend is returning to the room."

Dutifully, Milo took apart the phone and put the pieces under the mattress. He'd just lain down again and closed his eyes when the door opened. He sat up. Leticia walked in, not smiling, followed by a man in his early thirties, Latino, with a thin mustache on his long, dark face. His eyes were hidden by sunglasses. Before Leticia could speak, the man said, "Not much of a badass, is he?"

"Excuse me?" said Milo.

"The famous Charles Alexander."

This wasn't the only Tourist to mistake his checkered history for something glorious. There was no point arguing with the man, so he just said, "Hector Garza. Also known as José Santiago."

"At your service."

"Now all we need is Tran Hoang to round out the group. Is he still missing?"

"There's a joke," Leticia said, sounding impatient, "about two idiots with bad security in Hong Kong, but I can't remember the punch line. Oh, that's right! They end up *dead*." She turned and walked out of the room.

"I think we're in the doghouse," Garza said, then followed her. Milo grabbed his shoes and hurried to catch up.

Together, they left the hotel and walked up Nathan Road and crossed Salisbury to reach the trees in front of the Space Museum, opposite the Peninsula. Cars swept along between them and the hotel, and as they eyed the height of its tower, Leticia said, "What's he doing?"

Garza rocked his head. He had a habit of sucking on the side of his upper lip, as if digging for errant crumbs. "Staying in, apparently. All we've got is the hotel records. He arrived yesterday and hasn't left the room. Just like London."

"He's displaying himself," said Milo.

"Of course he is," Garza answered, "but to us, or to them? Or to someone else?"

"Doesn't matter," said Leticia. "We get his ass out of here one way or another."

Milo said, "Let me talk to him first."

Leticia looked at him. "What about Xin Zhu's men?"

"What?" asked Garza.

Milo said, "It doesn't matter now. We were marked as soon as we stepped into that lobby, probably earlier. I'm just going to have a talk with him, and if Zhu decides to pick me up on the way out, it won't matter—no one's been honest with me about anything we're doing."

"We're not here for a conversation," Garza said, and even with the sunglasses, Milo knew he was glaring at him.

"He's eluded you for weeks," Milo said, "and now he makes himself known to everyone. Give the man some credit."

"You'll get yourself killed," said Leticia.

"Look," Milo said, "you can both stand around here trying to figure out how to extract him without anyone noticing, or how to shoot him and escape without getting caught, but Alan knows all of this, too. He came to Hong Kong knowing he'd be trapped in there. He also knew that you wouldn't be able to get to him. The only thing he could conceivably want is a conversation. I'm the ignorant one here—I'm the least risk to your operation."

Garza faced Leticia, as if expecting some decision, but she just shrugged. Garza said, "If you try to sneak him out on your own, both of you are targets."

"Here," Leticia said. She took Milo's hand in one of hers and with the other removed a small pistol, a Baby Browning .25, from her purse and settled it into his palm. "It's a classic lady's gun, but it should do the work."

"I'm not going to kill him."

"I know that, Milo. But you might have to kill someone to get out of there alive."

Three minutes later, he was in the lobby. The lady's gun in his jacket pocket was heavier than it had looked. He didn't even try to find his shadows, because they were everywhere. All he knew was that He Qiang wasn't among them now. He took the stairs to the second floor.

There was a single open door halfway down, with a maid's cart. Room 212 was at the far end, beyond it. He walked slowly, easily, and as he passed the open door, he glanced inside. Standing on the other side of the cart was the man he believed to be He Qiang, staring at him. Milo stopped, his hand clutching the pistol in his pocket, but the man shook his head and waved him on. Milo wasn't sure what to do. He was being guided to the room, and he had an instinctive desire to turn and walk out of the hotel again, no matter what answers lay behind that door. Yet he continued forward. The answers were too compelling. Finally, he stood in front of 212. He knocked. "Alan? It's Milo."

There was silence, and he considered repeating himself, but he knew he'd been heard. He waited. Two minutes passed, and during that time he heard whispers behind the door. A conversation, but just one voice. He was on a telephone. Milo kept hold of the Browning. Then he heard the beep of a cell phone being hung up, and the door opened. It wasn't Alan Drummond. It was an Asian man with a low forehead, features that were definitely not Chinese. The man was Cambodian. Somehow, this did not surprise him.

"Is he dead?" Milo asked.

"Come in," said Tran Hoang, stepping aside to let him into the dark room.

4

Sung Hui was washing in the bathroom when Zhu's phone rang Sunday morning. He didn't recognize the number but guessed he'd find Shen An-ling on the line. The last thing he expected was the voice of Hua Yuan, Bo Gaoli's wife. They hadn't talked since that visit to her house at the Purple Jade Villas, and, with everything else going on, he had forgotten about her. She sounded peculiar, even for her, as if after more than a month she'd come out of her house and discovered that the world had been wiped clean during her absence. She said, "Comrade Colonel, we need to talk. Can you come here?"

"Today?" he asked, looking around for Sung Hui— she had left the bathroom, probably for the kitchen.

"Today, yes. Now, actually. It must be now."

She'd said it in a way that made Zhu think that, no, it did not have to be now, though he couldn't explain what gave him that feeling. "Can you tell me what this is about?"

"I was cleaning up his things. My husband's. And I came across a letter he wrote to you. Please, come to read it."

"I'm busy this morning," he said.

"Get here fucking now," she snapped.

He'd lied about being busy to see how she would react, but he wasn't sure how to interpret her reaction. "In that case, of course. I'll be there immediately." He lowered his voice, "Hua Yuan, you're afraid. Why?"

She didn't answer at first, and he heard noise in the background. Paper, perhaps the letter Bo Gaoli had written to him. Then he heard the unmistakable sound of weeping. Between sobs, she said, "Please." A sniff. "If you read the letter," she said after a moment, "you will understand. Hurry." She hung up.

He dressed and found Sung Hui boiling water for tea. They had made love the previous night, and there was a pleasant morning-after glow lingering between them—he could feel it. He kissed her forehead. "I need to run now. I'll be back soon."

"Let's go out to dinner tonight."

"As you like," he said, and she frowned at him. "What?"

"What do *you* like, Zhu?"

He began to say, *I like what you like*, or, *I'm happy to see you happy*, but he knew how inept those phrases were, so he just said, "What I like is you. Here at home or at a restaurant, or in the desert. It's all better with you."

Her frown faded away to nothingness.

His phone rang again as he was driving north on the ring road, and this time it was Shen An-ling, calling from Hong Kong. He Qiang had arrived to run things, but Zhu still wanted someone else there to help direct.

"Has he left his room yet?" Zhu asked.

"No, but Leticia Jones and Milo Weaver are now in town. They appeared at the hotel, then changed their minds and checked into the Kowloon."

"So they spotted you?"

"I was in the lobby, but it was He Qiang. Weaver saw him in New York."

"Sloppy."

"Yes," said Shen An-ling. "But we gave him a phone, and if you'd like I can patch you through to him once he's alone."

"Yes. That would be good."

"A woman came to his room."

"To Drummond's?"

"She was looking for someone named Charlie. Drummond opened the door a little and said a few words to her, then she left. Apparently, she had the wrong room."

"Is she a guest?"

"Yes. Jennifer Paulson."

"Let me know if she makes the same mistake again."

It was after nine by the time he reached the Purple Jade Villas. The guards had been told by Hua Yuan to expect him, so they gave his Guoanbu ID only a cursory glance, then sent him on. He remembered the drive to the villa from his earlier visit, but while everything looked the same, it felt different. Perhaps it was the sight of a laborer driving a lawn mower over one of the distant hills, reminding him that the beauty here took considerable effort to maintain.

Hua Yuan did not come out to meet him, so he parked and walked to the door on his own, noticing that the villas on either side were empty of cars. The air was damp here, as was the grass; his leather shoes came out in dark spots. Only when he knocked on her door did he get the feeling that this house was empty as well. It was as if, knowing that he was on his way, the Purple Jade management had sent in a team to evacuate the street.

There was no answer to his knock, or to the doorbell he rang twice. He looked at the heavy door and then, gingerly, turned the handle. It was unlocked, and it opened smoothly.

He stepped inside and instinctively slipped out of his shoes to pad around in socks. He stepped into the living room, with its square window framed in ivy, looking out at his car and the fields beyond, and called, "Hua Yuan? It's Xin Zhu." There was no reply.

Further back he found a dining room and, through a pair of double doors, a long kitchen tiled in white, with a counter stretching down the center of the room. It smelled of rust. The kitchen lights burned brightly, so that when he found her, arms and legs bent as if she were running along the floor, the pool of blood spreading out from the gunshot gash in her forehead created a perfect reflection of the fluorescent lamps in the ceiling.

She was wearing a floor-length robe, a different one than she'd worn before, and it hung behind her—again,

he imagined her running, the robe flung up by the wind—
and her bare, varicose legs were on display. A blood-
speckled white slipper hung off her left foot; the other
slipper was against the base of the oven, perfectly clean.

About an hour had passed from the time of her call,
which meant that the killer could conceivably still be
in the house. He went through the drawers until he found
a heavy Hattori cleaver, then walked slowly through the
house, from the bottom to the top. With his slow, deliberate pace it took twenty minutes to look into every
room, and on the way he wondered why he wasn't just
standing in the kitchen and calling Shen An-ling, or
the police, or even Purple Jade security. He knew why,
though. For the moment, he had silence and solitude.
As soon as he made the call, that solitude would be
broken, and he needed some time to figure out what
had happened, and who should receive his first call.

Back in the kitchen, he returned the cleaver to the
drawer, then crouched, groaning, beside Hua Yuan. He
took a corner of the robe and pulled it to cover her running legs, then checked the pocket—empty. There
would be another pocket between her and the floor, but
he didn't want to move her.

His phone rang.

"Yes?"

Shen An-ling said, "I'll connect you to Milo Weaver,
if you like."

"Go ahead."

As he threatened the health of Milo Weaver's wife
and daughter, he returned to the living room and looked
for the letter. If Hua Yuan had been expecting him, the

letter would be out, perhaps even on display, but it wasn't here. He peered around the kitchen, careful to step around the pool of blood as he looked in drawers. By the time Milo Weaver told him that Alan Drummond probably wanted to kill him, he was checking the tables in the foyer, and when Shen An-ling sent a message to his phone, signifying that Leticia Jones was returning to Weaver's hotel room, he was checking the dining room. After hanging up, he returned upstairs to check Hua Yuan's bedroom. He found many small items from her life—receipts, letters from girlfriends and family, and bills—but with each failure he became increasingly sure that he was going to have to roll over the woman in the kitchen.

So he returned and first tried to tug the robe out from under her, but when he pulled she slid with it. He stood, lifting the hem of the robe upward, and Hua Yuan rolled a little, farting loudly as the body resettled. Zhu closed his eyes, the robe tight in his fist, and reached into the damp hidden pocket. His fingers found moist, folded paper, multiple sheets, which he removed with his index and middle fingers. Then he stepped back, dropping the robe and backing away as the body expelled more gas. He withdrew to a bathroom, set the pages on the toilet seat, and washed his hands with hot water and soap, focusing all his energy on not being sick.

The moisture on the letter was not blood but urine, and Xin Zhu took the sheets to the dining room and laid them out individually on the long table. Her husband, Bo Gaoli, had written on only one side of each of the five pages, so as they dried Zhu could walk down the length of the table and read the entire message. Once he was finished, he returned to the head of the table and read it again. He pulled out a chair and settled down, then called Sun Bingjun.

"Apologies," he told the old man. "I'm sure you're busy."

"I'm always busy, Xin Zhu, or at least that's what I claim. What is it?"

"How well did you know Bo Gaoli, Comrade Lieutenant General?"

A pause. "We worked together on occasion. I can't say we were close."

"And his wife?"

"Hua Yuan? I didn't know her at all until after her husband died. I stopped by once to give condolences. She seemed to be taking it rather well."

"Comrade Lieutenant General, would it be possible for you to meet with me? I am at Hua Yuan's Purple Jade home."

"Are you interviewing her?"

"Please," Zhu said, "could you come?"

"Is this serious, Xin Zhu?"

"More than serious."

It took forty minutes for Sun Bingjun's Mercedes to arrive, parking behind Xin Zhu's Audi. By then it was ten forty-five. Through the square window, Zhu saw a tall, broad driver get out and open the door for Sun Bingjun, who walked alone toward the house, his face grim. Sun Bingjun had never been a man of smiles, and, as he approached, Zhu realized that he had known very few men of smiles, because those were the ones who inevitably sank out of view before long, their little grins wavering only at the last moment. Smiling was not Sun Bingjun's way, though drinking was, but even when he drank to excess, he never stepped too far. He had more self-control than anyone liked to admit.

Zhu met him at the door and brought him into the living room. The old man looked around, showing signs of impatience. "Where is Hua Yuan?"

"In the kitchen. She's dead."

Sun Bingjun's skin knotted around the eyes, then relaxed. "Did you do it, Xin Zhu?"

"She called me this morning about a letter she'd found among her husband's things. It was written to me. She was evidently scared but wouldn't go into details. I came as quickly as I could."

"But not fast enough?" Sun Bingjun speculated.

"Apparently," Zhu said. "I had to move her body in order to get at the letter in her pocket."

"Tampering with a crime scene," Sun Bingjun said. "I hope this letter was worth it. Oh," he added, looking out at their cars, "and next time, you might want to suggest I drive myself."

Sun Bingjun was only testing the borders of Zhu's stupidity here, for he was now, by his very presence, involved, and his driver was a witness. "Come with me," Zhu said and led him to the dining room. He retreated to a corner and waited, watching Sun Bingjun read the pages through and, like Zhu, read them again.

"Well," said the old man.

"You see why I needed you to come."

Sun Bingjun raised his head to look directly at Zhu. "You wanted someone to believe your desperate lie."

Perhaps inviting him had been a mistake. "That's not true."

Sun Bingjun walked to the first page again and read aloud, "*Comrade Colonel Xin Zhu, I am writing to draw your attention to a conspiracy that threatens the very foundation of our Republic.* Where did you get this from? One of those pulp novels the kids find so heartwarming these days? Page two," he said, taking a small step toward Zhu. "*I am coming to you because, as your adversarial history with Wu Liang is well known, I thought you might be able to view my evidence with a clear eye.*" Sun Bingjun smiled. "Very good, that. You turn your prejudice into a virtue. And here," he said, lowering a finger to point at a section of page three. "*I've been warned that Wu Liang is suspicious of my investigations, and that, within days, I might be called in to answer trumped-up charges, the same charges that I am preparing to level against him. This is why I'll be sending this by courier as soon as possible.*" Sun Bingjun opened his hands, flat, and tilted them from side to side. "Very chancy, that one. You show him to be wrong because, according to the date here—April 21—Wu Liang picked him up on that same day. This is the drama, of course, because the poor man thought he had more time before the devil caught up with him. Which is why he never sent the letter. Which is why it remained undiscovered until poor Hua Yuan came across it and, like a good wife and citizen, called you. But here," he said, raising an index finger, "this is the pièce de résistance, at least to my mind." It was on the second to last page, and the old man pointed a stubby finger at it. *"I realize that there will be resistance to you bringing these charges to light if, in fact, I am unable, and so I suggest going to Comrade Sun Bingjun, who is preparing to retire, and who would have fewer concerns about risking his position. He knows he is safe from ridicule.* Beautiful!" he said. "It directs you to do exactly as you have done—drag me into this foul mess of your engineering."

"Comrade Lieutenant General," Zhu began, but the old man waved at him to stop.

"I know what the stories are, Xin Zhu. I'm an old drunk who will fade quietly away upon retirement. I don't care about that. When I'm dead, my reputation will be entirely academic. What I *do* mind is when younger men listen to those stories and come to the conclusion that I am easily manipulated, that I can be a tool for their survival. The fact is that I've done something none of you young men have done, and that is to thrive into my dotage in the snake pit of Beijing politics."

Xin Zhu placed his hands on his thighs, saying nothing. He had no idea what he could say. It was the blood, the body, the urine, and the letter—they had made him stupid. He should have known that Sun Bingjun wasn't about to put himself out for . . . for what? For a thorn in the side of Chinese intelligence? For the story of a woman's death that was only that—a story? Why did he expect he would be believed?

Sun Bingjun sighed loudly and pulled out a chair, sitting in front of the final page of the letter, but he wasn't reading a thing—he was watching Zhu. He said, "This is how untenable your situation is, Xin Zhu. This is how easily Wu Liang could turn it around and throw it into your face. Every accusation is built on the foundation of a story, and before you speak to anyone you must learn your entire story, every detail." He grunted a half-laugh. "Why am I telling you this? You're Xin Zhu, the master of the narrative. You used a story to draw the Americans into a beautiful trap. Yet now you have entered this storyline unprepared. Who committed the murder in the kitchen? Where are the files that Bo Gaoli talks about here, the ones that prove that Wu Liang has been a CIA source for the last twenty years? I certainly hope it doesn't turn out to be a collection of e-mails like the ones you shared. And how do I really know that Bo Gaoli penned this letter?"

Sun Bingjun was right. He was getting ahead of himself, but, faced with a corpse and a urine-stained letter, time was no longer on his side. "I'm rushing," he admitted.

"And you've got too much to deal with already. What have you learned about the Americans' great act of vengeance?"

"We're still watching Alan Drummond's room."

"Enough, Xin Zhu. That man should be dead by now. You wait, and you appear complicit in his survival."

"Killing him will only make them change their plans."

"You don't even know their plans, Xin Zhu, so it makes no difference if they change them."

Zhu involuntarily rubbed his cheek, then told him about Liu Xiuxiu's report on Stuart Jackson and the *ferociously ambitious* wife of one of their colleagues.

"Hearsay," Sun Bingjun said, though from the look on his face he was taken aback. "Excellent hearsay, but still hearsay."

"And I have someone else inside," Zhu said, "Milo Weaver. He's working with them, but he's under my control."

"You didn't report that to the committee."

"Given the clues we now have in our possession, I believe I made the right choice."

Sun Bingjun looked momentarily irritated. Then, "Did you also leave something out of the report on the murder of Yevgeny Primakov? Did you kill him?"

"No."

"Who did it?"

"I don't know."

Sun Bingjun raised an eyebrow, perhaps signifying his disbelief. "Don't worry about Hua Yuan. My driver, happily, is loyal, and he knows better than to admit to seeing anything. I'll talk to the Jade gatekeepers and find out who else visited this morning."

"That's extremely generous."

Sun Bingjun pursed his lips, then shook his head. "It's pragmatism, Xin Zhu. If you're not constructing an elaborate scheme to protect yourself, then Wu Liang is truly dangerous and should be exposed. If I help you build the case against him, and it's successful, then my star rises just before retirement, but if it fails, I leave humiliated. Which is why I'm not going to let you do it on your own. Look at yourself. You haven't been sleeping enough, and I don't think it's only because of your young wife. You're trying to find a mole while fending off the forces of American retaliation. It's too much for one man."

"Either way," Zhu said, "your help is appreciated."

"Then let's make sure I don't live to regret it. Tomorrow you'll have a chance to tell the story to the committee, so get it straight. I'll make sure Wu Liang is in attendance."

Zhu nodded.

"Finish off these people in Hong Kong. You don't want their presence used against you at the meeting."

Again, Zhu nodded.

"Now go, Xin Zhu. I'll deal with this."

Zhu silently withdrew. He crossed the lawn and went to his car. Inside the Mercedes Sun Bingjun's big driver, with one of those clay faces that could be so easily forgotten, watched Zhu's progress, while Zhu noticed that various neighbors, up and down the street, had returned home.

As he drove, Shen An-ling called again to discuss Milo Weaver's twenty-minute visit to room 212 of the Peninsula Hotel. The microphones had only picked up a few spare words, the sound of a fistfight, and then silence as they switched, assumedly, to handwritten communication. "After Weaver left the room, He Qiang tried to give him another phone."

"Tried?"

"Milo Weaver refused. He told He Qiang to go fuck himself. Those words. I think the pressure is getting to him."

"Or he knows we don't have his family," Zhu said. It didn't matter, not now. Tomorrow, Wu Liang was going to have to answer for his collusion with the Americans, and perhaps he would offer answers to some of these mysteries. Zhu said, "Enough, Shen An-ling."

"Enough of what?"

"Everything. I want you to close them down."

A sigh. "Thank you, Comrade Colonel."

An hour later, in the office, he was connected to everything by a computer and a telephone linked to Shen An-ling, who kept watch in the lobby of the Peninsula. As there were only nine men at his disposal, they would first grab Alan Drummond and then collect the Tourists from the Kowloon. After Milo Weaver's exit, He Qiang had reported no other sounds from room 212 until, as he prepared to move in, Alan Drummond's cell phone bleeped an incoming message. Then, the sound of movement, of clothes being pulled on, of luggage being shifted. A door. Then, through the spy hole of his own door, He Qiang watched an Asian man, perhaps Vietnamese, walk past with nothing in his hands.

"It's not him," He Qiang reported to the others, as well as to Beijing, and gave a brief description. "But he came from the room. Heading for the stairwell."

"Don't lose him" was Xin Zhu's only advice, as he wondered who it could be.

With He Qiang on the same floor, they had two men—Xu Guanzhong and Wei Chi-tao—holding different corners of the lobby, while Shen An-ling observed from behind the concierge desk with two smart phones—one for communication, one for tracking his people. Five more men waited outside the tower, watching rear entrances on Middle Road, side entrances on Nathan Road, and the grandiose main entrance on Salisbury Road. Another kept an eye on the Kowloon lobby. However, after three minutes no one reported anyone leaving the Peninsula stairwell. Shen An-ling called He Qiang's phone, which rang seven times without an answer. Xu Guanzhong moved from the lobby to the stairwell, keeping an open line, and in that small Beijing office Zhu listened to Xu Guanzhong's breaths and feet echoing in the stairwell before the feet stopped and Xu Guanzhong said, "Oh."

"What is it?" asked Shen An-ling.

"I think he's dead. Yes. He's dead."

"He Qiang?"

"Garrote," came the unnerved reply. "His head is nearly . . ."

Zhu pulled at his lower lip. He Qiang was dead? There were only five floors to the Peninsula's original building, but thirty floors had been added in the midnineties with the construction of a modern tower. This could take forever. "Continue up the stairs," Zhu ordered. "Wei Chi-tao, you, too. Everybody else, move inside."

On his computer, Xin Zhu had a map of the two Hong Kong blocks that encompassed the Peninsula and the Kowloon, on which he watched his men's cell phones. Red spots on the screen, all in motion. Three red spots in the stairwell of the Peninsula, and five more closing in. Shen An-ling, in the lobby, began to deliver orders personally, and two more red spots moved into the stairwell.

Xu Guanzhong had more bad news. "He didn't go back to his room, and the other corridors are empty. We're going to check the maids' closets."

Shen An-ling's voice, irritably, "You didn't do that already?"

Xu Guanzhong didn't bother answering, and Zhu realized that while Alan Drummond might have checked into that hotel, he had probably never gone up to the room. He knew from experience how easy a trick like that was to pull.

On the map of the Peninsula, the red dots were moving through the corridors, and only one remained in the stairwell—the immobile He Qiang. Over the speaker Xu Guanzhong breathed heavily when, suddenly, there was a loud two-tone squeal. "Fire alarm. He pulled the fire alarm. The sprinklers are going." Noise, voices. "Evacuation."

"Keep looking," Zhu ordered. Shen An-ling had kept three men in the lobby. "Watch the crowd."

A woman's scream, and Xu Guanzhong stated the obvious. "Someone's discovered He Qiang in the stairwell."

Then, after a moment, Xu Guanzhong said, "Wei Chi-tao?"

No answer.

Xu Guanzhong said, "Wei Chi-tao, where are you?"

"He's on the fourth floor," Xin Zhu said, though he

could see that Wei Chi-tao's phone was as immobile as He Qiang's.

Then he heard, "Uhh," as if Xu Guanzhong had just lost all the air in his body.

"Xu Guanzhong," said Zhu. On the screen, Xu Guanzhong's phone, on the third floor, was not moving either. "Answer, Xu Guanzhong."

A voice spoke to him in English. "He's coming to get you, Xin Zhu."

"Who is that?" Shen An-ling shouted.

On the computer screen, Xu Guanzhong's telephone moved swiftly down the corridor and out a window.

Shen An-ling shouted, "Everyone! Third floor!"

The other spots around the Peninsula swept inward, toward the stairwell, slowed as they fought the evacuating crowds, but Zhu knew that didn't matter. They wouldn't find this Sebastian Hall. He was a Tourist.

"Stop them," Zhu said to Shen An-ling.

Shen An-ling said, "What?"

"Immediately. If he's still there, he's going to kill off all our men. Send everyone to the Kowloon, and we'll see if we can do better there."

"But—"

"*Immediately*, Shen An-ling."

5

In the Peninsula lobby, as before, he found it hard to spot shadows—rock gardens, as his father would have called them—but this time he wasn't able to see well because of the emotions. *They are safe*, just as the note in his father's pocket had said. Twenty minutes ago, when the door to room 212 had opened, his confusion had been compounded, but by the end of his talk with Tran Hoang the confusion had been cleared away, and with that so much of his anxiety. He'd felt it falling away in chunks as he left Tran Hoang, and when the big Chinese man, He Qiang, offered him a new phone, his joy told him just what to say, "Go fuck yourself." He'd taken the stairs back down here to the lobby and was blinded by the knowledge that they were safe. When, almost at the door, he spotted his sister sitting on a sofa, arms crossed over her stomach, staring at him, he gave her a smile and a wink before leaving.

Outside, his vision was clear enough to see across

Salisbury Road, and he saw that Leticia and Hector were no longer there. He had no doubt that they would find him on their own, so he turned the corner, walking up the packed sidewalk along Nathan Road, and at the intersection with Middle Road entered the Kowloon. Here, finally, he noticed a man who, he suspected, was all too aware of his entrance, but he let him be. His shadow would matter or he wouldn't matter, but in the end all the shadows in the world mattered so little. Really, none of this mattered now.

He took the elevator to the seventh floor and used his key on the door, and it was when he closed it behind himself that Hector Garza stepped briskly out of the bathroom, right arm extended, a Heckler & Koch USP pointed at Milo's face. Milo saw the emotions working through the Tourist's features. "On the bed," said Garza.

Milo sat on it, slowly raising his hands, and said, "Left pocket."

Garza reached into Milo's pocket and took out the lady's gun. His own pistol not wavering, he lifted the Browning to his nose and sniffed but smelled nothing other than gun oil. Then the door opened and Leticia strode in from the corridor, and the most worrying thing wasn't Garza's pistol but the expression on Leticia's face. It was the look of a Tourist, of someone who has disconnected herself from the emotional impact of what she's about to do. Only now did he realize how much he had been depending on her good moods to get him through all of this.

She took the Browning Garza offered her, then crossed to the television, turned it on—CNN was showing smoke and destruction from a bomb in a place called Kumarikata, in India—and raised the volume. She sat beside Milo on the bed and, without looking at him, said, "How long have you been working for him?"

So that was it. "This is the sixth day."

"You know what we have to do now, don't you?"

Milo didn't speak. He tightened his pelvic muscles to keep from urinating on himself.

Leticia said, "This isn't how it was supposed to end."

She seemed to be waiting for a reply, so he said, "No. I didn't think so either," for that was true. If she'd found out an hour ago, he might have even welcomed it, for a quiet death seemed the only real solution to his problems. Now, his own death had become pointless.

"How did you know? Did I give it away?"

"Probably," she said, "but I didn't notice. I got a call."

"Collingwood?"

"Yeah."

"And you think this was the first she learned of it?"

"What do you mean?"

"I'm not sure what I mean. Did she tell you to kill me?"

Her silence was answer enough. Finally, she cocked her head, regarding him, and Garza shifted his weight to his other foot. She said, "How did he get to you?"

"How do you think? My family. It's the same way he got Alan."

She twitched, turning to face him fully. "Tell me about Alan."

"Xin Zhu threatened his wife. Was running Alan since the end of May."

"Penelope Drummond is missing."

"Of course. Just like my wife and daughter, but now I know that Xin Zhu doesn't have them. Nor does Dorothy Collingwood."

"Who does?"

"They're safe."

She frowned, digesting this. "You couldn't have just told me about Xin Zhu?" she asked.

"What would you have done with the information?"

"Well, maybe I would've helped you."

"But not them. You wouldn't have helped them."

She lowered her brows until she was almost squinting. "So Alan says they're safe?"

"Alan's not in that hotel, Leticia. It's Tran Hoang."

Surprisingly, Hector Garza lowered his pistol. "He's dead."

Leticia rubbed her face, for she was putting things together quickly now. Her intelligence was another thing Milo was depending on. "No, Hector. We were told he was dead."

"By whom?" Milo asked.

"Collingwood," Garza answered, then looked at Leticia, who was frowning at him. "What does it matter?"

"Give me a moment to think," she said. "It might matter." Then she looked at Milo. "What does Tran Hoang say?"

Tran Hoang had said a lot of things, but Milo only shared what was urgent for them. "He says we should run. The Chinese will come for us at any moment."

"Of course he says that."

"He's just a distraction. By now, Alan should be inside."

"Inside where?"

"The mainland. Hoang is leaving, too."

Leticia closed her eyes and let out a quiet curse, then opened them and said to Garza, "There was someone in our lobby."

"I saw him, too," said Milo.

"That's good odds," said Garza.

"Wait," said Leticia. "What else did Tran Hoang tell you?"

"Not much else," Milo said.

"You were in there for nearly a half hour," Leticia pointed out.

"We were cleaning up," said Milo.

Garza looked tempted to raise his pistol again. "Cleaning up?"

"Because I tried to kill him."

Both Tourists stared at him.

"He admitted to murdering my father. I was angry."

"Well, *damn,*" said Leticia. She looked up as Garza worked his pistol into the belt under his jacket.

"Well, we're not going to kill him, are we?" he asked defensively. "And somebody needs to find out what's going on downstairs."

Leticia nodded. "So, we leave."

"It's the only play," Garza said.

"I agree," said Milo, but a look from Leticia told him his opinion wasn't of interest.

She said to Garza, "Five minutes. Call if there's opposition, and then cover us when we go down."

The Tourist gave her a smile and a wink and was gone.

"You're worried," Milo told her.

"Damned right I'm worried. What? You really think I'm a machine?"

"You're not an idiot, either, Leticia. Alan got Tran Hoang on his side, so to cover for it Collingwood told you he'd been killed. She's told you a lot of things. Don't imagine you have the slightest idea what any of this is about."

Her frown had deepened considerably, and she said, "What did Tran really tell you?"

"He told me the only thing that matters."

"That damned family."

He was about to reply, but they heard the loud *thump-thump* of two shots, muffled by walls, then the *tittit* of automatic fire in reply. Leticia was heading toward the door, her Browning held out in front of her. She checked the spy hole, then opened the door and jerked her head out and back in. A piece of the door frame exploded. She slammed the door shut, but it bounced back open again, letting in the noise of two more pistol shots and shouts in Mandarin. She grabbed a desk chair and wedged it against the door handle to keep it closed.

Milo was already at the window, prying it open, but he could see that the seven-floor drop to the street was no good. "No, baby!" Leticia called over the noise of the television and the explosions from the corridor.

"Duck!" She raised her pistol at him, and he dropped to the floor. Two shots, and the window shattered above his head. As he climbed to his feet, she was heading into the bathroom. He heard water running, then found her plugging a hair dryer into the socket beside the mirror as the tub was slowly filling with water. At the sound of two more shots, Milo turned to see two jagged holes in the door, just above the desk chair. "That's good," he heard Leticia say, shutting off the water, then she turned on the dryer and tossed it into the tub. A glow of hissing sparks. The lights snapped off, putting them in darkness. Briefly, with the television off and conversation in the corridor ceasing, there was silence. "See?" she whispered. "All you need—"

The lights flickered back on, the hotel's backup system kicking in, and he could now see her standing beside the tub, the pistol in her hand, looking dejected. "Oh, man," she said. "That was my only trick."

He wanted to laugh.

"What're you smiling at, Milo? We're dead now."

He shook his head, still smiling. "Toss the gun, Leticia. Let's go out there."

"I'm not suicidal. Not for this I'm not."

"Want me to go first?"

"If it pleases you," she said.

He turned to go, then paused. "Can you at least tell them what I'm doing?"

She sighed loudly as another shot from the corridor ripped another hole in the door. She shouted, "Děngdài!" There was silence; then she launched into a short stream of Mandarin that, he hoped, would save his life. To Milo, she said, "See you on the other side," and gave him a dry kiss on the lips.

Slowly, he approached the door and lifted the chair out of the way. Without the support, the door swung open on its own, revealing a slice of empty corridor. He placed his hands against the back of his neck. As he moved forward, his view widened, and he could see three Chinese men on the left, two on the right, all backed against the far wall so that if they fired at once they wouldn't hit each other. Two of them were on one knee. All five men were aiming at him. Three pistols, two small machine pistols.

They made no sign to him, so he chose the men on the left, approaching with purposeful steps. When he'd almost reached them, he heard Leticia shouting something else, and one of the crouched men motioned Milo to move to the side, which he did. One of the others lowered his gun and grabbed Milo's wrists, turning him around as he jerked his hands down behind his back and linked them with PlastiCuffs. Milo felt the pinch of a needle in his forearm but didn't fight it.

Leticia came out, her hands against the small of her back, and it was when she had cleared the door that Milo, and the man behind him, noticed that in her right hand was the Browning. The man shouted something beside his ear, a burst of hot air and noise, and simultaneously Leticia whipped out the pistol, getting off one shot before three bullets entered her. She fell, her empty gun hand writhing, and shouted a stream of curses. Milo's head flushed and burned as the drugs started to take over. Blood pumped from the bare shoulder of Leticia's black dress across the beige carpeting; then she was gone beneath a pile of Xin Zhu's men. Milo's own blood seemed to thicken and swell. His ears weren't working well—sounds smeared. They smear.

Stairs.

Lobby. Faces.

Street.

The back of a black BMW, crowded between two heavy men with bad breath.

The city.

Highway. Feet tingling. Outside, the sea.

Airport, but not Departures. An access road around the building, under catwalks, past vehicles with stairs leading nowhere, to a white twin-engine propeller plane idling far from anything.

Hands. Breath.

Cold wind across the tarmac. Two men talking, one in a pilot's uniform, at the foot of stairs.

Up. Hands lifting because feet no longer work.

Through the hole. No smiling stewardess. No "May I see your boarding pass?" Just two lines of grimy, padded seats. Only one other passenger. A pasty-faced Chinese with thick glasses, reading his telephone.

Down, in the seat.

Straps. *Not too tight, please*.

"Hello, Mr. Milo Weaver."

It's the pasty-faced one, putting away his phone. They're beside each other, the walkway separating them.

Can't raise hands, but not because of the straps.

"We will be there in three hours. About."

Where? It doesn't come out.

But where else could he mean?

And does it matter?

The engine rumbles.

The man is close now, his breath minty and clean. "No, no," he says, smiling. "Don't worry, we have time for talking. Later."

The man sits and buckles his seat belt.

They begin to move.

Yes, it matters.

6

The *People's Daily* that Monday morning ran a short notice announcing Hua Yuan's death "by stroke," reminding readers that she had been the widow of the esteemed Bo Gaoli, who was tragically felled by a heart attack in April. Zhu remembered Hua Yuan's suspicion of all officials who had reportedly died of heart attacks and wondered if this could be legitimately defined as irony.

She wasn't the only fresh corpse. Xu Guanzhong, Wei Chi-tao, He Qiang, and in the Kowloon Hector Garza had died, but not before killing He Péng, whom he'd recalled just for this job. Shen An-ling had arrived last night with their meager prizes for so many bodies—Milo Weaver and Leticia Jones. Things were as they should be—two enemies in custody, another one soon to be dealt with—but there was too much blood. It was time to be done with that.

Zhu had hidden the events of Sunday morning from

Shen An-ling, largely because he didn't want him distracted. Also, he'd entered a new kind of relationship with Sun Bingjun that required sensitivity. By helping Zhu, Sun Bingjun was risking everything, and there was no need to let that information move any further than was absolutely necessary. Sun Bingjun had told him to come to the Great Hall of the People at nine to present the narrative he had spent much of the previous night sketching out in his home office. It had to be complete, even when the facts were not known, and so he filled in holes with educated speculation. At eight, he put on his jacket. Sung Hui gave him a kiss, which he hardly even felt.

After the weekend rains, it was pleasantly clear-skied when he reached the Great Hall, and its damp steps were empty of schoolchildren. There were more guards than usual perched at the top, lugging their rifles, and he wondered if he had missed some announcement or other. Then he wondered if they were waiting for him.

In the Beijing Hall, he found Zhang Guo sitting with Feng Yi, both smoking cigarettes. He stopped a few feet away. Zhang Guo said, "I suppose you're announcing some breakthrough in the case, Xin Zhu?"

He shook his head.

"Maybe Sun Bingjun is," Feng Yi suggested, raising his cigarette. "He called the meeting."

As if on cue, Sun Bingjun strolled in, raising eyebrows at the three men and carrying a yellow folder. To Zhu, he said, "No notes?"

Zhu tapped his skull.

"Dangerous," Sun Bingjun said, then took a seat.

Zhang Guo and Feng Yi gave them questioning looks.

Wu Liang arrived with Yang Qing-Nian again, but this time both men looked flustered. "I almost didn't make it," Wu Liang told them all. "Some of us don't have the free time for last-minute assemblies."

"Apologies," said Sun Bingjun. "You needn't have come if you didn't want to."

Wu Liang noticed the coolness in Sun Bingjun's voice, and he shook his head. "I'm short on sleep. Excuse me."

They took their places, Zhu again sitting opposite the others, and after setting his own digital recorder in the center of the room, Sun Bingjun returned to his seat and began very simply. "Thank you all for coming here. You will have heard by now of the tragic death of Hua Yuan, the wife of Bo Gaoli, this weekend, and this is the reason for our meeting this morning. What you may not know is that she was murdered brutally in her kitchen, and the assailant has yet to be identified."

Though no one said anything, they all shifted, expressing their surprise through movement.

Sun Bingjun opened the folder on his lap. "The identity of her murderer can be set aside for the moment, but what cannot be ignored is something she had on her person when she died." From the folder Sun Bingjun took out the letter, now dry and crisp, kept safe in a plastic sleeve. He held it up for all to see. "It was written, days before his death, by Bo Gaoli. In it, he identifies an American mole within Chinese security."

More movement. Sun Bingjun ignored the reaction and began passing around stapled sheets of paper, photocopies of the letter. Zhu got up to receive one.

"Take a moment," Sun Bingjun told everyone, then closed the folder in his lap. As the others began reading, he watched Zhu, who ignored the letter and tried to read Sun Bingjun's face. There was nothing in there to read.

"Where did you get this again?" asked Feng Yi.

"From Hua Yuan's corpse," said Sun Bingjun. "The discoloration you see there is her urine."

"A letter," Yang Qing-Nian said, raising his voice. "A single letter? Who knows who wrote this?"

Wu Liang knew when to stay quiet.

Zhang Guo said, "I think, Sun Bingjun, that you should tell us exactly how you came across this letter."

Zhu listened as Sun Bingjun quietly and patiently told his story. He began in reality, saying that Hua Yuan had called Xin Zhu about a letter, before diverging. "Hua Yuan told him that it had to do with Wu Liang. Zhu, rightly suspecting that his involvement would be viewed with suspicion, called me before going anywhere. I promised to meet him at her house. He waited for me to arrive, and we entered together."

Zhu would have preferred if the old man had said he'd arrived first, but perhaps the surly Jade guards weren't amenable to changing their record of Zhu's entrance.

"We found her body in the kitchen," Sun Bingjun continued, "and that's when I noticed the letter in her pocket. I asked Xin Zhu to please remove it. Together, we read it in the dining room. I ordered Xin Zhu to leave the premises, because I wanted him involved as little as possible. I had my people clean up the mess. I've discussed the situation with Yang Xiaoming, and he asked that we perform a preliminary examination now before bringing him into it."

Which was entirely predictable, thought Zhu. Yang Xiaoming, the head of the Supervision and Liaison Committee, wouldn't want to touch this until it was set in stone.

"Unfortunately," Sun Bingjun went on, "under the circumstances it's impossible to leave Xin Zhu entirely out of the proceedings. He is the one who initially raised the worry of an American agent in our midst; it is he who has spent the past months warning us of our lethargy. And what have we given him for his efforts? Grief, largely. While we may believe we had reason, the fact remains that Xin Zhu is the only one qualified to establish if, and how, Comrade Wu Liang fits into the theory that Bo Gaoli apparently believed in before he was taken into custody by Wu Liang and, subsequently, died."

By the time Sun Bingjun paused, Wu Liang looked sick. His eyes nearly crossed with the effort of his concentration as he stared at Sun Bingjun, then at Zhu. Passively, Zhu met his gaze but said nothing.

"Given this new evidence," Sun Bingjun said, "I propose that we ask Xin Zhu for a report on his findings. Right now. Is this agreed?"

No one said a thing.

Sun Bingjun said, "To take a line from Wu Liang's

initial attempt to undermine Xin Zhu's investigations, I don't want to steer this particular boat. Please. Let us have a vote."

Everyone wanted to listen to Zhu's side of the story, including Yang Qing-Nian. Wu Liang abstained from voting, but after the vote he said, "May I say something?"

"Of course," said Sun Bingjun.

Wu Liang shifted in his chair. He had folded the photocopied letter down the middle, and now he ran his fingernails along the crease, squeezing. "This charade will go on no matter what I say. I know this. For the record, though, I have been, and I remain, loyal to the People's Republic. Like Xin Zhu, I have been worried about the prospect of an American agent, and it was only after serious thought that I decided the mole theory was an act of subversion by Xin Zhu, aimed in large part at me. We've seen how vindictive he is when personally attacked—the death of his son led to thirty-three American corpses—and so we have evidence that his vengeance is great. No matter how Comrade Sun Bingjun dresses this up, we all know that Xin Zhu has orchestrated today's sham. Either out of vindictiveness or because he himself is an American tool throwing suspicion at his enemies. I don't claim to know which, but I do intend to find out."

They knew he was finished because he finally laid the folded letter on his knee and sighed. Sun Bingjun said, "Your comments are noted, but don't assume I'm dressing anything up. I'm too old to stick my neck out for anyone I don't trust implicitly."

Wu Liang made no sign that he'd heard a thing.

"Xin Zhu," Sun Bingjun said, nodding.

Zhu rubbed his nose, sat straighter, and began, "Comrades, I wish I was here under better circumstances, and with better news, but such are the times we live in that I'm still catching up to the facts as I understand them, and the picture they paint is disturbing."

He began by rehashing his initial suspicions culled from the files of the Department of Tourism, the loose assemblage of intelligence that, when added up, pointed to an administrative mole. "There was a possibility," he admitted, "that, instead of a single higher-level mole, we were dealing with several—five or more—informants. That, of course, is still a possibility, but with the other facts swarming around us now it seems an unnecessary contrivance.

"Let us return for a moment to our first meeting in this room. You'll remember that Wu Liang told the sad tale that led to the suicide of Bo Gaoli in East Chang'an. I think we all found the story disturbing, none more than me, for I felt responsible. So, I visited Hua Yuan to find out what she knew. After a brief talk, I came away with three facts. One, that Bo Gaoli would not commit suicide. Hua Yuan made it clear to me that nothing— certainly not some minor indiscretion or the shame of being accused of something he hadn't done—would provoke that. She said this not out of respect, you understand, but with a kind of disgust. This was not a quality she admired. Second, she told me that, when she was cleaning out her husband's belongings, she found a box in a closet filled with cash. About three hundred thousand yuan. She had no idea where he'd gotten that kind of money, or why he would have kept it secret. The third matter of importance was that, on April 20, the day before he was picked up by Wu Liang, he was trying to get in touch with me, personally. I have verified this with phone records."

They shifted, all of them, even Sun Bingjun.

"I never claimed to be a friend of Bo Gaoli. We were no more than acquaintances. So why, I wondered, would he have been seeking me out? I can come up with no reason but one: He knew that, five days earlier, I had sent around a memo claiming that there was a mole in the Ministry of Public Security. Other than that, there was no reason for Bo Gaoli to have me on his mind."

Zhu paused, looking over the blank, passive faces staring back at him. Wu Liang's was the only one directed elsewhere; he was examining the fading green paint on the wall.

"We all know, from Wu Liang's own testimony, what followed. Wu Liang took Bo Gaoli into custody, and by the twenty-third Bo Gaoli was dead. He'd been in a cell for the previous three days, had no contact with the outside world, and, supposedly under round-the-clock guard, killed himself. I'm not going to waste your time with the problems in that narrative; just please note them.

"As I said before, I cannot claim to have really known Bo Gaoli, but I have every reason to believe that he had China's best interests in mind. If that is true, then let's consider a new narrative of that week in April. On Tuesday the fifteenth, I send my memo regarding the ministry turncoat. Bo Gaoli has been harboring suspicions of Wu Liang but has had no one to take those suspicions to. We all know that it is a rare administrator who will risk his career on unfounded accusations. By Friday the eighteenth, I had released my twelve-page list of compromised items from the Department of Tourism. Bo Gaoli, using that list, penned the letter each of you has, connecting his own suspicions of Wu Liang to a number of items. Bo Gaoli realized he had a potential partner in me. However, when he called on Sunday the twentieth, I wasn't available."

"What were you doing on Sunday the twentieth, Xin Zhu?" Yang Qing-Nian cut in.

"I was with my wife and, distracted by marriage, I let the battery on my phone run out. That's something I'll have to live with."

Yang Qing-Nian nodded, expressionless.

Zhu continued, "Realizing that things were going to come to a head very soon, Bo Gaoli sent his wife, Hua Yuan, to the countryside to stay with family, but it did him no good. By Monday, before he had a chance to send the letter to me, he was in the custody of Wu Liang."

Zhu frowned, scanning the crowd, but no one showed a sign of anything.

"One important question I cannot answer is this: What did Bo Gaoli admit to while in Wu Liang's custody? Did he admit that his letter existed? I don't think so, for the most expedient thing for Wu Liang would have been to torch his houses to assure the letter's destruction. It's what I would have done. However, I do think that Bo Gaoli at least admitted that he was able to connect Wu Liang to the items on my list, for it was after his arrest that Wu Liang arrived at my office to challenge everything I had written. Then, after disposing of Bo Gaoli, he set out to destroy my career, and perhaps even my life. That I'm still sitting here is not, as Wu Liang would have it, a testament to my political prowess, but a testament to the virtue of our system, which, though slow at times, nevertheless demands justice."

That last sentence had been a bit of agitprop for the virtue of the digital recorder on the floor, for they all knew that justice was all too rare in these halls. Survival was the only functional word.

"You mentioned money," said Zhang Guo. "Three hundred thousand. Was there a reason for it?"

"I don't know," Zhu admitted. "It's something I've not been able to tie into the storyline as I see it, though I have my suspicions."

"Perhaps you'd like to share those suspicions," said Sun Bingjun, looking very serious.

Zhu took a breath. He should have kept his mouth shut about that, for now he wished he'd brought notes. He hadn't wanted to look as if he were reading a script, though. "If forced into a position," he said, "I would call it the fruits of blackmail."

"Excuse me?" asked Yang Qing-Nian, irritably.

"The narrative," Zhu admitted, "could run essentially the same, but this way: Much earlier, Bo Gaoli discovers Wu Liang's allegiances but, instead of following the correct route of reporting him, goes to Wu Liang and demands payments for his silence."

Wu Liang, still staring at the wall, said, "Then why,

Xin Zhu, would he threaten his income by going to you?"

"Because he realized it was over. He saw that I was assembling evidence against the mole, and he knew that the value of those payments paled beside the political advantages of joining with someone who could bring you down. If he helped me, things would go much easier if his blackmail were discovered. What he didn't realize was that you would use the same excuse—namely, my memos—to take him into custody and kill him."

"Absurd," Wu Liang said to the wall, but his cheeks were flushed.

"Authenticity?" said Feng Yi. "We're basing most of this on a letter found on a dead woman. Has Sun Bingjun verified that it was, in fact, written by Bo Gaoli?"

Sun Bingjun said, "His fingerprints were found on the first and last pages."

"Not the ones in between?" asked Yang Qing-Nian, perhaps remembering that he was here to protect his mentor.

"Perhaps he was wearing gloves," Feng Yi said, stupidly.

Silence followed, until Wu Liang finally turned from the wall. "Is this really all you have?"

Zhu shook his head. "We could go back again to the list of compromised material. All of it is material you had access to."

"And you, Xin Zhu. You had access to the same material."

"As did we all," Sun Bingjun interrupted, "but none

of us have a dead man's letter with our names on it. Nor did Bo Gaoli die while in our care. Nor, I have to add, did any of us try to spearhead a campaign to crush Xin Zhu's investigation into the identity of an American mole."

"Which brings us back," Wu Liang went on, "to some very basic questions about the Americans. If, as you say, I am a mole—if, indeed, any of us are working for the Americans—then why are they sending agents to China to find out simple answers about Xin Zhu's private life? Why are they meeting with Turkestan zealots right under our noses? There's something happening here, and none of our finger-pointing has shed any light on it. Go ahead and arrest me, if you think it's necessary, but don't imagine that we've answered any significant questions here. What are the Americans up to, and how are they using Xin Zhu for their ends?"

"Would you like an answer?" Zhu asked him directly.

"Oh? So you have an answer?"

"By now I think I do, and this afternoon I hope to have verification. For a while, we've known that the Americans were playing an elaborate game of obfuscation. They are drawing our gazes elsewhere, playing on our fears, both to distract us and to discredit me. Our mistake has been the assumption that they were distracting us from a planned attack. We can call it my mistake, if you like. The truth, I now suspect, is that all of this effort has been a simple effort to lay cover for their agent in our midst. For you, Wu Liang. With us distracted by what they're up to, they are keeping you temporarily safe until . . . until what? Tell us, do you have an escape plan already in motion? Have they already bought you a nice house on the California coast? Will Chu Liawa be joining you, or has she outlived her political utility?"

"You're making this up as you go along, Xin Zhu. You're the one who's the master of distraction."

Zhu didn't bother answering. Wu Liang was sinking before his eyes. Even Yang Qing-Nian was unwilling to speak, for his mentor was too dangerous to defend. Zhang Guo caught Zhu's eye and gave an approving nod. Sun Bingjun's face expressed nothing except the emptiness that could defend you against an entire regime; then he said, "Wu Liang, don't think that any of this is settled. However, I believe that placing you in custody is the only path to take. Is there any disagreement?"

No one said a word.

Slowly, Sun Bingjun pushed himself up from his chair and walked to the door. He opened it and stood a moment talking to the guard posted outside. The guard left, and Sun Bingjun came back in, closing the door behind himself. As he returned to his chair, he said, "Wu Liang, shall we call Yang Qing-Nian your assistant in this case? I don't want you to be completely cut off in your cell, as Bo Gaoli was. He can represent your interests on the outside."

"If it's agreeable to Yang Qing-Nian," said Wu Liang. His face was red now, from his chin to his eyes. Zhu feared he was going to pass out.

Yang Qing-Nian nodded, looking less resolved than obliged.

When the guard arrived with two more men, Wu Liang allowed himself to be escorted out without any resistance or, really, any sign that he knew the rest of the world existed. Yang Qing-Nian followed him out. Feng Yi shook Sun Bingjun's hand, while Zhang Guo walked over to Zhu and whispered, "I'm honestly impressed. Congratulations."

"Thanks," Zhu said, though as soon as he said it he felt uncomfortable. He wasn't supposed to be congratulated for doing his job. That hadn't been Zhang Guo's meaning—he was congratulating Zhu for pummeling a political enemy.

"You're expecting something soon on the other front? The Americans?"

"I've had two of them in custody since last night. I didn't want to talk to them until this had been taken care of. Would you like to join the conversation?"

Zhang Guo laughed aloud, shaking his head. "My stomach couldn't take it!"

They shook hands; then Zhang Guo left with Feng Yi.

Sun Bingjun placed his folder under his arm and approached Zhu. They were alone now. "So how do you feel?" the old man asked.

"Feel?"

"You must feel something."

"I don't feel good, if that's what you mean. I've always known that Wu Liang is a self-serving cretin, but the world is full of men like him. To be honest, I'm still stunned that he was working for the Americans."

"You don't believe it?"

"I believe evidence. The evidence is there."

"Yes, and you found the letter yourself. Unless, of course, you fabricated it. Did you?" Sun Bingjun said, very seriously.

"No," Zhu said.

"Good. Then I haven't placed my trust in the wrong man."

7

He woke to a whitewashed, damp cell, cold and sick from the hangover of whatever had been in that needle.

He didn't know what time it was. Sleep had come on the airplane, the vibrations lulling him into a false sense of peace, and he'd woken here with urine-soaked pants, his arms aching. Someone had taken the laces from his shoes.

At some point, a slot in his low steel door squeaked open, and a tray was pushed through. Tepid tea. Flavorless rice and slices of salty chicken. He drank the tea and ate the rice but left the chicken untouched, not knowing when or if they would bring more tea.

He had nothing to do but think, yet the only thought that mattered had been settled. They were safe. That did not absolve Alan Drummond, though, for it was he who had put them in danger in the first place. More importantly, Alan's shoddy plan to kidnap Tina and

Stephanie had led to the murder of his father. No, Alan was absolved of nothing.

The door finally opened and, from the floor, he looked up at an enormously fat man following the guard inside.

"You are awake," said that by now familiar voice. "How's your head?"

Milo pushed himself back to the wall and got to his feet. His head was in terrible shape. "You look very pleased with yourself."

Xin Zhu grinned. "Do I? Maybe, but it's got nothing to do with you. More important things have gone my way."

"Congratulations."

Xin Zhu spoke briefly to the guard, who stepped outside but left the door open. The corridor, Milo saw, was made of rough-hewn stone. This was a basement. The guard returned with two low wooden stools and placed them in the cell. Only then did he step outside again and close the door but not lock it.

Xin Zhu grunted as he settled on one stool. Milo took the other—there was no sense acting defiant, not here.

Xin Zhu said, "Leticia Jones will live."

"Hector Garza?"

"Unfortunately, he did not survive the stairwell. The man in Sebastian Hall's room, I suspect, is just fine."

"He got away?"

An arched brow was all the answer he would get.

This wasn't quite the man Milo had expected to meet. He fit the description—overweight, comfortable with himself, an easy conversationalist—yet there was something lacking here. Where was the moral outrage that had defined the Xin Zhu he thought he knew? The man who had let loose his epic vengeance because of the death of a single young man, his son? The man comfortably staring back at him looked like so many other administrators he'd met during his career—cool, satisfied, viewing all of this as a clever game. Milo found it extremely disappointing.

"You have questions," Milo said. "So ask them."

"I'm not sure I do," Xin Zhu answered, rocking his head. "I do have some things I'd like to say. For instance, I'm sorry about Andrei Stanescu. Helping him put a bullet in you wasn't entirely . . . *professional*. I was guided by my empathy, and that's a mistake I'll endeavor to avoid in the future."

Milo stared at him.

"I'm sorry, too, that I had to carry on that ruse about your family. You do know, don't you, that I had nothing to do with their disappearance? Your father as well. From what I've heard, Yevgeny Primakov was a fine man."

Milo felt the urge to punch him.

"I assume Alan Drummond is responsible for all of them, as well as for the disappearance of his wife. His idea of keeping people safe so he can march out into the world and work without chains. How could he know that the man he sent for your family would be trigger-happy?" Zhu placed two fat hands on his knees. "Do you know where they are now?"

Milo said nothing.

"Of course. If you do know, you won't tell me. If you don't, you'd rather not let me have the satisfaction. But, trust me, I feel no satisfaction over any of this."

"I find that hard to believe," Milo finally said, for this man looked like the epitome of satisfaction.

"Again, the satisfaction is about something else." He got rid of his smile. "As for everything that you've been involved with, it is just as I explained on the phone. I learned someone was planning on doing not only me but my country harm. I've reacted to the best of my abilities. Now, I think I may have succeeded in neutralizing the threat."

"But you never learned what it was, did you?"

"It was nothing, Milo Weaver. That was the great magic trick. An elaborate fireworks display to cover something tiny—the movements of a traitor. Once you cut away the distractions, it's all clear. Even you and your Tourists were lied to."

As Irwin and Collingwood had made clear, it had never been about revenge.

Xin Zhu reached into his jacket and took out a box of filtered cigarillos. Hamlet brand. It was one of the few known facts that had made it into the CIA file on him.

Seeing that Milo was watching, he held out the box. "Would you like one?"

"No, thanks."

He took one out and tapped it against his knuckle, packing the tobacco. "So, do you know where Alan is?"

Milo shook his head and watched as Xin Zhu lit up

with a match, puffing at the flame, breathing smoke. "He's going to kill you, you know."

"Alan Drummond?" Xin Zhu laughed, more smoke spilling out. "Really? Well, that would be something."

"And if he can't do that, he'll go after your young wife."

All expression dropped from Xin Zhu's face. "What did you say?"

"He's a serious man. Don't underestimate him."

He considered Milo for a moment, then puffed on his cigarillo and stood up. It was evidently an effort for him. "Okay, Milo Weaver. I'm sure we'll talk again."

"How long are you going to keep me?"

"Not so long," he said. "We'll contact your people, set up a trade. You'll be home before you know it. Good-bye, Milo."

"Good-bye, Zhu," Milo said and watched the big man walk out, leaving puffs of smoke in his wake.

They came only five hours later, though to Milo it felt like ten. He'd eaten more rice and drunk a pot of tea, but his stomach was in knots and he was unable to sleep on the cool, damp floor. There were footsteps, a few words exchanged, then the loud squeak of his door's rusty hinges. Two soldiers entered in uniform, rifles over their shoulders, and one shouted at him in Mandarin. He took it to mean that he should stand. The soldiers grabbed him by the upper arms and hustled him down the stone corridor, past many more steel doors, to uneven stairs. There, the soldiers stopped him and pulled a bag made of soft black fabric over his head. He tripped as they headed up the stairs and through a pair of doors. Stop. A guttural conversation of half-words, then ahead. He tripped over something in the floor, and the soldiers caught him. Doors opened. Cold—they were outside. Wind buffeted him, then a voice in heavily accented English said, "Climb up." He reached blindly ahead and found the edge of a truck's flatbed. He climbed, and once up started to stand again. "Lay down," said the voice. The truck started up and began to move.

Forty minutes, an hour. Their path took them through a cacophony of car horns and engines and Chinese voices and food smells mixing with gasoline fumes. Eventually, the city noises faded away. The truck shook rabidly once they left the paved road, knocking him around, and after a while the truck slowed, then stopped, the engine cut. In the silence, he waited to be taken out, but all that happened was that someone walked toward him, crunching across gravel, then stopped near his head. A new voice, still heavily accented, said, "Tom Grainger was a friend of yours?"

He wasn't sure how to answer that. Tom had been more than a friend, but he'd been dead nearly a year. "Yes," he said.

The voice said, "We heard here that you were the one who killed him. Is this true?"

"No," Milo said.

"Do you know who did kill him?"

"Yes. That man is dead now, too."

"A Tourist?"

Pause. "Yes."

"Killed by Xin Zhu?"

"No," Milo said. "By me."

He heard the man sigh, then walk away again, gravel crunching. The truck was started again. He didn't hear another voice until, after a while, the road beneath them became smoother and the truck again slowed and stopped, idling. The original voice, the one he'd heard while being taken from the prison, said, "Take it off. We're here."

Milo sat up painfully, then tugged off the hood, expecting a flood of light to pour in, but he was instead faced with a nighttime field broken only by lamps laid out regularly in two lines leading outward. Behind him in the truck was a blank-faced Chinese soldier nodding him forward. He climbed down onto tarmac and saw, once the truck drove away, another twin-engine airplane with only a few internal lights on. Its stairs were lowered, but no one came out. Milo looked at the fading red lights on the rear of the truck, then the blackness all around, and realized the blackness was from trees on either side of the long runway. He approached the plane and waited at the foot of the stairs indecisively until a shadowy form filled the open hatch above. A woman's voice said, "Come on, Milo. We don't have all day." It was Alexandra.

As he climbed the stairs he felt the fear rising in him, but it was the fear he'd packed away in the back room of his head while in the prison. His legs were cold, the joints tough, and he felt like the Tin Man, too easily rusted.

She was smiling when he reached her, holding a

blanket that she wrapped around his shoulders as she guided him to the empty seats. As he settled down, she said, "You stink, Milo."

"I wet my pants."

"I think we have a change of clothes."

She started to walk to the rear, but he grabbed her forearm. "What's going on?"

"You're heading home."

"Please," he said, tugging. "Tell me."

She relented and settled into the chair opposite his. In the dim light, she looked even younger than thirty-two, so fresh and clean. She said, "We couldn't do anything about Hong Kong. We were there, of course, and I knew that Alan Drummond wasn't in that room, but once the Chinese started shooting I had to get out of there. I hope you understand."

He frowned at her, not quite understanding. What was she apologizing for?

"Anyway," she said, "Erika talked to a Chinese friend, but it didn't help. He needed something from the Americans—a simple trade would do the trick—but America wasn't ready to bargain. However, we'd learned enough by then to scare the pants off of that senator of yours. So I made some calls. You'd be surprised how much business you can get done by bluffing."

"Leticia?"

She shrugged, then checked a small wristwatch. "We'll see. We've got until three thirty to get out of here."

"What time is it now?"

"Five till two."

Milo turned to look out the bubble window but saw only blackness. "On the drive here," he said, "someone asked me about Tom Grainger."

She cocked her head. "Tom Grainger?"

"My old boss. A friend. He wanted to know if I'd killed Tom. I told him I hadn't, and that the man who'd killed him was dead."

"Good answer," she said, but neither bothered to speculate further.

A light appeared in the distance, at the far end of the runway, then grew, separating into two headlights. It was another military flatbed, and by the time it stopped, they were standing at the open hatch. "Don't go out," Alexandra warned. "It's part of the deal—we don't exit the plane. There's a sniper in the woods, just to make sure."

Two soldiers leaped out of the back and helped Leticia down, then assisted her to the steps. She was still in her black dress, with the addition of a soldier's heavy green coat covering her bandaged shoulder. Once they released her, she began to take it off, but the soldier shook his head and gave her a slight bow, saying something. Leticia gave an answer, flashed one of her notorious smiles, and kissed his cheek before beginning her ascent.

"Well, look at her," said Alexandra.

It took three hours to reach Hong Kong, where they took rooms at the Regal Airport Hotel to wait for their 8:00 A.M. flight to Tokyo. Milo fell asleep immediately and was woken by Alexandra banging on his door. She gave him fresh clothes that were a size too big, then asked if he'd seen Leticia. "I've been asleep," he said.

"Well, she's not here."

"Maybe she'll meet us at the gate."

She didn't, though, and they left without her.

In Tokyo, Alexandra waited with Milo for his connecting flight to Seattle, and then to Denver. "You should come, too," he told her.

She shook her head. "I'd rather pull a Leticia Jones." Then, "They'll be waiting for you, you know."

"I don't have a choice."

Alexandra smiled and took his arm in the crook of her elbow. "If there's one thing our father taught me, it's that we always have a choice."

8

He couldn't get Milo Weaver's statement out of his head. As he sat in the office, trying to feel joy over his newfound security, as he drove home and took that epic elevator ride to the thirtieth floor, and even as he told Sung Hui that he was taking her out to whatever restaurant she wanted, he could not stop thinking that it was true. Alan Drummond *would* try to kill him and, failing that, kill Sung Hui. It was how the world was. Things change. Nothing remains. The things we do not deserve are taken from us.

Over exquisite plates of dim sum at Sampan, they discussed a friend's impending wedding, and the groom's desire for a nontraditional ceremony. "Her parents are about to explode!" she said, laughing, and Zhu thought that if he could laugh like that, laugh with that same unhindered pleasure, he might just make a claim to deserving her. He tried but failed.

When they got back to their building at eleven

thirty, Zhu noticed an unmarked Ministry of Public Security Audi parked outside, and in the lobby found a pair of young men with ministry IDs who asked him to come with them. An angry look crossed Sung Hui's face, the unspoken accusation that he'd known this interruption would come, but he professed his ignorance as he walked her to the elevator and kissed her again.

They were just couriers. They knew nothing of their job beyond its definition: bring a single man to the ministry headquarters on East Chang'an. Not to the front door—no. Around the rear to a quiet entrance, where only the guards would be watching. That was when the worry began to flow freely through Xin Zhu. The young men took him to a small door, knocked, and waited until it was opened from inside by two uniformed ministry soldiers. They then left Xin Zhu to his fate, not even signing a release form, which was perhaps the most terrifying detail. When a Chinese soldier ignores paperwork, you know there is going to be trouble.

After being relieved of his cell phone, he looked into the faces of the soldiers, one of whom looked very familiar. A big man with a face of clay. "Do I know you?" he asked, but the soldier said nothing, only took him down a corridor of empty offices to a stairwell that led deeper into the earth. They stopped briefly at a metal detector beside a glassed-in desk. A guard looked up from his paperwork and, after a moment's examination, waved his hand for them to continue. They went through a steel door and down into the old stone basement of East Chang'an, where the cells lay.

Once he'd been locked inside one, he settled on the floor and, briefly, thought of 1969, when, as an eighteen-year-old mountain boy used to life in the Qinling range, he entered his first prison cell, corralled by boys and girls eager to teach him the errors of possessing a middle-school education. They'd come early, village kids he recognized, and pulled him out of bed, chanting Red Guard slogans. At first, he'd shared his cell with two others, but by the afternoon there were twenty. Tuan Gang, the asthmatic schoolteacher whose education had gotten Xin Zhu into this trouble, didn't survive the night, which, perhaps, was a blessing for the old man, for he never would have survived the next five years of farming the hard, selfish earth of Inner Mongolia. Nor would he have been able, as Zhu had been, to learn new lessons. Such as how to speak appropriately in public while creating an elaborate internal architecture of deceit, of finding ways of holding on to your individuality while showing all the outward signs of becoming one with the group. He certainly would not have received, after five years of labor, a visit from recruiters of the Central Investigation Division with a promise of a new life. No, Tuan Gang would have fallen over in those barren fields within three months and would never have lived to see what his favorite pupil was to become.

They had let him keep his watch, and so when the door finally opened he knew that four hours had passed. It was nearly four thirty. He hadn't panicked, for he knew what this was, and he knew that Yang Qing-Nian would stride in, barking threats. What would those threats consist of? Yang Qing-Nian was young and brash, but he was no idiot. If he was confident enough to pluck Xin Zhu from his home, he must have something powerful at hand. Zhu, however, couldn't figure out what it could be.

So it was a surprise when Sun Bingjun opened the door and, as Zhu had done with Milo Weaver, brought a guard carrying two worn benches. Slowly, Zhu climbed to his feet. Sun Bingjun sat down, threading his fingers together in front of his stomach, and then Zhu sat. Once the guard was gone, Sun Bingjun said, "How are you feeling, Xin Zhu?"

"Not well."

"I went to see Sung Hui, to put her mind at ease."

Zhu looked up at him, trying to read intent in his features, but Sun Bingjun was a virtuoso of the passive expression. "How is she?"

"Worried, of course. I told her you would be home by tomorrow." Sun Bingjun opened his hands. "I hope I wasn't telling her a lie."

It was an odd thing to say, and disconcerting to hear, but as Zhu stared back, wrestling with the possibility that Sun Bingjun's promise to Sung Hui might prove true, it came to him. It was instinct more than logic; for only after the realization hit him did he work backward through the things he knew to see if it was justified. The visits from members of the Department of Tourism, the nearly unbelievable slip by Stuart Jackson to Liu Xiuxiu, the fact that Sun Bingjun was clearly not the washed-up drunk he had so long pretended to be, and the remarkably timed letter from Bo Gaoli, along with his wife's murder.

Then he remembered the face of the soldier who had brought him to this cell—Sun Bingjun's driver was a ministry soldier with access to East Chang'an's cells.

He shifted, his legs aching, and moved his hands to his knees. He said, "You're here to make an offer."

Sun Bingjun just stared back.

Zhu said, "You helped me corner Wu Liang in order to divert attention from yourself."

"I did nothing," said Sun Bingjun. "You collected evidence. Hua Yuan called you before she was killed. I have nothing to do with any of this."

"Was your driver sitting with her when she called me?"

Sun Bingjun held onto his lifesaving face.

"Smart," Zhu said, for it really was. Sun Bingjun hired a ministry guard, who was able to get rid of Bo Gaoli. Bo Gaoli, who knew what Sun Bingjun was. Aloud, Zhu said, "Why didn't Bo Gaoli tell Wu Liang about you once he was locked in here?"

Sun Bingjun only blinked.

"Maybe because Wu Liang was my enemy, and he was afraid that Wu Liang would find a way to bury it, in order to hinder me. Perhaps he assumed Wu Liang would instead arrest him for blackmail—for, of course, he'd been extorting you. Or maybe he believed you would save him in order to save yourself. Whatever the reason, you made sure he didn't live to change his mind."

Sun Bingjun's face was remarkable to behold. Nothing fazed him. It was how you survived for years—for decades, perhaps—as an agent of capitalist aggression.

Add to it a reputation for drunkenness, and you were impervious to suspicion.

Zhu waited, expecting something, but Sun Bingjun wasn't interested in elaboration. Yet he made no move to leave. Zhu said, "What about the letter?" for it was the final, wild piece of evidence that, in retrospect, showed how desperate Sun Bingjun had become. "Bo Gaoli's prints were on the first and last pages—does that mean those pages were the actual letter he was writing to me? And everything in between, where the mole is named as Wu Liang, was the fabrication? That's sloppy, Sun Bingjun. That's the cracked brick that will bring down the whole house."

Sun Bingjun nodded, as if he'd made an excellent point, and finally spoke. "True, Xin Zhu. All it takes is a closer look at the letter—the one that you called to tell me about. In the committee meeting, I said that you were outside the house before I arrived, and you did not correct me. It's on record. How do I know what you did before I arrived?"

Zhu thought back, stopping at points along the way. The murders of Bo Gaoli and Hua Yuan. The committee meetings where Sun Bingjun had stepped up to ensure Zhu was given the time to keep pushing forward. The encouragement he'd given Zhu, insisting that he kill the agents in Hong Kong. "They know something," said Zhu.

Sun Bingjun blinked at him questioningly.

"Milo Weaver and Leticia Jones. One or both of them know something. You wanted me to kill them to silence them."

Finally, the reserve broke, and Sun Bingjun smiled. He leaned forward and patted the side of Xin Zhu's thigh. "As long as you believe it, I am happy."

"Where are they now?"

"On a plane. Heading home." Sun Bingjun raised his hands, palms out. "That is what you asked me to do with them, isn't it?"

Zhu exhaled, flipping rapidly through everything. Gradually, it all fit into place. There had always been a plot to attack Xin Zhu, but not in retaliation for the Tourists. It was to neutralize his hunt for Sun Bingjun. By orchestrating the illusion of an attack, they gave Wu Liang ammunition to go after Zhu, which gave Zhu no choice but to retaliate. Even the conspirators had become involved in the game, Stuart Jackson allowing himself to be seduced, then letting slip a few crucial words to Liu Xiuxiu. This old man had worked hardest to save himself—two murders, and years of maintaining a mask for everyone. "Weaver and Jones don't know anything, do they?"

"They never will," said Sun Bingjun. "You can be assured of that."

"I don't care if they do," he said.

"You will."

"What about Alan Drummond?"

"Funny," said Sun Bingjun, raising an index finger. "I did tell them that you were running him, but he had already confessed it to them. His disappearance in London was not part of any plan, though. The same is true of his appearance and disappearance in Hong Kong.

What they suspect is that in London he was running away from them, not you."

"Why?"

Blank-faced, Sun Bingjun said, "Because all Alan Drummond has ever wanted is your death, and they were taking that dream from him. Never take away a man's dream unless you're prepared to deal with the consequences. Of course, they never told him why you couldn't be killed."

He's going to kill you, you know. And if he can't do that, he'll go after your young wife.

"I lost four men in Hong Kong. They were good men."

"Aren't they all?" Sun Bingjun asked. "I'm afraid there's more, though. The pretty girl you sent to Washington, D.C., was found dead in the Potomac River, an apparent suicide."

Zhu rubbed his face. He no longer wanted to think about the tedium of the plot. Here in this cell, those things no longer mattered. What really mattered was that the bodies had been stacked in order to protect this old drunk, who now only wanted to show that he had Zhu's future in his hands. There could only be one reason for this performance: He was going to ask for something. Zhu said, "You want me to play along. Is that it? Convict Wu Liang?"

"You were already playing along, Xin Zhu. A couple more days and you would have happily demanded Wu Liang's execution." He shook his head. "You see, it may be that I'm not as helpless as I look, but this," he said, opening his hands to display the thin body inside his loose suit, "does not lie. I'm tired. I'm on the cusp of retirement, and that's how it should be. I've served the people long enough. What I would like is for you to take over my position."

It was an odd thing to hear. A promotion to the ranks of the Politburo? Then he stopped himself. That, obviously, wasn't what Sun Bingjun was talking about.

Sun Bingjun stared, waiting for him to understand.

How long had Sun Bingjun worked for the Americans? Had there been any outward signs that they'd all missed? Was there some stuffed bank account in Switzerland that, after his retirement, he would sail off to enjoy? Zhu wondered these things to avoid thinking about the subject at hand. He said, "You've never really served the people, have you?"

A sigh of impatience. "Don't lecture me on morality, Xin Zhu. Your history won't allow it."

"My history has always been guided by my ideology."

"Your recent history, Xin Zhu, has been guided by your guilt. The massacre of the Tourists? Tell me, who sent Delun to Africa to play around in the sand? Had you slept with her before that point, or was getting rid of him only the first step in her seduction? And when the Americans killed him, what were you thinking? Don't tell me you were a father enraged by your son's murder, because that's only part of the story. You were relieved that your son would never return to find out that you had stabbed him in the back."

Zhu felt sickness building up, deep in his intestines. His vision muddied by tears and swollen blood vessels, he could no longer see Sun Bingjun clearly, but he could hear the old man breathing heavily. "Is that your assessment?" Zhu asked. "Or theirs?"

"They've got excellent psychologists," Sun Bingjun said after a moment. "They collected as much information as possible from people you had spent time with, and they analyzed it. At first, I told them they were mad—I've never believed much in that pseudoscience—but then I looked at their data." A pause. "It was disappointing, to say the least."

And, of course, it was all true. Sending his son to Africa had been the first step in a seduction that he had bungled every step of the way, a seduction that only made headway once Delun was dead and grief had softened Sung Hui. Did that mean that their marriage was built on lies?

Yes, but whose marriage wasn't?

Zhu said, "I'm not worried about dying, you know."

"I told them that, too. They told me that, despite everything, your love for Sung Hui remains a motivating factor."

"So you've sunk to the level of threat."

"As you've done numerous times in the past, Xin Zhu. Unlike you, however, they are willing to give as well as take. Compensation. Security."

"Do you really think the Americans are going to let you walk?"

"Why not?" Sun Bingjun asked. "I've given them

most of my adult life, and now I'm giving them my replacement. They're not as irrational as you make them out to be."

"Of course they are. I am, you are. Everyone is. All they are is a collection of irrational individuals, just as we are."

"What is your favorite doctrine of the Chairman?"

Zhu stared, trying to get him into focus.

"Yes, I remember," Sun Bingjun said. "Perpetual revolution."

Zhu said nothing.

"You have a decision to make, Xin Zhu."

Part Five

THE AMERICAN EXPRESS

**FRIDAY, APRIL 4 TO
SATURDAY, AUGUST 9, 2008**

1

He sat across from George Erasmus Butler, the director's assistant—his "iron gut"—in a windowless room in the bowels of Langley. Irwin had said, *Remember that the operational flaws were in place before you even took over. Remind them of that.* However, he knew that such words would be wasted on someone like Butler.

So he cleared his head and stared across the table, wondering at what level in an organization's hierarchy a member's position began to change him physically. One expected it of Butler's boss, CIA Director Quentin Ascot, but under these fluorescent lights, he noticed the sheen to Butler's flesh, as if he were gradually becoming shrink-wrapped for the cameras. The politicization of the soul.

He was wandering again. *Focus!*

Butler leaned back in his chair, tapping an open file with his knobby forefinger. "Now, listen, Alan. Usually when something like this happens the conversation is essentially genial. Mistakes occur, but they're mistakes of flawed procedure, and our aim becomes fixing procedure. Here, though," he said, looking down at the papers and shaking his head, feigning exasperation. "Now, here it looks like we had the wrong man at the helm. Shoddy security. Opening your files to a goddamned *mole*. Instigating a contact procedure so rigid that even when you realized the Chinese were running every one of your people there was nothing you could do about it. I mean . . . *hey*, look at me. I'm not the enemy here. The enemy is yourself. Two months at the helm of a ship that's sailed for sixty years, and you run her right into the reef. You sunk it, man. You know how much we've spent on your unlikely little department over the years? Boggles the mind. The perks— the limitless credit cards, the first-class flights, the fucking *clothing*—it's just staggering how much you guys ate up. And this?" He lifted a single sheet of paper. "An *art heist* to add to the departmental coffers?"

"That was before I came on."

"Sure, that's convenient. However, it speaks more to the kind of operation you guys had going on West Thirty-first, doesn't it? I mean, here at Langley we've got to sign in triplicate for a new box of pens. See what I mean? Your cowboy bullshit has never gone over well with us simple desk commanders. We work for a living. We fly only when we have to. And as for shopping on the Company dime," Butler said, a smile flashing across his face as he lifted another sheet of paper showing a credit card statement with a balance of $22,927.58.

He read, "One afternoon's shopping in Paris: Dior, Prada, Louis Vuitton. I mean, am I just an old fogey here? Or have you people been living like kings off the Company's tit?"

Like plastic, he thought. *I can almost see myself in the man's cheek.*

The twinkle of lights, computerized. Red shimmers into blue. With each change the rumble of something in his stomach, growing sharper. Four lights, and it's like the point of a pencil trying to squirm its way out. Ten, and it's a pickax.

"What is it?" Penelope asked when he woke.

"Nothing."

"Don't tell me it's nothing, dear. I'm not one of your empty-headed bimbos."

The smile he gave her wasn't humor so much as the recognition of humor. She deserved at least that. In fact, she deserved a lot more, and he couldn't help thinking that their marriage, in sum, had been a little less than she'd hoped for.

Sensing that his trip to Langley was going to be a disaster, she had already reserved them four nights at a cottage in Croton-on-Hudson, close to the river, and they'd spent their days reading books and their evenings at expensive restaurants. He wasn't up for it, though. She knew better than to ask for details, but her patience was running out. "You know I can't."

"They canned you, Alan. You don't owe them anything anymore."

"I owe them everything," he said after a moment,

because he sometimes did that. He would take a seemingly rational statement, then reverse it completely to test its validity. The surprising thing was that it worked. "They put me in charge of something important. It might not be my fault that it failed, but if I'd been paying attention I might have avoided the disaster."

"What do you mean, 'disaster'?"

He'd said too much, he realized, and leaned over to kiss her. She pulled back. "Come on. Out with it."

She really was beautiful, and the intensity of her stare only magnified her exceptional features. He said, "Give me some advice."

"Not that you'll take it."

"I will. Really, I will."

"Okay, then."

He wondered how to phrase it, then settled on "In my work, I came across something that was dangerous to America, and—"

"To America?"

"Yes. Not *possibly* dangerous but actually dangerous. It's already caused destruction . . . *disaster*."

"Okay. Go on."

"Now, even though it's no longer my job, I think I can figure out how to neutralize it. It would take a lot of effort on my part, and require a little skullduggery, but I think it could be done—with proper planning."

She waited.

"Well?"

"Oh! You want me to tell you if you should do it or not."

"Exactly."

"Well, is it dangerous? For you."

"No," he said, the lie coming out before he had a chance to wrestle with it.

"Then, yes. I mean, if it's about saving America, you know I'm all about that," she said, grinning. "Is that the answer you wanted?"

He leaned forward to kiss her again, and this time she didn't pull away.

He'd known Dorothy Collingwood for three years; they'd met through his in-laws. Penelope's family had always gotten a rush mingling with America's power brokers, and with Democratic members of the Senate and the House to its credit, the Collingwood clan qualified. Dorothy, however, had chosen a different path from her relatives, using their connections to get herself placed within intelligence. When they first met, she'd been working in the support staff of the CIA's National Clandestine Service. She had higher ambitions, though, and once she realized that she could trust Alan, she promised that he would be part of her rise. "You're a smart guy, Alan. Solid. And you don't speak Beltway. Besides, your wife shows well at social functions." When she did move up, becoming an NCS staff operations officer, planning and running global counterintelligence and intelligence collection operations, she found herself faced with a new world—"a parallel world," she called it over drinks. "You wouldn't believe it, Alan."

"Of course I would," he'd said, for he had always played the unflappable war veteran with her. When she told him that there was an opening for the directorship of a hush-hush department on the fringe of the Langley beast, he'd tried not to show excitement. "What happened to the previous director?"

"Right now Senator Nathan Irwin's got one of his puppets in place, but he can't make that stick."

"The one before that, I mean."

"He was killed by one of his own men." She'd raised a brow. "Sound interesting?"

She hadn't been in the room when he'd been eviscerated by Butler, nor had she come to his defense, and when he told her he wanted to spearhead a retaliation against Xin Zhu he pointed out that she owed him this. She admitted that she did owe him *something* but said, "It shouldn't be seen to come from me, so take this to Irwin. We both know it's personal for him, so he'll go for it. Tell him to bring in Stuart Jackson."

"Who?"

"He's the old me. My predecessor. Retired, but still very much in touch. He's got China locked up, and you won't get far without him. He also knows the whole Tourism fiasco. Get them on board, and take it to my boss. They bring it in, and I lobby for it."

He marveled at how quickly she'd put the scheme together. "And that's it?"

"Essentially. But you have to bring in Stuart Jackson. He knows we can make this work on different levels, and he knows that in my position I have some helpful connections, because he's the one who set up those connections. If I'm right—and, as you know, I always am—it'll end up a joint project between myself, Stuart, and Nathan."

"What different levels are you talking about?"

She placed a hand on his arm. "You worry about your level, and I'll worry about mine."

Dorothy was never truly wrong, and so it was no real surprise when he found himself sitting with her, Nathan, and Stuart Jackson. The surprise was that they were sitting in a dusty safe house rather than some clean office in Langley, and then he learned the reason: Dorothy's superior had nixed the operation. "Then what are we doing here?" he asked the three of them, noting that there was no anxiety in any of their faces.

"We're going to make it happen anyway," Irwin said.

Dorothy said, "We've got access to funds, and you can contact your remaining Tourists. I'll have access to current intelligence."

Stunned, Alan said, "So no one's worried about losing their jobs over this?"

"I'm self-employed," said Stuart Jackson.

Nathan rocked his head noncommittally, and Dorothy said, "You know how ambitious I am, but ambition is empty without the ability to take risks. This is a large risk, but its rewards could be immeasurable."

"I don't understand," he said, for no one ever got a promotion over revenge.

"Remember what I said, Alan. We stick to our own levels, and we'll all be fine."

They largely agreed to his tactic of distraction, but when it came to the actual attack there was dispute. Alan, after toying with psychological warfare, had come to the conclusion that wet work was the best way to deal with Xin Zhu. "We know where he lives. Better yet, we know where his office is. We can wire the building and bring it down. A rocket launcher should do the job. Blame it on the Turkestan revolutionaries—they're already making overt threats. Ideally, we do this during the Olympic Games, when security will be focused on the venues, not on Xin Zhu's office. Zhu is eradicated, we disrupt the Games, and we also send a clear message to the Chinese Central Committee."

A week later, Alan was in Slovenia, taking a clean, modern train from Ljubljana, east to Sevnica, eyeing the cool, stylish Slovenians all around him. He'd mistakenly thought this would be a walk in the park. After all, he'd known Afghanistan, and when you left Afghanistan you left with the confidence that the rest of the world was a walk in the park. However, the impossibility of places had less to do with the places themselves than with what you were carrying in yourself; it had to do with the measure of your guilt. The guilt he was once able to measure with a yardstick now seemed to require a milestick—thirty-three of them.

There was no need for worry, though. The SOVA had no interest in someone who was no longer employed by the American government, and Tran Hoang had done his job well, piloting his plane from Budapest, flying low across the nighttime border to the landing field at Cerklje ob Krki. He'd driven himself and his drugged package in a waiting car north along the Sava River and just past Sevnica to a cabin in the foothills of Gavžna Gora.

When he arrived at Sevnica's small, provincial train station, Alan walked through the lobby and crossed the bustling morning street to reach, around a corner, a small pharmacy. Tran Hoang's ten-year-old Yugo idled at the curb, and it was a sign of the man's skills that pedestrians didn't even notice that a Cambodian man was in their midst, one who'd spent a time in Sri Lanka as he was being nurtured and then recruited by the Department of Tourism. Alan got in on the passenger's side, and Hoang put the car in gear. He drove west, toward the bridge that crossed the Sava. "How's our guest?" Alan asked.

Hoang rocked his head. He was chewing on gum.

"I suppose that means he's still alive?"

"Sure."

Of all the Tourists Alan had met, Hoang was the mutest. Talking to him was like dealing with someone who only had ten words left in him and had better uses for them than communicating with you. "Have you started the questions?"

Hoang shook his head.

"Why not?"

"We flew in last night," said Hoang, making no effort to hide his irritation.

"Is there something wrong?"

His jaw worked on the gum. He shook his head.

It took a half hour to reach the gravel road that snaked through the forest, and the temperature dropped as their elevation rose. The cabin, which Hector Garza, a.k.a. José Santiago, had tracked down, was a two-room affair, nestled against a boulder and surrounded by trees. A thin stream of smoke rose from a tin chimney. Hoang parked and led him into an empty room with a dirty kitchenette in the corner. The air was stuffy— someone had been smoking. They took off their coats. Against the far wall, beside a collection of faded, curling pornographic centerfolds, was a door. "In there?" Alan asked.

Hoang nodded.

Alan went to the door, took a breath, and opened it—another empty room, with the exception of a low cot. Henry Gray, American expat journalist, was sleeping on it, his right wrist cuffed to the bed frame. On the left side of his face was a purple bruise. Alan stepped back and went to Hoang, who was lighting the stove. "Why'd you hit him?"

"Fought back."

"Did you tell him you just wanted to ask some questions?"

No answer.

"Of course he fought back, you idiot. He's scared. Did you even read his file?"

Hoang gave him a look, just a look, but it was enough to stop his complaints.

Henry Gray woke up two hours later, and Alan handed him a chipped mug of coffee. Gray took it hesitantly. "Sorry about the face," Alan said. "He tells me you fought back."

"I tried to leave," said Gray. His voice was brittle from dehydration.

"Anyway, I'm sorry. I just need to have a talk with

you, and I had to be sure that no one else knew where you were."

"When you say no one else, who do you mean? The Hungarians?"

"No, Henry. I mean the Chinese."

Gray nodded slowly but said nothing.

"I'm here to talk to you about Rick."

"Rick."

"You spent a month with this man, and I'd like to know him as well as you do."

"I thought this was over."

"Did you really? A journalist of your stature?"

Henry Gray's face looked pained, and Alan wondered if he'd taken that statement for sarcasm. Gray's stature only meant something to conspiracy theorists, and Alan expected the man to begin a rant against international corporations and the CIA, with liberal doses of the military-industrial complex. Still, Gray had already been through more than most could handle. He had changed.

"I just want to go home," he said finally. "Ask me your damned questions."

"You worry too much," said Leticia. "I'm in, I do some shopping, I leave."

"But they'll spot you. Sooner or later, they'll spot you."

"I'll make sure it's later. Really, baby, you need to get some sleep. It's a good plan."

They were at a Mexican restaurant in North Bergen. She was done with her first margarita, while Alan hadn't

touched his. The lunch crowd was just starting to arrive. He leaned closer. "What's Collingwood been telling you?"

She, too, leaned forward. "What are you talking
about?"

"I'm not sure."

"She agrees it's a good plan. So do the others." Leticia
reached over to grab his hand, her bright red nails reflecting the ceiling lamps. "You're the master of deception.
That fat Chinaman is going to get vertigo trying to figure it out. And it all starts here. I go in. I tickle his fear."

His frown deepened, but what she said was true. It
was a good plan. A series of distractions to overwhelm
him as the pressures within his own government grew
against him. Either he panicked and made a mistake,
weakening him further, or he followed clues until he
was standing in the wrong corner of the room when the
door opened and they rushed in to kill him.

Leticia's face became serious. "You're really committed to this, aren't you?"

"It's the only thing I have left."

"That's not true. You've got a marriage."

"I won't for long if I don't take care of this. I'm fucking it up."

She pursed her lips. "It wasn't your fault, you know.
Not really."

"Milo tells me that, too."

"Did you convince him to join the great cause?"

Alan shook his head.

"See? He's got his priorities straight. People like you
and me, we don't know what's what."

* * *

"You're not listening to me, Alan. I can see it in your face. Just take a breath, cool off, and listen to what I'm saying."

"I can hear everything," he said.

They were sitting in the Georgetown safe house—a funny name for a house they knew the Guoanbu was watching—and he had been through two cigarettes. Dorothy had come alone, claiming the other two were busy, but he knew she just didn't want a scene. She didn't want them to think she didn't have control over him. She said, "Levels. At your level, this makes no sense. At my level, it's the only option. Things have changed."

"The whole point of this operation was to bring him down. Or was I missing something?"

"You know better than that, Alan. We never do anything simply to bring someone down. Not in politics, not in intelligence. Everything we do is to strengthen our position. Previously, the best way to do that looked like burying Xin Zhu. Kill him—then frame him. Now, the situation has changed."

"You'll have to do better than that, Dorothy. You know how much I've poured into this. You know how much it means to me."

"I can't," she said. "Don't ask for things you know I can't give. You're not *in* anymore. You're a private contractor. I'm your client." She leaned back, grabbing at her Evian. "Do you follow?"

"Then I'll sever our contract."

"And lose the few Tourists you still have? You'd be

dead in the water, Alan. You wouldn't be able to do a thing."

"I'll bring in Milo Weaver."

"Weaver?" She laughed. "He's over the hill. He's got a bullet hole in his gut. He's useless. And he wouldn't touch this with a ten-foot pole."

"He could be brought into it easily enough."

She stared at him a moment, then set down her bottle. "This is academic. You're not going solo, because in the end you're a patriot. So leave Milo Weaver alone. You'll just get him killed."

She was right, of course, but that was when he began to ask himself questions. *Could* he bring in Milo? And, if so, could he protect him? Probably not, but he could protect Tina and Stephanie, and that, in the end, was all that would matter to Milo.

"So the plan's changed," he said finally, because there was no other option. "We frame . . . what's his name again?"

"I didn't tell you his name."

"And you can't tell me how that gets us Xin Zhu."

"I'm sorry, Alan." She stared at him a moment. "It's what happens when you bring politicians in on your conspiracies; they take over."

"This is Irwin's doing?"

"We're *all* politicians, Alan."

He stared at her passive, political face. "If you think you can make a deal with Xin Zhu, then he'll humiliate you in the end."

"Please, Alan. It's not about deals, and it's not about

making Xin Zhu's life any easier than we'd planned. He will go down, but not the way we originally planned."

Alan flashed on lights, red lights turning blue. "There's only one way to take care of a man like that."

She leaned back, still staring, and furrowed her brow. "If you're not going to be on board, or if you're going to kick and scream the whole way, then tell me now. It'll save us a lot of trouble down the road."

"No," he said, and only afterward realized he was lying. "I just needed to get it out of my system. I'm on board."

She was shopping. The video feed was grainy, a little wobbly, but he could make out the shelves and the particular overabundance of Dean & Deluca in SoHo. What even the poor-quality picture couldn't hide was that she looked miserable. They'd fought that morning over . . . he couldn't even remember what had set it off. Not that it mattered. The reason for all their fights these days was him, and the shitty moods he brought home, the ones he took to the bathroom when he feared they would lead to outbursts, or worse. She could smell it on him, the misery and the secrecy and the raw hatred that ran his life now. She could see that he'd become a different Alan Drummond, one that was closer to the marine who'd been stupid with his courage in Afghanistan, the Alan Drummond she'd never known.

He was sitting in his home office, staring at the monitor, and in the phone pressed to his ear, Xin Zhu said, "I'm not an unreasonable man, Mr. Drummond.

Far from it. Like you, I only try to protect myself and my family. People like you and me, we understand that the safety of our country pales in comparison to the safety of our wives and children."

"Your dead son," said Alan.

"Exactly," said Xin Zhu. "What I ask is nothing so great. You'll describe the conspiracy to me, and keep me updated at regular intervals. I don't ask you to sabotage anything, not yet at least. I simply want to know."

It was his chance, he realized. He could undermine the others so that the only option remaining would be the full-scale war he had wanted in the first place. *Yet there is Pen, right there in front of me.* Or he could help them with a lie right now. He could tell Xin Zhu his own plans for a load of explosives to shatter his bones and organs, and let the others have their plot. *Right there, so close they can touch her.* Because Penelope was standing in front of one of Xin Zhu's men, he spoke the truth. "They're not telling me."

"They're not telling *you*?"

"That's right. They're giving the orders."

"Sounds like a step down, Mr. Drummond. I hope that the things I did had no hand in your decline. None of it was your fault, you know."

So this was how the Chinese gloated.

"You're serious," said Dorothy.

"Unbelievably so. This changes everything."

"Why?"

She'd asked that with a face full of innocence, the Evian halfway to her mouth. "He's onto us," Alan explained, as if to a child. "It's one thing if he's aware of Leticia, but another thing if he's moved up the ladder."

"We knew he would do this, Alan. As soon as she got back from China, we knew they would track her to the safe house."

"But he's threatening my wife."

"Don't think I don't understand that, Alan. I'm worried as hell about it—remember, I've known Pen longer than you have. But slow down. This is bigger than either of us now."

"What does that even *mean*?"

She shook her head, set down her water, and rubbed her forehead in a way that suggested she was posing for a camera hidden somewhere in this dusty safe house. "What it means is that things are already in motion. We're not shutting it down. We can't. Lives depend on everything moving forward."

"*Lives?*" he repeated, his mouth dry. His exasperation was getting to him, making him lose the half-assed argument he'd marched in here wielding. "My wife's life depends on me making sure she stays protected."

"Then send her away, Alan. We can help with that."

Had she made the offer immediately, or if it hadn't taken argument to bring her to that point, he might have taken it. However, like Milo Weaver weeks later, he no longer believed that, in a pinch, these people could guarantee Penelope's safety. Why would they? Why, in their position, would he?

He shook his head. "I can take care of her."

"Good," she said, crossing her forearms on the table,

gripping her elbows as she leaned closer. "Now, about you. You realize that this is a stroke of luck."

"Because you can play me back to him," he said in monotone.

"It's his biggest mistake, and he's walking into this. Why he thought you wouldn't bring this to us is a mystery for the ages."

"It's because he wouldn't bring it to his people. He knows better."

She smiled at that, then rocked her head. "Must be a holy terror working in their system."

"It must be," Alan said.

Two days later, he talked to them. Though he hadn't been around when the company was in regular contact with the Youth League, he had come across the old contact procedure in the Tourism files long before his life in that office ended. An ad in the *New York Post*, which was monitored by a Chinese exile living in the Bronx, then a rendezvous on the 9:15 ferry to Staten Island, leaving from Whitehall Terminal, with a volume of Charles Bukowski poems in hand.

Bukowski?

The things one does to be unheard.

2

Fear of failure haunted him during the flight to Seattle, as he worked his wedding ring off his finger, and again during the drive north toward the Canadian border. Not just a failed operation but a failed life. A week before, he'd struck his wife. As he groveled on the floor, crying real tears, she'd only stood over him, rubbing her face and staring, strangely devoid of expression. He'd expected anger and hatred, but by the evidence, she felt nothing.

Milo wasn't helping, pulling back from every attempt to bring him in voluntarily, so he'd done all he could, letting slip the location of where, in the future, he could go and find his family.

In Ferndale, a farming town north of Seattle, he met Tran Hoang on the long, low Main Street. The Tourist was sitting in a Mazda, sipping coffee from an anonymous white cup, parked outside of a stylist called Hair to Dye For. Alan parked two spots in front of him, using the car Hoang had left in the Seattle airport lot. Hoang waited a full five minutes before climbing out of his Mazda and getting in beside Alan. He said nothing.

"This is the deal," Alan said. "Once you're done with Korea, I need you to disappear, then go back to Manhattan and keep an eye on my wife, Penelope. You won't be the only one watching her."

"Who else?"

"The Chinese."

Hoang nodded.

"Figure out a good time, then extract her. You'll explain that I've sent you, and you'll show her this." He took his wedding band out of his pocket and handed it over. "Show her that ring, and she should cooperate. If not, try to call me directly, and I'll talk to her. Then you bring her to this place," he said, handing over an unmarked envelope. "Keep her safe."

"For how long?"

"Until I tell you otherwise."

Hoang opened the envelope and read the address that lay on the shore of Colorado's Grand Lake. Below it was an address in Brooklyn. Hoang sighed and stared out the windshield. In profile, he resembled a statue. He said, "You're changing tactic."

"I'm changing nothing," Alan lied. "The others are trying to change it."

"I'm sure they have their reasons."

"They've lost their nerve."

"Maybe they know something you don't."

Alan fingered the steering wheel. He wasn't sure why he'd expected Hoang to go along with this. He'd forgotten, perhaps, that he was no longer the one with power. He was trapped, though, and had no choice but to push forward. "Once she's safe, you'll return to New York and watch Milo Weaver. He lives there, in Brooklyn. We'll keep in touch, and at some point I'll ask you to take his wife and child as well."

"To Colorado?"

"Yes. They're friends of Penelope's, so once they're together you should be able to leave them alone. At that point, we'll discuss what comes next."

Hoang said nothing.

"Are you with me on this? If you aren't, then tell me now."

Hoang watched a pair of children with backpacks that looked too large for their small frames. He said, "Remember Henry Gray?"

"Of course."

"I spent a few days in Budapest, watching him after we put him back. I told you I thought he would go to the Chinese, or to the police, and if it looked as if he was going to do one of those things, I was going to kill him. I was wrong. He was so happy to be back, to be free of us, that he took his girlfriend on a trip to Lillafüred, a Hungarian resort in the mountains. Very picturesque. They had sex a lot, ate, and took walks. I felt like I was watching a bad romantic film."

Alan waited, not knowing what to say.

Finally, Hoang turned to him. "Is that what you have with your wife?"

Alan thought about his hand connecting with Penelope's cheek, of weeping on the floor, of Penelope's hard, apathetic stare, and felt his eyes moistening. He resisted the impulse to wipe them dry.

"Okay," said Hoang. "I'll help you."

She'd met him at Heathrow, coming up with one of her ubiquitous smiles, rubbing her decorated hands together as if preparing to dig into a steak. "Oh, honey, it's so great to see you again!" The hug. The kiss. Then guiding him to the taxi stand, whispering, "Dorothy's idea, baby. Sorry to cramp your style."

"Aren't you supposed to be talking to Sudan?"

"Delayed. They're getting cold feet. Might as well hang out with you, make it look right."

"No, Leticia."

"Gwen, baby."

"*Gwendolyn*, I don't need the babysitting, all right?"

"Dorothy thinks otherwise."

"Dorothy can go to hell."

Which, of course, only convinced her to stay, and left him with what felt like an age-old question: How do you plot and scheme when there's a Tourist breathing down your neck? Then, early Saturday morning, there was a knock on his door. "Charlie! I know you're in there!"

He was first struck by how beautiful she was, and then by the coincidence of her being Milo's sister. How the world folded in on itself. Then, as he listened to her, he was struck by the elegance of simply walking. He'd planned to leave later, but here she was, like an angel, offering him an exit. Penelope was his only worry, and only after Alexandra left did he realize that Xin Zhu would not touch Penelope if he could not find her husband.

It was as if God had sent him salvation, as if God wanted this, too.

"You realize that this is no longer easy," said the man his Staten Island contact had sent him to. He was young, midtwenties, but he had the movements and deliberate speaking manner of someone much older. Alan supposed political exile did that to you. "A couple of years ago, the Youth League was moving upward, and then— well, you know what happened."

Alan knew, and so did most politically aware Americans. A congressional committee had uncovered a CIA transfer of ten million dollars to the fledgling Chinese democracy group based in Guizhou province. Had the Youth League been part of the democracy movement that made itself understood through poetry and literary journals and hunger strikes, none of this would have troubled anyone very much. Yet the Youth League had watched the two post-Tiananmen decades slide by as if Tiananmen had never occurred and, as with so many armed groups before them, patience was no longer part of its vocabulary. The CIA had been crucified for its support of terrorists, first by outraged Chinese diplomats, and then by more congressional committees that made it a priority to dig as deeply as possible into the Company coffers.

"They're on the run now," said the man, "living in

the woods. They're still hungry, you understand. Their spirit is not diminished. However, they're on the edge of extinction, and they know it."

Alan had been ready for this. If the man wasn't at least a little resistant, then he wouldn't be trustworthy. "In this situation," Alan said, "a single victory could make all the difference."

"Or be the final blow that kills the movement," the man said quickly, as if the line had been on the tip of his tongue all along.

"I've told you everything," Alan said. "You have the details."

"You'll be in Rome for how long?"

"Two nights."

"Well," said the man, smiling elusively, "let us hope that everything is settled to the maximum of satisfaction."

Alan shook the young man's hand, then left.

He was staying in a small pension in the working-class neighborhood of Testaccio, where the Vespas buzzed and the sun baked the concrete and stones and encouraged his neighbors to shout at one another even louder until the afternoon siesta, when they fell into their sweat-soaked beds and made love or slept. It was during this empty period that he went down to a kiosk, bought a phone card, and went to the local post office to make his call. After two rings, Hoang said, "Hotel Manhattan."

"Room 9612, please."

Hoang didn't bother connecting him.

"Is everything all right?" Alan asked.

"Of course. She's in the next room. Do you want to talk to her?"

"Please."

He heard movement, a squeaky door opening, then Hoang's monotone, *It's him.*

Then Penelope's *Jesus!* "Alan? Alan!"

"Hey," he said. "Hey, Pen. You all right?"

"I—well, of *course* I'm not all right. I'm *shaken.* Who the hell is this guy? Where are you?"

"He's a friend, and I'm not in the country right now. But don't worry—you're there because it's safe."

"What do you mean, 'safe'? Is this about the apartment?"

"What?"

"The Company ripped apart our place, looking for something."

"Are you sure it was them?"

"I'm not sure of anything. Where *are* you?"

"I'm going to be gone a little while longer. Please, be patient."

"I don't have much choice, do I?"

"You always have a choice. But I'm asking you—please stay there until I get back. It's for your own good."

"Why does he have your wedding ring?"

"What—" he began, then remembered, rubbing the bald spot on his finger. "It was the only thing I could think to do. And, listen, Pen. I'm sorry."

A pause, then, "He told me about those thirty-three people."

"He?"

"Milo. I had no idea, Alan."

"Don't dwell on it."

She took a breath, a clotted intake, and he worried she was going to cry. Instead, she said, "Just come home, okay?"

"As soon as I can."

"When's that going to be?"

"It's not entirely up to me."

Silence.

"Pen?"

"I'm here."

"What's Milo doing?"

"Well, he's trying to find you, isn't he?"

"Has anyone contacted him?"

"The CIA. They're trying to figure out the same thing."

He thought about that, doubting that the CIA really cared where he was. "Okay, listen. You can't use your phone."

"He already took it from me."

"Don't be insulted if he doesn't give it back—he's not very trusting—but he's going to have to leave you alone for a few days. Go out with him and do some shopping—cash only—and make sure you're stocked up for a week. Okay?"

"Yeah, sure."

"When he comes back, he'll have Tina and Stephanie with him."

"*What?*"

"Listen, okay? They'll be scared, but let them know they don't need to be. They'll have to follow the same rules as you—no phones, no credit cards—but you'll all be fine. This shouldn't last long."

"Christ, you're mysterious."

She was starting to sound like the girl he had married.

With everything set up and ready to go, this was an unforgivable risk, but Hoang had been insistent. "You have to come—unless you want me to kill them, too."

"Don't touch them, Hoang. I'll be there," he said, then noticed what the man had said. "Wait—what do you mean: kill them, *too*?"

"There was an old man. He'd figured out where I was holding them."

"What old man?"

"A Russian. His accent, at least. He was in the Weaver apartment, but he came out and knocked on the apartment we were in. He said he knew they were in there."

"Jesus." Alan's stomach dropped an inch.

"What?"

"You killed Milo's father."

Silence. Finally, Hoang said, "I had no choice."

"Of course you did, you murderous shit."

Again, silence.

Alan closed his eyes, and the next day, as he descended into Denver International, he realized that, eventually, whether or not his plan succeeded, Milo Weaver would hunt him down and kill him for this.

He used the name Edward Leary for the flights, then used the name George Miller to rent a car, and by the time he reached Grand Lake he had been traveling for a day without rest. He didn't feel up for this, but there was no choice. Time was running out, and, given another day, he had no doubt that Tran Hoang would shoot everyone.

He parked beside Hoang's rental and walked up the lane to the two-story cabin that overlooked the lake. A chilly breeze rattled the trees. Hoang stepped out onto the porch to meet him but didn't offer a hand. "Don't worry," said the Tourist. "Everyone's breathing."

Alan pushed past him and found Penelope first. She gripped him in a desperate hug and began to cry. At first, he feared that Hoang had been lying and the tears were for two corpses upstairs, but when she began to kiss him frantically, he realized the tears were for him. She was full of questions, but he fended them off, saying, "Where are they?"

She led him upstairs, holding his hand, and in a bedroom he found Tina Weaver sitting in bed looking angrier even than when he'd first met her at New York Methodist, just after her husband had been shot. Again, Stephanie was leaning against her arm, half asleep, but then she blinked, waking, and said, "Hi, Alan."

"Hi, Stef. Tina."

Tina kissed her daughter's head and said, "Wait here, Little Miss. I've got some things to get straight with Alan."

Stephanie let her mother go, and once they were in the hallway, heading back to the stairs, Tina said, "I could fucking kill you."

Penelope said, "He's trying to *save* us, Tina," which he knew wouldn't help.

No one said anything else until they were downstairs. Hoang had stepped outside. Tina turned on him in the middle of the living room. "He told me you were crazy. He *told* me—but I didn't believe him. *You,*" she said, drilling a finger into his chest. "You're the one who got him involved. *You're* the reason we're stuck in the goddamned woods."

He wanted to tell her to shut up, but that was the wrong move here. Instead, he said, "Yes. It is my fault. All of this." Once he said it, it occurred to him that she didn't know about Yevgeny Primakov. Neither of them did. "Now," he continued, "I'm trying to clean it up. Milo's in trouble. The Chinese are threatening you and Stephanie in order to control Milo."

"How do you know this?"

"Because they did the same thing to me," he said, noticing a look of surprise cross Penelope's face. "What I've done is remove all of you from harm. Now, I need to do the same thing for Milo." That was a lie, but when you build a lie off a truth, the difference is hard to notice.

Proving, however, that she had an eye for such differences, Tina said, "I don't believe you. I won't believe it until I hear it from Milo."

"Don't call," he said. "You call him and his life will be in danger. Then they'll trace the call, and you and Stephanie will be next."

"You people lie so well."

What to say to that? Nothing, really, except "Of course we do. So do they. Everybody lies, Tina, so grow up. Don't risk your daughter's life by being rash."

That cooled her off, but only a little. "Then what's your glorious plan?"

"To get your husband back to you." Another lie.

She breathed loudly through her nose, then waved an arm around. "So we get *kidnapped*, and that's all you're going to tell me?"

"Yes, Tina. That's all I'm telling you."

She crossed her arms over her stomach and walked away, shaking her head.

"You're going to be left alone for a few days, so please just keep to yourselves. Either Milo or I will come back here, and by then it should be settled."

It was a kind of explanation, a sort of plan for the future, though when Penelope walked outside with him, she said, "What does it mean if Milo comes back and not you?"

He knew what she was getting at. "It means I'm not done with my job."

"Or that you're dead."

"Doubtful," he said and kissed her small, upturned nose.

They left Hoang's rental behind for emergencies, and on the road back to Denver, Alan said, "We're going to Hong Kong."

Hoang didn't seem to care.

"I'm going to check into a hotel, but I'm not going to the room. You are."

"How long until the Chinese come for me?"

"Not long, so prepare your escape."

"And you?"

"I'll be elsewhere. Just make sure they think I'm in that room."

After another mile, Hoang said, "So you've got an arrangement with the Youth League?"

Alan nearly lost control of the car. He hadn't mentioned a thing about them to Hoang, or to anyone. Their name had come up during the initial planning stage but had been cut because the group was too unpredictable. Alan considered bluffing his way out of it, but Hoang valued his words too much to waste them on idle speculation. "How did you know?"

"They were the only ones left, weren't they? At least, the only ones who would be desperate enough to raise arms. You walk in, to one of their old paymasters, and tell them the time has come to rise against Beijing." He paused, staring at leafy trees blur past. "It's intoxicating for people like them, even when they know it's doomed to failure."

"History is the only thing that's doomed."

"Man, did you read that in a *book?*" For the first time in Alan's experience, Hoang sounded exasperated. "You think any of them have thought more than five minutes past a successful revolution? They're suicidal, all of them. Maybe they want freedom, maybe not, but what unites them is that they want to be part of something enormous to make their lousy lives mean something. Hand them a country and they'll probably just go shoot themselves. What they want is *martyrdom*, Alan. And that's what you're going to give them, because it's going to blow up in your face."

After another half mile, still stunned by the unprecedented flow of words, Alan finally found his tongue. "Then why are you helping me?"

The rarest of all of Tran Hoang's expressions: a smile—a big, open smile that displayed a row of large teeth, two of them crooked. "You think I don't want martyrdom, too?"

Alan blinked at the road that was darkening with the descending sun. Two days later, even after flying to Hong Kong, checking in, and in the stairwell of the Peninsula, switching coat and hat with Tran Hoang and leaving again, after meeting with a stern Chinese woman he knew as Hu, waiting for dark and boarding a small fishing boat headed for Xiayong—even after all that, he thought that Tran Hoang, perhaps, was more insane than he was.

3

H e'd spent more than a month with them. That, perhaps, had been a mistake. He'd slept among them and eaten with them and cleaned with them and, through an interpreter, joked with them. He'd met their women and babies camped out in the forest, and he'd listened to stories of injustices that were so massive in their waste of human lives that he couldn't bring himself to share his own. He was a child of misery compared to their fully fleshed adulthood, and at times, he felt ashamed of the self-pity that had brought him so far.

Yet there really was no way out of it now. Upon arriving, he'd told their leader, Li Qide, that it had to be done soon, but "soon" was a different concept in the woods. Besides, they saw no point in doing it before the Games, when an action, even a failed one, would be so much more effective. He'd tried to argue with Li Qide, but, knowing their stories, how could he say aloud that he just wanted to get back to his wife?

He'd had no contact with anyone outside their camp for the past month, and by now their anger had supplanted his own. He was no longer exacting vengeance for his own insult but for the insult of the people he'd briefly joined. The smells they were familiar with were now familiar to him: the pungent cooking oil, the horse manure and the shabby outhouses, the aroma of human sweat mixed with pine and fir trees, the stink of sour pickles and fire-burned chicken.

Now, finally, it was the eighth of August, and he'd been traveling for nearly three days. A horse to Leishan, and then catching a ride to Guiyang, where he was introduced to a guide who drove him as far as Zhengzhou. There, he picked up this clattering old Mercedes and continued on his own with the aid of a map notated in English. He'd made it through three roadblocks populated by nervous soldiers, but his American passport, in the name of George Miller, and gift packages of Marlboro Reds made his progress smoother.

On the other hand, the roads were anything but, choked with holes and ridges like tiny mountain ranges, and he feared for his tires. They held, though, and he stuck to his route leading inexorably toward the capital.

"Me journalist!" he told a soldier at the last roadblock before Beijing's outer ring road as he held out his passport. The soldier, a short man with a wide face, looked confused as he examined the document. Alan pointed at his own chest. He was wearing the suit he had brought into the country and not worn again until yesterday, cleaned and pressed. He was painfully conscious of how loose it hung on him now. "Journalist! *New York Times!*"

For this, too, he had a press card and a forged slip of paper from the Foreign Ministry, both under the name of George Miller. Also, in a gutted catalytic converter, attached by two bolts under the car, were the disassembled pieces of a Chinese M-99B sniper rifle and scope, good for a distance of up to six hundred meters, though he wouldn't need that much range.

The soldier, still looking confused, went to confer with his comrades.

There was a second line at the roadblock, where trucks were checked over with mirrors on wheels and eager Kunming Wolfdogs. Though he didn't see how it started, he looked over at the sound of shouting to see a man being wrestled down from a truck with canvas walls so sooty that Alan couldn't make out the characters written on them. The young man was silent, though he fought against the two soldiers holding him—they were the ones who were shouting, possibly for help. Then one of the soldiers stumbled back and fell on his rear end, and the truck driver broke free, running madly away, in the direction of Beijing. Rifles were unslung, warnings shouted, then, when the driver was about a hundred yards away, the soldiers began shooting. The driver weaved, thinking he could swerve out of the way, but what he didn't know—and what occurred to Alan—was that soldiers the world over are bad shots. There's no point slowing yourself with evasive maneuvers, because there's no greater chance of them hitting a straight line than a swerving one.

After about ten seconds, the driver fell onto his face, as if diving into the road, and his left arm flopped for five more seconds before it also dropped.

Alan's soldier ran back and, breathing heavily, handed back his papers and started shouting. Alan stared back. The soldier slapped the roof of his car and pointed straight ahead. "You go! You go!"

Alan started up the car and drove ahead, past the corpse surrounded by five soldiers, all of whom seemed unsure what to do.

A tall Nigerian couple in colorful desert wear. Russians in tracksuits, singing. Australian tourists—spinsters—gawking. Drunk Argentineans waving soccer scarves. Austrian girls in traditional mountain dress, blond hair in Heidi braids, followed by short, immaculately dressed Sri Lankans walking mute. American shoppers creeping into crowded hutongs. Red Guards on Tiananmen, looking out of their depth among the hordes of foreigners. The Bird's Nest stadium, Gothic twisty modernism floating in a city of cubes. Painted cars, blaring horns, traffic police with white gloves waving desperately. Bicycles, thousands of bicycles.

Yet he kept thinking of a truck driver, and a left arm twitching.

He knew where he was going, but it was only noon. He drove carefully, taking in as much as he could before night fell and he would have to flee this place, never to return.

The problem with conspiracies—with functional ones, at least—is that each individual is only responsible for one small part of the overall plan. Trust is imperative. He had learned to trust the Youth League, even though their trust in him was misplaced. However, not even trust could ensure that the boy they had assigned to bring the truck of explosives into the city had succeeded. For all he knew, the dead driver he'd seen had been the one. So, more than trust, it took faith. Faith in events proceeding as planned, and the extreme faith that human error would not be an issue.

Of course, there wasn't only one truck; there were four. Each would enter through a different compass point, and if only one made it through there would be enough munitions to complete their task: four buildings, simultaneously. Nothing so grand or impossible as the Bird's Nest or the Great Hall, but important buildings that were nonetheless lightly guarded. Simultaneity was the key. "Like al Qaeda," Li Qide had said, eager to show his knowledge, as if Osama bin Laden had invented the concept of parallel attacks.

There were at least three more like Alan, men with nothing more than guns and scopes who, like him, would wait in prearranged apartments across from the main targets in order to catch the survivors. Alan had insisted on this. "Bombs are passive," he explained. "With this we show that the Youth League is not afraid to stay and fight. They won't be expecting it."

After an hour of battling traffic, he felt that he had absorbed enough of Beijing's new face. He headed over to the district called Haidian.

It wasn't easy finding the street, even with the help of Li Qide's notations, but eventually he found the

Haidian Theater, with its broad, flat face and Chinese characters running down the side, and followed Zhong-guancun north, past the ring road, to reach a leafy street whose sign matched the pictograms on the map. The apartment, as promised, was painted green, and an open archway led to a courtyard, where he parked among a scattering of old cars. An old woman slowly crossed the courtyard, carrying a paper bag blackened by grease. He waited until she was gone, then reached under his seat for the wrench. He slipped out and sank to the concrete, his cramped legs shouting back at him, and slid as far as possible under the filthy car. He worked on the bolts and soon held the blackened catalytic converter shell in his hand. He pulled it out, got up, brushed off his clothes, and locked the car door. Carrying the long cylinder like an architect with his plans, he climbed the iron stairs to the fourth floor and used a key to open the door to number 41.

He looked around the small, dusty apartment, with its cracked-tile kitchen, carpets rolled up into logs against a wall covered in water stains, the decade-old television, and the windows that looked across the narrow street to view the front of another low apartment building that Li Qide had been shocked to find on his target list. "What is this?"

"It's an office."

"No, you have bad CIA maps, like when you blew up our embassy in Belgrade. That's an apartment building."

"This isn't from maps, Li Qide," he said, then stretched

the truth. "It's from direct observation. In the basement level is a special Guoanbu center."

"But those are homes over it."

"Why do you think they installed it there? It's that important."

"What do they do in this special center?"

"They plan murders around the globe."

"For example?"

"I know of thirty-three."

"You don't want to share specifics?"

"I'd be happy to," he said and began to recite their names and the locations of their murders. "Sandra Harrison, Tallinn; Pak Eun, Daegu; Lorenzo Pellegrini, Cairo; Andy Geriev, St. Petersburg; Mia Salazar, Brasilia . . ."

Li Qide had accepted it, just as he'd accepted the other targets on the list: the recently completed Koolhaas-designed Central Television Headquarters on Guanghua Road, the Dongchen branch of the Beijing Municipal Public Security Bureau in the Daxing Hutong, and one Olympic venue, the main building of the Shunyi Aquatic Park.

It was one thirty, an hour before the moment. He unscrewed the pipe and laid out the rifle pieces. Outside, bicycles filled the street as people took care of last-minute errands before rushing home or to bars to watch the Games on television.

"It has to be before the Games," Li Qide had said.

"The whole idea was to humiliate them on the world stage, wasn't it?"

"That was before we knew you wanted to blow up an apartment building. No, we'll do it a few hours before the Games start, so that the civilian deaths will be minimal."

Not only were most people out of their apartments at this hour, but the crowds on the street would camouflage the young men and women with canvas backpacks full of C-4 who dropped them in calculated spots along the buildings' walls. Even Alan, as he tested the scope by examining the perimeter of the building, had trouble keeping track of people. Nor could he find those telltale backpacks against the corners of the building, but with an hour to go he knew better than to panic.

He'd gotten the rifle together when the *rat-a-tat* on his door started and an old woman's voice asked a hesitant, measured question. He ignored it, rechecking the scope, but the woman tapped again, then banged with her fist, prattling on and then, to his terror, trying the door handle. For an instant, he couldn't remember if he'd locked it, but he had.

There was a pause, during which she perhaps considered her options, then she banged again, following with a grating Mandarin singsong—some kind of demand. There was a definite sense of entitlement to her unintelligible prattle.

He got up and placed the rifle inside a creaky wardrobe, then stood beside the door. He interrupted her stream with a "Wǒ tīng bù dǒng"—I don't understand.

Silence.

He gave up on his phrasebook Chinese and said,

"I'm sorry, but I don't speak Mandarin. Do you speak English?"

She began with a long, surprised, "Oooh," then started up again, louder, angrier. He used the key on the door, pulled it open a crack, and as he moved his face to the opening the door crashed against him. It wasn't the force of an old woman but of a young man's boot. The handle struck him just below the sternum, knocking the air out of him as he stumbled back onto the floor, trying to catch air, and when he looked up at the four uniformed soldiers rushing in, shouting in mangled English for him to *Stay dair!* he saw the old woman between their forms, outside his door, against the railing, arms crossed tightly as if holding her old, heavy body together, and her face was filled with hate.

Then the bag was pulled over his head and they began to move.

He was dragged across concrete and dirt, thrown into a truck and driven through streets full of voices and car horns and smells of food that made him queasy, the stink of car exhaust and burning rubber, and then, surprisingly, the smell of fresh grass, and then concrete dust. Again he was dragged, this time into a building and up stairs, before being thrown onto a floor. The hood was removed, and he blinked in the sudden light of an overhead bulb, slowly adjusting to the sight of a small, dirty, windowless room. Concrete walls, concrete floor and ceiling. The soldiers left him there, then closed and locked a simple wooden door.

After about fifteen minutes, he still hadn't moved

from his awkward position on the floor, and he started to laugh. His whole life, he thought, had led to that apartment window and that rifle. It was funny, really, that something you'd worked your whole life toward could be so easily made pointless.

There were tears, too, and he knew he really had spent too long with those amateurs in the mountains. It was the same old story. One or two of them had been letting the police know everything, and they had all made the long journey to Beijing only to reach an ambush. No one had made it through. The mistake had not been theirs, for this sort of thing had to be expected. The mistake had been his, giving them an operation he knew they weren't ready for, and the whole folly had been the result of his desperation. The only reason he was still alive was because Xin Zhu would want some information from him. The others, the four in their trucks, the other three with their rifles—they were dead. The others who had been assigned to support the operation were probably dead, too, or soon would be. Twenty? Thirty? Thirty-three?

His hysteria had ebbed by the time a soldier opened the door and Xin Zhu came inside and told the soldier to leave them alone.

He really was enormous. All the reports had said this—Henry Gray had talked on and on about it, and Andrei Stanescu had been in awe of it—but that didn't prepare him for the way the Chinaman seemed to fill the small room, making Alan feel as if he should press himself against the wall. Yet the anger kept him from showing anything. Thirty-three spots turning from red to blue encouraged him to climb to his feet, step forward a little, and consider how to take the man down with his hands. It was possible, and once he'd even done such a thing in a pomegranate orchard west of Kandahar in the Arghandab district. It had been hard and long and brutal, but he'd done it and after getting sick in the dirt he'd slept that night without dreams. Anything was possible.

Perhaps aware of how he was making Alan feel, Xin Zhu didn't come close. He remained standing at the door and regarded him with resignation. Then he said, "You're a lucky man."

"Not as lucky as you, apparently."

Xin Zhu didn't bother replying to that. He said, "The bombs have been tracked and disposed of. Your comrades have been rounded up. Your little operation has been swept clean."

"Yet here you are. A chancy move."

"Oh, I'm not worried about myself. Not regarding you, at least. The men on the other side of this door will hurt you before you could ever hurt me."

It didn't sound like a bluff.

Xin Zhu said, "Before you go, I wanted to meet you. I wish I could apologize, but we both know I wouldn't mean it. I did as I thought best at a certain moment, and it's the nature of things that we have no choice but to live with the repercussions of our actions. I'll be living with mine for years to come. You'll probably have to do the same."

Philosophy in a cell, Alan thought. "Enough, okay? We're not here to make friendly. Just get it over with."

Xin Zhu nodded, looked a moment at his fat fingers, then said, "The favors are finished. I'm not going to live my life giving things to him."

"Who?"

"He hasn't earned it."

"Who?" Alan asked again, but Xin Zhu wasn't interested in explaining anything. He turned and opened the door and walked slowly out without another word. As he was shutting the door, though, Alan noticed that the corridor beyond it was completely empty. Xin Zhu had been bluffing after all.

By the time they came for him, he'd spent hours going through everything again. He saw his mistakes, saw how his emotions had gotten the best of him, but perhaps it was his military training that convinced him that regrets are to be buried. That which cannot be changed should not be changed. More philosophy in a prison cell. He did not think about what would come next, for that, too, could not be changed. Xin Zhu had made his decision, and everything else was beside the point.

One thing remained with him: his belief that when he was finally declared dead, either with or without the evidence of a corpse, Penelope would suffer the most, and he wished he could send word to her. He wished he had at least asked Xin Zhu for that.

Three men in plainclothes came for him. Two were armed with pistols, while the third only led the way through what he now saw was a bare apartment building. Outside, a nighttime field, the broken teeth of new buildings rising not so far away. The building he'd been in, he now saw, was an unfinished ten-story. Off to the left, over the city, he saw a distant display of fireworks opening the Olympic Games.

They drove him around the city, where the traffic was sparse. Not caring anymore, Alan asked the men if someone was videotaping the Games for them. He asked in English, French, German, and Arabic but received no reply.

Another field, a dirt road rough with holes, and a white twin-engine plane on a hidden runway. His three guides left him at the bottom of the stairs and drove off, and only as he was climbing toward the hatch did he truly understand that he wasn't going to die. A large, heavily muscled black man was waiting for him.

The man never introduced himself, but he was friendly. He offered Alan a drink and served the water Alan asked for with a modest smile. He had an African accent that Alan couldn't place, but when he asked the man said, "I'm from the dark continent. That's all you need to know."

"Is that where we're going?"

The man smiled in a way that made him want to laugh. "Strap yourself in."

While they were airborne, he washed as best he could in the small bathroom, then accepted a charcoal suit and pink tie that fit him perfectly.

He never saw the pilots, and when they landed in Hong Kong, the cockpit door remained shut. The man led him down to the tarmac, and they crossed to another twin-engine, a gray Lockheed Martin with French markings. The procedure there was the same—this time, a plate of salmon and mixed vegetables was offered—and he never saw these pilots either.

By then, morning had risen, and he could chart their movement westward over water and mountains. When they descended again it was to a runway half-obscured by red sand in what he thought from his vague navigation might be Pakistan. When he asked where they were, his host smiled and said, "You know? I'm not entirely sure myself. But I think we'd better get on the next one before it leaves without us."

The next plane was larger, an Airbus A320, with more than a hundred seats, but, as before, they were its only passengers. This time, Alan slept for a few hours before his guide woke him with a gentle shake of the shoulder. "We're here."

When he looked out the window, he realized they had already landed on a strip of old runway lined with overgrown grass and boulders. Around them were mountains. Instead of another plane, a red, windowless van awaited them, and it had Italian plates. Two grimy-looking men sat in the front with the engine idling, and he and the African got into the rear through a sliding door on the side. There were two benches, one against either side, and a wall between them and the drivers. When the man closed the door, they were in blackness. The blackness began to move.

"It'll be a long trip," he heard the man say. "Just try to bear it in style, okay?"

"Yet you still don't want to tell me where we're going?"

"He prefers security over comfort."

"He?" Alan said, thinking of the *he* to whom Xin Zhu wanted to give no more favors.

"Just a few hours," said the man; then a small light illuminated the dirty interior as he turned on his telephone. The man made a call, saying in French, "We're on our way." Pause. "Yes. Everything." Pause. "Okay." He hung up and, back in darkness, said, "He wants you to know everything's fine. I'm supposed to make sure you know that. Don't be scared."

"Why does he care what I feel?" Alan asked after a moment.

"I don't know if he does, but he seems to think that you're very good at escaping if you want to." Pause. "Is that so?"

"Probably the only thing I'm good at."

As promised, the drive did take a long time—more than four hours—and he felt the van shake over every bump and pot hole along the way. Sometimes they sped down highways, while other times they slowed for traffic, perhaps in cities, and by the time they finally stopped his legs were asleep. The man said, "Are we ready?"

Alan punched at his tingling thighs. "Sure."

The man pulled open the side of the van and stepped out. Alan squinted painfully, raising his hand to stop the flood of sunlight. All was white for a moment, then it faded to reveal a bank called BHI on a slice of stone sidewalk. "Come, please," said the man, reaching out a hand.

Alan didn't want to touch anyone, so he stepped down on his own and smelled water in the air. To the right and left an old European street ran wobbly along the edge of a harbor, and only when the man took him to a carved door beside the bank, the van now fleeing to expose buildings on the other side of the water, did he recognize that he was in Geneva.

His guide rang a bell and waited until it buzzed before pushing in and leading Alan up a narrow flight of stairs. A landing with two doors, then another flight of stairs. They took five sets of stairs to the top level, and on the way up another figure trotted down. As he neared in the semidarkness Alan had to squint to make out the face. When he did, he felt a sharp pain in his chest. The man said, "Hello, Alan."

"Hoang," Alan said, catching his breath. "What are you doing here?"

Tran Hoang placed a hand on his shoulder, reminding him of his sentimental question in Ferndale. *Is that what you have with your wife?* Then he was gone, and the pain in Alan's chest spread like a cardiac arrest before fading. Hoang, he suspected, was the reason Zhu had been prepared for him.

At the top, there was only one door. The African knocked on it, and a familiar voice said, "Come in."

Even though he could place the voice, he was still unprepared for the sight of Milo Weaver standing, just beyond a cramped foyer, in a living room full of sunlight. Around him, on the floor, were boxes full of files, and more files spread in a mess across a coffee table, a sofa, and two chairs as well as resting on top of a small television. A radio in the corner of the room was quietly playing French pop music. Milo didn't seem aware of the incongruity of the scene as he walked quickly over, saying, "Thanks, Dalmatian," and grabbed at Alan's hand, shaking it. "It *is* good to see you in one piece."

The black man—Dalmatian—said, "The street's covered," as he withdrew to the door.

"Good," Milo said over Alan's shoulder. "We'll have this cleaned up by midnight."

Dalmatian left the apartment.

"Come on," Milo said, pulling Alan into the room. "Sorry about the mess." He cleared one of the chairs, then guided him to it. Alan felt like an automaton, having over the last twenty-four hours only made moves dictated by others. Milo said, "Drink?"

Alan nodded.

Milo got up and went to a cabinet—also covered with files—and opened it to reveal a row of glasses and a lush variety of alcohols. After a month in the forests of Guizhou, Alan felt guilty sitting in the same room as them. Milo took out a limited edition Macallan, blew out the insides of two tumblers, and soon they were each holding a finger of amber liquid, neat. "To . . ." Milo began, then shrugged. "To." He tapped Alan's glass and sipped at his own.

Alan drank his in one swallow. Against the far wall, wide windows framed the not-so-distant mountains.

"Okay," Milo said, grabbing the bottle and refilling Alan's glass. He set the bottle on the floor and shifted enough folders on the sofa to make room to sit. He settled down and said, "Don't ask, Alan. Don't ask anything. I'll just tell you what I can, and by then you'll be ready to ask your questions."

Alan nodded, dumb.

"The only thing you really need to know is that he was ready for you. That was necessary. If he hadn't been, you would be dead now. I hope that's clear."

"Who told him?"

"Wait," Milo said, pointing. "What you did to me and my family was unforgivable, but Hoang has tried to argue your case. He's been partly successful. I understand why you made your mistakes. Irwin, Collingwood, and Jackson kept you in the dark, and from your perspective, there was only one way to finish this. Listen and believe: You were wrong. Xin Zhu is in a worse place now than if you had killed him."

"He looked all right to me."

"He's not," Milo said, all signs of pleasure gone from his features. "He's no longer in control of anything, least of all himself. And when the time comes, if it comes, he can be finished off with a simple leak of information. But it's not time for that yet."

Anger slipped into Alan's stomach, mixing with the hot whisky. "People are *dead*, Milo. Dozens probably. Because you told him. Doesn't that mean anything to you?"

"No one's going to be killed," Milo said, shaking his head. "I have assurances."

"Assurances? *Assurances?* Are you really so naïve?"

"Calm down, Alan."

Alan had been calm for too long. He'd been shuttled from one end of the planet to the other; his dreams had been smashed, the dreams that had justified his betrayal of so many people; and the world as he knew it was gone. Now, he was faced with this smug man who believed that, because of all these files, he understood everything, but he was wrong. Milo Weaver couldn't understand even a fraction of what he was feeling at this moment. "You don't know what you've done! You say you can bring him down with information. What information? From all these files?" he said, scanning a pile on the table. One label read AHMADINEJAD, MAHMOUD.

"No, this is all old intelligence. I'm catching up."

"Catching up to *what*? And why the excellent fucking mood?"

Milo shrugged in a way that only infuriated him more, then said, "Penelope's in Paris."

The anger subsided. Now, he only felt cold, the whisky barely even there. "What? Why?"

"I asked her to stay there."

"Is she all right?"

"Of course," Milo said. "She's with Tina and Stephanie."

Alan set his glass on Mahmoud Ahmadinejad and rubbed his face until stars appeared.

"Take it easy," he heard Milo say. "They're fine. Alex is with them."

"Alex?" Alan said, then figured it out. "Alexandra."

"We can go see them tomorrow," Milo said. "Unless you don't want to. I won't pretend to know what's on your mind, so it's your decision. If you don't want to see her, I'll cover for you however you like."

"Of course I want to see her."

"Good."

"But . . . *why*?" Alan asked, finally realizing the true source of his confusion. "Why are you helping me?"

"Aren't we friends?"

Alan blinked at him. "I wasn't sure."

Milo took a breath and rocked his head. "I haven't forgotten anything, if that's what you're wondering. I've got a lot of things going on now, and I don't think I can do it alone. Your help would go a long way toward repairing some of what you've done."

"Help?"

"Help," Milo repeated. "The question is, are you in or are you out?"

Alan stared at him.

"Don't be scared. It's a simple question."

"In or out of what?"

Milo smiled, his heavy eyes brightening for an instant. "I'm asking if you'd like a job."

Despite the smile, Milo wasn't joking. Alan leaned back in his chair and turned to look out at the mountains. Clouds were moving in. On the radio, a French girl was singing a hit from 1965. Christ, but he was tired.

Read on for a look ahead to
Olen Steinhauer's newest novel,

THE CAIRO AFFAIR

Coming soon in hardcover from Minotaur Books!

Chapter 1

Twenty years ago, before their trips became political, Sophie and Emmett honeymooned in Eastern Europe. Their parents questioned this choice, but Harvard had taught them to care about what happened on the other side of the planet, and from the TV rooms in their dorms they'd watched the crumbling of the USSR with the kind of excitement that hadn't really been their due. They had watched with the erroneous feeling that they, along with Ronald Reagan, had chipped away at the foundations of the corrupt Soviet monolith. By the time they married in 1991, both only twenty-two, it felt like time for a victory lap.

Unlike Emmett, Sophie had never been to Europe,

and she'd longed to see those Left Bank Paris cafés she'd read so much about. "But *this* is where history's happening," Emmett told her. "It's the less traveled road." From early in their relationship, Sophie had learned that life was more interesting when she took on Emmett's enthusiasms, so she didn't bother resisting.

They waited until September to avoid the August tourist crush, gingerly beginning their trip with four days in Vienna, that arid city of wedding-cake buildings and museums. Cool but polite Austrians filled the streets, heading down broad avenues and cobblestone walkways, all preoccupied by things more important than gawking American tourists. Dutifully, Sophie lugged her *Lonely Planet* as they visited the Stephansdom and Hofburg, the Kunsthalle, and the cafés Central and Sacher, Emmett talking of Graham Greene and the filming of *The Third Man,* which he'd apparently researched just before their trip. "Can you imagine how this place looked just after the war?" he asked at the Sacher on their final Viennese afternoon. He was clutching a foot-tall beer, gazing out the café window. "They were decimated. Living like rats. Disease and starvation."

As she looked out at shining BMWs and Mercedeses crawling past the imposing rear of the State Opera House, she couldn't imagine this at all, and she wondered—not for the first time—if she was lacking in the kind of imagination that her husband took for granted. Enthusiasm and imagination. She measured him with a long look. Boyish face and round, hazel eyes. A lock of hair splashed across his forehead. *Beau-*

tiful, she thought as she fingered her still unfamiliar wedding band. This was the man she was going to spend the rest of her life with.

He turned from the window, shaking his head, then caught sight of her face. "Hey. What's wrong?"

She wiped away tears, smiling, then gripped his fingers so tightly that her wedding ring pinched the soft skin of her finger. She pulled him closer and whispered, "Let's go back to the room."

He paid the bill, fumbling with Austrian marks. *Enthusiasm, imagination, and commitment*—these were the qualities she most loved in Emmett Kohl, because they were the very things she felt she lacked. Harvard had taught her to question everything, and she had taken up that challenge, growing aptly disillusioned by both left and right, so uncommitted to either that when Emmett began his minilectures on history or foreign relations, she just sat and listened, less in awe of his facts than in awe of his belief. It struck her that this was what adulthood was about—belief. What did Sophie believe in? She wasn't sure. Compared to him, she was only half an adult. With him, she hoped, she might grow into something better.

While among historical artifacts and exotic languages she always felt inferior to her new husband, in bed their roles were reversed, so whenever the insecurity overcame her she would draw him there. Emmett, delighted to be used this way, never thought to wonder at the timing of her sexual urges. He was beautiful and smart but woefully inexperienced, whereas she had learned the etiquette of the sheets from a drummer in a punk band, a French history teacher's assistant, and, over the space of a single experimental weekend, a girlfriend from Virginia who had come to visit her in Boston.

So when they returned to their hotel room, hand in hand, and she helped him out of his clothes and let him watch, fingertips rattling against the bedspread, as she stripped, she felt whole again. She was the girl who believed in nothing, giving a little show for the boy who believed in everything. Yet by the time they were tangled together beneath the sheets, flesh against flesh, she realized that she was wrong. She did believe in something. She believed in Emmett Kohl.

The next morning they boarded the train to Prague, and not even the filthy car with the broken, stinking toilet deterred her. Instead, it filled her with the illusion that they were engaged in *real* travel, cutting edge travel. "This is what the rest of the world looks like," Emmett said with a smile as he surveyed the morose, nervous Czechs clutching bags stuffed with contraband cigarettes, alcohol, and other luxuries marked for resale back home. When, at the border, the guards removed an old woman and two young men who quietly watched the train leave them behind, Sophie was filled with feelings of authenticity.

She told herself to keep her eyes and ears open. She told herself to absorb it all.

The dilapidated fairy-tale architecture of Prague buoyed them, and they drank fifty-cent beers in underground taverns lit with candles. Sophie tried to put words to her excitement, the magnitude of a small-town girl ending up here, of all places. She was the child of a

Virginia lumber merchant, her travels limited to the height and breadth of the East Coast, and now she was an educated woman, married, wandering the Eastern Bloc. This dislocation stunned her when she thought about it, yet when she tried to explain it to her husband her words felt inadequate. Emmett had always been the verbal one, and when he smiled and held her hand and told her he understood she wondered if he was patronizing her. "Stick with me, kid," he said in his best Bogart.

On their third day, he bought her a miniature bust of Lenin, and they laughed about it as they walked the crowded Charles Bridge between statues of Czech kings looking down on them in the stagnant summer heat. They were a little drunk, giggling about the Lenin in her hand. She rocked it back and forth and used it the way a ventriloquist would. Emmett's face got very pink under the sun—years later, she would remember that.

Then there was the boy.

He appeared out of nowhere, seven or eight years old, emerging from between all the other anonymous tourists, silent at Sophie's elbow. Suddenly, he had her Lenin in his hands. He was so quick. He bolted around legs and past an artist dabbing at an easel to the edge of the bridge, and Sophie feared he was going to leap over. Emmett started moving toward the boy, and then they saw the bust again, over the boy's head. He hurtled it into the air—it rose and fell. "Little *shit*," Emmett muttered, and when Sophie caught up to him and looked down at the river, there was no sign of her little Lenin. The boy was gone. Afterward, on the walk back to the hotel, she was overcome by the feeling that she and Emmett were being made fools of. It followed her the rest of the trip, on to Budapest and during their unexpected excursion to Yugoslavia, and even after they returned to Boston. Twenty years later, she still hadn't been able to shake that feeling.

Chapter 2

Her first thought upon arriving at Chez Daniel on the evening of March 2, 2011, was that her husband was looking very good. She didn't have this thought often, but it was less an insult to Emmett than an indictment against herself, and the ways in which twenty years of marriage can blind you to your partner's virtues. She suspected that he saw her the same way, but she hoped he at least had moments like this, where warmth and pleasure filled her at the sight of his eternally youthful face and the thought that, *Yes, this one's mine.* It didn't matter how brief they were, or how they might be followed by something terrible—those bursts of attraction could sustain her for months.

Chez Daniel, like most decent French restaurants—even French restaurants in Hungary—was cramped, casual, and a bit frantic. Simple tablecloths, excellent food. She joined him at a table by the beige wall beneath framed sepia scenes of the dirty and cracked Budapest streets that made for hard walking but wonderfully moody pictures. As they waited for the wine, Emmett straightened the utensils on either side of his plate and asked how her day had been.

"Glenda," she said. "Four hours with Glenda at the Gellért Baths. Steam, massages, and too many Cosmopolitans. What do you think?"

He'd heard often enough about the Wednesday routine she'd been roped into by the wife of his boss, Consul General Raymond Bennett. Always the Gellért Hotel, where Sophie and Emmett had spent part of their honeymoon, back when even students could afford its Habsburg elegance. Emmett said, "Anything exciting in her life?"

"Problems with Hungarians, naturally."

"Naturally."

"I tell her to ask Ray to put in for a transfer, but she pretends it's beyond her means."

"How about you?" he asked.

"Am I anti-Hungarian, too?"

"How are you doing here?"

Sophie leaned closer, as if she hadn't heard. It wasn't a question she posed to herself often, so she had to take a moment. They'd lived for six months in Budapest, where Emmett was a deputy consul. Last year, their home had been Cairo—Hosni Mubarak's Cairo. Two years before that, it had been Paris. In some ways, the cities blended in her memory—each was a blur of social functions and brief friendships and obscure rituals to be learned and then forgotten, each accompanied by its own menagerie of problems. Paris had been fun, but Cairo had not.

In Cairo, Emmett had been irritable and on edge—a backfiring car would make him stumble—and he would return from the office itching for a fight. Sophie—maybe in reaction, maybe not—had built a new life for herself, constructed of lies.

The good news was that Cairo had turned out to be a phase, for once they arrived in Hungary the air cleared. Emmett reverted to the man she had decided to spend her life with twenty years ago, and she let go of the puerile intoxication of deceit, her secrets still safely kept. In Budapest, they were adults again.

Emmett was waiting for an answer. She shrugged. "How can I not be happy? A lady of leisure. I'm living the dream."

He nodded, as if it were the answer he'd expected—as if he'd known she would lie. Because the irony was that, of the three cities they had called home, Cairo was the only one she would have returned to in a second, if given the chance. There, she had found something liberating in the streets, the noise and traffic jams and odors. She had learned how to move with a little more grace, to find joy in decorating the apartment with star clusters and flowers of the blue Egyptian water lily; she took delight in the particular melody of Arabic, the predictability of daily prayers, and the investigation of strange, new foods. She also discovered an unexpected pleasure in the act of betrayal itself.

But was it really a lie? Was she unhappy in Budapest?

No. She was forty-two years old, which was old enough to know good fortune when it looked her in the eye. With the help of L'Oréal, she'd held on to her looks, and a bout of high blood pressure a few years ago had been tempered by a remarkable French diet. They were not poor; they traveled extensively. While there were moments when she regretted the path her life had taken—at Harvard, she had aspired to academia or policy planning, and one winter day in Paris a French doctor had explained after her second miscarriage that children would not be part of her future—she always stepped back to scold herself. She might be sometimes bored, but adulthood, when well maintained, was supposed to be dull. Regretting a life of leisure was childishness.

Yet at nights she still lay awake in the gloom of their bedroom, wondering if anyone would notice if she hopped a plane back to Egypt and just disappeared, before remembering that her Cairo, the one she loved, no longer existed.

She and Emmett had been in Hungary five months when, in January, Egyptian activists had called for protests against poverty, unemployment, and corruption, and by the end of the month, on January 25, they'd had a "day of rage" that grew until the whole city had become one enormous demonstration with its epicenter in Tahrir Square, where Sophie would once go to drink tea.

On February 11, less than a month before their dinner at Chez Daniel, Hosni Mubarak had stepped down after thirty years in power. He wasn't alone. A month before that, Tunisia's autocrat had fled, and as Sophie and Emmett waited for their wine a full-scale civil war was spreading through Libya, westward from Benghazi toward Tripoli. The pundits were calling it the Arab Spring. She had health, wealth, and a measure of beauty, as well as interesting times to live in.

"Any fresh news from Libya?" she asked.

He leaned back, hands opening, for this was their perpetual subject. Emmett had spent an enormous amount of time watching CNN and shouting at the screen for the Libyan revolutionaries to advance on Tripoli, as if he were watching a football game, as if he were a much younger man who hadn't already witnessed civil war. "Well, we're expecting word soon from the Libyan Transitional Council—they'll be declaring themselves Libya's official representative. We've had a few days of EU sanctions against Gadhafi, but it'll be a while before they have any effect. The rebels are doing well—they're holding onto Zawiyah, just west of the capital." He shrugged. "The question is, when are we going to get off our asses and drop a few bombs on Tripoli?"

"Soon," she said hopefully. He had brought her over to the opinion that with a few bombs Muammar Gadhafi and his legions would fold within days, and that there would be no need for foreign troops to step in and, as Emmett put it, *soil their revolution*. "Is that it?" she asked.

"All we've heard."

"I mean you. How was your day?"

The wine arrived, and the waiter poured a little into Emmett's glass for approval. Sophie ordered fresh tagliatelle with porcini mushrooms, while Emmett asked for a steak, well done. Once the waiter was gone, she said, "Well?"

"Well, what?"

"Your day."

"Right," he said, as if he'd forgotten. "Not as exciting as yours. Work-wise, at least."

"And otherwise?"

"I got a call from Cairo."

It was a significant statement—at least, Emmett had meant it to be—but Sophie felt lost.

"Someone we know?"

"Stan Bertolli."

She heard herself inhale through her nose and wondered if he had heard it, too. "How's Stan?"

"Not well, apparently."

"What's wrong?"

Emmett took his glass by the stem and regarded the wine carefully. "He tells me he's in love."

"Good for him."

"Apparently not. Apparently, the woman he's in love with is married."

"You're right," she said, forcing her voice to flatline. The air seemed to go out of the room. Was this really happening? She'd imagined it before, of course, but never in a French restaurant. She said, "That's not good."

He took a breath, sipped his wine, then set it on the table. The whole time, his eyes remained fixed on the deep red inside the glass. Finally, quietly, he said, "Were you ever going to tell me?"

This, too, was not how she'd imagined it. She floundered for an answer, and her first thought was a lie: *Of course I was.* Before transforming the thought into speech, though, she realized that she wouldn't have told him, not ever.

She considered going on the defensive and reminding him of how he had been in Cairo, how he had treated her as if she had been a perpetual obstacle. How he had pushed her away until, looking for something, anything, to complement her feelings of liberation she finally gave in to Stan's approaches. Only partly true, but it might have been enough to satisfy him.

She said, "Of course I was going to tell you."

"When?"

"When I got up the courage. When enough time had passed."

"So we're talking about years."

"Probably."

Chewing the inside of his cheek, Emmett looked past her at other tables, perhaps worried that they all knew he was a cuckold, and the corners of his eyes crinkled in thought. What was there to think about? He'd had all day, but he still hadn't decided, for this wasn't only about an affair—it was about Emmett Kohl, and what kind of man he wanted to be. She knew him all too well.

One kind of man would kick her out of his life, would rage and throw his glass at her. But that wasn't him. He would have had his "little shit" moment as soon as he hung up the telephone; his day of rage was over. He needed something that could show off his anger without forcing him to break character or descend into cliché—it was a tricky assignment.

She said, "It's over. If that helps."

"Not really."

"Do you remember how you were in Cairo?"

His damp eyes were back on her, brow twitching. "You're not going to twist this into my fault, are you?"

She looked down at her glass, which she still hadn't touched. He knew very well how he had been in Cairo, but he wasn't interested in drawing a connection between that and her infidelity. Were she him, she would have felt the same way.

He said, "Do you love him?"

"No."

"Did you love him?"

"For a week I thought I might, but I was wrong."

"Were you thinking about a divorce?"

She frowned, almost shocked by the use of a word that she had never considered. "God. No. Never. You're . . ." She hesitated, then lowered her voice, pushing a hand across the table in his direction. "You're the best thing that ever happened to me, Emmett."

He didn't even acknowledge her hand. "Then . . . *why?*"

Anyone who's committed adultery envisions this moment, plots it out and works up a rough draft of a speech that, she imagines, will cut through the fog with some ironclad defense of the indefensible. Sitting there,

though, staring at his wounded face, she couldn't remember any of it, and she found herself grasping for
words. Yet all that came to her was hackneyed lines, as
if she were reading from a script. But they were both
doing that, weren't they? "I was lonely, Emmett. Simple
as that."

"Who else knew?"

"What?"

"Who else knew about this?"

She pulled back her untouched hand. He was being
petty now, as if it truly mattered whether or not someone knew of his bruised pride. But she could give him
that. "No one," she lied.

He nodded, but didn't look relieved.

The food came, giving them time to regroup, and as
she ate, cheeks hot and hand trembling, she reflected
on how betrayed he had to feel. Hadn't she known from
the beginning that she would do this to him? Hadn't
she seen all this coming? Not really, for in Cairo she'd
gone with the moment. In Cairo she'd been stupid.
Daniel had done an excellent job with her tagliatelle,
perfectly tender, and there was a pepper sauce on Emmett's steak that smelled divine. Emmett began to stab
halfheartedly at his meat. The sight made her want to
cry. She said, "What was it? In Cairo."

He looked up—no exasperation, just simple confusion.

"You were a mess there. Me, too, I know, but you . . .
well, you were impossible to live with. Paris was fine,
and here. But in Cairo you were a different man."

"So you *are* trying to blame me," he said. Coldly.

"I just want to know what was on your back in Cairo."

"It doesn't matter," he said as he lifted a bite to his mouth. He delivered it. It was like a punctuation mark, that move.

"Cairo was bad from the start," she went on, forcing the words out. "Not for me. No—I loved it. But you changed there, and you never told me anything."

"So you fucked Stan."

"Yes, I fucked Stan. But that doesn't change the fact that you became someone else there, and once we left Cairo you returned to your old self."

He chewed, staring through her.

"I'm not trying to start a fight, Emmett. I *like* the man you are now. I love him. I didn't like the man you were there. So let's get it out in the open. What was going on in Cairo?"

As he took another bite, still staring, something occurred to her.

"Were *you* having an affair?"

He sighed, disappointed by her stupidity.

"Then what was it?"

He still watched her so coldly, but she could see his barriers breaking down. It was in the rhythm of his chewing, the way it slowed.

"Come on, Emmett. You can't keep it a secret forever."

He swallowed, his wrist on the edge of the table, his fork holding a fresh triangle of beef a few inches above his plate. He said, "Remember Novi Sad?"

There it was. Yugoslavia, twenty years ago. *I saved*

you, Sophie. This is how you pay me back? She nodded.

"Zora?" he asked.

"Zora Balašević," she said, her throat now dry.

"Zora was in Cairo."

She knew this, of course, but said, "Cairo?"

"Working at the Serbian embassy. BIA—one of their spies. Not long after we arrived, she got in touch. Ran into me on the street." He paused, finally putting down his fork. "I was pleased to see her. You remember—despite everything, we got along well in the end. We went to a café, reminiscing about the good stuff, careful to avoid the rest, and then it came. She wanted me to give her information."

To breathe properly, Sophie had to leave her mouth open. This wasn't what she'd expected him to say. Her sinuses were closing up. She said, "Well, that's forward."

"Isn't it?" he said, smiling, not noticing anything. Briefly, he was in his story, looking just like her old husband. "I said no, so she put her cards on the table. She blackmailed me."

She didn't have to ask what Zora had blackmailed him with, and at that moment she had a flash of it: A filthy leg in a black army boot, spastic, kicking at the dirt of a basement. "The bitch," she snapped, but she could feel herself reddening. It was so hot.

"You know what would happen if that came out. I'd never work in the diplomatic corps again. Ever. But I still said no."

She was burning up. She grabbed the collar of her

blouse and fanned it, drawing cool air down her shoulders. "Good for you," she managed. He shrugged, modest. "My mistake was that I didn't report it."

She tried to empty herself of all the heat in a long exhale. "You could have. You could've told Harry, or even Stan."

"Sure, but I didn't know that then. I'd been at the embassy less than a week. I didn't know anything about those guys. Neither of us did. By the time I realized my mistake, it was too late. It would've looked like I'd been covering it up."

He wanted affirmation, so she said, "I suppose you're right."

"Living under that cloud certainly didn't help my mood. But that didn't compare to later, when the whole thing came back to bite me."

She waited.

"About a year ago, last March, Stan started asking questions. Not very subtle, your Stan." A faint smile. "It turned out that loose information had been floating around, intel that originated in Cairo—intel I'd had access to. I was under investigation for most of last year."

She moved back in time, remembering the fights, the moods, the drinking, the anger. It all played differently now. "Why didn't you tell me?"

That faint smile returned. "I didn't want to burden you," he said. "You were having such a good time. Of course, I didn't know *why* you were so happy, but . . ." A shrug.

She didn't know how he could have said that without hatred, but he had. She felt a hard knot in her chest.

He said, "It turned out that Stan already knew about Zora. His guys had been watching me when we first got there—normal vetting procedure. He'd seen me with her, and when the compromised intel came to his attention he followed up on it. So I told him what happened. I told him what she tried to do, and I told him that I refused."

"Did you tell him about . . . ?"

"I left the blackmail a mystery, and he finally let that go. He never asked you?"

She shook her head, but she wasn't sure. Maybe he had.

"Anyway, I told him that Zora hadn't tried again. I never even saw her after that. But he didn't believe me. He sat me down for more talks, trying to trip me up on my story. Eventually, he brought Harry into it. Stan showed him his evidence, but no one ever showed it to me. I was lucky—Harry wanted to believe me. Still, he couldn't afford to have me around anymore, so he suggested I put in for a transfer. Make me someone else's problem, I suppose."

"Stan never told me any of this," she said, but it was getting harder to find air, and the last word barely made it out.

"Secrets are his game, aren't they?"

Silence fell between them, and Emmett returned to his steak.

People talk of conflicting emotions as if they're a daily occurrence, but at that moment Sophie felt as if it were the first time she'd experienced them. Honesty pulled from one side, while the other side, the one that was motivated by self-preservation, held a tighter grip. She stared at her pasta, knowing she wouldn't be able to taste it anymore, maybe not even be able to keep it down, and it occurred to her that maybe her husband deserved to know. To *really* know. Exactly what kind of a woman he was married to. It would be the end, of course. The end of everything. Yet when she thought back to their honeymoon, it was obvious that he was the one person on the planet who deserved to know it all. He was probably the only person who could understand.

She was still trying to decide when the restaurant was filled with a woman's scream. It came from the table behind her. She began to turn to get a look at the woman, but instead saw what the scream had been about. It was at their table, where their waiter should have been standing, a large man—bald, sweating, in a long, cheap overcoat. Upon looking at him, she understood why their neighbor had screamed, for she had the same impulse herself. He was all muscle—not tall but wide—with muddy blue prison tattoos creeping out from under his collar. A man of absolute violence, like those tracksuited Balkan mafiosi she occasionally saw in overpriced bars. He wasn't looking at her, though, but at Emmett, and he was holding a pistol in his hairy hand.

It was the first time she'd ever seen a gun in a restaurant. She'd seen hunting rifles disassembled in her childhood living room, then put to use outdoors when her father went hunting for red stag deer in West Virginia. She once saw a pistol hanging from inside a jacket in their Cairo kitchen when an agent of one of the security services had come to have a talk with Emmett. In Yugoslavia, they had been on soldiers and militiamen and in one grimy kitchen that still sometimes appeared in her dreams, but she had never seen one in a restaurant.

Now she had, and the pistol—a modern-looking one, slide-action—was pointed directly at her husband.

"Emmett Kohl," the man said with a strong accent, but it wasn't a Hungarian accent. It was something Sophie couldn't place.

Emmett just stared at him, hands flat on either side of his plate. She couldn't tell if he recognized the man, so before she had a chance to think through the stupidity of her actions she said, "Who are you?"

The man turned to her, though his pistol remained on Emmett. He frowned, as if she were an unexpected variable in an equation he'd spent weeks calculating. Then he turned back to Emmett and said, "I here for you."

Mute, Emmett shook his head.

Behind the man, the restaurant was clearing out. It was surprising how quietly so many people could retreat, the only sound a low *rhubarb-rhubarb* rumbling through the place. Men were snatching phones from their tables and holding women by the elbows, heading toward the door. They crouched as they walked. She hoped that at least one of them was calling the police. A waitress stood by the wall, tray against her hip, confused.

Sophie said, "Why are you here?"

Again, the look, and this time she could read irritation in his features. Instead of answering, he glanced at the gold wristwatch on his free hand and muttered something in a language she didn't recognize. Something sharp, like a curse. He looked back at Emmett and, his arm stiffening, pulled the trigger.

Later, she would hate herself for staring at the gunman rather than at her husband. She should have been looking at him, giving him a final moment of commiseration, of tenderness, of love. But she hadn't been, because she hadn't expected this. Despite all the evidence to the contrary, she hadn't actually expected the man to shoot Emmett twice, once in the chest and, after a step forward, once through the nose, the explosion of each shot cracking her ears. She supposed it was because she was still dealing with the shock of Zora Balašević, of Stan, and the novelty of a gun in a restaurant. It was so much to deal with that she couldn't have expected more novelty to come so quickly. Not that night.

Yet there it was. She turned to see Emmett leaned back against the wall, his hazel, bloodshot eyes open but unfocused, sliding out of his chair, his face unrecognizable, blood and organic matter splashed across the wall and a sepia city scene. Screams made the restaurant noisy again, but she didn't look around. She just stared at Emmett as his body slid down, disappearing gradually behind the table and his plate of half-eaten steak. She didn't even notice that the gunman had jogged out of the restaurant, pushing past the remaining witnesses—this was something she would be told later.

For the moment, it was just Sophie, the table with

their wine and blood-spattered food, and Emmett slipping away. His chest disappeared, then his shoulders, his chin pressed down against the knot of his tie, then his face. The gory face that was missing the short, almost pug nose that, more than his hair or his clothes, always defined her husband's look. The table rocked as he fell off the chair, leaving a mess on the wall. She didn't hear him hit because her ears were ringing from the gunshots, and she felt as if she were going to vomit. There was more screaming and the distant sound of weeping, but she soon learned that all of it was coming from herself.

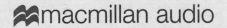